Blood Identity

Jack Paskvan

Again, my many thanks go out to
Ellen Leidl and Steve Meredith for their ardent support and their
extraordinary creative and technical skills, which contributed to
the publication of this novel.

CHAPTER ONE

June 18, 1990

"C'mon, don't be scared. We can make it."

"It's too deep. The water's too fast."

"No, it's not. Don't be a scaredy cat. It won't even be up to my waist."

"I'm not going."

"Then I'll go by myself if you're afraid to wade to *our* little island. I'm not afraid, and I'm a girl. Why are you so scared?"

"It's *your* island. And I'm not scared."

"Look, I'm already in the water."

"Don't go!"

"You coming?"

"Alright! I'm coming with you!"

****

When Charlie Johnson wasn't selling cars for a Spokane Ford dealership, he spent most of his free time trying to cheat on his wife. But this night he wasn't having much luck.

After hitting the happy hour hot spots with not a single decent prospect to show for it, not unlike his sales figures of late, Charlie was driven out of desperation to the Stockyards, a local watering hole for singles that well lived up to its name. If Charlie couldn't score there, then he had best pack it up and go home to the family. By nine-thirty it didn't look like this was going to be Charlie's night.

The air was muggy when he stepped outside, heavy and stifling, unusual for that part of the country, and the parking lot pavement glistened with a shimmering glow where the night lights cast their stark illuminations. Hot and frustrated, Charlie snatched his already loosened tie and ripped it away from his collar with the finality of resignation as he headed toward his car, a slight stagger in his walk. Fumbling for his keys, Charlie unlocked the door, tossed his tie on the passenger's seat and slumped down behind the wheel with a heavy sigh of self-pity. "Shit," he said aloud and started the car.

On the way home he stared thinking up explanations for his wife, not that he had to give her any, but she would smell the booze on his breath and start in on him again. Tonight he just didn't want to put up with her crap.

Suddenly, out of the progressively dense fog and his half groggy state of mind, he spotted someone alongside the road just ahead. Charlie's reaction time was slow; he was already past the person when he realized he had just seen what appeared to be an attractive woman hitchhiking in that relatively remote neighborhood. His foot hit the brake. He searched the rearview mirror, saw someone back there who was but a ghostly image silhouetted in the heavy mist by a nearby streetlight. Wondering what the hell she was doing out there all by herself, Johnson shifted into reverse and started to back up slowly, his mind questioning his initial impression all the time. He stopped twenty feet from her, and she began to walk toward his car.

As he leaned over to the passenger window he had rolled down, Charlie peered into the thick night air and looked into the face of one of the most beautiful women he had ever laid eyes on. Although her features were streaked with shadows, it was nevertheless clear she was an exceptional one with those heavy folds of wavy dark hair that blanketed her shoulders and eyes that shined bright in the night. When she spoke to thank him for stopping, her voice was but a husky whisper, and her lips parted slowly and sensuously into a smile. Charlie was momentarily stricken speechless out of competing waves of shock and lust.

"Where you heading?" he managed to ask.

"To my car. It's not far from here," she answered in that low, exotic tone. "I've been walking at least a mile."

"Hop in. I'll take you to it."

"Thank you. You're very kind."

Unable to keep his eyes off her, Charlie's furtive glances shot back and forth between the woman and the road. "Charlie Johnson's my name," he announced to break the silence. "How about yours?"

"Kimberly," the woman replied softly, her look fixed straight ahead. "I go by Kim."

"Kim what?"

"Huh?" She seemed totally lost in distant thoughts.

"Your last name," Johnson hastened to add. The urgency in his voice betrayed his ulterior motives. "What's your last name?"

"Oh...Brown," the woman answered. She managed a thin smile for Charlie, which he took as a sign of encouragement.

Johnson returned her smile with a broad, leering grin. "How come you out here all alone?" he asked.

There was a moment of silence before Kim answered, "I went somewhere with someone, and it didn't work out...so I left alone."

"Yeah, that can be a real drag," Charlie sympathized in a manner totally void of sincerity. "I've been there."

"I'm sure you have," Kim added in a voice barely more than a whisper.

"What?"

"Please take the next right up ahead."

Charlie was a little taken aback. "Uh, yeah...sure." He made the turn, and Kim told him her car was just a few blocks further. She had him make a couple more turns which took them to a gravel road bordered on one side by vacant wooded lots and a steep embankment on the other. Just ahead a car was parked on a dirt turnoff to an open field. Charlie pulled up behind it, blocking its exit, shut off the engine and laid his arm across the passenger backrest with his hand draped closely to Kim's shoulder. "Kind of a strange place to park, I'd say," he noted. His hungry look was back again.

This time Kim returned his suggestive smile. "It's a long story," she told him.

"I have time on my hands," said Charlie.

"Then let's not waste it talking about where I park my car," Kim responded in a manner unmistakably seductive. Her hand reached across the console and came to rest lightly on Charlie's crotch, which immediately began to bulge. Before he could even react, she bent over and pressed her mouth firmly to his. Her other hand clutched the back of his head, and her fingers began to claw through his hair and signal to him her willingness.

Charlie's eyes went wide with pleasant surprise as Kim smothered him with passionate kisses. Her right hand skillfully undid his zipper and slipped inside to stroke his rigid penis. With a little groan, Charlie anticipated what would come next. He closed his eyes and let his head fall back against the headrest.

Charlie's eyes exploded wide open with shock and the horror of what had just happened. He felt no pain other than a slight stinging sensation that ran across his throat, but he was all too aware of the hot wetness that drenched the front of his shirt. His head grew cloudy; all he saw through the haze of his mind was her smile looming out of the dark confines of his car. Then he knew he was trying to scream, but he heard nothing, no sound whatsoever. It was not the sensation of his throat being slit from ear to ear but the pain of the knife plunging into his crotch, twisting, then slashing back to cut off his cock that brought the gurgling screams to his lips just moments before Charlie died.

****

Detective Sergeant Joe Rummel had his mind set equally on routine paperwork and retirement when the lieutenant barged into his tight little office tucked away in a corner of the squad room. He was fed up with doing the paperwork anyway, fed up with nineteen years of paperwork for that matter. Now that his daughter was going to be a senior in college, he was definitely pulling the plug next year. Nineteen years in this business was as much as any man should have to put up with. The only bright side now was the fact he no longer was working in Chicago where he had spent his first twelve years as a cop before landing this job in Spokane, the result of a divorce and a lucky break all in the same year. Perhaps, if he had been offered the Spokane job the year before, he and Julie might still be together, but probably not. She had always hated his line of work; Spokane or Chicago, it made no difference to her. Now it all came down to his working just to help his daughter finish college, and then that was it--no more investigating homicides, no more dealing with the scum of the earth, no more police work. If he needed the extra bucks, he'd take a seasonal job in Alaska on a fishing boat.

Lieutenant Jim McCoy was not his typical easygoing self that day. He even looked a little shaken, which for a man with his many years on the force was unusual. "I just got a call from the sheriff's department," he said. "They asked me to send someone out from homicide to look over a murder scene. You're elected, Joe."

Rummel was a bit surprised. "Why don't they put their own people on it?" he asked.

"They want us out there too," McCoy replied. Pausing a moment, Lieutenant McCoy started chewing on his lower lip, a habit of his when he was thinking, then he stated, "This is not going to be pretty, Joe. We've got a real sicko out there...big time."

"Where is it?"

"Out in Glenrose at the end of 21st."

As Rummel pushed his report to one side, he offered his lieutenant a concerned look and inquired, "What we got?"

"Some knife happy creep," sighed McCoy. "Cut the victim's throat and then proceeded to slash up his groin area. The sheriff's people say it's a real fuckin' mess out there."

For a moment Rummel was carried back to Chicago. That's where he would expect that sort of thing, had in fact seen something very similar to it when he was a rookie on the force. This was the kind of shit he didn't need at this stage of the game. Slowly he pushed his chair back and stood up. As he looked at McCoy, he showed him the years of frustration etched in the lines across his face, the exhaustion written in his soft brown eyes.

Detective Rummel was a big man, close to six-four, pushing two forty, a little bit of that being middle age spread but not much. At forty-seven, he was still reasonably good looking with solid square features and a quick, broad smile of perfectly positioned teeth dulled slightly by age and cigarette smoke. He had the look of a retired NFL linebacker, a wall coming at you or one to run through, but his slightly elongated head diminished his American ex-jock appearance and transformed it into a bit more refined, European jock look instead, a soccer player. Rummel had thick, dark hair, tight waves that formed a near curl flecked evenly throughout with touches of gray. What aged him were the deeply furrowed lines around his eyes and across his brow that gave him a sad countenance of perpetual weariness, and a saga of scars that topped his eyebrows, dissected his left cheek, formed a matched pair on his upper lip, and a prominent one that ran across the bottom of his chin. Given his size, Rummel had always been expected to be in the thick of it, a role he dutifully observed, but Joe had a tendency to be a little clumsy and accident prone. That's where he got the dubious nickname of Hit Man in Chicago, the guy who always took the hits, a name he gladly left behind when he moved to Spokane. He looked like a man who had seen too much in his lifetime already, and those gentle eyes reflected that with their vacant, sad stare. For a moment, that look was back, but then, just as quickly, his smile returned to cover up what was really eating away at him piece by piece, day by day. "Police work sucks," he told McCoy.

"Now's a fine time for you to come to that conclusion," McCoy noted.

"I came to that conclusion a long time ago," Rummel said as he grabbed his navy blue sports jacket and headed out the door.

****

The crime scene had attracted an unusually large number of uniformed and plain clothed personnel. Not that Spokane was any stranger to violent crime, figured Rummel as he drove up to a uniformed sheriff's deputy and flashed his badge out the window, but this certainly had all the markings of a celebrity event. The deputy stepped aside and motioned him toward a place to park his car.

George Sept, one of Rummel's counterparts from the sheriff's office, spotted him and hurried across the road to greet him. "This is the shits, Joe," he puffed as he placed a hand on Rummel's broad shoulder and started to lead him toward an '89 blue Mustang parked precariously on the shoulder of the road. "I've been on the force close to seventeen years, and I've never come across anything like this…never. This is fuckin' sick."

Great, Rummel thought. Sooner or later big time troubles had to catch up with what was left of a once relatively wholesome city. There was no escaping it these days. The scum had infested every corner of the country. Retirement again settled into his mind.

It was 10 a.m. and already getting downright hot. As Rummel approached the car, he could smell the pungent scent of decaying death, the same heavy obnoxious odor of fresh road kill that saturated the air around it, compounded now even more by the sweltering heat inside the victim's car. Other officers present stood a respectful distance from the vehicle to avoid the unpleasantness, allowing the two detectives ready access to the scene. The passenger door was open, and Joe looked inside. The sound of hundreds of flies buzzing in those close confines annoyed his ears, and the sight of a body that was already bloating tormented his eyes. A twisted grimace torn across the man's face nearly matched the cruel gash etched over his throat. One arm dropped helplessly by his side, and the other dangled across the backrest like it was still trying to reach out for something or someone. His white shirt was soaked red, and the dried blood in his crotch was so thick it was almost black.

"See, I told you this was a fuckin' mess," Sept remarked over Rummel's shoulder.

Joe didn't respond right away as he inspected the interior, and then he asked, "Anyone touch anything in here?"

"We dusted the doors for prints," Sept replied. "That's it."

"How about him? Anyone touch him?"

"Just to get his IDs," said Sept. "Guy by the name of Charlie Johnson. We've got people checking him out as we speak. Otherwise we didn't touch a thing."

"I thought so," grumbled Rummel. "Shit…they don't pay me enough for this." The detective dug into his coat pocket and produced a pair of latex gloves, which he slapped on, with the precision of a seasoned surgeon. He took his jacket off and handed it to Sept, which left him down to a short-sleeved shirt. Stretching across the seat and reaching inside the dead man's open fly, he started to grope around as if he were looking for lost silverware in dirty dishwater.

"The passenger door handles were wiped clean," noted Sept.

"Uh-huh, so someone had their wits about them," Joe concluded as he continued to dig around in the man's pants.

"Looks that way," said Sept. "What the hell you after, anyway?"

"See if anything's cut off," Rummel growled.

"That's disgusting," Sept commented. "Let the coroner do that." The revulsion that had captured his expression momentarily was quickly replaced with a smile. "Say, Joe, when you pulling the plug?"

"Not soon enough," Rummel answered. He withdrew his hand and backed out of the car.

"What did you find in there?"

"It's what I didn't find," Joe noted. "Someone cut his dick off."

"Well, doesn't that just beat all," Sept moaned. "What the fuck's next in this town?"

"Feels like he's been cut up pretty bad," Rummel continued, offering his colleague a concerned look. "Probably multiple stab wounds, but that's up to the coroner to decide." He took a few moments to look over the crime scene again, then turned again to Sept and added, "This is some real bad shit, George…real bad."

The sheriff's detective nodded in agreement. "Yeah, I ain't never seen anything like this around here. Suppose it happens in the big cities, though."

"It does," Joe said softly. "And it happens here too. I'll hang around until we get the body removed."

Sept decided to go back to his original subject. "When you getting out?"

"Next year."

"Lucky bastard. I got three more to go." While Sept continued to talk about retirement, Rummel leaned forward into the car again and began to examine the slash across the victim's throat. He started to make a sweeping motion with both hands as he followed the angle of the cut. "What are you doing, Joe? Giving the guy last rites or something?"

For a time Rummel was preoccupied and didn't answer as he continued to reenact the murder, then he said to Sept, "Let's assume the sucker was taken face on. Right now there's no reason to believe he wasn't…you say you found him this way and all."

"That's right."

"Okay, look at this, George."

Detective Sept peered inside over Rummel's shoulder.

"The cut angles slightly down from his left to his right, and it digs in a little deeper on the right side. You can see that here when I pull the skin away a bit."

"Yeah, so?"

"I'm assuming it wasn't made forehanded, which right now is an assumption," Joe continued, "and assuming this was a backhanded cut facing the victim, then the killer was probably left-handed."

"I'll buy that."

"It's up to the coroner to buy that first. That's what he gets paid for."

"Looks like it came as a complete surprise to the poor bastard," noted Sept.

"That brings me to the other part," Rummel continued. "This guy's got someone in the car that close to him…someone he obviously trusts from the looks of it, considering he might have been allowing that person to play with his pecker, then what we're looking for is either a woman or a faggot…a left-handed one."

"Nice piece of work, Joe," Sept commented, smiling. "I'll check out Mr. Johnson's sexual proclivities and let you know."

"Do that, George. Might be of use." Rummel backed out of the car and took in a breath of air. He carefully removed his gloves and delicately held them arm's length. "You got a bag for these?" he asked Sept.

"Just drop them on the ground. I'll get one."

"You come across anything else?"

"We think the car might have been moved," Sept replied.

"How so?"

"Well, you can't really follow tracks on this gravel, but there's a little dirt turnoff about twenty-five yards back, and there's a couple of little digs in the gravel right there like someone was jerking the car down the road."

"Driving from the passenger's side?"

"Exactly."

"Why's that?" asked Rummel.

"Because there could've been another car parked on that turnoff, and this one blocked the way," Sept explained. "Looks like some pretty fresh tracks in the dirt there."

"Can we get a make on the tread?"

"Too dry and dusty."

"So maybe this guy is taking somebody to his or her car when he gets killed," Rummel concluded.

"Could very well be," commented Sept.

"Let's go back over that spot with a fine-toothed comb," Joe suggested.

"We're already doing that," Sept said.

"Let's take another look at it anyway. I want to find this creep before this happens again."

Sept looked worried. "Think it will?" he asked.

Rummel shook his head sadly. "Things like this usually do," he answered.

The sheriff's detective handed Rummel's jacket back to him, and the two men started to walk back to Joe's car. George Sept tried to lighten up the mood a little. "So what are you going to do when you're not engaged in fascinating and fun work like this anymore?"

"Go fishin'," was Detective Rummel's only reply.

****

Marty Vaughn was out the door of O'Reilly's just minutes before closing time, a quarter ounce of cocaine in his pocket, the fruits of a deal he had just completed inside. He had consumed a few too many beers and wasn't careful where he was walking. Rounding the corner on Bernard, he bumped into a woman he swore was one of the most beautiful he had ever seen. The night lights made her eyes glisten and cast neon ribbons of radiance to her heavy waves of long dark hair. Apologizing to her, he couldn't help but notice her cover girl perfect lips and the friendly smile she seemed to have just for him. "Hey, sorry," he said. "I wasn't watching where I was going, but I'm glad I wasn't. The name's Marty Vaughn."

The smile remained. "Apology accepted," the woman answered in a low, sexy voice. "My name is Kim."

CHAPTER TWO

She was his only source of hope for the future now, his daughter Kim. Lately, it seemed, Joe thought about her constantly. Julie, his ex-wife, was gone for good. She had stayed back in Chicago and remarried, and when she had given birth to a child late in life from that marriage, that had finalized everything in Rummel's mind. Actually, it had ended long before that with their fights, mostly about his job and his drinking, but it had taken the new baby to close the door permanently. Julie had given birth to a boy, which in its own way made up for the one she and Joe had lost years before to a drunken driver. All that remained for Rummel of their lives together and apart was his daughter, who at times seemed to be his sole reason for going on. She was the one he thought about now, his complete source of pride, his last remaining breath of freshness in a cold, empty life. It had been much too long since he had seen her or even talked to her. The detective made note to himself to call her tonight just to hear her voice, just to reassure himself there was at least one decent thing left in his life.

A sudden interruption over the phone intercom rattled Rummel back to an unwelcome reality. It was McCoy, and he wanted to see him right away. Forcing himself to his feet, Rummel squeezed from behind his desk, as he always had to do in that cramped, corner office. He reminded himself, however, that this squad room was still a vast improvement over the cold hole he had called home in Chicago all those years. Here, at least, he had a window and clean, ivory colored walls. Never once had he regretted moving to Spokane, other than the fact he was separated from his daughter much more than he would have preferred. No doubt McCoy wanted to discuss this Johnson case, which had every cop in town talking, everyone but him. Joe was having difficulty involving himself in it at all. It was like taking a step backwards to the streets of Chicago.

McCoy was biting his lower lip again when Rummel entered his office. The lieutenant was a cop's cop, streetwise, a man who had earned his way up through the ranks with almost as many scars to show for it as Joe had. He was tough looking with his barrel build and thick arms covered with a layer of silky, black hair. He was dark complexioned, dark eyed, nearly bald and not very tall, pushing it at five ten, and he wore a full black moustache that formed a near semi-circle precisely trimmed at the corners of this mouth. McCoy was hard working to a fault and as fair as a man could be with not the slightest bit of bureaucrat in him. He had earned the respect of practically everyone on the force to the point he was their armor clad leader at the forefront of battle, but the chinks were beginning to show now in his battle gear as he faced this new threat to his streets. It was as if he saw the thin walls of decency finally crumbling down all around him, and he had at last run out of ways to keep that from happening.

It took a second or two before Rummel realized someone else was in the room sitting in a corner chair.

"I want you to meet Brad Curtis," McCoy said.

Curtis stood up, and Rummel found himself face to face with the exact opposite of himself. The man appeared to be in his early to mid-twenties, although the detective would later find out he was actually thirty-two, and the last thing anyone would ever guess was that this guy was a police officer, which Rummel assumed he was because he had seen him around the building a couple of times before. He had been dressed in expensive looking suits with spiffy shirts and ties when Rummel had spotted him previously, maybe a lawyer instead of a cop. Today he looked a little more ready for the field with solid gray slacks, a charcoal blazer and open collar. Still, he made Joe feel a bit shabby in his old, worn J.C. Penny's navy blue sports coat and tan Dockers. Curtis was only five foot eight at best and couldn't weigh much more than one-forty if that. He was too good looking to be a cop, Rummel thought, not in a traditionally handsome sense but more like a ballet dancer or Bloomingdale's sales clerk. Christ, it looked like he didn't even shave. He had thick, boyish locks of light brown hair that fell in a single loose wave across the right side of his forehead, and his pale blue eyes shined with innocence. His features were carefully sculptured, bordering on delicate, and he had the smile of a freshly minted politician. Something told Rummel he was going to be working very closely with this young police officer, and based on his initial impression, he wasn't all that sold on the prospect. "Nice to me you," Joe said with a friendly handshake and a clear look of reservation in his eyes.

"Pleasure's mine," replied Curtis. "I've heard a lot about you, and all of it is good."

"You must've been talking to the guys who cleaned me out when I bet against Gonzaga last season."

"That *was* stupid," McCoy butted in.

"No, seriously," Curtis continued, his smile broadening even more. "I'm told you're one of the best. I look forward to working with you."

"I'm assigning Brad to work with you on finding this knife happy creep," McCoy said. His look took on the gravity he was carrying inside. "We've got another one, Joe."

"I knew that was going to happen," Rummel groaned. "I just knew this shit would come up again."

"We had three similar murders in Seattle last year," Curtis added. "I was working vice, but I had occasion to be in on one of the investigations. Sounds like a very similar M.O."

"We hired Brad from the Seattle P.D. a month ago," McCoy explained. "He comes highly recommended."

Rummel couldn't help but look at his new partner with a glint of skepticism. 'Highly recommended for what?' he wondered. 'Figure skating?' He momentarily put his preconceived notions aside, however, and stated, "Glad to have you on board." To McCoy he asked, "Where's this one located?"

"Same thing, in a car...this time in the city limits over at Mission Park off East Sharp. We have a patrol car there right now."

"Then I'm on my way," said Rummel. He turned again to Curtis. "You ready to take a tour?"

"I'm with you," Brad replied, and the two men left McCoy, who was again chewing his lower lip.

****

What Rummel found was almost identical to what he had seen four days earlier. Except for one thing. He knew the victim this time.

"This like anything you've seen in Seattle?" he asked Curtis as he held the car door open for him to take a long, hard look.

As he leaned into the car, the young detective appeared to be unfazed by the blood soaked corpse that was sprawled out against the driver's door and stared back at him with vacant eyes that still held their last look of terror. In addition to his throat being cut, the man had been slashed badly in his groin area, and Curtis automatically assumed he had suffered the same fate of the previous victim. "This resembles a couple of the murders in Seattle," he replied matter-of-factly.

Rummel was impressed with the young man's composure. "You say resembles...but not exact?"

"Hard to say until we compare coroners' reports," Curtis noted, "but it looks like we have a lefty here, just like two of the Seattle cases. Look at the way that cut on his throat runs downward from his left to right. That's the sign of a left-handed attacker."

'Very nice,' Rummel thought. 'The kid's got talent.' "What else did you discover in Seattle?" asked Joe.

"Not much," replied Curtis as he backed out of the car and faced his partner. "Trouble is we could never find any prints or anything to do a blood workup on...at least that's what I heard, anyway. Remember, I was in vice," Brad added with a frown. "I only came across the one victim because it appeared to be prostitute related, and I was on call at the time. I just did the preliminary investigation. That was the third one, and there weren't any after that."

"How long ago was that?"

"About a year."

That made Joe think. Something might have scared off the killer at that point and driven him out of town, if in fact it was a him. It very well might be a her. Marty Vaughn was a lot of things, all of them not very nice, but Rummel was quite certain he was not a homosexual or even bisexual. Vaughn had always thought of himself as a real hotshot with the women and had prided himself on his numerous girlfriends, although that was no real measure of straight these days. But something inside told Rummel that Vaughn was straight alright, and that whoever he had let get this close to him had to be a woman. He would check with Sept to find out what he had dug up on Johnson just to be certain. "Nothing after that, I suppose," he said absently to his partner.

"Not a thing. We had half of homicide working on it and not even one decent suspect to show for it."

"Let's call in the forensic team and get this car dusted down," Rummel suggested. "I know we won't find anything, but we've got to do it. Then we're gonna pay this little slime ball's friends a visit tonight when they crawl out from their holes and see if we might be able to dig up a witness."

"I look forward to it," said Curtis. His face beamed with youthful enthusiasm.

'Jesus,' Rummel remarked to himself as he reached inside his pocket for his examination gloves. 'Was I ever like that?'

****

Maybe he had never noticed it before, but it struck Joe that night that the streets of Spokane were beginning to smell like Chicago's. Likely as not, it was the unusual humidity that had caused the connection. Whatever the reason, there was heaviness to the air, an oily feeling from it that covered everything and accented the pungent odors of exhaust fumes and stale debris. The alleys had their own special smell that wafted onto the streets from the dumpsters and urine soaked bricks. Here and there an empty bottle of Thunderbird or MD 20/20 stood guard in vacant doorways and next to abandoned stair steps in mute testimony to the dead souls who had been there hacking away at their lives inch by inch. Others still huddled around in groups of twos or threes and, as the two police officers passed by, they shifted submissively to the edge of the sidewalk, their loud drunken talk falling to murmurs.

They had hit several of Vaughn's known hangouts looking for someone who might have been with him that night, starting with the quaintly respectable O'Reilly's and working their way down. Now they were in the heart of skid row, which even Vaughn had tended to avoid if he could help it, but it was also home to some of his associates in the drug world. Rummel had been informed the victim had been seen with Ray Hill the night he had been murdered and was told where Hill might be found. Hill was someone else who was well known to the detective. One more stop was on their list before they'd call it a night--The Pit, a basement dive that well lived up to its name.

The two detectives entered the dingy, smoke filled bar to be greeted by suspicious stares and an uncomfortable silence as a pool game in the corner came to an abrupt stop, and the three players, all biker types, stood tall with pool cues held menacingly at port arms. Curtis stood out like a college student slumming it. He wore well fitted jeans and a camel colored windbreaker. Joe was still in one of his many pairs of trusted Dockers but had on a lightweight tan trench coat to go with them this time, one that hung noticeably high on his towering frame. Rummel ambled over to the bar as if no one else was in the room, followed right behind by his partner who acted just as nonchalantly. The owner and bartender, an emaciated shadow of a man with thin, greasy strips of black and gray hair that languished in strings, just then appeared from the back room. A look of surprise filled his face, followed by a slow, broad grin. "Rummel, you dumb son of a bitch. What the fuck you doin' in here?"

Joe laughed. "Well, if it isn't Mr. VanTighem...look what the goddamned cat drug in. I heard you were off drying out somewhere."

"What's that bullshit all about?" the owner answered. "My candy ass cousin tell you that?"

"Fact is he did," Rummel said with a smile.

"I just can't figure a guy like you hanging out with a pampered little asshole like that."

"He's the only friend I've got."

"You two deserve each other then," VanTighem sneered. "If you weren't a fuckin' cop, you'd have a lot more friends." The owner paused briefly to look over Curtis with a critical eye. The young police officer noticed right away that hidden behind the shabby exterior was a distinct look of intelligence. "Where'd you get the pretty boy here? You change your ways, Rummel?"

"This here is my new partner," said Joe as he wrapped a burly arm around Brad's shoulder and moved him forward like a proud father showing off his son on graduation day. "This is Detective Brad Curtis, and, Brad, what we have here is Alan VanTighem, bottom feeding cousin of my best pal, Jack VanTighem."

"He's a pontificating cocksucker, that's what he is," the man grumbled to conceal his twisted sense of humor. "Ever since the chickenshit quit drinking, he ain't been worth a lick of fun."

"You be nice to him, Alan, and maybe he'll give you some of his money to help clean up your act."

"That's good enough reason not to be nice to him," VanTighem remarked. "He's just about dumb enough to do just that, and I don't want my act cleaned up. Besides, I haven't spoken to him ever since he got religion."

Rummel broke out laughing. "He hasn't got religion. Religion's got him…and it's driving him nuts."

"Good for the peckerhead," VanTighem snorted with a lopsided grin of bad teeth. "But you didn't come here to talk about my cousin. What do you want?"

The detective's expression shot serious. "Guy by the name of Ray Hill…we're looking for him. Heard he was a friend of Marty Vaughn's, and he was with Vaughn just before he met his end."

"Vaughn didn't have any friends," snarled VanTighem. "Served the little prima donna right. Heard he got his cock cut off. That true, Rummel?"

Thinking word gets around fast, Joe chose to ignore the question. "You seen Hill around?"

"He was in here earlier."

"You know where he might have gone?"

"He might have gone home," VanTighem answered. "He lives just around the corner…Churchill Apartments."

"Appreciate it, Alan. I'll tell Jack you said hello."

"Don't bother."

"Nice to meet you, Mr. VanTighem," Curtis added with a friendly smile.

'Please give me a break,' thought Rummel.

"Where'd you find this guy, Joe?" VanTighem asked sarcastically.

"Never you mind," replied Rummel as he was already heading toward the door.

On their way out, neither man paid any attention to the pool players who were still standing by the table, but both men moved their hands a little closer to their weapons just in case.

In the rundown hallway outside Hill's apartment, the detectives could hear loud voices inside, partying from the sounds of it, though not very sociable, and it also sounded like there were at least three of them in there. Motioning for Brad to step to one side of the door, Rummel flushed himself up against the wall opposite him and banged on the door, shouting, "Police...we want to talk to Ray Hill!" For a moment there was silence, then panicked scurrying inside and desperate orders exchanged which were intended to be muffled but nevertheless came across clearly from fear driven mouths. "That's it!" Rummel announced. "We've got a drug bust on our hands!" He leapt in front of the door and gave it his best kick with all his weight behind it, then jumped aside as the door flew open.

Rather than a hail of bullets, a chair flew into the hallway, which at least told them there may not be guns inside. Weapons at ready, both officers barged through the doorway, Rummel swinging right and Curtis hunkering low and to the left. Before he even saw it coming, a lamp sailed across the room and hit Joe squarely in the forehead, knocking him backwards into a wall. He wanted to shoot the bastard who had done that, but he was too dazed to see or hit anything. All he made out was a shadow streaking toward what must have been another room, and he heard Curtis shout, "Stop!" The next moment his partner charged after the man. Rummel mustered all of his strength, managed to pick himself up and staggered after them.

They had tried to make it out the window and down the fire escape, but with all three of them going for it at once, there was nothing but chaos at the half open window. Rummel couldn't quite believe what he witnessed next.

Two of them turned on Curtis, while the third rolled off the pileup and over the bed to head for the bathroom. A lightening kick straight and high in the air caught one of them under the chin, and an instant later Brad's other leg rotated and shot out to slam the second assailant in the groin. With one smooth motion, Curtis lunged forward and threw an elbow to the temple of the second man who had dropped to his knees, bowling him over, and then he nailed the first one with a sharp, backhanded chop to the throat. Both were on the floor and out of commission in a matter of seconds.

Suddenly Rummel realized he had one in the bathroom to take care of. He turned and lurched through the open door. The man was bent over the toilet with one hand in the bowl and the other reefing at the handle. Rummel kicked him squarely in the butt and sent him crashing forward into the upright toilet seat, which fell forward on him. With his big hands, he seized the man by the collar and pants waist, pulled him back and rammed him headfirst into the toilet tank. The man went limp, and Joe tossed him to one side like a used dish rag. He pulled up his coat sleeve and searched the toilet bowl for its contents. A quart freezer bag containing pills and plastic vials of crack was lodged just inside the opening. The detective withdrew his prize and put the drugs down for a moment so he could thoroughly wipe off his soaking hand and arm against the man's face. "Mr. Hill, we meet again," he said when he was finished.

Curtis already had his two men cuffed, although they weren't going anywhere for awhile anyway, and he was on his radio calling in for assistance when Joe stepped back into the room. "Jesus, look at you," Brad told him.

Rummel was still a little dazed and confused. "Huh? What do you mean?"

"Your head…it's covered with blood."

For the first time Joe felt a stinging sensation. The detective raised his left hand and brushed it gently cross his brow and temple. It hurt. He inspected the back of his hand and found it covered with blood. Rolling his eyes to the ceiling, Rummel moaned, "Ah, man, I'm too short for this shit."

His partner found no humor in his remark. "We'd better get you to the emergency room for some stitches," he said. "I've got help coming. Think you'll need an ambulance?"

"Nah, no ambulance," Rummel replied as he backed up against a wall and slowly slid down it to sit on the floor. "You can drive me there when the backup gets here. Besides…we have to wake these assholes up and read them their rights." Hesitating a moment to catch his breath, he added, "We'd better do it by the book. No doubt these boys are going to be screaming police brutality in a couple of hours."

On their way to Deaconess Medical, Rummel looked at Brad with an admiring, though weak smile, saying, "Where'd you learn that shit back there?"

"What shit?"

"All that fancy kicking stuff. You a black belt in karate or something?"

"No belts," Curtis replied. "I've taken a lot of lessons in various martial arts, but most of it has been self-taught."

"Jesus, you kick like a mule."

"When you're my size, you have to come up with some kind of advantage," Curtis answered. "You do if you're going to stay in one piece in this business."

"You got a name for it?"

"I suppose the majority of it is called savate."

"Sir what?"

"Savate…French style kick boxing mixed with a Korean brand of martial arts called Taekwondo."

Staring straight ahead again, Rummel nodded his head, remarking, "That I've heard of." There was a momentary pause before he added, "Yes, I must say, I am impressed." More silence followed by another comment. "I hope you noticed my own particular brand of self defense…how I use my head to stop flying objects."

Curtis laughed. "What do you call that?"

"Stupidity," Rummel scoffed. "The best brand of self defense would've been quitting this business years ago."

Quiet fell over the two occupants of the car for a minute or so as the truth of Joe's words touched them both. Suddenly the older detective asked, "What the devil brought you out this way? Spokane's actually kind of a dead town…especially compared to Seattle. I'd think a young guy like you would want to stay where the action is."

"My girlfriend took a promotion here," Curtis explained. "She's a vice-president now with Seafirst Bank."

Rummel smiled. "Hanging around with a pretty high powered woman it looks like," he observed.

"She's great," Brad said with a proud grin. "She got the job six months ago, and it's taken me this long to catch up with her."

"What's her name?"

"Kim…Kim Wintrode."

"Good name," Rummel said, nodding. "I've got a daughter named Kim."

****

The next day Detective Rummel and his new partner went to county lockup at the Spokane Public Safety Building to interrogate Ray Hill. Rummel's head throbbed as the pain pills began to wear off, and he could feel the stitches starting to pull. If he had known his head was going to feel like this, he figured he should have at least gotten drunk and deserved it. "Sorry to bust in on your little social event," he told Hill. "If you would've invited us in nice like, we probably wouldn't be having this conversation."

"You had no fuckin' right, Rummel," Hill sputtered. "Where was your fuckin' search warrant anyway?"

"You ever heard of probable cause?" Curtis offered.

Hill wouldn't even look at him. He knew what Curtis had done to his two pals, and he wanted nothing to do with the young detective. Glaring up at Rummel from his chair, he sneered, "I'm gonna sue your fuckin' ass for police brutality."

Joe laughed. "From my end of it, I see resisting arrest and assaulting a police officer. That, along with the drugs we found, will buy you some real time, Ray ol' boy."

Hill clammed up, stared at the floor and sulked.

"Tell you what, though, Ray," Rummel went on. "Seeing as how both parties seem to have gotten off on the wrong foot, what do you say we start all over and be nice to each other?"

"What do you want, Rummel?" Hill grumbled.

"Just a little information, Ray. Nothing that would even hurt you or ruin your upstanding reputation."

"Like what?"

"Like were you with Marty Vaughn Tuesday night?"

Hill suddenly looked scared and very willing to talk. "I had nothing to do with that, Rummel...I swear I didn't."

"I didn't say you did," the detective said. "I just want to know if you were with him that night or saw anybody with him. That's all we wanted to know in the first place until you beaned me on the head and got yourself in all this trouble."

Hill asked for a cigarette, and Rummel offered him one and a light. Taking a deep drag, Hill explained in a shaky voice, "We had a little business that night, and I saw him for maybe a half hour or so."

"Little business like the quarter ounce of coke we found on Vaughn," added Curtis.

Rummel glanced over to his partner and gave him a slight nod to cool it. "Go on," he said to Hill.

"We were at O'Reilly's. He left alone, and I was out the door a couple minutes behind him." Hill paused, and the two officers waited patiently for him to continue. "I was headin' down the street the opposite way, and I happened to look back and see him on the corner talking to this chick."

"You recognize her?" asked Rummel.

"Nah, it was too far away. Looked like she had dark hair, though...body looked great from a distance. I just figured it was some hooker he met up with or one of his girlfriends he was always bragging about."

"You notice what she was wearing?"

"Jeans I think...how the fuck would I know?" Hill was becoming very agitated. "I didn't pay any attention...alright? All I know is what I heard on television and what the word is on the street, and I'm telling you right now, Rummel, I want nothin' to do with that kind of shit. I hope you get the fuckin' bastard."

"Did he leave with her?" inquired Rummel.

"I don't know," Hill stated. "I just kept on walking."

Turning to Curtis, Joe asked, "What do you think? We need any more from our friend here?"

"Not that I can think of," Brad concluded.

"Hey, what about me?" Hill demanded. "You said we could talk."

"We just did," answered Rummel.

"C'mon, man, I mean about this bust." Hill's eyes were pleading.

As he managed a smile for someone he held in total contempt, Rummel said to the man, "Tell you what...you talk to your lawyer and tell him to cool it on pursuing the rough stuff, and we'll see to it the D.A. drops the charges of resisting arrest and assault. The drug bust, on the other hand, you plead it out any way you want to." Turning to Curtis, he asked, "That sound fine to you, partner?"

Brad grinned like a boy scout. Joe just couldn't get over how delicate and harmless he appeared after what he had witnessed the night before. "Sounds fine to me," Curtis replied.

"That okay by you?" Rummel asked Hill.

Hill just grunted and shook his head yes.

The detective couldn't resist rubbing it in. "Next time we come to a party of yours, Ray ol' boy, you might be a little more sociable and invite us in...save yourself all this trouble."

"Fuck you, Rummel," said Hill under his breath.

"See ya, Ray," Rummel responded.

As soon as he left the interrogation room and entered the hallway, Joe really became aware of his splitting headache. He knew it wasn't going to get any better when he saw McCoy hustling down the hall toward him, chewing his lower lip. "Joe, we got reporters outside, and they want to talk to you."

"I don't want to talk to them," Rummel argued. "I've got a helluva headache, and I just don't want to deal with their shit right now. Let Brad do it."

"I'll be happy to talk to them, Lieutenant," Curtis cheerfully offered.

"No, Brad," McCoy replied. "Joe's been on this since the beginning, and they want to talk to him." To Rummel he asked, "You got a tie to wear?"

"No."

"Figured as much. Brad, loan him your tie."

The young detective loosened his tie, pulled it over his head and handed it to Rummel. Joe gave them both a pissed off squinty look but said nothing as he opened it up farther to fit over his head and cinched it up under his collar, a bit crooked just to spite them.

"Goddamnit, you get out there and spend a couple of minutes telling them absolutely nothing," McCoy commanded. "And then go home and rest up that head of yours for a couple of days. That's an order. You've probably got a mild concussion. What did they say at the hospital?"

"I probably have a mild concussion," Joe deadpanned.

All three men headed to the main entrance of Spokane's Public Safety Building where the press anxiously awaited just beyond the doors. The cameras were already aimed at them when they stepped outside, and immediately reporters started clamoring with questions. Rummel thought of his friend Jack VanTighem, who a few years back had worked for *The Spokesman-Review* until he had become a successful writer of New Age novels. He could just picture Jack out there hating every minute of the job, cursing his colleagues under his breath rather than attending to business. At that moment he wished his friend was still working for the press so he could count on some support in the crowd.

As Rummel approached the television cameras with a little nudge in the back from McCoy, the reporters pushed toward him, and he heard two or three of them all shout the same question, "Do you have any suspects in the case?"

To the nearest microphone Joe said, "At this time we have no suspects."

"Do you know if there's any connection to the killings?" one asked.

"We think it was done by the same person if that's what you mean. As for the two victims, we see no connection at this time."

"Could this be the work of a serial killer?" another shouted.

"That is always a possibility," Rummel replied.

"Any clues? Leads?"

"We're following up on every piece of evidence. Right now that's in short supply."

"Are these killings tied in with any similar murders elsewhere?" asked one of the women television reporters.

"There may be a connection to some murders currently under investigation in Seattle," stated Rummel. "We're looking into that now."

"Then this *is* the work of a serial killer," noted a reporter from *The Spokesman-Review*.

"I haven't reached that conclusion yet," Rummel answered him with a noticeable tone of irritation. "If and when I do, I'll let you know."

"Isn't it true the genitals of both victims were severed?" asked another.

Rummel wanted to avoid that one. All they needed now was a copycat killer, to say nothing of the added sensationalism his confirmation would give the case. "Each victim suffered a series of lacerations in the groin area," was all he would say. "I'll leave the rest up to the coroners' report."

"Detective Rummel…do you think the murderer is a man or a woman?" asked the same female television reporter.

"That we don't know yet," Rummel lied in light of his own way of thinking.

"What do you know?" the *Spokesman* reporter shouted.

"I know I have a headache, and I'm going home to do something about it," Joe responded curtly.

"How did you get that cut on your head?" inquired another.

"I slammed it into the car door." There were a few chuckles in the crowd, and Rummel concluded, "I'm sure the Lieutenant here will be happy to handle the rest of your questions. I've got some things to do." With that, he pushed his way through the crowd. The reporters swarmed forward to surround McCoy, who was waving his hands and insisting he had nothing further to add.

Rummel was halfway down the sidewalk when Curtis caught up with him. "Anything you want me to do?" he asked.

Sighing, Joe replied, "Start a computer check through the FBI and see if they've got anything else like this across the country. Go back ten years if you have to. Right now I need to be left alone and maybe have a couple of beers. I'll help you with it first thing in the morning."

"You look like you could use a longer break than that," Brad sympathized. "Say...Kim and I are going out to dinner tomorrow night. You care to join us?"

"Not this week, Brad."

"Got any suggestions for a good restaurant?" inquired Curtis.

"You're asking the wrong person. Fine dining to me is going to The Onion for a burger and rings."

"We'll find something. You take care of yourself, Joe. You don't look all that hot."

"I don't feel all that hot," Rummel answered. "You two have fun." The detective turned and walked slowly away toward the parking lot. He was glad his partner had brought up his girlfriend. He had forgotten the promise he had made himself to call his daughter, and the mention of Kim had jogged his memory. First thing, once he was home, he would call Kim and see how she was doing.

****

"Hey, Sandy, this is Joe Rummel. Is Kim there?"

Stunned silence took hold of Rummel when he heard his daughter's roommate ask, "Isn't she there yet?"

"Isn't she where?" Joe inquired, dumfounded.

"In Spokane. She was planning to come out and see you."

"I haven't heard from her...I had no idea."

"It was going to be a surprise. I'll bet she stopped and visited some friends along the way. She said she was going to spend some time in Missoula."

Rummel was still in shock. "Does her mother know about this?" he asked.

"To be honest with you, Mr. Rummel, they haven't been getting along too well. I think Kim wanted to talk to you about that. I'm sure that's one of the reasons she left Chicago."

"Left Chicago? For good? How long's she been gone?" Joe pressed.

There was a long pause on the other end, followed by the hesitant explanation, "Maybe a week...or two...I guess."

The detective had been in the people business long enough to know when someone was not being completely truthful with him, but he didn't push it with Sandy; perhaps he didn't want to hear the truth. Instead, he said, "She didn't call, let me know...nothing."

"Like I said, Mr. Rummel...it was supposed to be a surprise."

"Oh, I'm surprised alright, Sandy. Thanks for telling me."

"No problem, Mr. Rummel."

"Talk to you later, Sandy. Goodbye." Joe hung up and wondered just what the hell would happen next. He was totally unprepared for this. He knew full well he would be worrying about Kim every minute of the day until she showed up on his doorstep, and when she did he was going to give it to her both barrels for taking off like she had and not letting him know what she was up to. Rummel hoped desperately nothing had happened to her so he would indeed have that opportunity to give her hell.

CHAPTER THREE

Rummel couldn't quite believe he had agreed to this, but here he was on a Sunday afternoon parked in front of Brad's apartment, which looked a little pricey for a cop's salary. The banker girlfriend must be giving him money, Joe figured, or else he was just plain family rich, which had been the detective's first impression anyway. No way could he be on the take. He would suspect Sister Theresa before this kid.

What he had agreed to was Sunday dinner and the chance to meet this superwoman girlfriend Kim. Normally, this time of the year, Rummel would have been fishing with his buddy Jack, but VanTighem was out of town that weekend on business. Besides, Joe had to admit to himself that crack on his head was still bothering him. His resiliency had vanished with the advent of middle age. About all he would have done anyway would have been toss a couple of burgers on the grill and watch TV, likely as not an outdoor sports show, so why not let someone else do the cooking. It had to beat his standard fare of burgers, frozen dinners, pizza or fried chicken, and it would do him good to crawl out of his shell and be a little sociable for a change. At least that's what he kept telling himself. In actuality, he figured he'd rather stay home.

Rummel grabbed the six pack of Heineken he had purchased especially for the occasion, climbed out of his battle scarred, white '84 Toyota pickup and headed up a very countrified stone walkway surrounded by lush green shrubs and a well manicured lawn. As he prepared to ring the doorbell, he felt a little nervous about it all, almost like he was on a first date. Deep down he wanted to be accepted, he wanted to know right then and there that he would fit in. Cops spend too much time together, and their wives and girlfriends are well aware of that fact. The approval of a partner's spouse or significant other was important, so important that many a working relationship hinged on it. Suddenly, Joe caught himself wishing he had a girlfriend he could have brought with him to even things out a little, to take him off the hook and away from too much scrutiny. With situations like this, it definitely helped to be attached. That was something he had not been for a very long time, and being completely on his own was a feeling he had never quite grown accustomed to.

Rummel rang the doorbell and waited. Moments later it was answered by one of the best looking women he had ever seen. Her hair was sensuous, shoulder length and wavy, soft brown with a hint of auburn, and it framed sculptured high cheekbones, a dazzling wide smile and bright blue eyes that were richly colored. His first thought was this had to be the perfect European beauty right out of central casting. The smiles and eyes held him speechless for a few seconds. There was genuine sincerity in her warmth, particularly the smile, and in her eyes burned intelligence. Instantly, Rummel liked her, and just as quickly he realized this was a woman not to be taken lightly, one who could handle her own under any circumstance.

"Joe Rummel," Kim said as she extended her hand and gave him a firm handshake. "I've heard so much about you that I really looked forward to meeting you. Please come in."

"You've been the main topic of conversation on the other end, Kim," Rummel replied, feeling strangely inadequate in this woman's presence and a little uncertain of himself, emotions he thought he had outgrown years ago. "Now I can see why."

"You flatter me. Don't just stand there…come inside. Brad's working on dinner."

Somehow that seemed to make sense, Joe thought as he entered the expensively appointed apartment. The walls were covered with signed prints, mostly modern impressionist and Asian works. Joe preferred wildlife and western art, but these looked damn good, very classy, as did the rest of the furnishings—a plush, dark blue patterned sectional, a few pieces of heavy duty white wicker and a generous helping of rosewood tables and cabinets, most of which he suspected were antiques. The view from the living room of Brad's South Hills apartment encompassed downtown Spokane and was no doubt among the best available for city lights at night.

"Hey, I'm in the kitchen, Joe," Curtis called from around the corner. "You guys can come in here and keep me company."

"The chef must not be kept waiting," Kim announced as she motioned to Rummel to follow her.

Joe did follow her and found his partner decked out in a Kelly Green full apron fussing over a steaming pot on the stove. "What's for chow?" Joe asked to tease the man he was starting to view as a friend.

Curtis turned around with a feigned look of irritation. "Chow! You think you're still in the Army or something?" With a gracious gesture, he went on. "Today we are serving rack of lamb with a wine and mushroom marinade, steamed asparagus with cream sauce, potatoes rissole, and for appetizers we have Greek spinach turnovers, all to be concluded by my very special Grand Marnier soufflé for desert."

Rummel was truly astounded and impressed. "You gotta be kiddin' me," he answered.

Curtis put on his annoyed expression again and said to Kim, "Please get this barbarian a beer to stuff in his face."

"Hey, Brad, I brought my own...Heineken...class, don't you think?"

"I'll take one of those if you don't mind," said Kim. "I could use a beer right now after listening to all this bullshit in the kitchen."

"A woman after my own heart," Rummel stated. He opened two beers with the bottle opener Kim had handed him, gave her one and asked, "How about a glass?"

"Bottle's just fine with me," Kim replied.

Grinning, Rummel clicked his bottle against hers and took a healthy swig, his eyes finding it difficult to let go of her while she drank also. "Ahhh," he said as he lowered the beer from his lips. "That's good stuff, though I must admit an ice cold Pabst or Miller is hard to beat."

"Miller's my choice," Kim added.

"I don't suppose either of you two give a damn I have a bottle of vintage Bordeaux to serve with dinner," Brad added.

"What's that?" Joe teased.

Kim laughed. "Yes, dear, we care," she said. "If it wasn't for you, we'd be missing some of the finer things in life...like your great cuisine and charming company." She reached over and gave him an affectionate pinch on the butt.

"That's better," Brad sniffed, still sticking to his little act.

At that moment, Rummel flashed back on the other night when this young partner of his had systematically dismantled two hefty opponents with apparent ease. He sure had his different faces, Joe thought, and judging from the smell in the kitchen, the kid was as good a cook as he was a fighter.

The three of them chatted another half hour in the kitchen before dinner was served. During dinner they carried on their many topics of conversation ranging from life in the big cities they all had left to Joe's eloquent tale about landing a sixteen pound steelhead from the Clearwater River. As the time passed, he found himself liking both of these people more and more, to the point he was actually becoming attached to them. That was something he didn't often do, and he wondered if it was wise for him to let these feelings take hold so early in their relationship.

There was a fifteen year difference between him and Brad, eighteen with Kim, and Rummel couldn't help but assume the role of a father figure, at least that's how he viewed himself, and he hated that. It was bad enough to reach middle age with little to show for it, let alone having to admit that fact to himself and playing the part in the presence of others. He was still in good shape, he looked good and might have even passed for a few years younger were it not for the furrows and scars on his face. He didn't want to sound like an old man telling fish stories, but he was doing just that. He didn't want his marriage, his career, past adventures, his youth to be behind him, but it was. And he was pushing it even farther behind him as he sped headlong toward his highly anticipated retirement.

He wanted a woman like Kim. He wanted Brad's vitality and enthusiasm again. He wanted a piece of their youth, and had he not grown to like them both so much, Rummel might have, at that point, resented them. But Joe knew also he couldn't have it both ways. At best, he could only pretend to retain some of his youth while reality constantly and cruelly shoved him forward. It suddenly dawned on him this was the reason he had resisted coming to dinner in the first place; he had somehow known deep inside he would confront his own lost youth and inevitable mortality in the faces of these two people. It was a tough pill to swallow, but by the time the meal was over, he had decided it was all well worth it.

Kim and Rummel cleaned off the table and filled the dishwasher, much to the objections of their host, but they told him to shut up and sit down-- they were going to do this despite his protests. Then all three adjourned to the deck, lounged on the patio chairs and topped off a perfect meal with another bottle of wine, which Joe had to admit as damned good, though he wasn't much of a wine drinker.

Kim started off the conversation. "Brad tells me you have a daughter named Kim."

"Yeah, the little twerp," Rummel grumbled.

"What's the matter?" asked Curtis.

"Oh, I just found out she took off sometime back and was heading out here to surprise me with a summer visit. But she's not here yet. Now I can worry myself sick about her whereabouts until she gets here."

"I'm sure she's alright," Kim hastened to say. "How old is she?"

"Twenty-one."

"That figures. When I was that age, I was all over half the country and didn't much give a damn who knew where I was."

"I know it doesn't do any good to worry," Joe sighed as he slouched back in his chair, his eyes cast downward on the wine glass he balanced in both hands. He looked back up and added, "But I'm her dad, and dads are supposed to worry about their daughters. And this one's a real pistol."

"Sounds like someone I'd like to meet," Kim noted.

Rummel managed a smile. "I have a hunch you two would hit it off," he commented. "Hopefully she'll get her little butt in town in the next day or so, and you'll have that chance."

"Perfect excuse for another dinner party," Brad suggested.

"But this time I get to put it on," Rummel said as he sat upright again. "How's Pizza Hut sound?"

All three laughed, and Joe felt a little better now about his daughter's mysterious wanderings. Their confidence seemed to rub off on him and he was, momentarily at least, able to set aside his worries and think the best of the situation. Kim would be in Spokane shortly, and she would be alright. If this rotten world can produce a couple like this, he figured, then things do work out. That's the way he had to look at it, for now anyway, and his new friends made it easier for him to believe.

It was seven o'clock when Rummel finally left. Once he was back in his pickup, he paused to think for a few moments before starting the engine. They were perfect, the two of them together. There was a Ken and Barbie if ever they existed, but with brains and character, and that's what made him take the extra time to mull them over in his mind. As a couple, there was one key element that distinguished them from each other, that actually set them apart, and he knew what it was. Brad had a good head on his shoulders, certainly well above average in intelligence, and a personality that could charm a wolverine into laying over for a belly rub, but the control belonged to Kim. It wasn't just their conversation which had told him that either, although that had been a part of it. It was the look in her eyes, the same one he had spotted right off, and the way she carried herself that said she was the one in charge. Kim had briefly talked about her meteoric rise in the banking business and her previous financial management experience, and Rummel had a stronger than ever hunch that's where the money came from in Brad's life. There was no doubt about it. In that relationship the real power and brains were solely in Kim's domain.

****

When Joe arrived home, he found a note stuck in the door. Opening it, his heart jumped with relief as he read:

> Pops,
> I arrived this afternoon and you weren't home.
> Wanted to surprise you, but this note is probably
> surprise enough. I'm going out for something
> to eat and do some grocery shopping. See you
> later.
> Love, Kim

Rummel raced inside his apartment to straighten the place up before she arrived, a task he quickly realized he should have undertaken when he had first heard of her coming. But he did manage to wash a stack of dishes, store away a pile of dirty clothes, put on new bed sheets in the small guestroom where he would put Kim and make up his own bed before he heard the doorbell ring. It was nine-thirty.

There was a little hesitation in his steps as Rummel approached the door. He paused, took a deep breath before opening it.

Although it had been almost a year since Joe had seen his daughter, coming face to face with her now and realizing what a lovely woman she had become made it seem like a lifetime since he had last laid eyes on her. Kim's hair looked a bit longer and a little lighter brown than he had remembered it, thick with loose curls that spread over her shoulders and tumbled a few more inches down her back. Her pale green eyes were as bright and full of laughter as ever, and that huge smile of hers made Rummel want to break out with a shout of joy. She had inherited that smile from him, and the hair color and texture, and also her square features which gave her a wholesome farm girl look polished with just the right amount of cosmopolitan glamour. The eyes were here mother's contribution. Kim was tall, five foot ten, which was something else she had received from her father's side of the family, and though she was stocky like an athlete in the shoulders and upper body, she was also well proportioned with a distinct feminine shape and long legs. She was her father's girl.

Rummel stood there in the doorway, stunned silent for a second or two, then he spread his big arms and shouted, "Where the hell have you been?"

Diving into his grasp, throwing her own solid hug, Kim laughed and asked, "You knew I was coming?"

Joe held her back arm's length to take a good long look at her. "I talked to Sandy," he explained, paused for a moment, and then remarked, "Damn, you look good, young lady."

Kim again hugged her father tightly and replied, "You too, Dad...you look great."

"C'mon in," said Rummel as he wrapped an arm around his daughter's shoulder. "It's been a while since you've visited the old badger's nest."

"Looks like you cleaned it up, Pops."

"Nah, never touched a thing. Your bags in the car?"

"I've got it loaded down front and back. Some groceries too, but nothing that will spoil."

"Let it wait a bit," Rummel told her. "Here, grab a chair. Can I get you anything...coke...a beer?"

Kim chose to remain standing for the time being. "I'll take a beer," she said.

For a split second, Joe had to remind himself she was twenty-one now and a full-grown woman, and that thought rushed a shot of sadness to him. But it was also nice he could sit down and have a beer with his daughter, finally share some things in the adult world with her and perhaps learn what the little girl turned woman was all about. He disappeared momentarily into the kitchen and returned with two bottles of Pabst and one glass. Kim accepted the glass and poured her beer with skill that came only from experience. Rummel motioned again for her to take the chair closest to the couch where he plopped down. "Okay...tell me all about it," he began. "Why the big surprise visit, and where have you been?"

Kim didn't sit or answer right away. She looked down at her glass and briefly toward the living room window before turning back to her father and saying, "I've decided to drop out of school for awhile, Pops. I'm not going back to Chicago. This past week I've been staying in Missoula with friends thinking this over, and this is the conclusion I've come to. I can't go back right now."

Joe felt like he had been punched between the eyes. For a few long seconds he said nothing in response until he managed to ask at last, "But, Kim...why? The University of Chicago's one of the best schools in the country, and you've just got a scholarship and just a year left before you graduate. What the hell's going on out there, Kitten? You running short of money? If so, I..."

"It's not that," Kim interrupted. Once more her eyes lowered, and some long, silent seconds passed before she abruptly looked up at her father and stated point blank, "There was a guy...and it didn't work out. Right now I don't feel like being in school while he's there. When he's gone, then I'll go back...or finish college here. That I promise you, Dad." Her eyes pleaded with Joe to understand, and Rummel could see the hurt etched in them. "I...I'd like to stay here with you if that's alright," Kim continued. Her voice was soft and on the verge of breaking. "I can get a job and help out. The truth is I needed some time away from school anyway, and a chance to live in the real world." She paused to collect her thoughts and then concluded, "At this point, a full-time job would do me good. And I just need this time to think. I'm sort of mixed up right now."

Joe put his beer down on the coffee table and leaned forward with his elbows resting on his knees, his hands clasped in front of him. There were some quiet moments before he spoke. "What about your mother?" he asked finally.

"What about her?" Kim countered defensively.

"Does she know about this move of yours?"

"The question is does she care," stated Kim.

Rummel pinched the bridge of his nose and closed his eyes. This, on top of the entire week's events, suddenly made him very weary and feeling old. Clasping his hands again, he looked straight at his daughter and told her, "I'm sure she does care, Kim. You're part of her old life, and right now she's hung up with the new. That doesn't mean she doesn't care or love you." But in his mind Joe cursed his ex-wife for shutting out their daughter like she had. It appeared all support both financial and emotional had fallen on his shoulders, and he was more than happy to assume that responsibility, but the least she could do was show a little more concern now and then. This, he figured, was in a twisted sort of way Julie's revenge, even though it was her own daughter who was being hurt the most. "I'll tell you what," he continued. "You stay here this summer. I'll talk to your mother. If, at the end of summer, you still want to stay out of school, then we'll work out something else, like you finishing college here. Agreed?"

Kim managed a smile. "Agreed."

Rummel decided it was time to lighten up the conversation a bit with a little friendly harassment, so he puffed up, pasted on a phony glower and made the comment, "So, you've been hanging out in Missoula and didn't even give your old man a call. I've been worried sick about you."

"I'm sorry, Dad," Kim responded with an apologetic smile. "I know I should have called."

"Who the devil you been staying with over there in hippieville?"

"You remember Karen Williams…the redhead you met two years ago when you came back to visit."

"Yeah…sure."

"Her and her husband. He's in environmental studies at the university there."

"But, Kitten," Joe insisted, "Missoula's less than four hours away. You could have called or even run over here to let me know what you were up to."

"I just didn't want to upset you," Kim replied. "I took the chance you wouldn't find out I had taken off. But you did…and I'm sorry."

Rummel stood up, moved to her side and placed a hand on his daughter's shoulder. "You're forgiven this time, Kid," he said softly. She laid her cheek against his bare arm and gently placed her hand on his. "How's the beer doing?" Joe asked. "You care for another one?"

"Not right now, Pops."

"Good. I don't want to see you taking after your old man when it comes to beer."

"You could always quit," Kim suggested.

Maybe not, Rummel thought. Not while he was still working for the department anyway. He had considered the prospect more than once lately, whether or not the beer was taking over and becoming his only companion, the sole constant he could count on in a world filled with deception and ugliness. But right now that was a subject he wanted to avoid. "You're starting to sound like Jack," he answered her. "You remember Jack VanTighem, don't you?"

"How could I forget," laughed Kim. "You call Missoula hippieville. There's an old hippie if ever there was one. You remember the summer after high school when you two took me fishing in Montana? That was a hoot." Showing her father a surprised look, she remarked, "But he was drinking then. What happened?"

"He quit, but I'll let him tell you about that if he wants to."

"I read his latest book," Kim said. "Neat stuff, but a little weird."

"Weird is one of the words I'd use," Rummel agreed with a grin and a nod. "Speaking of Jack and fishing," he noted, "I've got some vacation time I have to burn, and both of us are heading over to Helena next week to catch some salmon, but I can always put that on hold since you're here."

"Don't you dare," Kim said. "You're not going to make any special plans or change anything just because I showed up. I'll be just fine here all by myself."

"You can sure come along with us if you want to."

"And get in the way of your male bonding," Kim commented with raised eyebrows. "I wouldn't think of it. Besides, it'll give me time to go out and look for a job."

Rummel pursued the matter just to be absolutely sure it was okay by her. "I know Jack wouldn't mind."

"Maybe not, but this is something you guys planned on for yourselves, and I don't want to interfere. I like the idea of being here alone. Really…there's some things I want to do right here in Spokane."

"Okay…if you're sure."

"I'm sure."

Joe beamed, took another long look at his daughter. He was delighted to have here with him despite the circumstances. She had become everything he had hoped for, every bit the woman he had envisioned from the time she had been a little girl.

One thing troubled him now and only one. The thought of her having been involved so deeply in a relationship that she had been driven to him by its failure hurt him. He still found it hard to picture her with a man, though he had already reminded himself over and again she was a grown woman who had every right to sexual intimacy. Practicality and common sense told him it was ridiculous to hold on to her that way. But that's the way he was, old fashioned in many respects, and Joe couldn't change that if he had to, as much as he hated to admit it. All he could do was avoid the subject and hope that his overly protective feelings would diminish and go away, as one day sooner or later they would have to. He decided it was just another of the realities fathers had to face with their little girls, and he also concluded most were just as uncomfortable with it as was he. "You make yourself right at home," he told Kim. "Enjoy yourself here while your old man takes off. Whatever you want, help yourself. It ain't much, but I guess the two of us can make do here...as long as you don't take over the bathroom completely."

"Thanks, Pops," Kim said as she gave her father a big hug. A tear streaked her cheek and dampened his collar. For the first time in weeks, Kim felt really safe, actually not afraid of the constant torment that grew out of her painful memories. This was the only man she trusted, the only one she could ever count on. "I needed to hear that. I needed to come here to you."

Again Rummel held her back arm's length, saying, "You know you can always come to me. I'm a cop...the good guy...remember?"

"You're about the only good guy too," Kim tried to joke, sniffing back another tear and forcing a smile. "I'm beginning to think there's not many left these days."

"Ah, don't let one jerk give us all a bad rap," Joe answered.

"Men deserve a lot more than a bad rap," Kim griped.

That was as much as her father wanted to hear of it. He pasted on a big smile and said, "What do you say I fix us up a couple of dishes of ice cream."

"You got chocolate sauce?"

"Of course, still do. I'm a helluva gourmet cook, you know."

"Alright, we're in business!" Kim exclaimed. "Anything good on TV tonight?"

"How about we go out and pick up a video?" Joe suggested. "You have dinner yet?"

"No, I was waiting on you."

"I'm stuffed from having dinner at my new partner's place. But I can pick up a pizza for you along with the video."

"No love stories," Kim pointed out.

"And no cop shows," added Rummel. "Comedy or horror?"

"Horror," Kim growled with a look of evil delight.

"You're on. Horror it is. Let's take my truck. We can unpack your car later."

Kim's look was radiant. "You got it, Pops," she said and was already on her way to the door ahead of her father. The thought crossed her mind again how much she really loved this man, the only one she would ever love the way she was feeling, for the present anyway. It was like old times again.

CHAPTER FOUR

Even after four years Kim would have recognized that self-assured grin anywhere. As she greeted Jack VanTighem at the door, she immediately whipped up a warm, welcoming smile of her own. With an extended hand expected of a professional young woman, Kim said, "Long time, no see, Jack. I hear you're going to give Dad a fishing lesson."

VanTighem took her hand with a firm grip, answering, "I knew you'd be back to straighten out the old man sooner or later. It's good to see you, Kim."

"You too, Jack." Kim found herself again fixated by his eyes, which had mesmerized her from the day they had first met. They were an alarming pale green although, surprisingly, void of the arrogant streak she had remembered. Apparently they had mellowed over the years, possibly even grown a little tender, yet they were still as piercing as ever and just as intriguing. She told herself if he were fifteen or twenty years younger and not her father's best friend, she would definitely be interested.

The man carried himself like an aristocrat in a part of the country where a more relaxed posture was the norm. That was his way, not his intent. He had fine European features, a little on the exotic side to be considered typically handsome in an American sense, more like striking, perhaps a touch beautiful, and definitely sexy--an eyeful for the cultured taste. Jack was clean-shaven, although Kim recalled he had worn a moustache before. He had a full head of soft brown hair, and though graying heavily at the temples, it was styled youthfully with a natural wave to both sides. His nose was a bit long and slender with a slight hump at the bridge that lent itself well to his foreign look. His mouth was narrow and slightly upturned at the corners, which gave him a kind of perpetually knowing smile that could look a little cruel at times and cocky always. He had a strong but not overly masculine chin, and at a shade under six foot, he was built a little on the slender side with very delicate hands and wrists for a man. Kim thought he exuded pure sex appeal. No way did he look forty-five years old, just two years her father's junior.

"So what's the deal? We going to stand out here all day, or are we going to get your dad's ass in gear?" That intriguing smile, one that could either be construed as sly and seductive or genuinely warm and friendly, was back again.

"Come on in, Jack. He's in the back room getting his gear together."

VanTighem entered the house just in time to hear his friend holler from out of sight, "Kim, did I leave my fishing boots out there?"

"What the hell you need your fishing boots for?" Jack yelled back before Kim could answer. "We're taking a boat for God's sake, and the lake is like bath water this time of the year."

"When did you get here?" Joe called out.

"A couple of minutes ago, and if you don't hurry up and get moving, I'll take Kim with me instead. If I recall, she caught more fish the last time than you did anyway."

"Come to think of it, I did," Kim added.

Rummel appeared around the corner decked out in khaki shorts and his well worn, two tone purple Hawaiian shirt. "I'm ready," he announced.

"One of these days I'm going to burn that damn thing," Jack muttered to Kim.

"What?"

"Nothing. What about your boots?"

"You said I didn't need them."

"Just seeing if you were paying attention." VanTighem turned to Kim, observing, "He hasn't been well lately, you know. Little absent minded…Alzheimer's coming on, I suspect. Probably too much beer."

"If beer was the cause," Joe butted in, "you'd be in a nursing home by now. Just because you think you've cleaned up your act, doesn't mean I have to. Besides…you're boring now. I don't even know why I hang around with you."

"I know I'm boring," Jack countered. "I'm boring myself to death. That's why I associate with boring people."

"You two going to start in on each other already?" Kim interrupted. "You have a six hour drive ahead of you to do that."

"She's right," VanTighem noted. "We should spread it out and savor it a little, don't you think?"

"Sure," Rummel agreed. "I don't want to hurt all your feelings right away. You do have feelings, don't you?"

"Not anymore," VanTighem quipped. "They're too expensive to feed."

"Out, you two!" Kim ordered.

"We're going," Rummel said, and he threw his big arm around his friend's narrow shoulder and spun him toward the door.

"And don't come back until you've caught a mess of fish and lowered your blood pressure."

"Have to be back by Sunday night, Kitten. McCoy would have my butt in a ringer if I wasn't there Monday morning."

"Forget about work," VanTighem scoffed.

"Easy for you to say with your bank account," Rummel remarked.

"Will you two get out of here?" Kim urged them.

"Good idea," Joe said as he grabbed his canvas bag. "Fishin' and camp gear's all stacked up outside."

"Already packed it," Jack said. "Let's split."

****

The northern lights swept overhead in pulsating waves like sheets of bright silk shimmering in the wind. Beyond the foothills and behind the mountains they filled the sky with a glow that rivaled the radiance of a full moon on a perfectly clear night. It was three a.m., and the two men appeared to be the only anglers left on that portion of Hauser Lake. The lights from their Styrofoam floats spread an eerie, opaque green fringe in the black water around both sides of the boat and attracted thousands of minute creatures that swarmed just below the surface. All was totally still and peaceful, other than the now infrequent flicker of a rod tip, which would suddenly cause the silence to be shattered with a mad scramble and hoots of instant excitement as a two pound kokanee salmon exploded into view and cleared the water by four feet. Otherwise, the only sounds came from nocturnal creatures triggering small rock slides along the step banks, their ominous eyes peering out of the darkness when captured by a searching flashlight, and the soft voices of two good friends sharing the predawn hours together.

"We should be two short of our limit," Rummel said after a prolonged period of silence.

"So?"

"I suppose I should count them again to make sure."

"Are you going to be forever the cop?" VanTighem asked. He was trying to be sarcastic, but his mind was too far off and his voice too gentle to come across as such.

"Well, shit, it'd be embarrassing for me to get picked up on a fishing violation."

"Yeah, you're right," Jack said. "There's fifty game wardens out there in the night waiting for us right now. It's three fifteen...if we wait another forty-five minutes, we might be able to sneak past them when they change shifts."

Ignoring Jack's remarks, Rummel was already counting fish from the five-gallon bucket they had filled to capacity. "Yup, I was right...we've got eighteen...two more to go."

VanTighem was lying back in his seat with his feet propped up on the gunnel of his sixteen-foot Crestliner, his face planted straight skyward. The last thing he wanted right now was to have a fish bother him. The action had been hot and heavy earlier in the night, and now was a time for contemplation and the enjoyment of a vast, star encrusted Montana sky featuring God's very own light show. He let Joe finish stuffing the fish back into the bucket and told him to settle back and relax. They could worry about two more salmon later. Besides, Jack wanted to stay out for the coming of dawn.

Rummel lumbered into the seat next to him, let out a big, relaxed sigh and kicked his feet up on the side of the boat also. True to his sport, however, and unlike his friend, Joe continued to hold on to his rod just in case. He reached into the cooler and grabbed another beer, opening it with a distinctive pop that punctuated the stillness of the night.

"While you're there, would you mind fetching me up another 7UP?" VanTighem asked him.

Joe handed him a can and inquired, "You ever miss it?"

"What? 7UP? Fuck no."

"Beer, smartass. I'm talking about beer."

"Don't I wish," Jack replied. His tone was pensive. "Sometimes I think it would all be so easy just to knock down a six pack and be home free again. But I can't do it. I really can't do it. All those years of believing in the unlimited powers of the human mind must've finally come to good use."

"How's that?" Rummel was truly curious. One day he might also be faced with the choice his friend had made.

"Creating realities and all that crap...it works. I shut booze out of my life by making that my new reality." VanTighem snickered ironically, more to himself than to his friend. "One day the party ended, and the need took over. I went through the motions of seeking help, but my mind was already made up. I quit. I did learn you can twelve-step anything from quitting drugs to picking your nose in public, but personally I'm not buying into it. Besides...I resented the religion involved."

Rummel broke into a grin. "Boy, things sure have changed, haven't they," he noted.

"People change," was all Jack said.

But Joe's curiosity was aroused now, particularly about the original topic in which he had a personal interest. "So why don't you drink in moderation?" he asked.

"Because I hate the stuff," VanTighem replied. "I hate it and myself for fucking up the last ten years of my life, keeping me stagnant while I stayed on working in the newspaper business. Journalists are the most obnoxious, self-centered, self-serving, backstabbing, egotistical assholes to ever set foot on this earth...and I was the worst of the lot. Their only redeeming trait is they're right much of the time and more than not stand up for what is right."

Rummel laughed out loud. "No one can ever fault you for your honesty, Jack."

VanTighem cracked a smile. "You want to know how rotten I was? I'll tell you how bad. I voted for Reagan twice just in hopes his policies might wipe out half the human race. And I did it out of pure drunken meanness. Thank God for Gorbachev. I'll be spending the next couple of my lifetimes in the Black Hole of Calcutta for that little stunt. Being a drunk and voting Republican is the Mount Everest of meanness."

"Don't be so hard on yourself," Joe told him. "I was raised Democrat and Catholic. I learned to question nothing or get the crap beat out of me if I did. At least you had the courage to explore."

"That I've done," Jack agreed with a note of sadness in his voice.

Rummel backtracked again and inquired, "Why do you say you wish you could drink again?" He was looking right at Jack, and in the dim light VanTighem could see the interest and concern on his friend's rugged face.

Jack stared up at the brightly lit night sky, saying nothing for a moment. Then, without taking his eyes off the heavens, he answered quite simply, "Because sometimes it hurts too much."

"Cindy?"

"Yup."

"You're going to have to get over her sooner or later," Rummel gently counseled. "I know. I went through it, and it was tough. But it had to be done."

"You really over Julie?" VanTighem asked.

"For the most part." Joe paused, then added, "You never really get past it, I guess, particularly when there's a kid involved. But it doesn't hurt anymore."

"I don't want to give the *idea* of her up," VanTighem flatly stated. "I know if I do, I'll have lost everything...all the changes and feelings will be gone for good."

"But you think the booze would make it easier," Rummel concluded.

"It would."

"How?"

"It killed everything in me before her, and it would kill the memory of her now."

"But you said just a minute ago you wish you could drink again. I don't get it."

"I only wish I could kill the pain," VanTighem quietly answered. "But I can't. I'm being held back."

Now that just didn't make sense to Rummel. "Who's holding you back?" he wanted to know. "Sounds to me like it's nobody but you."

There was no answer forthcoming, just a long, patient silence between the two men. After a deep breath, VanTighem finally spoke. "I keep hearing voices," he said.

"You're hearing voices?" Joe repeated with a blank look.

"That's right...I'm hearing voices." More silence, followed by VanTighem's evasive explanation, "I know it sounds loony. Tough shit...I'm loony then."

"I suppose it makes sense," Joe commented. "You're a writer, and writers are supposed to have over active imaginations."

"Writer of trashy novels like you always say."

"I just say that to get your goat."

"Well, just listen up," said VanTighem defensively, "because I'm gonna tell you about my overly active imagination. And you're the only one outside my shrink who's heard this."

"Lay it on me," said Rummel.

Jack took another drink of 7UP, stuck out his tongue at the can, cleared his throat and began. "Shortly after I quit drinking, I jumped squarely in the shit of everyone who I thought was fucking with my life. I told my boss and co-workers to piss off and Cindy to hit the road...we were through. Then I took off, lit out of town to go look up an old girlfriend in Tacoma." VanTighem paused for another drink and took a moment to collect his thoughts before he continued. "I didn't get more than thirty miles down the road when suddenly I hear this voice clear as day telling me to just relax and cool it, everything was going to be okay. That didn't bother me because I'm always talking to myself, but the feeling that hit me afterwards was, for the lack of a better description, like one helluva drug rush. I mean I melted right into the seat. I even had to pull over off the road. Don't ask me what the hell it was, because I don't know...or at least at the time I didn't think I knew. Since then it's happened a few other times, always comforting...sort of leading the way."

"And you figure maybe this is God talking to you?" Joe inquired.

"Or his Son, or both," VanTighem replied, his expression deadly serious. "In the seven years you've known me, Joe, you've also known I've been about the farthest thing from being a Christian a man can get. Cindy and I used to constantly argue over the subject. Hell, I was an atheist in

Vietnam, so that ought to say something about the integrity of my convictions. I've read The Bible, twice, once for research and this last time to see if I might have been wrong. I'll tell you right now, the way I see it, the Old Testament is pure bullshit. Genesis contradicts itself within the first four pages by allowing for the fact others existed outside the so-called first family. The Old Testament is nothing but a history of the Jews and Arabs written by the Jews... period... and a pretty biased one at that. The so-called children of Abraham, no matter what religion they lay claim to, are just deluding themselves into thinking they're something special. They're nothing more than a long, windy chapter in a very fat history book."

"Would you mind holding it down a bit," Joe suggested with a phony worried look. "There's been some storm clouds brewing in the North."

Jack just ignored him, took another swig of 7UP and went on. "For the next few weeks after my so-called epiphany...never did tie up with the old girlfriend...I found myself meditating a lot, even praying. Bit by bit the answers started to come. I started to see my former self through the eyes of some of my old romances who claimed to still care about me but were still emotionally afraid of me after all these years. And then there was this one kid, someone I hired to do some work around the house, nice kid, and after the first couple of minutes talking to him he says to me, 'You look like a man on the road to Damascus.' I was getting blindsided every which way I turned. Finally I just got tired of running and turned myself over to Christ, or the Christ Being, or whatever. I hate to admit it, but it feels kinda good for a change. Not that I gave up my Eastern beliefs, mind you. But as far as my belief in Christ and the New Testament goes, I have to think He's the one holding me back and keeping me away from the booze. Now He's holding me up by the collar just a kickin' in the breeze waiting for the next move."

There was no judgment one way or the other written on Rummel's face. He simply noted, "You said you told your shrink about this. What'd he say?"

VanTighem chuckled. "He said he could give me a list of scientific explanations for what happened to me. But in my case, considering my track record, he figured it was God talking to me."

"Sounds to me like you've developed a conscience without asking for one," Joe quietly observed.

"Oh, I asked for it alright," grinned VanTighem. "I just don't know what to do with it now that I've got it."

"I see your dilemma, old buddy. Wish I could help you out, but God and me ain't exactly been on speaking terms over the years."

"Neither was I, Joe," VanTighem reminded him.

"I guess I'm not afraid of death," Rummel commented out of the blue. "When I was younger and should've been scared, like in Vietnam, I wasn't really. Now it's getting that way again. It's only when you've got someone in your life, someone to love and care for that it seems a guy gets scared. Don't get me wrong...Kim's my life now, but she's grown, and if one these clowns should off me, she could take care of herself." After taking a few seconds for his beer and some thoughts, Joe added, "As for God, I guess I just have to let the chips fall where they may. Maybe I did screw things up pretty badly with Julie and such, but at least He knows I'm trying to do right by it now. I guess whatever happens after I croak, that's the chance I have to take."

VanTighem didn't respond right away. Finally he said, "No, I'm not worried about my soul either." For a time his stare seemed lost somewhere across the lake. Then he turned to his friend, looked him squarely in the eyes and said, "But I'll tell you what I am afraid of. I'm damned well afraid of getting old, and we're both heading that way too fuckin' fast. But worse yet, strangely enough, I'm *not* afraid of growing old alone. Something's still missing in my makeup."

That hit home with Rummel, very hard. There were a few moments of dead quiet before he replied, "I think I know what you mean. My job's kinda turned me cold too."

Dawn began to touch the night sky with its first signs of pallor that quickly washed away the northern lights and turned the glassy lake surface an ashen grey. Long minutes without conversation passed as the two men turned their attention to their rod tips and waited patiently for the slightest movement that might signal the return of another school of salmon. All was still, save the sound of shore birds awakening and the occasional high-pitched shriek of a lone nighthawk that had lingered to hunt to the very last minute. It was beginning to appear this might be the end of it, and they would be going back two fish short. But that made no difference to either man. They were where they wanted to be at that point in time, doing what they wanted to do.

VanTighem finally broke the silence. "You still working on that psycho case?" he asked.

"Don't remind me," Rummel growled. "It's too nice out here to be reminded of that shit."

"So I take it you are then."

"Yup."

"You come up with anything yet?"

Rummel hesitated a moment before answering, not that he wanted to keep any secrets from his best friend, but he was wondering himself if, in fact, he actually did have anything. "I think it's a woman," he said at last. "A left-handed one."

Jack was intrigued. "Why do you say that?"

"Cause both victims were straight near as we can figure, and they were taken out from the front, probably while having their dicks played with. That tells me it's a babe. The angle their throats were cut indicates a left-handed murderer. Are those fuckin' fish ever going to bite again?"

VanTighem wasn't about to change the subject. He had been doing some thinking about this, and he had a proposal to make. "Who you got working on it with you?" he inquired, his tone showing signs of the old reporter coming out.

Rummel stared at his friend with a suspicious look. "A new kid by the name of Brad Curtis," he replied. "You wouldn't know it by looking at him, but he's one tough little son of a bitch. Why do you ask?"

"You got room for a civilian on the case?"

"Who? You?"

"Who else?"

Joe leaned back in his seat, resting both arms over the back of it, and measured his friend's expression closely before he asked, "What brought this up? You writing a book or something?"

"Maybe," Jack answered. "Thinking about it. I've never done a cop story before, and I figured it might be a nice change from my standard fare. This serial killer thing you have is plenty juicy, and you could more or less show me the ropes and the technical stuff."

"McCoy would have a coronary," Joe stated. "He's still pissed at you from the time you were a reporter. And don't call it a serial killer case. I don't even want to think about that crap."

"You're a short-timer. What the hell do you care what anyone thinks? Besides, you know I'd treat the cops right. You can be my technical advisor...anything not right, out it goes." VanTighem waited a moment to let his suggestions sink in, then he said, "Tell you what...I'll cut you in for half. There's your retirement sweetened for life. Kim's education settled."

That last remark did it. The offer was totally appealing the way Rummel viewed it, and perfectly legal if he held off until after his retirement to collect. Not much anyone could do about it anyway, not if he put his foot down and insisted that his friend be allowed to help out. Worse they could do was take him off the case, which wasn't likely. The Spokane Police Department needed him more than ever now, and they had to make the very best of his services while they still could. Besides, he could use all the help he could get, and a good investigative reporter might come in damned handy. A sly smile crept across Joe's face. "Sure...why not," he agreed. "Do you good to go to work for a change. It's been a long time."

"Whatever you need, you got it...as long as I get to tag along, and you clue me in as to what's going on along the way."

"I'll run it by McCoy on Monday," Rummel promised him.

"Think he'll object? You said he was pissed at me."

"He is. And of course he'll object, but in the long run he'll do what I want because he has no other choice. He wants this thing tied up fast, and as long as I can convince him you'll be a good little boy and not get in the way, and maybe be a real asset to the case, he'll go along with it, as long as it doesn't cost the department anything."

"Great," VanTighem said, his look glowing with satisfaction. "I'll be ready to roll whenever you give me the high sign. But there's one other thing."

"What's that?"

"Look at your rod."

Rummel's rod tip was twitching frantically. "Holy shit!" he shouted as he scrambled to set the hook.

****

"I told you we'd make it. Aren't you glad we tried?"

"I like laying here looking up at the clouds."

"This will always be our island. Just for the two of us."

"That one up there looks like a dog. You see it?"

"I see it. It does look like a dog. I wish we could stay here forever."

"Maybe we can if we pretend hard enough."

"Pretend is for little kids. Someday we'll have to go."

"I want it to always be the two of us together. Nobody else."

"I want it that way too."

"Make a promise? We'll always be together?"

"I promise."

****

Gary Keating had a little too much to drink and was on his way back to his motel when he came across her standing at the bus stop. It was late at night with no one around and not much traffic on the streets. Wondering first if such a good looking woman shouldn't be a little paranoid out this late alone, he concluded next she must be a hooker, although she didn't look like one. Finally he figured she must be waiting for someone, probably a boyfriend. She sure was a beauty--tall, built, sexy long brown hair. That was one he definitely would like to have a shot at. Since he was an out-of-towner in Spokane on business, and since he fancied himself a ladies' man even though he was, in reality, a middle-aged, overweight ex-college jock with thinning blonde hair, and since he had already fortified his courage with alcohol, Keating decided to give it a try. He walked right up to her and said, "Excuse me. I'm on business in town and a stranger to Spokane. By any chance you know of a good night spot nearby?"

She smiled at him, which was encouraging. "The Red Lion up the street has a nice quiet lounge," she answered. Her voice was soft yet also a bit raspy, coming across as being very sexy.

"That's where I'm staying," Keating commented with a broad smile of his own. He hesitated, then inquired, "You waiting for the bus?"

"No," she replied.

"Someone picking you up and giving you a ride or something?"

"Doesn't look like it," the woman sighed.

At that moment Keating knew he was in luck. "Say, how about joining me for a drink at the Red Lion? You can call for a ride there if you want, or I can give you a lift."

"I'll pass on the drink, but making that call sounds like a good idea," the woman said with a look that was warm and clearly inviting, Keating thought.

"Great." I'll walk you there. My name is Gary Keating."

"Nice to meet you, Gary," the woman said as she offered him her hand, which he took in his and held too long. She didn't seem to mind. "I'm Kim...Kim Robinson."

By the time they reached Keating's hotel, he had convinced her to make her phone call from his room. They seemed to be hitting it off very well. She laughed at his jokes, and she told him she appreciated him escorting her this late at night. Keating figured it was all falling into place just perfectly.

In Keating's room, Kim made two phone calls, both of which appeared to be no answers. Showing only a slight sign of frustration, she sat on the edge of the bed and crossed her legs to reveal the perfect contour of her tight Levis. She asked Keating if he had a drink.

"Sure, I keep a bottle with me," he eagerly replied. "Bourbon okay?"

"Bourbon and water sounds just fine," Kim answered him.

Keating produced a bottle from his suitcase and dashed off to the bathroom for two glasses. "I'll go down the hall and be right back with ice," he said as he reappeared with two drinks.

"Don't bother," Kim told him. "This is just fine the way it is."

Keating sat down on the edge of the bed next to her, handed her a glass and raised his. "Here's to good times."

"To good times," Kim repeated in that low, sexy voice of hers.

Keating loosened his tie. "Hot in here," he commented. He was nervous, a little edgy. Perhaps this seemed to be going just a little too well.

"Why don't you get comfortable?" Kim suggested as her lips parted into a suggestive smile. "If you don't mind, I have to use the bathroom for a few minutes." Before he could say anything, she stood up, picked up her purse and headed toward the bathroom. Keating kept his eyes pasted on her tight buns the whole time. Kim disappeared, closing the door quietly behind her.

Keating had his shirt off in an instant, choosing, however, to leave his tee shirt on to cover up the flab lines in his gut, which he tried to suck in. He heard the bath water start to run, and he knew then this was going to be it.

The minutes passed, and the water kept running. Thinking the tub must be full by now, Keating still chose to wait some more. The water continued to run. Easily ten minutes passed. Finally he stood up, sucked in his stomach once again, and approached the bathroom door, rapping on it lightly. "You okay?" he asked.

No answer, nothing but the sound of running water. There didn't appear to be any overflow coming out; she must be okay. Maybe she didn't hear him. Keating again asked, a little louder this time, "You okay in there?"

Still no answer. The water was still running.

Tentatively, Keating pushed on the door. It opened a few inches, and he applied a little more cautious pressure to it until finally he decided to open it all the way.

Kim was standing right there in front of him, and it startled Keating. His surprise instantly turned into fear as he saw a look and a face he scarcely recognized, wild eyes and a sadistic leer that sent shivers racing down his spine and tears to the corners of his eyes. It was the look of a beast crazed with blood lust and poised to sink its fangs into unsuspecting prey, who he realized at that very moment was him.

His life was but seconds away from ending, and somehow Keating knew that very clearly. But fear froze him in place, paralyzed him completely, made him totally helpless as the events unfolding before him became stop-framed in a series of millisecond movements that seemed to take an eternity. A knife flashed in the picture, long and narrow, glistening in the bright bathroom light, and held high in a latex gloved hand it fell toward him with a roundhouse swing. All Keating wanted to do was get the hell out of there before that knife cut his face, but it disappeared from his vision, and there was the sting of it biting across his throat, and suddenly it was all no longer slow motion. It was an explosion of rapid reality instead. He saw blood from his severed jugular spray white tile and the mirror alike. Then Keating blacked out and died.

CHAPTER FIVE

McCoy was waiting for Joe at his desk when he showed up for work Monday morning. They went straight to the lieutenant's office where they spent a half hour behind closed doors. When it was over, Joe approached Brad at his desk in the squad room and said to him, "We've got another one." Curtis was right in the middle of taking a bite out of his orange while going over some faxed reports he had received from Seattle. He dropped everything. "Out at the Red Lion Parkside," Rummel added. "Sounds like our friend again."

"Let's go," Brad said as he shot to his feet. He was wearing that boyish, enthusiastic grin of his again, which Rummel could never quite become accustomed to.

"I'll meet you downstairs in a few minutes," Joe told him. "I have to talk to McCoy about a few other things, and there's a phone call I've got to make before we take off."

"See you in a few," Curtis replied and was gone.

McCoy was not taking this well, Rummel told himself as he reached for the telephone. This was now a full-fledged epidemic, the work of a serial killer, the stuff national news sinks its teeth into, and that above all else was what McCoy feared most. A hungry press meant big time pressure from above, and McCoy's nerves were just too shot to handle that. Now was not the time for Joe to tell him he was contacting VanTighem and arranging to meet him at the Red Lion.

Two uniformed officers were already there when the detectives arrived. One of the officers, a woman, was comforting a hysterical room cleaner, who was both crying and babbling wildly about what she had seen inside the room. As he walked by her, Rummel picked up enough between her gasping sobs to tell him he was about to encounter an all too familiar sight. He asked the officer to try calm the woman down and informed her he would be back later to ask the maid some questions. Rummel entered the room with Curtis right on his heels.

The bathroom door was open, and the victim lay spread eagled on the floor, his head and upper torso sticking out in the entryway. His eyes were wide open, the fear still etched in their dead stare. A gaping gash ran across his neck, blackened with caked blood that had filled the obscene slit and clotted. The floor was filled with a pool of sticky dark red, grotesquely contrasted art deco by the shiny white tile and a blood splatter that marked a path across the mirror and bone colored wall. The victim's trousers and underwear had been pulled down around his ankles, his penis removed. Blood covered the insides of his thighs and his groin, making it difficult to determine the exact extent of mutilation. But even without a detailed inspection, which Rummel opted to forego this time, the detectives could still identify the same pattern of crisscross cuts that lacerated the lower abdomen, inner thighs and testicles. There had to be a good twenty slices, just like the others. Joe was sick of it all, this whole case and the job too.

The enthusiasm was gone in Curtis' expression also. Instead, a strange, distant look had taken over as if he had stepped outside this reality in order to live with it. This clearly had taken Brad over the top too, and Rummel wondered right then if his partner would ever be young again. Perhaps he had just crossed the same bridge Joe had crossed somewhere, sometime a long time ago, the bridge between the end of innocence and the beginning of callousness and regret. Next stop middle age.

"Forensics been notified?" Joe asked absently.

"On their way," Brad said.

"They sure won't have any trouble finding prints in a motel room. Problem is won't be the ones we want."

"We might get lucky," Curtis offered.

"Don't think so," Joe said as he bent over the body. Rummel dug for the victim's wallet in his crumpled pants, found it and went through it for identification. Gary Keating obviously had a family, judging from the picture of a rather attractive brunette and two kids, a boy and a girl. If Gary Keating had kept his dick in his pants, along with his wallet, Joe speculated, he would still have a family. A sickening thought suddenly hit the detective. Was there a collection of male parts out there somewhere, trophies the murderer had stashed away to take out and admire in the privacy of his home? No, it wasn't a him. There was just too much evidence now pointing to a female. These victims were letting a woman get very close to them and paying the ultimate price for that bit of indiscretion. Joe swore to himself he'd get the bitch if he had to hold off his retirement to do it.

He went over the rest of the body very carefully, looking for even the slightest clue that might break this deadlock. The forensic team would do the same, but Rummel hoped he might at least find a stray hair, a fingernail, any fragment of evidence to get the ball rolling and give him some promise right now without having to wait for the same negative reports he had received on the other two.

But there was nothing he could discover on the body without a more thorough lab investigation. It made sense because, like the others, there were no signs of a struggle. Possibly the only physical contact made had been in the genital area, and that was nothing but a bloody pulp, something only a lab examination could sort out anyway. The victim's wallet revealed no names or addresses that might offer a lead. He had Idaho identification, appeared to be from Boise, his credit cards seemed to be intact, there was close to two hundred dollars in his wallet, robbery was definitely out of the question. Same story as the others right down to the angle of the slice across the victim's throat. For now Rummel would seal the area off and wait for the forensic people.

Outside the room there was a commotion. He heard Brad's voice telling someone he couldn't go in there and the response, "The fuck I can't...I was invited." VanTighem had arrived.

Rummel stepped outside and told his partner, "It's okay, Brad. I asked him to come here."

"Who is this guy, Joe?" Curtis demanded.

With the sudden realization he had tossed a couple of pit terriers together without intentionally meaning to, Rummel grinned and said, "Brad...Jack VanTighem. Jack, this is my partner Brad Curtis."

"Yeah, nice to meet you, Jack," Curtis abruptly commented, then turned to Rummel and added, "But that still doesn't tell me what the hell he's doing here."

"Jack's a writer," Rummel explained. "He's also my best friend. He asked me to cut him in on this investigation, and I told him I would."

Curtis was momentarily stricken speechless. "What about McCoy?" he finally managed to ask.

"Fuck McCoy," Rummel snapped. "He's up to his ass in a big mess here, and I'm one of his best hopes for getting him out of it. If I want to bring in some outside help, I'll damn well do it. Jack here is a former newspaper man, and at one time one of the best bird dogs in the business." Joe paused a moment, then concluded, "We may need all the help we can get to track down this nasty little broad."

"So you're sure it's a woman now," VanTighem jumped in.

"Not absolutely," Curtis said in a sullen voice.

"Yes, we are," Rummel stated. "If not, then all three of our victims were fags, and the way I see it that's just not the case."

"Mind if I come in and take a look?" VanTighem asked. He appeared eager, which Rummel was quite certain would change in the next few seconds.

"Go ahead. But don't touch anything."

VanTighem stepped past the two detectives and went inside. He looked down at the head by his feet and was momentarily mesmerized by the nasty cut across Keating's throat. Then his eyes drifted farther down to survey the real damage. He had seen a lot of things in Vietnam, a lot as a reporter for that matter, but nothing like this. Nausea briefly swept through him causing his forehead to sweat and his eyes to tear, and VanTighem suddenly wanted to turn away. But he couldn't. Perhaps it was, in part, morbid fascination that locked his eyes on that sight, although surely it was the horror of it all that kept his stare fixed there. At one time he might have even comprehended such an act, at one time perhaps during his darkest hour, but not anymore. This was purely incomprehensible to him now. And yet, at that very moment, he knew also he would have to grasp it if he ever wanted to capture it in writing. This would be his next book.

Turning to his friend who had joined him, Jack remarked, "Makes me kind of thankful I've dropped out of the dating scene for awhile."

"It can be dangerous out there these days," Joe solemnly agreed.

VanTighem just shook his head with amazement and disgust. "What do you do with a mess like this?" he asked finally.

"You mean from a cop's perspective?"

"Yeah. What do you do with this?"

Rummel stepped to one side to view the body again and remind himself this was reality not theory. He had to think a bit before he could get back on track with an explanation for something so disgusting. "Well, first," he began, "you go over the body for any signs of foreign material...a hair, a piece of cloth, whatever...and you want to make sure you go through the victim's belongings and identification very carefully not to disturb anything to see if there might be some small clue. You have to wear these stupid gloves when you do that. I checked his wallet for names and addresses, particularly a female's. None, of course. Just like the others...a big fuckin' blank." Joe took a deep breath and went on. "Next, we'll have the investigative team in to look for prints, particularly on things like that glass and bottle of booze sitting over there on the bed stand. Of course, there's only one glass and you can bet your sweet ass there was another one, which is missing now. They'll examine the body more carefully, and when they find nothing, which will probably be the case, then they'll bag him up and ship the poor bastard's carcass off to the coroner who will also probably find nothing, other than to substantiate my theory the murderer is left-handed."

"Then what?"

"Then you go back to square one like I've done with the other two, but this time we may have a little more luck."

"How's that?"

"Romeo here was taken out in a well frequented location, unlike the other two dummies, and we have security cameras here and maybe a witness floating around who can place him and his girlfriend together last night. We'll get the tapes from the hotel, and somewhere in or around this building we should come up with a snapshot of our two love birds."

"What's next?" Jack asked.

"Interview time," Rummel said. "You ought to be good at that. You did it enough years yourself."

"I'll watch this time."

"First place we start is that motel maid out there in the hallway...once we get her to calm down. She stumbled onto this thing probably a good eight hours or more after this guy was killed, but we have to check with her anyway just to make sure she didn't mess with anything in the room. Then we find out who was on duty last night and go to them one by one, plus the hotel guests and any bar customers if we can get their names. The uniforms can handle some of it. Like I said, we might get lucky this time. Maybe someone saw them together last night, and if not, we should come up with at least a couple of security images."

"What if we don't?" Jack inquired.

Rummel cracked a cynical smile. "We'll cross that bridge when we get to it. Let's put it this way, if we can't get a clear picture of her or an eyewitness account, and if we can't make an identification somewhere along the line through computer searches with departments nationwide, then you'd better pack your bags and spring for some plane tickets for yourself, because we're going to take a little trip all across this country and track down every single crime that even remotely resembles what we've seen here." The detective's smile vanished. He looked at the body one last time, then around the room and finally back to his friend. His expression was cold and as determined as VanTighem had ever seen it. "We're gonna nail this fuckin' bitch's hide to the wall." With that last remark, Joe began his methodical search of the room.

****

The pressure was now on and coming down on Rummel from all quarters. City Hall was demanding an all-out investigation, the press was going wild with the biggest crime event to hit Spokane in memory, civic leaders were up in arms and decrying the general decay of the inner city, whereas church leaders were bemoaning the overall decline of morals in general. Three teams of city detectives worked around the clock, and an equal number of county investigators were also on the job. Yet Rummel felt it all centered on him, and in fact a lot of it did. Between the press, his superiors and the other detectives on the case, his phone rang day and night at the office and at home. Everyone was going nowhere fast, and they came to him for answers he just didn't have.

The crime lab and coroners' reports bore out what Rummel had feared-- they had a third murder on their hands with no physical evidence to show for it. Even more disappointing, they had come up with three different security images of Keating and his companion, and in every one of them the woman's face was obscured, cast downward to the ground. It was a woman, though, confirming Rummel's original assessment, and it was one who was either very lucky or very smart to know exactly where the cameras would be placed, their angles, even in the parking lot, and manage to avoid them by keeping her head lowered.

The interviews with staff and patrons of the hotel had also come up empty. Joe and Curtis, with VanTighem tagging along, had conducted some of them for two days straight. On the third day, Rummel opted to let Brad handle some of the remaining interviews on his own while he hung around the office. He had made arrangements with VanTighem to meet him at the police station after McCoy had gone home in order to give his friend a little on the job training with the computer systems. That particular evening the lieutenant was accommodating and left work shortly after five. Rummel waited until Brad had checked back in and left for the day. It was almost seven-thirty when Jack arrived.

"One of the things the FBI computer does," Rummel explained to his friend, "is match up violent crime patterns...signature aspects we call them. You know, some guy wearing an orange ski mask and carrying a sawed off shotgun blows some people away while taking down a convenience store in Biloxi. We fax in the particulars and see if the signature aspects, like an orange ski mask and sawed off shotgun, don't come up in, say, Cleveland. It's called ViCAP, and we run our information through the FBI in Quantico."

"What's ViCAP stand for?"

"Violent Criminal Apprehension Program. That's Fed talk."

"I gather that," VanTighem noted. "I read recently somewhere that in the next few years all computers will be tied in together with some kind of communication system that allows them to talk back and forth to each other. Even home computers. Police departments might even be able to access the Fed computers directly."

"I can hardly wait," Rummel remarked sarcastically. "There goes my travel allotment."

"You might even get a computer at home that will be able to contact somebody in England or India."

"I don't want a computer at home, and I don't want to contact anybody in England or India."

"You don't want to contact anything. You don't even have an answering machine."

"I don't need one," Rummel growled. "I have my police pager, and that's all I need. Anyone wants to get hold of me at home, they can wait until I'm there."

"God, what a fuckin' dinosaur."

"You want to see what we found out through ViCAP or not?"

"So I take it you've already done this ViCAP thing," VanTighem concluded.

"Oh hell yes," Rummel replied. "Brad ran it right after the Vaughn killing. In fact, the report just arrived yesterday. Brad has it on his desk. I haven't seen it yet, but he mentioned something about Seattle, which we already knew about, and Houston."

The two men went to Curtis's cubicle, and Joe rummaged through a stack of papers on his desk. Not finding what he was looking for right away, he tried the drawers and grumbled about how this stuff always gets shuffled around. After a minute or so of sorting through folders, Rummel produced a file of FAXs and said, "Here we go." They began to read over the information together with Joe explaining out loud, "We've got the three in Seattle, two in Houston, one in New Orleans, and that's..." Suddenly Rummel stopped dead in his tracks. "What the hell?" he said.

"What's the matter?" VanTighem asked.

"I don't remember him saying anything about this," Rummel commented, more to himself than to Jack.

VanTighem was puzzled by it all. "What's going on there?"

Rummel didn't answer right off. He was still preoccupied with the information on the very last sheet. Finally he said, "We've got another one...and just two months ago." The detective looked up at his friend and stated, "We're not going to Seattle right away. We're on our way to Chicago."

****

Kim had grown accustomed to her father being in and out like a stray dog since her arrival. In fact, she rather liked the situation the way it was. Those precious moments they could spend together were all the more enjoyable and very close, treasured because they were so sporadic. She thrived on the special attention and the laughter they shared, yet Kim also liked the freedom she found from being on her own in a new town. And this was the first time in her life she truly felt independent, no longer reliant on her father for school, although she also had the luxury of anchoring herself to his heart and never being too far from the security he provided in the event her new found freedom should betray her.

She had landed a job in a clothing store at a nearby strip mall, walking distance from her father's apartment, and she was rapidly settling in, removing herself from the memories of Chicago and her past. Although Kim had already made a few new friends at work, she didn't allow herself to become too close to any one person for reasons she really couldn't identify. Everyone treated her very well, and she found Westerners far more friendly and helpful than her native Chicagoans, but something just held her back from involving herself too deeply with others. She had done that back East; her attachments had been there, and one by one they had been shattered--her mother with the new marriage, her boyfriend who had dumped her, her two closest friends who had married and moved elsewhere, even her father when he had left. Now she had him back, and for now that was all she needed.

Kim was pleasantly surprised when she answered the phone--just a couple hours after her father and VanTighem had left for the airport--and became introduced to Brad Curtis on the other end of the line. "My dad's had some very good things to say about you," she told him.

"Glad to hear that," Brad responded. "Personally, the guy's kind of a hero of mine."

"Mine too," Kim said.

There was a brief pause on the line, then, "Listen, I have the day off, and my girlfriend and I are going to hit the matinee, and we figured you might be a little lonely. We wondered if you'd like to come along."

"Sounds great. What time?"

"We'll pick you up at two-thirty."

"What we seeing?" Kim asked.

"*Pretty Woman*," Curtis answered. "You seen it?"

"No, but I heard it's good. I'm looking forward to it, Brad. I really have wanted to meet you."

"Same here," Curtis said. There was another pause. "By the way, my girlfriend's name is Kim too."

"I already heard. Dad was very impressed with her."

"Yeah, she's a cool lady. See you at two-thirty."

"You got it." Kim said goodbye, looked at her watch and went about finishing a few chores around the apartment before they arrived.

When Kim opened the door and saw Brad standing there, she had to do a double take. In her mind, cops were supposed to look like her father, big and rugged; they had all seemed that way when she was growing up anyway. This man was just the opposite, and despite his overall delicate look, he was the sexiest man she thought she had ever seen. His broad flashy smile with its touch of impishness and those vivid, startling blue eyes staggered her momentarily, and during that second of silent hesitation, she seized the time to admire also the soft waves of hair that plummeted playfully over his forehead. Congenial charm oozed from the man. Obviously he was accustomed to such reactions from women. He continued to maintain the sincere warmth of his expression without blinking an eye, saying finally, "Hi...I'm Brad." His voice was gentle and melodic.

Kim recaptured her composure and quickly responded with an outstretched hand. "And I'm Kim Rummel," she said. "Finally we meet."

Brad shook her hand firmly, asking, "You ready to go?"

"Let me get my purse and we're gone." Kim disappeared briefly, returned and followed Brad out the door, locking it behind her. Curtis was already heading toward his car, a classy looking white Chrysler convertible with red interior, and as he walked away from her, Kim couldn't help but admire his exquisitely tight buns packaged to perfection in faded 501 Levis.

As she approached the car, Kim quickly discovered the other half of that relationship was equally attractive, downright gorgeous in fact, which sent a fleeting shot of envy through her. But Kim Wintrode's graciousness quickly overcame that as she opened the door and stepped out of the car to introduce herself. Kim instinctively liked her, just for her confident and open manner if nothing else. The woman impressed her as being purely straight forward, and that she admired in anyone.

Curtis handed his girlfriend the car keys and slipped into the back seat while she motioned Kim into the passenger's seat and went around to the driver's side. Already all three were chatting away like old friends. As they drove away, Kim remembered one of her father's comments and had to agree with him that Ken and Barbie were indeed alive and well, living in Spokane, Washington.

CHAPTER SIX

Rummel and VanTighem had done about all they could in Chicago after reviewing time and again the information the detective had obtained from the city's 2nd District Homicide Division.

The victim had been a student at the University of Chicago, a sort of campus Don Juan by reputation, based on statements made by his fraternity brothers anyway, which were probably overly exaggerated. Additional interviews with people associated with the victim were still ongoing.

It was all textbook identical--the angle of the cut, the pattern of mutilation, the total absence of any foreign substances which might link up a suspect. It was as if the murderer carefully planned out her settings in advance so she could get close enough to her victims to commit the act but not close enough to leave any traces of contact. So far she was a perfectionist, and that troubled Joe more than anything else. He was beginning to wonder just how much knowledge of police investigative procedures she actually did have.

Rummel had gone over all the photographs and reports at district headquarters by himself, then he had taken VanTighem on a tour of the crime scene, which was an alley just off campus. He had also brought his friend along with him for an interview with the coroner who had examined the body. The best Rummel could come up with was that the crime had been committed by the same person almost two months before the Spokane murders had begun. Possibly, the murderer had moved from Chicago to Spokane in that time frame. That was something to go on anyway. He would have Brad contact the motor vehicle bureau and utility services in Spokane to ferret out any new customers from the Chicago area within the past couple of months. All this he had explained to VanTighem very carefully so the writer could truly grasp the monotony of detective work.

****

Joe had fortified himself with three beers before picking up the phone in his hotel room to call Julie. He would be leaving tomorrow for the West Coast on the redeye flight, and he had put this conversation off long enough. As he heard the phone begin to ring at the other end, he almost hoped she wouldn't answer. By the same token, he equally dreaded he would encounter an answering machine and be forced to make his presence known without the opportunity to speak to her directly, risking the chance she might ignore him and not return his call. She wasn't working anymore. This was the middle of the afternoon, and she should be home with the kid. On the fifth ring, Julie answered.

There was stunned silence on her end of the line when Rummel spoke. "Julie…this is Joe. I've been in town the past couple of days. I wanted to talk to you about Kim before I go back."

"Is she alright?" the voice on the other end hesitantly asked.

"She's with me," Joe replied. "I don't know if she's coming back to school or not. You busy? Can we meet somewhere for coffee?"

"Shawn's taking his nap," Julie said. Her voice had suddenly assumed control and grown cold. "Let me see if I can get a neighbor to stay with him. What's your number, and I'll call you back."

Rummel gave her the main desk number of his hotel and his room number. Julie hung up. He had nothing left to do now but wait.

****

They had decided on The Village, an Italian restaurant that featured high backed booths, classic terrazzo tile floors and some privacy, an old hangout of theirs during better years. Joe had arrived first and was almost finished with his Miller Draft when Julie walked in. He was amazed at how little she had aged, in fact how beautiful she still was with her classic high cheekbones, aristocratic nose and thick brunette hair that today was tied up into a severe bun behind her head. The cold expression written across her face came as no surprise, however.

Julie was gracious, extending a hand to him which he took as he awkwardly stood up to greet her, and she in turn gave him a curt handshake, then abruptly sat down opposite him. Her manner was clearly very reserved and intended to set the tone for this meeting. Rummel squeezed himself back into the tight fitting booth with about as much grace as he had shown standing up, which was exactly the way he felt about everything at that moment--clumsy. "What can I get you he asked?"

Julie eyed his beer. "I thought this was supposed to be for coffee," she remarked coldly.

Joe decided now was as good a time as any to stand his ground and not let her get to him. "I'll order you a coffee, then. As for me, I'm sticking with beer."

"I see things haven't changed much."

"I drink less now," Joe countered.

Pausing a moment, Julie sighed and softened a little. "There's no sense us starting in on each other again," she conceded. "You said you wanted to talk about Kim. Is she okay out there?"

Rummel eased up a bit himself and even showed the hint of a smile. "She seems to be happy," he told Julie. "Of course, I'm not real crazy about the idea of her not finishing school when she's that close." He stopped briefly to think it over, concluding, "But, she is twenty-one...and I suppose it's her life to do with as she wants."

Julie looked surprised. "I never thought I'd hear that come from you. You're the one who never wanted her to grow up in the first place."

"I don't think that's really true," Joe commented. "Fathers are just naturally like that with their daughters, and I don't think I was any worse than your average guy."

"You wouldn't," Julie scoffed. "On second thought, forget the coffee. Order me a gin and tonic, would you please?"

Raising his hand, Rummel summoned a waitress, placed their order and waited for her to return with the drinks before diving back into their conversation. After she had departed, he took a quick gulp of beer and watched Julie as she toyed with the straws in her drink before removing them and tipping the glass to her lips. She had never been much of a drinker, and he could see in her behavior how this meeting was affecting her. The last thing Joe wanted to do was cause her any pain. In a way, he still loved her, but it was a very distant love and one he would not allow to stand between him and his daughter. "I guess you're right," he allowed finally. "Maybe I did put more into Kim than I did our marriage."

"Nice to hear you admit that after all these years," Julie remarked. Her tone was cool at best and clearly sarcastic.

Rummel ignored her caustic comment and continued. "That's the past," he noted. "It's now and the future I'm more worried about. Kim's only got her senior year left, and I've been planning on just one more year of work before retirement so I could still help her out now, which..."

"You'd better figure on working a little longer then," Julie interrupted.

Puzzled, Joe asked, "What do you mean? She did finish second semester...didn't she?"

Julie broke out with a cynical laugh. "Kim dropped out of school two months ago," she said, and her expression quickly darkened again.

Rummel was dumfounded. "Why…why didn't you tell me?"

"Don't blame me," Julie told him, both hands held up in a gesture of innocence. "She had me just as fooled as you." She took a stiff drink and said, "I'll be the first to admit we don't communicate like we should…never have for that matter…but I called a couple of times, and Sandy always told me she was out but she'd give her the message. Well, when she didn't call back, I just let it slide. Probably shouldn't have, but I did. I guess I figured she was still mad at me for some damned reason." Julie paused a moment to gather her thoughts while her ex-husband lit a cigarette. "Finally, I got suspicious and cornered Sandy," she went on. "She seemed to be hiding something so I called the school. By that time, I found out Kim hadn't been to classes for over two months. I tried getting hold of you a couple times, but you were never in, and I guess I put it out of my mind for awhile." Julie suddenly cut her explanation short and glanced around the room. Her eyes had started to form tears, and Joe could see them clearly when she looked back at him. "No," she said in a voice very subdued, almost breaking. "No, that's not the truth. The truth is I just didn't want to deal with you over it." A forced smile appeared as Julie added, "Like you say…she's twenty-one, and if she wants to disappear for whatever reason, I guess that's her business."

Rummel was still astounded. He took a hasty drag off his cigarette, put it in the ashtray, had a drink of beer and demanded, "What the hell brought all this about? She told me about some guy, but I had no idea she actually dropped out of school over it."

"Well, apparently she did just that," Julie stated. "When I finally got Sandy to fess up, it sounded like a pretty messy relationship."

Joe didn't need to hear that. He winced, reached for his cigarette and rested back against the booth. "You have any idea if he's still around here or not?" he inquired.

Julie just shrugged. "I suppose not anymore. The way Sandy sounded, he split. To be honest with you, it was tough getting anything out of her. I think Kim had her pretty well coached."

Rummel shifted forward, leaned across the table now as he strangled his beer bottle in front of him with both hands, and he spoke with forced control in his voice, his anger inside screaming to be unleashed. "She's been gone two months, and you had no idea? Even though she's right in your own backyard? You have any idea what goes on out there? You have any idea how fucking dangerous it is out there for a full grown adult male to go wandering around…to say nothing of a young woman out on her own?"

"Don't you blame me, you bastard!" Julie shouted. She could be heard throughout the entire bar which, fortunately, was nearly empty. "Just where the hell were you these past two months? Obviously *you* haven't kept track of her either for I'm sure the same goddamned good reasons you always used! Your precious goddamned job takes up too much of your time, and if it isn't that, then the rest of your time's spent feeling sorry for yourself!" Although her voice had lowered, Julie's rage still burned through. "You're a real champ, Rummel," she smirked. "A real fucking champ. You're out to save the world from itself, but you couldn't even save your marriage or yourself from boozing it up. And that was alright with you because you could always make yourself into the good guy for your daughter. When it got just too damned tough on you, you could always hide behind her and show the whole world what a good daddy you were.

"Did it ever occur to you, Joe, you left me out of it entirely? What little time we did spend together, it was always you and Kim, and I was made to feel I didn't account for a goddamned thing. Sure I could discipline her and be the bitch mother, and you could be the wonderful father of convenience…when it was convenient for you to be home and not at work or out drinking with your buddies on the force.

"Don't you ever turn it back on me, you fucking bastard," Julie continued with mounting anger. Her expression had twisted into a nasty sneer, and her tone was biting. "It's hard enough for me, as it is, to live with the fact I almost grew to hate my own daughter because of you, and I can't remember a moment when I could honestly say I had any kind of relationship with either of you. You both left me out in the cold. Yes, I've been a lousy mother to Kim…particularly since I've remarried and found a family who cares for me. You get that? They care for me…someone cares for me and not always the other way around. I needed that all my life, and I sure as hell never got it from either of you."

Her long suppressed feelings now freed, Julie was compelled to stop for a time. A tear streaked her cheek. She took another drink, then suddenly grabbed for one of Rummel's cigarettes, saying as she lit it, "I quit these fucking things two years ago. You see what you do to me, Rummel?" Joe opened his mouth to say something, but Julie wouldn't let him talk. "I'll admit," she went on, the control in her voice now present again, "Kim and I have no relationship anymore. I don't want it to be that way, but I have to take care of myself now. I'm sorry it turned out like this. She's a grown woman now, and we really don't communicate. Maybe someday we will. Maybe now it's your turn to do some more communication and less blind support for anything she decides to do. I wish you luck with it, Joe. I'm through. I'm sorry I lost her…but I'm through."

Rummel swallowed hard, and his look mellowed. Painfully silent moments passed before he found the courage to respond to his ex-wife's tirade. "I know I wasn't much of a husband," he confessed. "There's nothing I can do to change that now. It's too late for that, and I'm not going to go around beating myself up over it. Maybe that's why I've started to take it out on my job instead. Maybe that's how come I hate it so goddamned much. I mean it, Julie...I really hate police work."

"I never thought I'd hear that from you," Julie commented.

After he took another drink of beer and placed the bottle on the table, Joe added, "Well, I just don't give a shit anymore. I've got less than a year to go before retirement, and then I'm getting the hell out. I should've done it fifteen years ago, but I didn't. I should've done a lot of things, and I didn't. That's the way it is." His stare turned to the bottle on the table, and he held it up for inspection, noting in a distant tone, "As for the booze, I've been drinking like this since the Army, and I expect I'll continue to do so until something forces me to stop...or I croak. It's no big deal anymore."

"It should be," Julie told him. "It'll kill you, Rummel. One way of the other, it'll kill you."

Joe sighed, stubbed out his cigarette. "So will these things," he remarked.

"You're too good a person, Joe, to let yourself just fall away," said Julie softly.

"That wasn't the way you were talking a couple minutes ago," Rummel chuckled.

"You just piss me off...that's all," Julie replied. "I still care what happens to you, Joe."

Rummel didn't want to venture into that. There was still so much feeling for her inside him, so much confusion as to how he should feel, so much regret, yet he also lacked the desire to go back to the way it was, even if he could. It was best to take the safe route and return to the original reason for their meeting. "At any rate," he said, "I'll take this matter up with Kim when I get back, and I guess I'll leave the decision about school up to her. She's just going to have to face up to the fact that after next year, there won't be any more financial support."

Julie was happy to hear that, to know that for once her ex-husband wasn't going to be there to catch Kim when she fell. "When you going back?" she asked.

"Tomorrow morning bright and early," Joe answered. "But I'm heading straight to Seattle first to do some more work on this murder case that brought me here. Ugly one."

"I don't want to hear about it," Julie said.

"I don't want to talk about it," Rummel concurred.

Julie finished her drink and noted, "I should be getting back. The neighbor's probably wondering what happened to me, and Jim will be home in an hour."

"Yeah, I have to get back to the hotel myself. I drug a writer friend of mine along with me, and he's going to wonder what happened to me."

"Is that the novelist Kim told me about?"

"One and the same."

"Kim gave me one of his books a couple years ago. He's quite good. You're hanging out in some pretty high circles these days, Rummel."

"I'll tell him you said that."

Julie stood up and made ready to leave. Rummel squeezed out of the cramped booth and was right behind her. He paid the check and together they left the restaurant. On the sidewalk outside, Julie turned to her ex-husband and offered him a handshake, saying, "I'm sorry for the outburst in there, Joe. It's been building up a long time."

"I understand," Rummel replied. Finding his words hard to come by, he looked to the pavement, then back to Julie as he noted in a quiet voice, "It's the past. The best we can do is try to keep the past where it belongs and go on with our lives."

"When you see Kim, give her my love will you?"

"I will."

"I mean it. Tell her I really do care."

"I know you do. I'll tell her."

"And take care of yourself, Joe," Julie added.

"Always do," Joe said with an empty smile.

Julie was uncomfortable with their parting. She looked around nervously, wanting to find the right words, but they seemed stuck in her throat, the right actions that might lay all of this to rest once and for all, but the years of bitterness and pain still inside her prevented her from doing or saying anything, other than offer a simple goodbye. "See you around, Rummel," she said finally.

"I won't be hard to find," was Joe's only reply. She turned and walked quickly away, and Joe watched her until she disappeared around the corner. He admitted to himself then what he had always known, that he still loved her, that he missed her, that there would probably not be another love in his life at this stage of the game. It was this last realization which hurt him the most. His own selfish nature suddenly became very clear to him, written right across his mind's eye for him to read over and over. He had been a failure at his marriage, hated his job and wanted to love someone without the necessary skills to do so. He could neither express his feelings nor make the sacrifices required for a successful relationship. What Julie had said about him was absolutely true.

Standing there on a busy Chicago street, Joe felt very much alone and empty. He needed another beer, thought about going back inside for one, then thought better of it. He turned and walked away, wondering how VanTighem had whipped his drinking problem with such apparent ease. Rummel knew it wouldn't be nearly so easy for him to do.

CHAPTER SEVEN

Kim Rummel and Kim Wintrode had become instant friends. Wintrode was the kind of woman Kim could look up to, yet still be very comfortable with as a peer. Despite the fact she had all the trimmings of success, she was, in reality, very down to earth and open, traits Kim felt she shared with her.

Three days after their initial meeting, they were having dinner together at Commellini's, a well-regarded and popular restaurant located on the outskirts of the city. Brad was on duty that evening, so it was just the two of them enjoying the opportunity to know each other better.

That night Kim Wintrode was wearing a very expensive, grey glen plaid suit with a richly purple, high neck blouse and matching pocket-handkerchief. Kim had come up with the best she could from her budget wardrobe, a well-fitted beige suit and matching cream-colored blouse, but not near the name brand attire she knew her friend had on. It was obvious Wintrode had money, and Kim wasn't about to pry into the woman's resources, although she was surprised during the course of their conversation that Wintrode did volunteer some information about her boyfriend's finances. "Brad fell into some family money a few years back," Kim Wintrode started off, "and I've been managing his portfolio for him. I used to work as an investment counselor before the banking business, but to be honest with you, Kim, I really get tired of finances…it's boring. I'd like to do something creative, but I haven't got a creative bone in my body…not one."

"Oh, I'm sure you have lots of hidden talents," Kim offered cheerfully.

Kim Wintrode raised both hands and said, "Honest, no I don't…not a one. I'd love to paint or write or play music, but all I can do is make money for people."

"You poor soul," teased Kim.

Wintrode laughed. "I'm telling you, it's boring, Kim. It's a real drag, but it pays the bills, so to speak, and then some."

"You'll just have to go out and buy your art," Kim suggested.

"I do."

Something in the conversation had made Kim curious, and she asked her new friend, "Since he doesn't have to, why does Brad work as a cop?"

Sighing, Wintrode leaned forward on the dinner table, cupped her chin in both hands and explained, "Cause the dumb shit's an adrenalin freak, and he loves it." She abruptly sat upright again. "I tried to get him to quit in Seattle, but no way. So, I figure he's a big boy and can make his own decisions, although I worry about him a lot."

"I worry about my dad too," Kim added solemnly.

"There's nothing I can do about it," Wintrode went on. "I love him and don't think it'd be right to leave him because of his chosen career. His parents used to worry themselves sick too, but they're both gone, so it's up to me to look after him now."

"You knew them?" Kim asked. "What happened to them?"

"Plane crash. Oh sure, I knew them. Brad and I have been together a long time."

"It must have been tough on him," Kim noted.

"On both of us," Kim Wintrode replied sadly, but she quickly recaptured the spirit of the evening with a smile and changed the subject. "I'm sick of taking about money and sad things. Tell me more about you."

"Well, you don't have to worry about money when we talk about me," Kim laughed. "My dad and I are constantly broke."

"How about your mother? What's she do?"

Kim's expression suddenly darkened. "She's a housewife right now. We don't get along all that well, so I don't keep close track of her."

"Sorry to hear that."

Kim forced a little smile. "It's okay. I know some of it is my fault, and I know she's still bitter about my dad. She has her own world now with a new husband and a little boy, and she seems happy. I just feel like I'm intruding when I get in touch with her. I get the sense from her I should be feeling guilty about her and dad splitting up. For a long time, I did feel guilty about it, but I'm not buying into that anymore." Kim paused to gather her thoughts, then went on, "You know, the time comes in a person's life when sometimes they have to choose sides, right or wrong, just because they like one parent more than the other…or they're needed more by one than the other. It's like that with my parents. Sure, my dad has his faults…he drinks too much, although I've never seen him really drunk or mean when he drinks, and he's a big chicken when it comes to showing his true emotions. He's gone out there on the streets and risked his life for close to twenty years, but you just try to get him to sit down and talk things out. It's like trying to catch fish by hand."

"Men are like that," Kim Wintrode observed.

"Is Brad that way?"

"Brad's very special. He's a lot different than most men. Your dad's of the old school."

"And I know that," Kim quickly agreed. As she paused again, her look drifted off, and her words were slowly chosen when she tried to explain her father to her friend. "I remember when I was little," she began. "He was the biggest thing in my life. I mean just take a look at him…to a little girl that's *big*, but it goes beyond that. He was my dad, the center of my life. I knew I could always go to him for whatever I needed. He was my security blanket, and he was a good guy. It was like he included me in everything. He was always the one to take me to the museum or the zoo, and I couldn't have been much older than eight when he took me with him on my first fishing trip on Lake Michigan. That's the way it was with us…he shared everything with me. Sure, I remember the fights he and mom used to have, but they never scared me because I knew when it was all over he'd still be there, and it could be the two of us again. Now I can almost understand my mother's resentment of me."

"Sounds like you two really have something special," Kim Wintrode noted. "I lost my father a few years back, but we were never close. To be honest with you, I didn't like the man, but that's a long story."

Kim decided she wouldn't pry into that last comment. "Some of it changed I guess around the time I turned thirteen," she went on with a touch of sadness in her voice. "He started to put up a barrier between us, like he had created this imaginary line that separated my childhood from the time of growing up. But I still wanted him close to me like it was before…you know, the roughhousing and holding tight, and I couldn't understand why he suddenly became so physically withdrawn from me. We were still buddies, but the closeness was gone…and I missed it."

"Maybe that's the way responsible fathers think they have to act," Wintrode told her. "I, for one, wish mine would have behaved that way."

Lowering her eyes to the table, Kim said, "I'm sorry. I guess I don't have much to complain about."

Wintrode grabbed her hand and gave her a big smile. "Hey, it's okay. I've learned to deal with it, and it's not a problem anymore. I like hearing about you and your dad. It tells me there is such a thing as good family relationships out there…something I wouldn't have believed a long time ago."

"The more I talk to people," Kim said solemnly, "the more I believe families only differ in their degree of dysfunction. It makes me wonder if I ever want to take on the job myself."

"There's no crime in thinking that," Kim Wintrode said with a reassuring squeeze to her new friend's hand. She let go and took a sip of her Sauvignon Blanc, then added, "I remember a time when the outcome looked pretty damn bleak. You just have to hang in there and keep on slugging for what you want out of life." Her look took on a warm glow as she commented, "Tell me…an attractive young woman like you must have a boyfriend or two stashed somewhere. Anyone special?"

"There was," Kim replied, her look again downcast. "We split up a few months ago." Suddenly her eyes shot back to her friend. "No…that's not true. *We* didn't split up. The son of a bitch left me flat cold for another woman."

"I suspect that happens to all of us sooner or later, Kim," Wintrode observed. "I know it probably doesn't seem so now, but you'll get over it. There'll be another one down the road who's a whole lot better for you. But for now…I know the feeling. You want to kick the bastard squarely in the balls and leave him squirming."

"A whole lot more than that," Kim remarked with a wicked smile.

"Whoa!" Wintrode laughed. "Ol' mellow Joe's daughter's got a mean streak in her."

Kim laughed too. "You bet I do," she stated, saluting with her glass of wine.

"What you need is a guy like Brad," Wintrode suggested. "Now there's a real pussycat. He'll cook for you, pamper you, talk to you when you feel like talking and leave you alone when you don't."

"Sounds great to me," Kim nodded agreeably.

"To say nothing of the back rubs and his soft hands," Wintrode said with a hungry glint in her eyes.

"Enough…enough!" Kim exclaimed. "Sold. When do I take possession?"

"Hey, I'm not finished," Wintrode joked.

"I don't want to hear any more. I'm about ready to have an orgasm as it is."

"That too," added Wintrode with a sly chuckle.

Kim groaned and said grinning, "You're not playing fair,"

Kim Wintrode grew a little more serious. "The point I'm trying to make," she said, "is that, believe it or not, there are still some out there like that. You have everything going for you, Kim…looks, brains, and I'll bet you even have some of those creative talents that bypassed me in life. Just be patient…he's out there."

"I suppose so," Kim conceded. "But right now I'm not looking. I'm still pretty bitter."

"It just takes time," Wintrode told her softly. Suddenly she sat upright, pressed her hands together with eager anticipation and suggested, "What do you say we order. I'm starved."

"Call me a lot of things," Kim beamed, "but never late to dinner."

Both women laughed, and their conversation continued nonstop throughout the meal and late into the night.

****

Unlike their procedure in Chicago, this time VanTighem accompanied Rummel to precinct headquarters in Seattle. Along with the detective, Jack had connections with the police department there himself, and since they had three separate killings to investigate, Rummel figured he might actually be of some real help.

They had spent nearly two days poring over the police and lab reports, going over every little detail again and again. One thing became clearly evident by the end of the second day--either the same person had committed all the crimes, including Spokane and Chicago, travelling and taking a break in-between, or there were some killers out there on exactly the same wave length, and all of them were left-handed. Rummel ruled out the latter assumption. There was one other certainty. At this rate, it wouldn't be long before the FBI stepped in, which didn't hurt his feelings one bit. He was amazed they hadn't been involved already. Unlike some of his co-workers, Joe had no problem with the FBI whatsoever, never had. He had always been appreciative of the extra help, although this time if they did show up he'd have to stash VanTighem away more carefully.

One fact did come out of the Seattle investigations Rummel hadn't picked up on before arriving there. All three murders had occurred within one month, June of the previous year, and then the killings had abruptly stopped, very close to the same time frame in Spokane. With the exception of Chicago, it appeared the murderer was on--what Joe darkly referred to--a vacation spree. As much as he hated to admit it, the black humor of that remark appealed very much to VanTighem, and he jumped on the idea as a plot premise.

On the third day, they were ready to tour the crime scenes. Both men waited in the hallway outside the briefing room for the homicide detective who had been assigned to accompany them, someone by the name of Terry Long was all they had been told by the civilian desk clerk. A few minutes later the briefing room cleared with the usual noisy banter and bad jokes, and Rummel pushed forward into the group, asking one of the patrolmen the whereabouts of a Detective Long. "Back there by the door," the officer told him.

Rummel looked back and forth through the crowd trying sort out the officers in street clothes. "Which one?" he inquired.

"The tall blonde," said the patrolman as he hurried on.

Puzzled, Joe asked VanTighem, "Tall blonde? What tall blonde?"

Jack shook his head, laughing. "The woman, dummy," he answered. "How can you miss her? It's the two meter broad standing over there."

"A woman homicide detective!" complained Rummel.

VanTighem let out a little howl of delight. "What's the matter? Haven't you ever worked with a woman detective before?"

"Yeah sure, plenty of times, but they make me nervous."

"Stop being such a damned sexist," VanTighem scolded him.

"Me!" Rummel demanded. "Look who's talking. You're the one who called her a broad."

"Hang tight...she's looking this way," Jack alerted him with a hushed voice.

"Don't call me a sexist, asshole," Rummel growled out of the side of his mouth.

"Sorry for pointing out the obvious," VanTighem snickered, adding, "Last name sure does suit her, though."

"C'mon," grumbled Rummel as he pushed forward with his friend close behind.

As he approached her, Joe realized she had to be a good six feet tall because he was just about staring her eyeball to eyeball, and she was wearing flats. She was a woman who looked to be in her mid-thirties and well proportioned to say the least, very athletic in fact, yet her feminine qualities far outweighed any masculine traits that might be due to her size. She was in street clothes, a matching solid grey skirt and jacket with a light blue blouse, no frills. Her features were narrow and somewhat plain, a little tomboyish, but altogether she made a rather attractive cop. Her long hair was naturally straight and pulled tightly back in a bun. She had bright blue eyes that shined like her light complexion and a crooked little smile that spoke of a streetwise attitude and a down-to-earth sense of humor. That smile broadened and leveled out when she realized the man coming toward her was her new assignment. "You must be Detective Rummel," she said cheerfully when Joe came up to her.

"That's me," Joe replied. She wore no name tag so he had to punt. "I take it your name is spelled with an *i* and not a *y*," he added.

"A lot of people are a little surprised when they first meet me," she told him, her smile still in place.

Grinning a little sheepishly, Rummel said, "Count me among them." He turned to VanTighem. "This is Jack VanTighem. He's helping me out with some things."

Terri shook VanTighem's hand, told him it was nice to meet him and asked, "You with the Spokane Police Department too?"

"No," Rummel broke in. "Jack's a close associate of mine with a specific set of skills that might prove helpful with this case. I hope you don't mind him tagging along."

"Not at all," Terri said. "What sort of skills are those, Mr. VanTighem?"

"I'm a writer."

"He's a researcher," Joe butted in.

"I'm a writer and a researcher."

Terri didn't miss a beat as the two fumbled over each other. "What sort of things do you write?" she asked. "You're name sounds familiar. Maybe I've read something of yours."

VanTighem opened his mouth to answer, but Rummel was there first. "Actually, Jack here was an investigative reporter who has lots of experience in criminal cases. I've known him a long time, and I'm using him to do some leg work. I hope that's okay with you."

Terri smiled at Jack and then turned her smile to Joe, saying, "That's fine by me, Detective. It's your case." Her look grew serious. "They tell me you've had some problems in the hinterlands...same as ours."

Rummel glanced around the busy police station, then inquired, "Can we go somewhere quiet for coffee and talk?"

"That's what I'm here for," replied Terri, "to show you around. Coffee sounds like a good place to start."

"Good. Lead the way."

"I have to pick up something in the office, and I'll be right back," Terri told them.

"We'll be here," Joe said.

"Really nice to work with you, Detective Long," VanTighem added.

"No formality here...Terri is fine."

"Terri it is," said VanTighem with that playful grin of his. "I'm Jack. And by the way...the Detective here goes by Joe."

A little flustered, Rummel responded, "Sure...call me Joe."

"Okay, Joe," said Terri with a warm smile for him. "I'll be right back."

As she walked away, VanTighem nudged his friend in the ribs, noting, "I think she's got the hots for you, ol' buddy."

Rummel was embarrassed. "Ah, get off it. Next time I'll leave you back at the hotel."

"No, I'm serious," Jack tormented him. "I've seen that look before. Remember...I used to be in the business."

"Used to be, bullshit," Rummel countered. "Behind that Christian exterior of yours, there's still the same old weasel."

"Okay, okay," VanTighem conceded with raised palms as he pretended to back off. "Have it your way. I know nothing about these things."

"She's probably a dyke anyway," grumbled Rummel.

Jack had a sly look about him. "I don't think so," was his singsong reply.

****

After a stop at a strip mall coffee shop, where Terri detailed her work while she was a detective in training with the investigative teams on each of the Seattle cases, and where they went over the extensive notes she had compiled at the time and brought along with her now, the three of them made a tour of the crime scenes. They were at the final location, Lowman Beach, a small oceanside park bordered by a narrow curved road, when Rummel turned to Detective Long and said, "You've seen all this before…probably plenty of times. You've gone over all the reports. In your estimation, what's the bottom line?"

VanTighem was somewhat surprised his friend trusted her judgment. She must have impressed him somehow, maybe in more ways than one.

Terri surveyed her surroundings, the ivy covered retaining wall that bordered the road and the thick vegetation that flowed down a gentle slope to the public beach. She kicked at the bits of loose gravel in the parking lot where they had stopped, all the time reviewing and thinking about something she had spent months pondering already. "The bottom line is," she answered, addressing both men, "nothing…nada. Not a single shred of evidence. No hair samples we could identify as not being accounted for, no broken fingernails or skin traces, nothing to track the killer or killers. No fingerprints or footprints. No clues in the form of personal items found. No motive of robbery or revenge. All three victims had their wallets intact, and none had police records or appeared to have any real enemies."

"Any of them homosexual?" asked Rummel.

"We thought about that first thing," Terri replied. "Straight arrows…two of them married."

"Go on," Joe urged.

"In two cases where cars were involved," Terri continued, "fingerprints had been wiped from the passenger's door only. Nothing else had been rubbed." Hesitating a second, Terri corrected herself. "Wait a minute…that's not quite true. Their zippers were cleaned off too," she added with a smirk. "It's like the killer knew in advance what he or she would touch and either wiped the object clean or took something of evidence with them."

"You say he or she," noted Rummel. "Any thoughts on that?"

"Personally, I think it's a woman," Terri told him. "The way these situations were set up, it'd almost have to be...considering these guys really were straight which, as I said, we have no reason to believe otherwise."

"That's pretty much what I figured too," Joe concurred.

"If it is a woman," Detective Long continued, "she's damn fast with her hands. These guys were taken out completely by surprise. No struggle whatsoever." She looked at Rummel with a pensive expression, and she gestured with her hands when she commented, "You know...it's this total lack of evidence that, in a weird sort of way, seems to be the only evidence in itself."

Joe was interested, and so was VanTighem. "What do you mean?" asked Rummel.

"I can't really put my finger on it," Terri replied, scrunching her face up in deep thought, a habit of hers Rummel had already found to be sort of cute. Suddenly she pointed to the ground. "It's like this," she remarked.

"Like what?" VanTighem asked, puzzled.

"Well, it took me awhile to figure it out," Terri said. "But you know, we get a lot of rain around here, and these three murders were committed in remote areas where there's grass and dirt, and even here there's a couple of places that could hold a footprint if anyone moved around outside the car at all...providing there was any moisture on the ground. I went back and checked the weather records, and all three of the killings were committed under relatively hot, dry conditions. Like I said...it's like everything right down to the weather was carefully planned out to prevent even the slightest shred of evidence from being left behind. It's too perfect." Detective Long paused, then went on. "I realize some of these sickos might have high IQs, but this one seems to know what she's doing, or not doing as is the case...like she had written the book on it. She knows what we're looking for, and she's not leaving it."

Rummel told himself he liked this woman, and he saw what she was getting at, something he had completely overlooked himself. "You saying she could be or was a cop?" he asked point blank.

Smiling, Terri answered, "I doubt it, but you never know. More than likely, though, I'd be inclined to believe she had or has access to police procedures...maybe experience around cops. No doubt she has done her homework."

This was fascinating, VanTighem thought. He was making mental notes of every word spoken.

Joe turned to him and asked, "What do *you* think?"

"Who? Me?"

"Yes, you. You've been hanging around police headquarters for years, more so than a lot of cops I know have. You have any ideas on this?"

VanTighem needed some time to ponder the question. He rubbed one side of his face, then folded his arms and stared off somewhere. "It's always a possibility," he said as he looked at the ground and started to pace a little half circle around them. "I know there's plenty of books available on investigative procedures...anyone could get their hands on them. But it sure does make sense that someone awfully close to police work would have a real edge. Especially someone who might've had some kind of training, maybe even training with the Feds. My experience has been, however, that when cops screw up they do some really dumb, obvious thing while paying attention to the little details. From what you've shown me so far, there's been no screw-ups whatsoever." He cracked a smile and remarked, "But what do I know...I was just a reporter. You're the ones who gave me the material to work with."

"Good point," Rummel said as he poked a finger at his friend in fun. But his humor quickly vanished, and his expression clouded as he observed, "Unless, like Terri pointed out, the glaring screw-up is none at all."

"That's all I could come up with," Terri commented, shrugging. "We're still working on it, but it's been a year since the last one. To be honest with you, the FBI is probably more involved with it now than we are."

"Just like you said, Joe," VanTighem pointed out, "a hit and run vacation murderer."

"A what?" asked Terri.

"So far they've occurred in relatively short spans of time during the summer," Rummel explained. "Except the Chicago case, and we still have Houston and New Orleans to check out. To be honest with you, I don't know what we'll find there."

"That where you heading next?" Terri inquired.

"If the Department approves the travel, I am," Joe replied. "Jack here will have to arrange it on his own. But we'll go back to Spokane first. My partner in Spokane and I will spend some time there piecing together what've we've got before I head South." Something suddenly dawned on Rummel, and he was amazed he hadn't thought of asking her about it earlier. "Speaking of which, I've got this new partner who just recently left the force in Seattle and came to work for us. You by chance wouldn't know a Brad Curtis, would you?"

"I've heard of him," Terri said.

"Nothing bad I hope."

"Not really," she answered. "I know some guys who worked with him in narcotics."

"Narcotics?" Rummel said, surprised. "He never mentioned anything about that. I thought he was in vice."

"He was," Terri explained, "but first he worked narcotics before he was transferred over. These guys really liked him, said he was one helluva good cop."

"Why vice then? Who'd ever want that?"

"Well, I don't think *he* did," Terri replied. "I'm not sure I should talk about it since this is all secondhand information."

"No, go ahead," urged Rummel. "I want to know. I work with the guy, and I should know."

Terri remained silent for a moment, making that odd little expression with her face again. "The word had it," she said finally, "he's a little heavy-handed."

"How so?"

"He likes to use his fists," she answered.

"And his feet," Joe added with a grin. "I've already seen him in action."

Detective Long went on. "Like I said, these guys stuck up for him, but there were some complaints, and he ended up in vice. I guess they figured he wouldn't be so rough on the hookers and pimps. I heard he didn't like it, and that's probably why he went to work for you guys."

"He has a girlfriend he followed out there," Rummel told her.

Terri looked a little annoyed. "Oh yeah, I heard about her too," she said. "These guys all had the hots for her. That's all they talked about was Brad's little Southern Belle."

"That's funny," Joe commented. "She never said anything to me about being from the South, and she sure as hell doesn't have an accent."

"You know her?" Terri inquired.

VanTighem thought he saw a little flash of disappointment hit her face, but he was always reading into emotions like that.

"Sure, I've met her," Rummel said. "She's a real sweetheart, but then I think they're both great together. I call them Ken and Barbie...behind their backs, of course."

"That was pretty much the same opinion around here from what I've heard," Terri remarked. "Like I say...nothing but good things except for a few customer complaints, and you know how those are. It was probably just politics."

"I'd guess that," Joe agreed. "Same old story everywhere."

"You ought to try the newspaper business if you want a good dose of politics," VanTighem said.

Terri decided to change the subject. "Say, when are you guys leaving?"

"Tomorrow morning," VanTighem replied.

"You two got any plans for dinner tonight?"

Both men looked at each other and shrugged. "Nothing we can think of," Rummel said. "Maybe grab some seafood and have a couple of beers.

Except Dudley Do-Right here doesn't drink, so I'll have to entertain myself while I listen to his lies."

"I know a great little sports bar that puts on a dynamite feed," volunteered Terri. "Fresh seafood and the works. You want to make it a threesome?"

Rummel started to stammer, "Well…I…"

"We'd love to," Jack butted in as he placed a hand on his friend's shoulder.

Terri beamed. "Great," she said. "It's not expensive, and I think you guys will love it."

"We'll buy," Rummel hastened to add. "You've been a big help, Terri."

"Let's go Dutch," she said.

"We'll see," VanTighem noted with a confident wink.

The three started toward the rental car, and as they were about to climb in, Terri asked them, "You guys do much fishing out your way?"

Rummel was a bit shocked. "Yeah, sure," he answered and glanced back to VanTighem. "Jack and I live for it. You like to fish?"

"Love to. My uncle's got a boat, and we head out for salmon or bottom fish every chance we get. I caught a 36 pound king last year. Maybe sometime, if you two guys get some vacation, you can come out here, and I'll take you out. Sound good?"

Joe was still a little astounded. "Why…yeah. Sounds great!"

Terri started to reach for the back door handle, but VanTighem grabbed it instead, saying, "I'll get in back. You two stretch out in front." Without any protest, Terri hopped right into the passenger seat. Thoroughly amused by her response, Jack flashed his buddy a smartass grin over the roof of the car. Rummel just rolled his eyes and growled to his friend, "Get in, please."

CHAPTER EIGHT

When Joe arrived back in Spokane, he was at least relieved to find out there had been no additional killings. McCoy, on the other hand, was experiencing no such feelings of relief.

Rummel had no sooner hit the squad room when McCoy walked in. "I want to see you in my office right now, Joe," he said and headed down the hallway. The detective just shrugged at his fellow officers in the room and started down the hall behind him. "Close the door," McCoy said when Joe entered. His tone was curt, cold, unlike him. McCoy didn't bother to take a seat, and he didn't offer Rummel a chair either. "What the hell's this I hear about you dragging a reporter along on your trip?" demanded the lieutenant.

"Word gets around fast," Rummel remarked.

"You goddamned rights it does!"

"He's not a reporter anymore. He's a writer and a friend of mine, and he picked up his own expenses."

"That supposed to make some kind of fuckin' difference!" McCoy shouted.

After quickly making a mental list of possible snitches, Brad at the top of it, Rummel explained, "Look, Jim, I intended to tell you. Fact is I was going to come to you about it first, and then that Keating murder hit, and I just forgot." That last part was a lie, and about as lame as it could get, but it was the best he could come up with on the spur of the moment.

"Bullshit!" McCoy raged. "I've got enough fuckin' reporters hanging around here that I don't need another one sticking his nose into this goddamned investigation!"

The best defense is a good offense Rummel always figured, and here it comes. "I told you he's not a goddamned reporter!" the detective shot back. "I'm going to use all the outside help I can get to crack this son of a bitch once and for all! VanTighem's got contacts and money, and we ought to be damned happy to have him on our side when there's at least three police departments I know of that can't pull a single fuckin' clue out of their asses!"

"He's a goddamned civilian!" McCoy argued.

"Yeah, and one who's got enough juice in this town he could go straight to the mayor if he wanted to and get approval to work on this in a heartbeat. Then you'd have him in your office every day. Right now he's under my wing."

McCoy was taken aback for a moment. He wasn't sure Rummel was bluffing or not, or if in fact VanTighem actually had those kind of connections, but the last thing he needed right now was to find out. Inside he mellowed at bit, and outwardly he started chewing his lower lip again. He said nothing for a few uncomfortably long seconds, then demanded, "Suppose you tell me how I'm going to explain to the rest of those loon brained journalists that we're letting one of their fellow writers...that is the term you used, isn't it...tag along on the most important investigation to ever hit this city. And they can't come!"

"Tell them they're more than welcome," Rummel snapped. "All they have to do is pay for it out of their own pockets like VanTighem's doing and have fifteen years of hard investigative experience to back it up."

"That's not funny, Joe."

"I didn't intend it to be."

"I don't want to see that guy around here."

"You won't. I'll work with him on my own time." Rummel hesitated a moment, then added, "If it makes you feel any better, we'll take separate planes."

"Oh? Where are *we* going now?" McCoy asked sarcastically.

"Houston...then New Orleans," Rummel answered.

"Little late for Mardi Gras, isn't it," McCoy said as he plopped down in his chair behind the desk. "What makes you think we have that kind of money in the travel budget?"

Rummel chose reason over argument. "If you don't, then we'll have to work it over the phones, but we won't get what we need. We've got two very similar cases in Houston that happened about four years ago and one in New Orleans a year before that. They all fit the pattern."

McCoy just shook his head and pinched his eyes shut for a few seconds. "What'd you come up with in Chicago and Seattle?" he inquired finally.

"Chicago, I can't figure out," said Rummel. "I can see a proximity connection between here and Seattle...and New Orleans and Houston also.

Other than that, they all occurred during the summer months...with the exception of Chicago."

"What's that got to do with it?" McCoy asked as he looked back up at the detective.

"Beats me," Joe replied, shrugging. "Maybe it's a summer spree thing with this maggot."

McCoy just rolled his eyes and sneered, "Great. If we're lucky, maybe we can book tours for next summer's murders in Salt Lake City." He leaned forward with his hands clasped on his desk and glared up at Rummel as he inquired, "By some chance did these little pearls of illumination drop from the mind of our illustrious fiction writer?"

"No, they dropped from *my* mind," Rummel retorted.

With his hands held up as a gesture of truce, McCoy nodded his head wearily and observed, "Okay, Joe, I know this thing's got you as wound up as any of us. It's no joking matter. You come up with anything at all in Seattle?"

Rummel paced over to the window and back, looked around the room as if he was checking out the office for unwanted ears. He appeared to be a little uneasy with the situation, and McCoy picked up on it right away. "You got something, Joe?" he urged gently.

"Ah, I don't think it's a damned thing," Rummel answered, shaking his head in frustration. "There's a cop out there...a female detective of all things...who planted a little seed in my mind, and I can't quite seem to shake it."

"Let's have it."

"Okay," Rummel complied. "For what it's worth, here goes." He paused another couple of seconds before pointing out, "Everything's too clean...no traces whatsoever. Terri...that's her name, Terri Long...she made this offhand comment that it was almost like a cop had pulled this off...a very smart one."

Shocked by what he had just heard, McCoy shot upright in his chair and said, "Whoa! You got anything to back that up?"

"Not a goddamned thing," Rummel admitted. "And I, for one, don't think it's a cop. But I do think it might be someone who knows police procedures like the back of her hand."

"You're convinced it's a woman then."

"I am. And so is this Detective Long. Let me give you some examples of what I'm talking about."

"Go ahead."

Joe took a deep breath and began. "In two cases here and two in Seattle, a vehicle was involved. Every single time the passenger door handle was wiped clean but nothing else in the car. This tells me the murderer was fully conscious about leaving prints, and I'm inclined to believe gloves were used right after the killings took place just to make sure. That's one example. Here's another. Most of the murders took place where footprints likely wouldn't be left, except the first one here, and that little dirt turnoff had been kicked over to eliminate any signs. No hairs, no struggles that might leave skin traces, nothing. Somebody's been reading the books, or else knows how to fuck up police work pretty damned good through association with cops."

McCoy leaned forward again and observed, "Pretty farfetched, Joe."

"Damn right it is, but right now I'm not going to overlook anything."

"No, I don't blame you," agreed McCoy with a nod. "What's next?"

"Houston, then New Orleans if the department authorizes it," Rummel replied. "And this time we're going to do it a little different."

"We? You mean VanTighem and you."

"Separate planes if need be."

McCoy just let out a long, exasperated sigh and asked, "How do you mean different?"

"This time we're personally going to do a complete background check on the victims. I'll put Jack to work on the newspaper files to start with."

For the first time McCoy showed the slight glimmer of a smile. "That's a good place for him," he noted. "But he's not to step foot in any police precincts. Agreed?"

"Agreed," Joe said. He was about to ask his lieutenant if that was it when an afterthought hit him. "You wouldn't be inclined to say who ratted me out, would you?"

McCoy's smile widened as he answered, "No, I wouldn't. I have my contacts, and we'll leave it at that. But I'll tell you who it wasn't."

"Brad?"

"You got it. When I cornered him, he clammed right up and played dumb. I should have his young ass in hot water for that, but I know all about partners and their personal ethics."

That was a relief, Joe thought, but just as quickly he started to suspect Terri, and that bothered him just about as much.

Either his face revealed that, or McCoy could read minds. "And it wasn't Detective Long either," the lieutenant added. "By the way, she comes highly recommended."

Rummel knew right then the pipeline had been with someone in Seattle headquarters. Jack had said he had his contacts there, and one of them must have spotted him, but by then Rummel didn't give a damn who had leaked the information. Let the brass get tight ass about it, he figured. He had his way and would soon be off and running, he hoped.

McCoy grew serious again. "The FBI has been contacted," he told Joe. "It came right from the top."

"Good," Rummel said. "You let me go out of town to do my thing, and they can work with Brad here. I have no problem with the extra help."

"You'll get your travel," McCoy told him. "The Feds have their local people working on it right now, and I don't expect the big guns until next week at the earliest."

"I want to be gone by then."

"You will be. And make sure your *associate* doesn't travel with you."

"He won't. And he'll probably want to fly first class anyway."

McCoy just groaned and said, "That fucker just pisses me off."

****

Rummel spent the better part of the afternoon with Brad going over what little he had come up with and laying out various projects for his junior partner in his absence that included a heads up about the FBI. He told Curtis to check motor vehicle records for any new licenses issued to Illinois transplants and follow up on the utilities companies for new customers from that area also. That, in addition to working with the other teams assigned to the investigation, would keep him busy while he was gone.

Next, Joe made arrangements for a flight out, booked a hotel in Houston and phoned VanTighem to tell him about the plans, advising him he would have to take a different flight and where to meet him in Houston. First he wanted him to meet at his apartment that evening and go over some details in advance.

When Rummel arrived home, Kim wasn't there. He figured she must be at work. He went straight to the refrigerator, cracked a beer and then began to pack some clothes for the trip. Finished with his packing, he kicked back on the couch, reached for the remote and turned on the TV for some mindless late afternoon viewing. His head still spun as he tried to piece together a puzzle missing everything but the twisted faces of the victims. Periodically, Terri's face cropped up also to provide him a welcome break from his haunting images.

He must have fallen asleep, but he wasn't sure if he was actually awake now or just dreaming he heard voices and laughter outside the door. Shaking himself from his groggy state, Joe looked up just in time to see his daughter and Kim Wintrode walk through the door.

"Pops, I didn't expect you back until later," Kim said.

"I had to get some things done before I take off again tomorrow, Kitten. Hi, Kim."

"How was Seattle, Joe?" Wintrode asked

"Big, like always. Is Brad with you?"

"No, he's working late tonight, you slave driver. Your daughter and I met for a quick drink after work, and we're going to take in a movie."

"That sounds like fun," Rummel yawned, still a little dazed from his unscheduled nap. "What the hell time is it, anyway?"

"Six-thirty," Kim said.

"Jack was supposed to meet me here at six. Wonder what the devil's keeping him."

"VanTighem's coming!" Kim exclaimed. She turned to her friend, saying, "Hey, this guy you have to meet."

"This the famous author I've been hearing about?" asked Wintrode.

"Infamous is more like it," Rummel grumbled.

No sooner had those words come out of his mouth when the rumble of dual straight pipes was heard outside. Kim hurried to the window and motioned for her friend to come take a look. Peering over Kim's shoulder, Wintrode took careful note of the '65 black Mustang convertible parked out front and the driver in snug Levis as he started up the walkway. "Looks interesting," she announced.

"Don't you be feeding his ego," Joe told her. "It's not starving to death by any means."

Both women stepped away from the window and awaited VanTighem's arrival.

"Door's open," Rummel hollered.

"What are you…psychic or something?" Jack asked as he stepped inside.

"No, it's that twenty-five year old Ford of yours that could wake the dead what gave you away. I should bust you for that thing."

"Don't be talking that way about…" VanTighem stopped mid-sentence when he spotted Kim and the stranger in the room. "Hey, Kim, how's it going?"

"Jack, I'd like you to meet my friend Kim Wintrode."

"A pair of you, huh," VanTighem said, and he stuck his hand out to greet the woman who had stepped forward. Jack was instantly captivated by her uncommon loveliness, those eyes and that long silky hair which, like a siren's call, beckoned him to touch. He would have had difficulty taking his eyes off her were it not for the sudden realization of Kim's qualities also, the high school kid he had known now grown up. Side by side, they stood nearly the same height, the one whose looks were classic, the other's wholesome youth and beauty, each in her own way totally striking and very appealing, both traps for a man's heart. It was Kim Rummel's appearance and manner he was more comfortable with because she reminded him more of Cindy, but this other woman had an air about her that was purely magnetic, mysterious, even dangerous. The latter VanTighem had always found hard to resist.

Kim Wintrode had also formed her own immediate impression. This man was interesting, she thought, very exotic and attractive, a challenge and dangerous in his own right, something she too had difficulty resisting. With Brad she was comfortable, and she was growing weary of comfort. "Mr. VanTighem," she said. "A pleasure to meet you. It's not often in my line of business I have the chance to meet a successful writer."

"They're all neurotic," commented VanTighem with his patented impish smile. "Formality makes me nervous. Call me Jack."

Her inviting smile equaled his in attraction. "Alright, Jack, I will."

VanTighem figured he'd be standing there all night staring at her if he didn't tend to business. Turning to Rummel, he asked, "What we up to next?"

The detective had spotted that little exchange of looks between Jack and his partner's girlfriend, and he decided it best to pull him out of there right now. "I want to go over this Houston trip," Rummel said. "The ladies here are taking off to a movie."

"Oh-oh, serious cop talk," Kim noted. "Best we hit the road. I just came home to see if you were back and let you know there's some homemade chili in the refrigerator, Pops."

"Thanks, Kitten. Jack and I will probably get into it later."

"Well, we're off then," Kim said.

"Have fun," her father told them both.

"Nice to meet you, Jack."

"Pleasure's all mine, Kim."

With her hand locked under her friend's arm, Kim Rummel started them toward the door. "Bye, guys," she said.

"See you later, Kitten."

Wintrode stopped for a moment at the open door, turned to VanTighem and pointed outside, saying just one word. "Classic."

"Finally I meet someone who appreciates the finer things in life," VanTighem replied.

"Twenty-five year old Ford," Joe growled, and with that the two women left.

After waiting a minute or so just to make certain they wouldn't return for something they had forgotten, Rummel wrapped his heavy arm around VanTighem's shoulder and said with a big grin, "Jack, ol' buddy, you mess around with that, and her boyfriend's gonna kick your sorry ass into the next century."

"I'm trying to quit," VanTighem laughed. "Remember?"

"Yeah...right."

****

Joe picked up VanTighem at Houston Intercontinental in a rental car and drove him straight to the Howard Johnson Inn where they were staying. One more time he went over their itinerary. He would check all the police records and review the crime scenes, while VanTighem's job was to go over the news accounts and obits to develop a list of anyone connected with the victims. This meant library time--city directories, phone books, things Jack hated to do but had a knack for just the same. He groaned, accused Rummel of having all the fun, and Joe reminded him that if he thought police and coroners' reports were so much fun, he could have his job when he retired. Then McCoy could chew *his* ass out for associating with such low-lifers as reporters and writers. Point well taken, VanTighem noted.

The more recent Houston murder presented precisely what Rummel was looking for and had feared he would find, a carbon copy of all the others, completely devoid of any concrete evidence. A neighborhood bar owner with a history of alcoholism and spouse abuse had been out on the town one night alone and never returned home. His body had been found in a small residential park, cut up the same way and featuring a left-handed angle to the slash across his throat, no signs of a struggle, no prints, no traces of fiber, no lost hairs, nothing. The interview which VanTighem and Rummel conducted together with the widow, now remarried, revealed the victim had enough enemies--including the anything but bereaved widow--to keep them busy for weeks if they saw fit to follow up on them all, which they didn't. While they talked to her as she stood in the doorway of her modest suburban home, a dirty faced three-year-old tugging at her arm, it occurred to both men the victim probably didn't know anyone smart enough to have pulled off the crime. Nevertheless, they chased down a few of his associates just to make sure and proved their point, discovering in the process there was only one common thread in the case. The victim died owing everyone money.

Their investigation of the first murder victim, however, a Robert Bryson, brought about a twist that rocked both men back on their heels.

Following a phone call to set up an appointment, they found themselves standing outside the door of a very expensive, upscale downtown condo. The victim had been single, successful, and--in addition to his mother--he had designated as a primary beneficiary the person who owned that condominium apartment.

The moment the door opened to reveal a slightly built man in his late forties, someone with dyed blonde hair, one whose voice floated with a soft, fluid Southern accent, both men knew they could just about throw their heterosexual murder case right out the window. Rummel introduced himself by name and police department and then introduced VanTighem, referring to him only as his associate, which he had done all along as a matter of policy. When he stated his business, the man's expression quickly saddened, legitimately from the looks of it, and he invited them both inside.

His name was Ron Gillette, a boutique chain entrepreneur of considerable standing in the Houston community. Among other things, he was on the board of directors for the leading local theater company, active in a half dozen prominent charities and a member of the mayor's advisory committee for the arts. Now Joe knew why the police reports had been so hush-hush about any homosexual involvements with the deceased.

Gillette offered them seats and asked them if they would like something to drink, perhaps coffee. Rummel declined, but Jack said he would take a cup if it was already made. Their host graciously excused himself and returned shortly from the kitchen with two cups of coffee. He sat down in a chair opposite his two guests, who had seated themselves on an extravagantly huge and luxurious leather couch that looked like something straight from the prop department of a larger than life Texas soap opera. VanTighem took a moment or two to look around and admire the apartment's tasteful and very expensive décor, but Rummel wanted to come right to the point. "We're reopening this investigation," he explained, "because recently we've had very similar cases in Spokane and Seattle. We think there may be a connection. What we need from you, Mr. Gillette, is as much information as possible about Robert Bryson, who I believe you knew fairly well."

"I knew him very well," Gillette said softly. "But it's been four years since that happened. I told the police everything I knew back then."

"I know you did," Mr. Gillette," Joe replied. "But the case was never solved, and it looks like his murderer might have surfaced again. I'm sure you'd want to see the killer apprehended and brought to justice."

"Of course I would."

"You mind if I ask you a question up front, Mr. Gillette?" inquired Rummel.

"Please feel free."

"Was Robert Bryson a homosexual?"

Gillette laughed lightly, the first signs of life they had seen in the man. "Is the Pope Catholic?" he responded, then added, "The preferred term is gay."

Rummel was not amused. "Would there be any chance he might have been involved with a woman?"

"I think not," Gillette flatly answered. "We were lovers for ten years."

That certainly threw a monkey wrench into this particular case, Joe figured. Everything else had fallen right in line, identical to the others, and now this. If the same killer was involved here, then they had a real charmer on their hands.

"Did Robert have any female friends?" VanTighem interjected. "Anyone close?"

Gillette looked a little surprised. "We all do," he said. "We don't live in complete isolation, you know. Robert had a lot of friends of both sexes. He was a very warm man...very gentle and kind."

"I take it no enemies then...not that you know of," noted Rummel.

"None whatsoever."

This was taking them nowhere fast, the detective told himself. If he had decided to intentionally dream up a single circumstance that would make this investigation worse than it already was, this would have to be it.

"I'll tell you gentlemen the same thing I told the police four years ago," Gillette volunteered. "I think this terrible crime was the result of the hatred and violence we harbor in our society against those who differ from the majority, and that especially applies to the gay community. It's the same thing I have fought against all these years and will continue to fight right up to the end."

"How do you account for the fact there were no signs of a struggle then?" Rummel asked point blank.

Again Gillette was caught by surprise, and this time he looked a little hurt also. "I didn't know that was the case," he answered.

"Well, it was," Joe said. "I don't want to bring up old wounds, but Robert let someone get very close to him without a struggle. And he was killed in a very intimate setting...the backseat of his car." Rummel paused a few moments to let his words sink in and then went on. "Now if you say it wasn't a woman, then it must have been a man he allowed that close to him...or a woman who looked like a man. Were you two having problems at the time which might have resulted in him seeing someone else?"

Staring over his shoulder out a picture window that afforded a panoramic view of downtown Houston, Gillette chose not to respond right away. When he looked back at the two men, there was sadness in his eyes that spoke of troubled memories never healed. "I suspected Robert had other relationships," he said quietly. "I never knew for certain, but I suspected it. He was just that way. I guess he was naturally flirtatious, but it was just his insecurities that needed reassuring. He was quite beautiful, you know."

Not from the picture Rummel had seen, but he wasn't about to tell him that. "Could you give us any names?" asked the detective.

An ironic smile crept across Gillette's face. "I'd be the last to know," he said.

"I suppose so," Rummel agreed.

Turning to VanTighem, Gillette inquired, "Why did you ask if it was a woman?"

Jack cast his friend a questioning look to see if he should answer that. Rummel gave him the go-ahead with a nod. "The victims in the cases we're investigating all appear to have been straight," VanTighem told their host.

"You're sure about that," Gillette said with a sly smile. "Don't you think there's a little bit of the question mark in all of us...maybe to the point those poor men crossed over to find out?"

"Interesting observation," VanTighem noted. He suddenly grew a little uncomfortable under the gaze fixed directly upon him. Time to go, he thought.

"Yup, interesting," commented Rummel. "But the law of averages says not in every single one of these cases." He abruptly stood up, thanked Gillette for his time and announced they would be going now. Gillette had already passed the test of scrutiny many times over in this particular case, his innocence and sincerity clearly beyond question, and the man could be of no further help. Rummel knew he could chase down a list of people as long as his arm in the Houston gay community and come up with exactly the same thing in this four year old murder case he had found with the others--nothing. The person he wanted was in Spokane right now, and he knew damned well that person was a woman.

As they were leaving, Gillette cast a parting look at VanTighem, which Rummel caught. Once the door closed behind them, Joe turned to his friend in the hallway and said, "You remember that remark you made about Terri in Seattle?"

"Which one?"

"The one about her having the hots for me. Remember? You said you could always tell by that look."

"Yeah?"

Rummel cracked a smile. "Well, I saw that very same look back in there, ol' buddy. I think Ronnie has the hots for you."

"Oh go fuck off!" VanTighem said, and he stormed off.

Joe followed him to the elevator, chuckling the whole time.

CHAPTER NINE

New Orleans was VanTighem's kind of town. He had been there many times before, although some of his trips remained only vague memories seeping from an alcoholic haze. When he had been drinking, this had been one of his favorite places to party. Now that he was sober, the city had taken on more of a rundown, decadent air, but he still enjoyed it. The architecture alone and the bizarre blend of both a laid back and frenzied pace never ceased to fascinate him, to say nothing of the long legs in silk skirts that breezed up and down the streets. Like it or not, New Orleans brought out the old devil in him, something he sort of missed from time to time. Rummel, on the other hand, thought the city was a dirty scum hole, and he couldn't wait to get back to his beloved Northwest.

They dived directly into their routine, Joc to the police department to review files and VanTighem to the city newspaper and local library for a background search on the victim, this one a man by the name of John McConey who had been killed five years ago.

Rummel had to chuckle while he went through the files in the supervising detective's office. Sitting behind a desk across from him, Lieutenant Steve Clark, a round faced, overweight jovial sort of man with a crew cut and a sweaty forehead, kept him thoroughly entertained with a steady stream of parables laced with old style Southern wisdom. "I was the investigating officer on that case," Clark was saying in that distinctive New Orleans accent that sounds more Brooklyn than Southern. "That was a little trip into the dark side of human nature."

"This guy was a scumbag," Rummel announced. "A list of aliases, sexual assault, suspected child molester, pornographer, con games, forgery, drugs, alcoholism. What'd you do...throw a party when he got offed?"

"Let's just say the Good Lord works His justice now and then," Clark responded, smiling.

Rummel read further, still shaking his head. "So this is his real name...John McConey?" he asked finally. "The information here...birth date, social security number and the like...it's all legit?"

"In that report it is," Clark answered. "He'd been known to use a few others."

"I see he came here from Houston not long before he was killed, and before that he was all over the place...Dallas, Kansas City, St. Louis."

"Originally from Indiana, as I recall," the lieutenant noted. "I remember wonderin' how a good Midwestern boy like that could turn out the way he did."

"It's right here," Joe said. "Auburn, Indiana, but no mention of any family there."

"That was a tough one at the time," recalled Clark. "Our man was married and divorced three or four times, but we had one helluva time tracking down any next of kin. First wife committed suicide, and I believe there were a couple of kids from that marriage."

"You contact them?"

"Nope. Never could find them."

"How about the other wives?" asked Rummel. "Any other kids?"

"Nobody we contacted would own up to having anything to do with him. The only person who'd claim the body was his girlfriend here in town."

"What's her name?"

"Pam somethin'," Clark replied. "It's buried in the file there somewhere."

Joe took a few minutes to read on and review some of the material he had skipped over. "Yeah, here it is," he said finally. "Pam Andrews. While I'm in town, I'll definitely look this Andrews woman up."

"About as cooperative with us as a cornered gator," Clark commented as he put his hands behind his head and sprawled back in his chair. "At first, we thought she was the one who had done it, but she come out clean right away. First place, she had a string of alibis. She wasn't even in town when ol' John got hisself killed. And she was left-handed," Clark added.

"What?" Rummel bellowed.

Lieutenant Clark was a little shocked by the detective's outburst. He leaned forward, pointed at the file in Joe's hands and told him, "Looky there at the coroners' report. It says right there the killer was probably right-handed."

As he quickly thumbed through the pages, Rummel reviewed the autopsy photographs again and read carefully word for word the coroners' report. Somehow he had completely overlooked the angle of the cut across the victim's throat the first go-around, probably because he had just assumed it was the same, and he mentally kicked himself for that oversight. "I'll be damned," he groaned upon completing the coroners' statements. "Right-handed." First the homosexual slaying in Houston and now this, he thought. The whole thing's getting worse, not better.

"Something wrong there, Detective?" Clark asked.

Rummel caught himself chewing his lower lip just like McCoy. He shook his head, stared off toward some pictures on the wall and answered, "It's just that we've been chasing this left-handed killer in four different cities, and now this. Looks like a dead end."

"Maybe he's ambidextrous," Clark suggested.

"Maybe *she* is," Joe muttered. He looked back at Clark, noting, "She…it's a she."

"You know, I always thought that myself," observed Clark as he leaned back in his chair again. "I worked on that case more than a year, and one thing I did find out…Mr. McConey had hisself a real trap line goin'. I imagine any one of them could've done it, but we could never prove it. They're all listed there, right along with the Andrews woman," the lieutenant said when he again gestured toward the folder in Rummel's lap. "You know, you sure can't tell it from that photograph, but ol' John was a pretty handsome feller. I had occasion to come across him once or twice before he was killed. He definitely was a ladies' man."

"So were the other poor bastards," remarked Rummel. "All but one."

"Huh?"

"Oh, one in Houston was a fag," Joe stated.

"Queers, hookers and pissed off girlfriends always topped my list of suspects," Clark commented. "Maybe you've got a switch-hitter here."

"Yeah, an ambidextrous one," grumbled Rummel.

Slowing rising to his feet, Lieutenant Clark announced, "Well, Detective, I've got other business to attend to. You just help yourself to that file and copy anything you want."

Rummel stood up also. "I will. And thank you for all your help."

Clark ambled around his desk, placed a hand on Rummel's broad shoulder and walked him out to the squad room where he pointed out the copy machine, then left the disgruntled detective to his own devices.

****

That night Rummel and VanTighem compared notes in Joe's hotel room. Jack had acquired a small list of names of people associated with McConey from newspaper crime reports, public records and the media coverage of his slaying, and Rummel had Pam Andrews he wanted to contact.

"Any of these people from Houston?" Joe asked his friend.

"Not that I can find," VanTighem answered. "Any family mentioned was from the Midwest, and the rest were fellow crooks from around here. Why do you ask?"

"Oh, I guess I was just hoping for a Houston connection," Rummel said wistfully. "Call it wishful thinking."

Neither man said anything for a few long moments until VanTighem suddenly jumped to his feet and proclaimed, "We're gonna get the hell out of here! C'mon, I'll take you to the Chart House and buy you the best damned mahi mahi you ever sunk a fork into."

"I don't know," Joe hedged. "I was just thinking we'd eat at the hotel and get a fresh start in the morning."

"Bullshit. This is New Orleans, and we're going out on the town tonight." VanTighem was already on his way out the door to freshen up in his room. "It's less than a ten block walk to the heart of the French Quarter, and we're going whether you like it or not. It's time you stop stewing about this shit."

"Maybe you're right," Rummel conceded.

"You bet I'm right," Jack called out from the hallway. "Now get your butt ready and wash some of that cop smell off."

A half hour later the two men were outside the Warwick Hotel where they were staying, suited to Rummel's budget not Jack's, and heading toward Canal Street. They strolled down the broad, featureless boulevard of Canal until they came to the narrow confines of Bourbon Street, then turned left toward the bright lights ahead. It was already too hot and muggy for Rummel, and once they were on the cramped sidewalks of Bourbon Street, closed in by row upon row of two and three story buildings adorned with the ironwork frill of another century, the air seemed to grow even more stifling, hotter than before. VanTighem appeared to bask in it with his brisk walk and incessant chatter, and Joe just shook his head in wonderment; would this man ever grow up? He was beginning to think also this was a long walk just for a piece of fish.

"Now when we hit the main section up here," Jack was telling him, "these little black kids will be all over you, and they're going to bet you money they know where you got your shoes."

"They are, huh," was all Rummel had to say.

"Yeah," Jack said, his excitement spilling over. "You just tell them I got these shoes on my feet on Bourbon Street, and that'll take the wind out of their sails."

"Thank you, Robin Leach, for your take on the lifestyles of the rich and famous."

"Ah, stop being such a fuckin' grouch."

The street quickly began to fill up with people and seemed to widen a bit as they entered the French Quarter. Hot sounds of jazz mingled with laughter poured through the night air, and tourist trap lights glowed even brighter to display their wares. The old bricks beckoned to be walked upon, and VanTighem did just that, dragging his friend along with him down the middle of Bourbon Street to join the hundreds of revelers on that steamy, sensuous night. It was a blend of the beautiful and the bizarre, low-cut silk dresses and punk hairdos, black tie and beggar, women dressed to taunt men's desires and transvestites trying their best to compete with them, college kids sporting fraternity T-shirts and street urchins scrambling for an extra buck. There was a beat and a mood in the air that was even beginning to draw Joe into it. It made him feel young again.

"Well, I'll be a son of a bitch," VanTighem suddenly remarked.

"What's the matter?"

"Up ahead," Jack said, pointing. "That tall guy."

A half block away in the middle of the street, a young man stood head and shoulders over everyone swarming around him. He carried a placard raised high on a lath which he clutched close to his heart. He had to be nearly seven feet tall, and even from that distance, Rummel could see he was well dressed in a dark suit, white shirt and tie. "Yeah, what about him?" Joe asked. "He promoting LSU basketball or something?"

"That kid was here six years ago," VanTighem explained. "Some people really know how to keep the faith."

As they approached, Rummel saw that the sign read, 'The Wages of Sin is Death', and on both sides of the street two zealots were handing out pamphlets to any who would take one, shouting hell and damnation for all to hear. VanTighem grew strangely somber. The two walked right past the stoic young man who continued to stare straight ahead, his mere presence and serene silence commanding attention. One of his companions raced up to VanTighem with a pamphlet, and the writer took it, saying quietly, "Peace…and to your friend there."

"Peace be with you, brother, and to your friend too," the man replied.

After they had passed, Rummel inquired with a puzzled look, "You know those guys?"

"Nope," VanTighem said as he stuffed the pamphlet into his hip pocket.

Joe's expression turned serious, and a little concerned. "Don't you think you might be carrying this business a bit too far?"

VanTighem had a distant look about him, and he didn't respond right away. Finally, he answered his friend. "Like I said, six years ago when I was down here, just before my first book was published, I was hanging out with a bunch of drunken reporters right in this very same spot."

"You were the ring leader, of course," laughed Rummel.

"Of course."

VanTighem's mood prompted Joe to grow solemn again. "Well, what happened then?"

"We were shitfaced and being assholes in general when one of those guys came running up to me and started jabbering about the Scriptures. I don't think it was the same one…maybe it was. But the tall kid is the same person."

"So what'd you do?" asked Rummel. "Punch him out?"

"No," said Jack sadly. "I just stopped, looked him close up square in the face and said, 'Fuck God'. He came unglued and started bouncing all around screaming 'blasphemer'. I just laughed. And my friends laughed, and we all walked away…laughing."

A long silence followed both men as the continued to walk up Bourbon Street, broken finally by a sober observation Rummel made without the slightest tint of humor in it. "No wonder you're hearing voices," he remarked.

"Yeah…no wonder."

****

The next morning they took their rented car and headed out to see Pam Andrews. She hadn't been hard to find. The file on McConey had provided an old address, and she was still in the phone book at the same location, living in Algiers across the river. As they crossed the Huey Long Bridge, leaving the skyline of New Orleans and the Superdome behind, both men seemed lost in their private thoughts. Rummel was mesmerized by dilapidated housing projects, war zones actually, and he wondered how anyone could live like that. VanTighem's thoughts drifted back and forth between the past and the present as he delved into personal questions how he could have ever found a shit hole like this so much fun. Once in awhile one or the other would make a comment about their surroundings. Rummel wondered out loud if the fishing was decent in the river, and Jack told him there were monster catfish in there that would eat him alive. That recharged his interest in the area, a little at least.

It took them close to an hour to find the place. They cruised up and down narrow, bumpy streets lined by a monotonous sequence of small houses, either framework or brick, all on block foundations to combat the perpetually soggy earth. Their cancerous sores of peeling paint bore witness to an endless struggle against humidity, heat and torrential rains. Postage stamp yards were strewn with litter, and discarded toys lurked in the cover of uncared for lawns that were but mere patchworks of clumped grass and trampled earth.

Finally, they stopped in front of a white cracker box house, its only distinguishing feature being some brickwork along the front. Both men climbed out of the car and approached the front door, careful not to trip over some gaping faults in the sidewalk. As Rummel knocked on the screen door, he thought it might fall off its hinges. No answer. He opened the screen door and knocked again, louder this time. A long minute passed before he heard movement inside.

The door opened and a woman, who was actually in her late thirties but looked a good ten years older, answered. Her blonde hair hung in long, stringy curls, and her eyelids were half shut, partially concealing what might have once been pretty light blue eyes that were now bloodshot and vacant. She was very slender, nearly anorexic, with pronounced sharp features that appeared to be due largely to emaciation from substance abuse and neglect. Rummel could smell the booze on her breath, and he suspected drugs also. "Yeah?" she asked in a husky, cigarette voice.

Rummel flashed his badge and said, "My name's Joe Rummel, Spokane Police Department, and this is Jack VanTighem. Are you Pam Andrews?"

Eyeing the detective suspiciously, the woman inquired, "Spokane? Where's that?"

"Washington," answered Rummel in his best official tone. "Are you Pam Andrews?"

"Yeah...so what of it? What do you want?"

"May we come in?"

"When you tell me what you want," answered the woman defiantly.

"We're here investigating the murder of John McConey," stated Rummel.

Pam Andrews laughed, but was quickly cut short by a raspy cough. When she was through hacking, she croaked, "You gotta be shittin' me. I buried that bastard five years ago, and you guys are still looking for the killer? That's one for the books. Well, it ain't me."

"We know it's not you," Joe replied. "Now may we come in?"

The woman looked over both men before answering, her eyes resting on VanTighem, and she asked, "Is he a cop too?"

"He's working on the case with me," was all Rummel said.

Andrews hesitated a moment or two longer, then said, "Yeah...come on in." As they stepped inside, she remarked with a smirk, "It's a bit of a mess, but today's the maid's day off."

All three stood a minute or two in the cramped living room, its furniture scarred with rips and cigarette burns. Finally Andrews offered them a seat on the couch and a couple of beers. The latter both men declined. She took the faded and dilapidated easy chair across from them. "So what was it about ol' John that brings you two out of the woodwork and this far? I'd hardly think he was worth it."

"We're investigating some similar incidences in the Seattle and Spokane areas," Rummel explained. "The murderer has a particular style, and we're looking into all the cases that are similar."

Pam winced. There was still some hurt there. "It made me fuckin' sick, that's what it did," she told them. "I don't even want to think about it. I hope you get the bitch that did it."

That hit a chord with both men. "You think it was a woman?" asked Rummel.

"Sure it was," Andrews sneered. "John was a lot of things, but he wasn't no faggot. He was out whorin' around, and some bitch nailed him when he wasn't looking. Cops here figured the same thing, and that's why they'd liked to have pinned it on me, but I was visiting relatives out of state when it happened. Could've been any one of a dozen women in this town." Pausing briefly, she inquired again, "Hey, you sure you guys don't want a beer?"

Rummel said no, and VanTighem informed her he didn't drink.

With a disapproving look at Jack, Andrews stood up and announced, "Well, I'm gonna have one anyway. It ain't nice to make a lady drink alone." She disappeared into the kitchen, returning moments later with a can of Lone Star beer in hand and a fresh cigarette. Sitting back down, she concluded, "That's all I can tell ya."

"You know if McConey had any relatives around here?" Joe asked.

"Not around here," Pam answered. "He didn't talk much about relatives. I know he had a couple of ex-wives just from the smartass remarks he made…and some kids. He had a daughter in Houston…I think a boy there too. Like I said, he didn't talk much about it."

VanTighem shot a glance at Rummel, and the detective returned it. "What do you know about these kids in Houston?" Rummel quickly asked.

Andrews took a healthy gulp of beer and then a drag off her cigarette. She leaned her head back and blew smoke slowly toward the ceiling, an act she might have, in her own mind, thought was sexy and coy, but it didn't wear well on her at this stage of the game. Looking back at her guests, she responded in a harsh voice, "All I know about for sure is a daughter there. I think he mentioned something once about a son there too, but I can't be sure. Christ, he had kids all over."

"How about the daughter then?" Joe pressed.

"He wouldn't talk about her…I know that. It wasn't too long before he got killed when this letter arrived. There was no return address, I remember that, but it was postmarked Houston. The reason I remember was because of the woman's handwriting, and I hit on him about it when he got home. He told me it was none of my goddamned business, but I kept after him, and finally he said it was his daughter, and he wanted nothing to do with her." After another hit off her cigarette and a swig of beer, Pam went on. "After that, there was a couple of phone calls I answered, and this woman on the other end of the line said she was his daughter in Houston, and she wanted to talk to John."

"Did you ever get a number?" VanTighem jumped in, taking the words right out of Rummel's mouth.

"No, she wouldn't give me one. I think I asked, but she always just hung up."

"Did John know about this?" inquired Rummel.

"Yeah, I told him," Pam replied. "To tell you the truth, he seemed kinda scared, and I wondered about that at the time. But he always told me just to ignore it. He said she was trouble, and she just wanted money from him."

"And you let it slide," Joe concluded.

"John wasn't one to be pushed," Andrews stated. "He could get kinda mean."

"What about the police?" asked Rummel. "You tell them about this?"

Hesitation raced across the woman's expression. For a moment, it appeared she wouldn't answer as her gaze lowered, but finally she said, "No...no, I didn't." She glanced back up and explained, "I didn't want any more hassles. You know what I mean? I didn't want to be connected with any of his kids or his past. It was over. He was dead, and like I said...I just figured it was some whore here in town that did it. I buried him, and it was done. That's it."

Again Rummel saw the sadness in her look. In her own twisted way she must have loved the creep and probably still did. "Anything else?" he asked.

"I told you everything I know," Andrews responded.

Rummel abruptly stood up, and VanTighem did the same. "We won't be bothering you anymore, Miss Andrews," the detective told her. "Thank you very much for your help."

With a weak smile, Pam asked, "You sure you guys don't want to stick around for a beer? I don't get much company around here...respectable company anyway."

Rummel smiled warmly, more out of compassion for the woman than anything else. "Sorry, we can't," he said. "Police business, you know."

"Yeah," Andrews drawled, "you guys are all so straight."

"It's an occupational hazard," VanTighem commented, nodding at his friend. "You've been a real help, Pam."

"Ah, I don't know about that," the woman answered as she reclined in her chair. She was trying to be cheerful, but her look suddenly darkened, and she said in a bitter tone of voice, "You guys get that bitch. Okay?"

Rummel's reply was dead serious. "We will, Pam. That you can count on."

"I *will* count on it, Detective," Andrews smiled.

Both men said goodbye and left. Once they were back at the car, Rummel turned to Jack and remarked, "I've got a gut hunch about this one."

"So do I," VanTighem said.

"When we get back, I'm going to need your help," Joe told him. "Maybe I'm getting paranoid, but let's just keep this between the two of us for the time being. I want you to use every trick in the book to track down this McConey's past and find that daughter."

"What are you going to do?" asked VanTighem.

"Once we get home, I'm going to drive over to Seattle and spend some time trying to find any kind of Houston connection with those victims. If we can place that daughter in Seattle, then sure as hell we can track her to Spokane."

"You sure that's the only reason you're going to Seattle?" Jack inquired with a sly smile.

Normally Rummel would have found some humor in a question like that, but he was too intense right now to find humor in anything. "Business, my friend," was all he said.

"You going to let Terri in on this?" VanTighem asked.

"We'll see," Joe replied. "Maybe when the time comes."

CHAPTER TEN

Rummel checked in with McCoy first thing when he showed up at division headquarters. The lieutenant didn't look any the worse for wear from his absence and was actually cheerful when he informed Joe there hadn't been any new killings. "You think it's over, Joe?" he asked, hoping for some insight that might confirm his optimism.

"Maybe here in Spokane," Rummel said. "But it ain't over. Not by a long shot."

McCoy's expression darkened. "Okay, let's hear it. What you got from your travels down South?"

Rummel explained in detail what he had uncovered, emphasizing the discrepancies--the homosexual killing in Houston and an apparent right-handed murderer in New Orleans, except no mention of McConcy's daughter. At this point he couldn't even prove McConey actually had a daughter and, without confirmation of that fact, it still seemed like too much of a wild goose chase to anyone except him and Jack. None of it sounded very encouraging to McCoy. And he was completely baffled by Rummel's next request. "I want to take a drive out to Seattle," Joe told him.

"You were just there," stated McCoy.

"I know, but I want to dig deeper into the pasts of the three victims there. I'll even throw in some of my own time for this one. I'll do it one better and pick up the travel tab in my own rig," the detective added.

McCoy started in on his lower lip again and eyed Rummel suspiciously. "You on to something, Joe?"

"Not a damn thing," Rummel lied. "That's why I want to go to Seattle…to narrow this down by process of elimination. We started on the assumption all these crimes might've been committed by the same person based on M.O. Now we've got some discrepancies. What we're missing is a common thread, and the only way I see of finding one is dig deeper into the backgrounds of the victims. Maybe we can link Seattle and Spokane and concentrate on it regionally." That last remark raised another thought, and Joe asked, "How's Brad doing with the Chicago connection?"

"He's been running around like a one armed paperhanger," McCoy replied. "So far he hasn't been able to come up with anything substantial on our new arrivals from the Chicago area. But he's still working on it, and I know the FBI is too."

"Good," said Rummel. "I've got a feeling about that one." He paused a few moments to think, rubbed the side of his face and glanced around the office with tired, squinty eyes. "I'm going to turn him loose on a complete background check of the victim there also. That's another reason I have to go to Seattle. We can track it from both ends...hopefully right to the middle here in Spokane."

"It's your call," McCoy sighed. "I was hoping you'd bring me a little better news from down South."

"I did," Rummel declared. "I may have eliminated it altogether. And if not, if Brad digs up something from Chicago, and I find a connection in Seattle, anything that points to the South, then we'll get the FBI to help us backtrack it right from the beginning in New Orleans. But for now, that all depends on the victims."

"That's not very encouraging," McCoy noted.

"You're tellin' me," Rummel agreed.

McCoy stood up and shifted to his window which afforded him a glimpse of Riverfront Park. After some silent moments of just standing there with his hands clasped behind his back, he remarked finally, "This town doesn't need this sort of crap."

"No town does," Joe commented.

Turning around, McCoy said, "Okay, see what you can find in Seattle. Don't take too much time doing it, though. I need you here."

"I'll do my best," Rummel promised him.

McCoy cracked a thin smile. "You taking your old buddy with you?" he asked.

"Nope. He's staying here this time. I gave him a homework assignment to do just to see if he can live through the boredom. If this doesn't cure him of police work, then we've got a real crusader on our hands."

"How'd he do down there?" McCoy inquired.

"Great," Rummel said with a big grin. "Daddy's little helper all the way. Saved me a bundle of time and effort." Chuckling to himself, the detective just had to rub it in a little, suggesting as a postscript. "We ought to put him on the payroll."

"Fat fuckin' chance," McCoy growled.

Joe left McCoy's office knowing he had bought VanTighem some time. Already his friend was phoning all over the country, checking vital statistics and courthouse records to trace McConey's past through every alias on record. Somewhere down the line he was going to stumble across that daughter, and when he did, Rummel would take over from there. He told himself if he even heard the word Houston mentioned in Seattle, he was going to zero back in on McConey's daughter like a kamikaze pilot diving for the smokestack of a battleship.

****

Rummel was packing again when Kim came home. "Hi, Kitten, what you been up to?"

"Kim and I went out after work," his daughter answered.

"You two are getting real tight," he noted.

"She's great," Kim replied, and then a puzzled look crossed her face. "What are you doing?"

"Back on the road again," Joe told her with a sheepish grin. "I'm off to Seattle tomorrow."

"Pops!" Kim exclaimed. "You just got back. You're going to let this job kill you."

"Duty calls, Kitten."

Kim looked a little hurt. She was definitely worried about her father burning the candle at both ends. "Can't you take it easy a day or so?" she pleaded.

"In less than a year I'll take it easy forever," her father assured her.

That wasn't good enough, but Kim wasn't going to press him. She had seen too much of that while she was growing up to make the same mistake her mother had made. "What do you have planned for tonight?" she asked.

"Well, I have to go over some things with Jack before I leave...but I can do that over the phone. What you got in mind?"

"How about a movie?"

"Haven't you and Kim seen every movie in town already?" Joe asked with a wink.

"Almost," Kim laughed, "but we can rent one."

"Sure."

"I can whip us up something for dinner, and..."

"No," her father interrupted, "tell you what. I'll spring for takeout. What sounds good...pizza?"

"You and your pizza," Kim said. "How about Chinese?"

"Sounds fine. I buy, you fly. Deal?"

"Deal."

"Okay, let me finish packing, and you go out and get the Chinese." Rummel dug for his wallet and pulled out two twenties, handing them to Kim. "That should more than cover it. Your choice on the movie."

"You trust my taste then," Kim said slyly.

"I trust you emphatically," Joe beamed. He couldn't help but feel a glow of pride as he looked upon her. She had certainly become the light of his life now that they were together again, and he felt guilty he couldn't spend more time with her. Someday soon, he promised himself.

Kim hung around the apartment a few minutes longer to call in their order and tidy up some odds and ends, then she left, but not without first giving her father a kiss on the cheek and a slightly biting tease, "Welcome back, Pops."

After she had gone, Rummel dialed VanTighem. "How's it coming?" he asked when Jack answered.

"Man, you really are a slave driver," came the response.

Rummel ignored the remark. "You come up with anything?"

"I've got McConey tracked to Indianapolis so far," VanTighem told him. "That was easy. He had a surviving cousin back in Auburn who said he left town when he was sixteen, more like kicked out of town, and took off for Indianapolis. The guy said he heard from him once a couple years later, and he was still in Indianapolis. I put in some calls to check marriage and birth records there, and I should be hearing back on that shortly. It isn't easy to get people to cooperate," Jack added.

"You're tellin' me," Rummel sympathized.

"Actually, Indianapolis is kind of a stroke of luck," noted VanTighem.

"How's that?"

"I went to public information school at Fort Benjamin Harrison, and I've got an old Army buddy back there who went to work for the *Indianapolis Star* when he got out. He's doing some of the leg work for me right now."

"You tell him anything about this?" Joe asked, concerned.

"Not really," said VanTighem. "I just told him I needed it as a personal favor for a book I'm writing, and there'd be a couple hundred bucks in it for him."

"Must be nice," Rummel pondered out loud.

"Yeah, it is," Jack teased and then went on. "I wanted to order a complete social security work record on our man, but that's going to have to come from you or the FBI if you want results any time in the near future. Of course, I could always tell them I was you and give them your badge number."

"I'll take care of it when I get back, old pal...thanks just the same. I don't want any of this stuff rolling into the office in my absence."

"My, my...we are being the cautious one."

"Like I said…just between you and me for the time being."

"I got ya."

"You're doing good, Jack," Rummel told him, and he meant it.

"Thanks," VanTighem replied. "Like I said, my old chum's doing all the leg work. The way I figure it, this daughter should be in her late twenties to early thirties by now, and McConey wasn't that old when he got killed, which means he had to have started a family early. That should just about put him in Indianapolis about that same time and her too when she was a baby."

"I like it," Rummel commented.

"Figured you would," VanTighem said. There was a pause, followed by, "So, you're taking off tomorrow for Seattle, then."

"Yup."

"Well, don't do anything I wouldn't do."

Rummel knew what was coming next, but he had to ask anyway. "Like what?"

"Like bang six foot cops."

Envisioning the shit eating grin on the other end of the line, Rummel shot back, "Someone's got to do it. At least I don't have religion as an excuse to stay away."

"Ouch," VanTighem pretended to wail. "The man just bit me right on the ass."

"You just keep up the good work, and your ass will heal soon enough," Rummel chucked. "I gotta go. Kim and I are having a father-daughter evening."

"Good for you. About time. Say hi to the little twerp for me."

"Will do. Thanks again, Jack."

"My pleasure."

VanTighem hung up, and Joe placed the receiver down, remaining there by the phone for some time to think about what his friend had just said. Terri's face came to mind, and he tried to remember the details of it. He hadn't decided yet whether he would contact her right away or not--or at all--but something told him that was just a game he was playing with himself. Deep down he knew he would call her at some point while he was in Seattle. He actually caught himself hoping his investigation would go quickly so he might squeeze in an extra day or two there, maybe even get out on that fishing boat she had talked about.

CHAPTER ELEVEN

Seattle turned out to be another dead end. After three days of going through a list of names Terri had previously provided him from the files and interviewing all the primary next of kin of the victims, Rummel found absolutely nothing that would indicate a Houston connection. He had taken the approach with each family member to first ask general background questions in hopes Houston would crop up in the conversation. When that had not happened, he had asked them point blank if they or the victims had ever lived in Houston, or had anyone they were associated with ever lived there to their knowledge. The best he could come up with was one twenty-two year old nephew who had moved there.

Rummel was thoroughly frustrated. It appeared all the victims had been nothing more than random targets, textbook typical for serial killers. Except the first one. That contact by McConey's daughter just prior to his death still troubled him, and it placed a person in Houston who could have conceivably committed the crimes both there and in New Orleans, despite the fact one was an apparent homosexual killing. Although the pattern was consistent now, no concrete connection to a person or place could be found.

The time had come to call Terri. Over a beer in a downtown pub, Joe wrestled with himself as to how to go about it. Sure, he had plenty of things to discuss with her, but it would be nothing more than going over all the same old information again to come up with absolutely nothing, beating a dead horse. He felt foolish coming right out and saying he wanted to see her, and he felt just as foolish telling her he had been in Seattle three days chasing down a nonexistent Houston connection for whatever it was worth. She did ask him to contact her when he came back. That was the least he could do, he figured. Just say hello. He looked at his watch. Four o'clock. If she was on day shifts, this would be a good time to catch her at work. Feeling like a big awkward kid, Rummel rifled through his wallet for her card and went to a pay phone to make the call.

"Joe, why didn't you tell me you were in town?" Terri asked after he had explained what he had been doing.

"I wanted to snoop around on my own a couple of days," he offered as an excuse. "This thing's got me running around in circles. I just didn't want to drag anyone else into it."

"When you going back?"

"I figured I'd head out tomorrow morning. I drove my own rig this time."

"Can you stay an extra day?" Terri asked.

"Oh, I don't know. I should get back. Why do you ask?"

"I've got three days off," Terri informed him. "My uncle and I are taking the boat out tomorrow to do a little fishing. It'd be great to have you come along."

That was tempting. That was so tempting, Joe thought, that it hurt, but no way could he stay away three days. "I really appreciate the offer, Terri," he said, "but I can't stick around that long."

"You don't have to," she insisted. "We're going out to The Straits, and we could meet you at Port Angeles. We're leaving at six in the morning, and we should be there by, say, ten. It'd give you plenty of time to drive out, and we plan to moor there anyway. If you want to stay overnight in town, great. You'll have a fresh start the following morning."

Rummel had to think about that one, but he couldn't for the life of him figure out why. Hell, he wanted to go, and it would only be an extra day. He kept telling himself he was too short to work around the clock on this case anyway, but what he was really trying to say was that he wanted to see Terri. Not to mention the opportunity to catch a salmon or two. "Sure, why the hell not," he finally agreed. "You sure your uncle won't mind?"

Terri chuckled over the phone. "He'd love to have a male companion for a change. Do him good to take a break from me and my war stories."

"No shop talk I take it," Joe said, cracking a smile at his end. "I guess that just leaves the Seahawks."

"Better not," Terri warned him. "He's an Oilers fan. That's where he made all his money before he retired...down in Houston."

Rummel felt like he had just been punched in the chest. By now he was so suspicious of everyone and everything, even the mere mention of Houston sent the hackles on his neck rising. Suddenly, this was a trip he wouldn't miss for the world. His old gut instincts told him he had to be on that boat tomorrow. "As long as you don't think he'll mind," he repeated slowly, his voice now subdued. "I'll meet you at Port Angeles at ten."

"Fantastic," Terri replied. "Meet you there at the docks."

Rummel forced himself to cheer up. "Sounds great, Terri," he said. "I look forward to it."

"Gotta go. There's some loose ends around here I want to tie up before the trip."

"See you tomorrow, Terri." Joe hung up and went back to his table to order another beer. This would take some thought, how to avoid going into all the details of his recent trip down South, but one way or the other, the subject of Houston would soon come up again. That he would make certain of.

****

The drive the next morning out the Olympic Peninsula served to remind Rummel he had made the right decision to move out West. The fog was lifting in delicate wisps off the ocean, and the morning sun gently coerced the clouds away to expose a bright blue sky and the rugged snowcapped peaks of the Olympic Mountains. Along the way, rich emerald fields coated with morning dew cut sculptured paths through the forests and up the mountainsides. Everything was clean and pure, laid out in a sequence of visual delights like an artist's canvas that captured rural life from a time long gone by with its subtle animation through dairy cows that grazed rich pastures on both sides of the road. Joe rolled down his window to let the cool sea breeze shower him with its freshness and rich aroma. It smelled like life, free and exhilarating life. It was a good day to be alive.

Upon arrival at the unpretentious, working class seaside town of Port Angeles, Rummel drove straight to the public parking lot located next to the docks just like he had been there before. A good fisherman runs on radar, he told himself, and when it came to finding the place to go fishing, he was the man to do it. He looked at his watch--five to ten, right on time.

Joe stepped out of his pickup, locked it with his luggage inside and ambled down a ramp to the docks, his eyes searching for a tall blonde somewhere amid the boats and fishermen still left there that morning. Then he heard a voice call out, "Joe, over here!" Rummel looked around, and again the voice called his name. At the far end of the long, narrow dock he was standing on, he spotted Terri waving at him off the stern of a thirty-two foot cabin cruiser, a veritable yacht by his standards. They were just coming in. He quickened his steps to catch up with them before they had to moor and inhaled, as he rushed, deeper breaths of cool, moist air rich with the pungent smells of ocean life and gasoline.

"Can you make it, Joe?" asked Terri as the boat cut sharply to port and nudged its way parallel toward some open slips at the end of the dock.

"Sure, do this all the time," Joe laughed. "Maybe not with as big a boat, however," he added as he teetered on the edge and looked down at the dark water beneath his feet.

Terri reached out a hand, and Rummel grabbed it, pushing himself up and over the side of the boat with what he hoped would have been a little more grace. He felt the strength in her grip and of her arm as she hauled him in. "Welcome aboard," she said.

Regaining his feet but feeling a little jittery in the knees, Rummel took a few moments to glance around and allow his legs to settle down a bit. "Nice boat," he commented.

"We sure like it," beamed Terri. "C'mon, I want to introduce you to my uncle."

The boat had already started to back away from the dock and was now making a tight semicircle in the backwater to direct its bow seaward when Terri led Joe into the cabin. Intent on steering the craft, Terri's uncle looked over his shoulder to warmly greet the detective and then turned his eyes back to the water. He was tall and lean, which figured, at least six-four, ruggedly handsome and very distinguished looking. He had a glorious head of long silver hair that was wildly matted from time spent in ocean breezes and salt air. The man shared his niece's blue eyes, though his had sunken and mellowed with age and no doubt years of hard work, and his smile was as broad as Rummel's and hugely welcoming. Joe's expectation of a big, rangy Texan was confirmed right down to the slow, soft drawl that was a blend of life spent both in the Northwest and the South. When they had cleared the marina, Terri made the formal introductions, and her uncle opened with, "Glad to have you aboard, Joe."

"My pleasure, Mr. Long."

"You call me Byron, yah hear?"

"Will do, Byron."

"Ready to give these fish a little hell?"

"Always," Rummel replied with an eager grin.

"Then let's kick this baby in the ass, and we're off."

Joe settled back on the padded compartments that lined the gunnels in the stern, and Terri sat opposite him. Twin engines roared into full power, and they headed out to sea. He could scarcely hear her above the engine noise and the pounding of the waves alongside as she explained how they rigged up their rods for this type of fishing. One thing was for certain; the woman knew what she was doing. She told him about the right lead from the flasher and how to hook a herring or anchovy so it had just the right action in the water. Rummel couldn't help but be fascinated by her. He tried to listen, but his real attention was on her face, those alabaster cheeks which withstood frequent shots of spraying water without a flinch, bright blue eyes sparkling in the sunlight, and her flag of long blond hair that streamed freely in the wind. She was at home in this type of environment, as natural to the outdoors as were the sea birds that soared gracefully overhead.

It couldn't have been a more perfect day with the sun warming them from a nearly cloudless sky and the ocean surface a glassy calm, all of it mellowed out even more by the lazy drone of powerful engines near idle while they trolled off the rocky points. A cold beer, good company, everything was as it should be. Except for one small hitch.

The best Rummel could come up with was a three pound silver salmon, which he released, a fish no bigger than the ones he had caught in Montana, whereas Byron had already boated two Chinooks in the eight pound class, releasing them also, and Terri had a fifteen pounder to her credit. Somehow he had known in advance this would happen, but today he didn't much care. His thoughts were still drifting back and forth between the pleasures of the moment and the problems he faced back home. Catching a fish was, for once, the farthest thing from his mind.

It was nearing three o'clock, dead time for their lines in the water. They had just consumed an excellent lunch of gourmet sandwiches and potato salad Terri had prepared in advance, the credit for which her uncle had been quick to point out. During the course of their conversation now, Joe learned that Byron had raised Terri from the time she was eight until she had entered the University of Washington, both her parents having been killed in a car accident. Only after she had enrolled in college did he relocate to Houston, and it was the mention of that move which prompted Rummel to crack a fresh beer, lean back in his cabin seat and remark casually, "I was just down there."

"Oh?" Byron said. "Business or pleasure?"

"Unfortunately, not pleasure," Rummel replied.

"Joe's been tracking some nasty homicides here and in Spokane," Terri interjected. "And maybe he found something in Houston also," she added with raised eyebrows and a questioning look.

"Well, Houston's a good place for that," her uncle commented.

"You ever hear of a guy by the name of Ron Gillette?" inquired Rummel.

Byron Long broke out with an amused laugh. "Everyone in the business community knew little ol' Ron," he stated. "Hell, Joe, what business you got with that little fairy?"

Rummel took a drink of beer and elaborated. "A boyfriend of his got himself killed a few years back. It has almost all the earmarkings of these murders here in Washington."

"You remember," Terri reminded her uncle. "The knifings I was working on last year."

"I remember you never caught that creep," Long chuckled over his shoulder. He was behind the wheel, and he looked back at the water to check his course. "I thought I raised you up better than that."

Terri chose to ignore that remark, turning to Joe instead and saying, "I know Houston was one of the places on your list, but you didn't say anything about finding something there."

"I didn't find anything to speak of," Rummel covered up. He wanted to slip into this conversation through the back door. "For one thing, we're talking about a homosexual murder there."

Byron Long was thinking now. He turned his captain's chair back around, left one arm draped over the wheel and said, "I remember that. As I recall, it was a pretty sticky mess. They kept it real hush-hush in the community. But I thought Gillette was completely exonerated."

"He was and is," Rummel told him. "And they never found the killer."

"You find out anything about the victim?" asked Terri.

"Just that he was gay as a lark," Joe answered.

"From all the rumors floating around town at the time, he was a lot more than that," Long added. "The way it was told, he was one kinky son of a bitch."

Rummel's curiosity was aroused. "Oh, what'd you hear?"

"Gillette's little boyfriend was a real social butterfly," Long noted. "He had money, family money, and he used it to get into all kinds of scrapes. I know for a fact he knocked up some young socialite in Houston because I used to golf with one of her old man's business associates. The truth was some of us even thought her father might've had the jerk knocked off."

Rummel didn't even pay attention to that last comment. Already his mind was whirling with the realization he may no longer be stuck with a gay killing in Houston.

"You should ask Brad if he remembers it," suggested Terri.

"What?"

"Brad Curtis," Terri repeated.

Joe was leaning forward now, hanging on her every word. "What's he got to do with it?" he inquired. His look revealed both bewilderment and surprise.

Terri was a little unsettled by his reaction, and she grew more serious. "That's where he's from," she informed him.

"He never said anything to me about it," Rummel quickly pointed out.

"After I talked to you the last time," Terri explained, "I did a little checking around with the guys he worked with. They told me he had moved here from Houston, same reason you gave me for his move to Spokane…to follow his girlfriend. I remember specifically they said she was originally from that area because they started laying some of their Southern Belle crap on me again." Terri paused, then added, "Hell, it'd be easy enough to check out. Brad used to work for the police department there."

That did it. Rummel's mind was running wild, and he was trapped by a sudden onslaught of his own conflicting emotions. The trail was practically right there in front of him, laid out beautifully, yet he refused to believe it. The best he could do for the time being was lean back again and take a healthy swig of beer, allow himself a few minutes for his thoughts to clear.

"Why's it so important?" Terri asked.

Joe had to gather his wits about him to come up with an adequate reply. "Probably isn't," he said pensively. "I'm just a little surprised Brad never told me anything about being from Houston when he knew I was going down there. You'd think he would've mentioned it anyway."

"Maybe he doesn't want to be reminded," Long chuckled as he turned from his skipper duties to face them again. "Not that I minded it all that much, but it sure isn't the great Northwest."

For now, Rummel had to put this behind him. He forced a smile and said, "You've got that right, Byron." Struggling to his feet against a lightly rocking boat and cramped spaces, he announced, "Think I'll step out back for a minute and check those rods." Without another word, he left the cabin. Terri and her uncle just traded perplexed looks and shrugged.

****

That evening they dined on a hearty seafood smorgasbord in town although Joe didn't have much of an appetite. His thoughts were still elsewhere. He tried to pick up the tab, but Byron wouldn't hear a word of it. Joe was his guest, and he had enjoyed his company very much that day. Both men had taken to each other.

By the time they left the restaurant, the sun had already set, leaving only a narrow strip of pale blue sky in the West. Joe was planning to go straight to his truck and head for the motel room he had rented shortly after their return from the fishing trip, but Long had a different suggestion. "Why don't you two stay out awhile and hit a few night spots," he said. "It's still early, but old farts like me have to hit the hay."

"You staying on the boat?" Rummel inquired.

"We almost always do," Terri said. "But I'm good for a couple more hours if you're game, Joe."

Rummel wasn't sure he was. "Well...I've got to be heading out early in the morning," he hedged. "I don't know...maybe one more beer wouldn't hurt."

"Or else we could take a walk and look around," suggested Terri.

Why not, he thought. He was too wound up now anyway to consider serious sleep.

"You two do that," Byron insisted. He stuck out his hand, and Joe took it with a solid grip. "Joe, it's been a pleasure having you on board. I expect to see you back soon."

"You can count on it," the detective told him. "I enjoyed the trip and the company."

"Sorry you didn't catch a decent fish."

"Win some, lose some," said Rummel philosophically. "That's fishing. Next time."

Byron Long offered him a big grin. "Next time it is, Joe," he agreed. "Catch you later, Terri." He turned away and started to walk down the road that would take him to the docks.

"You want to grab a couple more beers, Joe?" asked Terri.

Rummel glanced around at the haze that was starting to drift in, took in a deep breath of cool night air and replied, "Nah, I don't get much opportunity to be in a place like this. That walk sounds like a good idea."

"There's a little chunk of beach and a park down the road," Terri suggested.

"Sounds fine to me."

Terri cracked a big smile. "Let's go check it out."

They headed in the direction of a point of land scarcely discernible in the twilight, their course aided by the orange beacons of three sodium lights that marked a parking lot in the vicinity. As they left the bright lights of town behind them, they talked about themselves and their respective pasts. Terri made it all seem easy for Joe with her straightforward questions and her own openness about herself.

She was actually thirty-nine, had never been married, came close a couple of times, but her dedication to police work had brought about an end to both relationships. Joe could relate to that. He told Terri the time might come in her life, however, when she would look back on her choices as mistakes, something he was wrestling with currently. She agreed that could be a possibility.

Rummel spoke mostly of Kim and recent events with her coming to live with him. Also, when asked about his friend, he told Terri the real reason he had brought VanTighem along on the previous trip and requested that she keep it under her hat around police headquarters. Terri agreed, but she couldn't resist informing him that she had already discovered who Jack really was. Rummel laughed and remarked it was impossible to keep secrets between cops.

They approached the narrow, rocky point which was separated from the main highway by the parking lot and a flat portion of land dotted with the shadows of some scattered picnic tables. A well traveled path led down to a thin sandy beach that ran halfway up the point and back toward the road where it disappeared in the darkness. Lights from the parking lot and a few residences nearby illuminated their way.

Deciding to forego the path and beach in favor of a little adventure, they tackled the point instead and found a crude trail through the rocks which had been worn down by others before them. Rummel held Terri's hand now, leading the way as they scrambled single file over a particularly treacherous section of boulders. Twice before, while they had walked closely together, their hands had brushed, and both times Joe had felt compelled to reach for her, but his years of reserve and deep-seated fears had prevented him from doing that. Now it was easy; they had an excuse. They were like two kids exploring, and the circumstances warranted their touching, made it all okay in Joe's mind.

Finally they could go no farther. They were at the end of the point, and all around them the surf washed gently against the rocks with a steady, rhythmic beat. Across the water they could see the bright lights of Victoria on Vancouver Island, and the smaller villages in the area too, and the occasional twinkling of ships' lights as they silently passed through the Strait of Juan de Fuca. A soft haze overhead secluded the stars, and the moon had yet to appear over the nearby hilltops. All was very still and peaceful, punctuated only by Rummel's heavy breathing. He coughed and said, "I've got to quit these damned cigarettes."

"I haven't seen you smoke that much," Terri commented.

"I don't. But I still should quit the damned things altogether. They've taken their toll on me just coming out here."

"I used to smoke," Terri remarked. "Chewed Cope for awhile too."

Rummel broke out with a laugh. "You?"

"Sure," Terri said with a smile he could see clearly in the dark. "It's one of the curses of modern women. But I quit them both."

"That's what I have to do with these things one of these days," repeated Rummel. Suddenly he became self-conscious about holding her hand, and he let go of it as he pretended to need both hands to comb out his hair which had become matted and curled even tighter by the salt air. He simply couldn't escape the idea he felt foolish holding hands with a cop, but that was just an excuse, and he knew it. Joe was afraid of the contact. It had been so long since he had shared intimacy.

"You got anyone back home, Joe?" asked Terri out of the blue. "Anyone other than Kim I mean?"

"Just Jack," he answered with a chuckle. "Between the two of them, I've got more than I can handle."

"You know what I mean," Terri laughed but quickly grew serious again. "Anyone special?"

Joe's smile faded. "No," he told her. "No one special." He paused, then added, "It's been a long time...and sometimes I wonder if there ever will be someone special again. Jack and I were just talking about that recently. We both have our demons and curses, but they all go by the same name. It's called middle age."

"It goes both ways, Joe," said Terri solemnly. "Women suffer from it too."

"Never much thought about that," Rummel admitted. "But I suppose they do." He let his eyes drift out to sea. "I guess after you spend so much time in life hurting and getting hurt, one day it just doesn't seem worth it anymore." He turned to Terri and asked, "You know what I mean?"

Terri nodded her head and said yes.

"Everyone must hit that point in their lives at one time or other," Joe continued. "Some a little harder than others. I guess I don't have it so bad when you take a look at some other folks. You take Jack now. That poor battle scarred son of a bitch has been duking it out with women all his life…two marriages, a new girlfriend every time you turned around, and he pushed them all out before any of them got too close."

"I feel sorry for someone like that," Terri quietly observed.

"No sorrier than he's feeling for himself right now," commented Rummel. "He thought he had them all stomped into the ground and then, whamo, he got blindsided by a sweet little Christian girl who, by the way, wasn't all that sweet. Actually, from what I knew of her, she was Jack VanTighem in a woman's body. She had his act down better than he did."

"What happened?"

"He fell crazy in love with her, and she dumped him. Actually, it didn't quite go that way. He fell crazy in love with her, quit drinking, then wised up, and he walked out on her. He was doing pretty well for himself until he got religion, and then he kind of got goofy. She sucked him back in, and *then* she dumped him."

"Sounds like we all have our war stories," noted Terri.

"Actually, I feel kind of lucky," Rummel told her. "I've got Kim and a good friend. Julie, that's my ex-wife, we sort of made our peace recently the best we could, and that makes me feel a little better." Joe showed Terri a warm smile and concluded, "Less than a year to go for retirement, and I'm home free to do a lot more of what we did today."

Terri looked into his dark eyes, which seemed to glisten in the night, and she felt herself drawn to his gentle nature and the strength of his character. This man was a mountain that had been battered by the storms of life, chipped away, eroded, but still stood tall. She sensed the goodness in him, and also the hurt that had been deeply buried away so he could survive and take one more good swing for decency at those cruel realities that hit back. In that, she was with him all the way. Her own disappointments now seemed to fade in the company of this man. She realized now what she had suspected all along. She wanted him; she wanted to be with him. Only her own fears and insecurities stood in the way. It was time to push them aside. "I'd like to see you again, Joe," she said as she attempted to overcome the hesitation in her voice. "I like you. I'd like to spend some time with you."

If her words came as a shock, it was only because Rummel felt unworthy of such feelings. But there was no place he could run and hide. "I like you too, Terri," he said. "I like you a lot...even though you beat my pants off today fishing." The smile was back to cover up the trembling inside.

Terri seized the moment. She bent forward and kissed him gently, and there was a lightheaded tingle for Rummel as he pressed his lips against hers and reached around her to pull her close to him. Their lips parted and consumed each other with a tender passion, reserving the complete fulfillment of pent-up emotion for later. Their kiss lingered, and they savored its delicate touch until slowly it subsided and both of them withdrew to delight in and review their euphoric sensations. Terri leaned back a little, still holding Rummel around the waist, and she said, "I suppose we should be going back."

"I suppose so," Joe answered softly.

"To your room?" Terri added with a coy smile.

Rummel wasn't quite prepared for that. "What about your uncle?" he asked.

"He'd kick my butt if I returned to the boat early," Terri laughed.

Joe's bewilderment showed clearly on his face. "What do you mean? I don't get it."

"All he's heard me talk about since I first met you is you," Terri explained. "He's been waiting years to hear that."

Rummel chuckled. "No wonder I got the red carpet treatment."

"Yeah, we ganged up on you, Joe," Terri replied as she turned him around toward the road with her arm wrapped tightly around his waist and laid her head against his shoulder. She kissed him one more time close to his ear and whispered, "Let's talk more about me beating the pants off you."

CHAPTER TWELVE

VanTighem was one of the featured guests for an annual charity banquet held downtown at Spokane's Davenport Hotel. He did indeed strike a very handsome figure in formal black tie for the occasion, but he would have been much happier staying home and lounging around in jeans. Yet duty called, this time in the form of a personal invitation from the mayor's office. He hated these things. He had always been uncomfortable with the public, and his extroverted nature covered up for that fact. Worse yet, he had been forced to make a brief speech which had really put him on edge. Public speaking had never been his forte; that's why he had become a print journalist rather than a television reporter. But he managed to handle the job well that night, although the whole time he had wished he could have been more himself. VanTighem realized, however, if that had happened, they might have either thrown him out or carted him off to be committed.

Following the presentations and the speeches and all those things that made Jack want to go home, he was at last free to mingle briefly and then bail out. He was about to do just that when she approached him through the crowd. She was stunning in her strapless white evening dress cut very low in front.

"I enjoyed your presentation, Jack," Kim Wintrode said. "Nice to see you again."

VanTighem couldn't help but be mesmerized by her utterly disarming beauty and elegance, which was even more evident tonight than he had remembered it to be. "Good to see you too, Kim," he replied with a playful smile he couldn't help. "I was afraid I might have been a bit boring up there."

"Not at all," said Kim. Her gaze was locked onto his intense green eyes. "You gave us all a couple good moments."

"That's show biz," VanTighem joked.

Kim came right to the point. "What are you doing right now?" she asked.

Jack was caught a little off guard. "Uh, nothing, I guess. I was just on my way home."

"You want to get out of here and go for a drink? My treat."

"Sure," he said. "If you don't mind the company of a teetotaler."

"Not at all," Kim smiled. "I like a man who has his principles."

VanTighem laughed. "Principles can also turn a man into a first class bore."

Wintrode smiled warmly. "I think perhaps you come down too hard on yourself, Jack." She winked and added, "Come on, let's get the hell out of here."

They left immediately, took the staircase down to the lobby and went outside two blocks down the street to Flaherty's, a fun little night spot complete with bowls of peanuts and a honky-tonk piano. VanTighem had spent many of his drinking years in that bar so for him it was like returning home, right down to a shouted greeting from the bartender when he entered. They found an open table in back, somewhat secluded and away from the noise. Kim ordered a Virgin Mary for Jack and an Amaretto Sour for herself. While awaiting their drinks, she started off the conversation. "It's not often I have the opportunity to be in the company of a celebrity."

"Celebrity hell," VanTighem scoffed. "According to Joe, I just write trashy novels and make good money at it."

"You're too modest."

"Modesty and humility are long overdue in my life, Kim," the writer stated.

"You mind if I ask you something?"

"Go ahead...shoot."

"How long have you been off drinking?"

"Close to three years," VanTighem proudly answered. "Why do you ask?"

"Oh, no reason really," Kim said. "I've become very close friends with Kim Rummel, and she's told me a few stories. You know...things she picked up from her dad mostly." She showed him a concerned look. "I hope you don't mind me bringing it up."

"Not at all," Jack told her as he fixed his smile on her and looked right into her inviting blue eyes. He was very interested to see where this was leading. His old instincts started to tug at his insides. "So, what'd you hear?"

"I hear you used to be a holy terror," Kim bluntly said to him.

"Just holy now," VanTighem nodded modestly. "My reputation exceeds me."

Offering him a tender and understanding smile, Kim said, "I've had my days too."

"It builds character," Jack commented. "Especially if you can break away from it."

Kim took a deep breath and admitted with cool precision in her voice, "I must confess...I've been attracted to you since the first day we met, Jack."

All his years of experience handling remarks like that from women and his cultivated calm detachment in those situations could not come to his rescue this time, particularly now that he was face to face with easily the most beautiful of them all. VanTighem was stricken dumfounded. Once again he was being challenged to the contest of a new relationship, but this time he was without any of the weapons that had become long lost in his past. And here was a woman who clearly knew what she wanted and would do or use anything at her disposal to have it. His response momentarily stuck in his throat, and might have lingered there too long had he not been saved by the waitress who brought them their drinks.

After she had left and VanTighem had regained his composure, he asked Kim directly, "What about your boyfriend? I heard you two were inseparable."

"We are," Kim replied casually. "But we also have an open relationship."

"How's that?" VanTighem asked, although he already knew the answer.

Kim offered him a knowing smile, the seductiveness in her look apparent. "It means, quite simply, we don't allow relationships with other people to interfere with our own. We both freely admit our attraction to others, and occasionally, if the situation permits, we act on those attractions. That's one of the reasons we keep separate residences."

"And you're acting on that right now," VanTighem noted.

Taking a sip of her Amaretto, Kim's eyes never left him. She put her glass down and said, "That's right, Jack."

VanTighem took a drink also. "Ahh, they make them nice and hot here," he commented, then dabbed his lips with a napkin and bought a little time. A few empty seconds passed. Finally, he told her, "Well, Kim, I must say I admire your candor." She nodded with a pleasant smile, and Jack went on. "There's one thing I finally learned over the years and throughout my relationships...probably too late, I might add."

"What's that?"

Jack leaned forward, his elbows on the table, cupped his chin with both hands and responded, "I'm not afraid to lay it on the line with women. I don't always like it, and often it makes me uncomfortable, but I'm not afraid to be honest with them."

"That's good to hear," Kim said.

"Yeah, right," VanTighem remarked as he sat upright again. He took a deep breath and continued, his expression clouding slightly. "What you might see on the exterior here, someone you find attractive, maybe even sexy, is not necessarily the person I am now."

"I'm interested," Kim said as she folded her arms on the table and bent forward. "Tell me more."

VanTighem cracked a cynical smile, shook his head a bit over what was going on in his mind, and then came right out with it. "I don't know how I would handle intimacy anymore." He paused before adding, "It's gotten to the point I don't think I can handle the emotions anymore, and just the thought of it scares the daylights out of me. To be honest with you, I'm pretty much afraid of any close contact with the opposite sex, both emotional and physical."

Kim straightened right up with a look of surprise and pure admiration over what she had just heard. "I was all prepared to hear you tell me you were gay," she laughed.

"Nope, trying to quit," VanTighem joked.

Reaching across the table, Kim placed her hand on top of his. "I've heard a lot of things in my time," she commented, "but never have I heard this kind of honesty from a man."

"Well, I'm not particularly proud of it," Jack managed to chuckle with a forced grin. His look suddenly grew serious. "There was a time, not long ago, when I thought of sex as a weapon, used it or withdrew at my whim to screw with their emotions. You see, I'm fully aware that women, not all but most, crave the intimacy, the closeness, the touching, the loving so to speak. I abused that, and now I'm paying the price."

"What happened?" Kim asked. Her concerned look reappeared.

Jack wasn't about to get into that. Instead, he simply said, "I guess I developed a conscience somewhere along the line."

Taking another sip of her Amaretto, Kim allowed the momentary silence between them to soften his defenses a little. Then she asked quietly, "Who was she?"

"You're very perceptive, Kim," VanTighem responded with a wink and a smile.

"You care to talk about it?"

"Not particularly."

Kim Wintrode's hand slid across the table again and touched VanTighem's as he cradled his drink and stared pensively into it. "You said you weren't afraid to be honest with women. Maybe it would help to talk about it."

"I also said I wasn't always crazy about it sometimes," Jack flatly replied. "I do talk about it. I talk to my shrink."

"Is your shrink a woman?"

"No."

"Well then...I'm a good listener."

VanTighem looked up at her. If ever there was a woman he wanted on the spur of the moment, this was the one. Her eyes were filled with understanding and intelligence, her face beckoned to be touched, those lips sought to be kissed. A couple of years ago and he would have been out of there with her like a shot. What was holding him back now? he asked himself. Had he torn himself apart so much that he could never go back now? Was he still so much afraid? Still afraid of being hurt after he had dished out so much of it himself in his lifetime? Another long breath, and Jack confessed, "She left me because she couldn't reconcile the age difference between us. It made me feel old," he added, "like there was something wrong with me."

"How much difference?" Kim asked, her curiosity aroused.

"Fifteen years," VanTighem said.

"Bullshit," snapped Kim. "That's pure bullshit. If she was really in love with you, that wouldn't have made a damned bit of difference. There was something else she was afraid of. Probably something in herself, not you."

"I wasn't buying into it either," VanTighem agreed. His voice had taken on a cold tone. "As much as I hate to admit it, I'm not really sure she ever did really love me."

Kim saw the hurt in his eyes, the moisture subduing their intensity. She could also see that at one time those light green eyes might have burned with such independence and danger that they had challenged any woman, with the nerve to try it, to reach into their soul. There was none of that now. There was only defeat and pain. She wanted this man more than ever, and she would have him. "You ever see her?" Kim asked.

"No, she moved away."

"Figures," Kim observed.

"Why do you say that?" inquired VanTighem.

"Some women are runners. They run away when it gets too close."

"You sound like you're speaking from experience," Jack noted.

"I've been there," Kim said. "Not anymore."

VanTighem leaned back against his chair and commented with a note of resignation, "I can't say I blame her. We were both very similar in too many ways."

"So this is your way of running now too," remarked Kim.

"I guess it is, Kim. The truth is I was just as afraid as she was."

VanTighem took another drink, and when he put his glass back down, Kim took him by the hand again. "I'm not a psychiatrist," she told him, "and there's nothing I can do to stop anyone from running away. Except for tonight. I can stop you tonight…if you'll allow me to."

No matter what his reservations were at that moment Jack could not say no. He was just too drawn to this woman, too captivated by her to walk away from her now. Otherwise, he would never know, and that would be worse than disappointment. He reached for a napkin and asked Kim if she had a pen in her purse. She found one for him, and he wrote down his address, handing it to her. "It's in Wandermere," he said. "Meet you there in a half hour or forty-five?"

Kim took the napkin and put it in her purse. "I know the area," she said. "I'll be there."

"Are you sure you know what you're doing?" VanTighem asked.

"Are you?" Kim countered.

"To be honest with you, I don't know. I just don't know." Pausing to look into her eyes, Jack added softly, "I do know I want to make love to you."

"Then we have nothing to worry about," Kim said.

VanTighem finished his drink and stood up to leave, Kim joining him. As they left the bar, he felt uncomfortable even putting his arm around her. They hardly knew each other. Again he questioned his judgment. She must have sensed that because she reached for his hand, saying nothing to him, and let her touch convey her message while he walked her to the parking garage where they both had their cars.

As they approached a white Chrysler LeBaron convertible, VanTighem remarked, "Nice wheels."

"It's Brad's," Kim said. "Mine's back in the shop. I've been borrowing this one a lot lately."

Her nonchalance about using her boyfriend's car to have an affair with someone else troubled VanTighem, but he shook it off, realizing he had pulled similar stunts in his time also.

Kim unlocked the door, opened it and then turned to Jack, and without any hesitation she kissed him tenderly on the lips. He felt an erotic rush from that brief encounter, an excitement and a mysterious sense of adventure he had not experienced in a very long time. "See you shortly," was all Kim said to him as she gently touch his mouth with her forefinger and climbed into her car.

"See you," Jack said when she rolled down the window. His old, self-assured smile was back.

****

Kim had no trouble finding VanTighem's home, an elegant, large Cape Cod yet modest compared to some of the neighboring residences located in one of Spokane's most exclusive districts. It was what she would have expected of the man. She parked her car in the driveway, walked up a curving, well maintained stone path to the front door and rang the doorbell, only to be answered immediately by loud barking inside. A few moments later Jack came to the door, along with two Brittany Spaniels who greeted her by poking their heads out the narrow opening he tried to block with one leg. "C'mon, kids," he said. "Get back."

Kim squeezed inside while VanTighem juggled the door and his dogs at the same time. "They won't hurt you, Kim. They're real sweethearts, but they will jump on you so bear with me while I ride herd on this tribe." He turned to the spaniels, ordering them, "Now stay down. Go on...get back."

"They're beautiful!" Kim exclaimed. "What's their names?"

"The lady there on the left is Bridgette, and the good looking fellow here is Woody."

"What great looking dogs. Do they hunt?"

"They live for it," Jack answered, and then he turned to the two spaniels, "Okay, you guys. Kennel up." He pointed to a doorway at the far side of the spacious sunken living room. Reluctantly, the Brits did as they were told, and two sets of intense amber eyes set behind big pink noses watched Kim from the kitchen entrance as she stood in the foyer and surveyed her tastefully decorated surroundings.

She was instantly captivated by a huge, full length portrait centered on the far wall over a massive stone fireplace. Without another word, Kim took the one step down into the living room and crossed it for a closer look. VanTighem remained by the door watching her. As she stared up at the imposing figure highlighted in a richly detailed, gold Florentine frame, she fell entranced by the look, the proud pose, the piercing green eyes that seemed alive. It was a painting, she thought, of a man in his early twenties, dressed in a conservative, olive three piece suit, and it appeared to be very Wall Street boardroom and very old. "Who is this?" she asked. "Your grandfather?"

Grinning broadly, VanTighem walked across the room to join her. He placed a hand on her bare shoulder and said, "No, Kim, that's not my grandfather."

"Who is it then?"

"That's my college graduation picture."

Kim's eyes shot back and forth between VanTighem and the portrait. "It's a photograph?" she asked, astounded.

"Sure is with some kind of hand painting...airbrushed I think. I had it taken just before I was drafted."

"I can't believe it," Kim said, shaking her head. "I mean I can see it's you now, but it looks like it's a hundred years old."

"I sometimes think it was taken a hundred years ago," VanTighem chuckled. "Can I get you anything to drink?"

"What do you have?" inquired Kim.

"Full bar."

"You know how to make a White Russian?"

"Coming right up," Jack said. "First let me put the pooches out in their kennel, or we're going to have visitors at all hours." VanTighem disappeared for a couple of minutes, came back and prepared her drink behind a classic mahogany bar located near the kitchen entrance. He poured himself something he had taken from the compact refrigerator beneath the bar and returned to her with a drink in each hand.

"What's that?" Kim asked, pointing at his glass.

"Cherry Kool-Aid," VanTighem replied sheepishly. "I'm hooked on the crap."

Kim laughed warmly. "So it's true, then. The mighty have fallen."

VanTighem couldn't help but crack a smile over that remark. "Sad but true," he said. "You keep that up, and we'll get nowhere tonight."

Placing her glass down on the nearby coffee table, Kim took Jack's from his hand to do the same, and she wrapped her arms around his neck and said to him softly, "Yes, we will." She kissed him, tenderly at first, her lips parting ever so slightly, and VanTighem again felt that long lost thrill race through him and lift his emotions to soaring heights. He returned her gentle kiss in kind, his own touch as light and as sensitive as any Kim had ever experienced. The excitement and taste of him shot through her and sent out a signal that this would be different, that this man instinctively keyed into a woman's needs and was completely capable of being at one with a woman. Her passion fired, Kim opened her mouth to his, finding his tongue waiting for hers, and together the pressed hard to satisfy their hunger for each other, their bodies swaying in sensuous dance. Jack's hand swept through Kim's hair, and he teased her with little nips on her lower lip, which drove her even more out of control. Already she was moist, and she clawed desperately at the back of his head to pull him impossibly closer to her. That was enough, and Kim pulled back. Out of breath, she whispered, "Which way to the bedroom?"

The soft glow of a full moon flowed into the expansive master bedroom through twin cathedral windows and bathed their embraced bodies in pale blue light. VanTighem slowly undid Kim's dress, planting behind the descending zipper delicate kisses across her bare back. He ran his tongue up her spine to focus on the back of her neck, and he nibbled playfully on her earlobes. Savoring every moment of it, Kim tossed her head back. Her hair showered over Jack's shoulder, and her dress slipped to the floor. She unsnapped her bra and allowed it to do the same, stepping out of the crumpled folds around her ankles. Kim turned to him, unbuttoned his white formal shirt with trembling fingers and kissed his chest, running her tongue through the sparse patch of soft hair centered there. Pulling his shirt away from his shoulders, she pressed her nakedness hard against him and kissed him passionately, almost violently. Both felt the sensations swell again to new heights.

Kim eased away from Jack. She quickly slipped out of her panties and allowed Jack the time to completely undress also. Taking him by the hand, she led him to the edge of the bed, pulled back the covers and slid underneath them, urging him with an outstretched hand to join her.

For a few long moments, Jack remained there by the bedside, standing naked in the moonlight over her as he absorbed her loveliness nestled among the covers and held mysterious in the dark. Suddenly another face came to mind, her smile filling his heart, and a warning shot from the pit of his stomach told him to stay back. He felt his desire slowly subside.

By his look alone, Kim knew something was wrong. For the first time in her life, she was stunned by a feeling of inadequacy. She had run up against something she had never encountered before, and suddenly she hated that woman, whoever she was. Though she could not deal with her directly, she would now do everything in her power to kill her in this man's mind tonight and forever. In a matter of fleeting seconds, her sensual passion had been transformed into outraged jealousy, not because of another woman, but over this man's love instead. She had never before come face to face with such a depth of love, and she wanted that love all for herself more than anything else at that very moment. She would have it, even if she had to give completely of herself in order to obtain it, and that was something Kim was not inclined to do.

Kim reached up for VanTighem's hand, which he offered, and gently drew him to her. Reassured again by their naked warmth together, they did nothing for awhile but touch. Kim ran a finger across Jack's brow and down the side of his face, feeling a single tear there. "Don't say a word," she whispered. "Not a word."

****

The next morning VanTighem awoke to find Woody and Bridgette sprawled out on the bed beside him. 'What the hell?' he thought. 'How'd they get in here?' Jack made a move to sit up but was instantly pummeled back down by his two spaniels. One chose a cheek and the other an ear to lick. "Okay, you two, down! Go on, get down." Dutifully the two Brittanies hopped off the bed and waited for Jack by the bedroom door with tails going full speed.

VanTighem was groggy, felt drugged, even hung over--how could that be? He struggled to sit up and look at the clock, but something hid the dial.

It was a note from the looks of it, and then it all began to come back to him. Last thing he remembered it was well past four-thirty when he drifted off to sleep with Kim in his arms. That had been a night reminiscent of his youth, and he couldn't help but smile when he thought about it. No wonder he felt groggy and exhausted. But where was she now? And why were the dogs in here? Jack staggered to his feet and picked up the note:

> Jack--I let your two friends in to keep
> you company. Hope you don't mind.
> Had a fantastic time last night, but today
> is a work day, and I must try keep up
> appearances. I hope to see you again soon.
> Very soon. Kim

Jack VanTighem again smiled. Last night had been an unexpected surprise in his life, one he had often wondered if he would ever experience again after his last relationship and one he now fully intended to experience a whole lot more. Now the question loomed in his mind could he let go after this. By the tone of her note, it appeared Kim was not prepared to let go either, not yet anyway. They had experienced too much intensity, too much passion together to merely chalk it up as a good time. But one or the other, perhaps both, could get hurt. Jack realized this woman could be dangerous in ways he could only sense, in ways he found very exciting, and he was not about to cut and run now.

VanTighem was wide awake now and oddly full of energy. He tossed on his clothes and told his dogs all three of them were going downstairs to the kitchen for a hearty breakfast.

CHAPTER THIRTEEN

"You have to go now. We can't stay together anymore."

"I'm not going to leave you."

"You have to for now. You have to get away while you can."

"And leave you alone?"

"I can manage. I can handle myself. And we'll be together again."

"How can you be so certain of that?"

"I just know. We'll always be together. You have a chance to start new now, and you need to take advantage of it. Here, take this to remember me by."

"What is it?"

"A rose from the park. Keep it safe and know I will always be with you."

"Will you stay here so I know where to find you?"

"We're not going to lose touch. Do you hear me? We're not losing touch."

"I'll be back for you when this is over."

"You don't have to. I'll come to you first."

****

David Ewan was out on the town raising hell and making a general nuisance of himself, along with his two buddies from Eastern Washington University. Ewan was one of Spokane's rich boys, top of the heap, and a thorn in the side of just about everyone with whom he came into contact. Except his doting parents; especially his father. David Ewan Sr. had made it big in the real estate business and had plenty of the wherewithal to bail his son out of scrapes with the authorities, which he had done on numerous occasions in the past.

This particular night had started out no differently than any other for Ewan--a few pitchers of beer and the bullying of a random patron or two in a local college pub, then a ride through the city to find some action. They were cruising out West Pacific on route to the various parks in the area to smoke some joints when Ewan spotted a woman ahead on the sidewalk walking briskly toward them. "Pull over next to her," he ordered the driver.

The car slowed and came to a stop on the side of the road just a few yards in front of her. Ewan rolled down the window, stuck his head out and said to her, "Hey, foxy lady, you shouldn't be out here all alone this late. Want a ride?"

Her eyes fixed straight ahead, the woman ignored him as she walked on by the car.

Again Ewan turned to the driver. "Hack a U-turn up here and swing around," he said. "I want to follow this bitch."

"Hey, man," the driver argued. "I don't think we ought to be doing this kind of shit."

"I ain't going to hurt her!" Ewan shouted. "Now, damnit...do as I tell you! I'm just gonna have a little fun here...spook her a bit."

The driver shook his head with resignation and slowly drove away to turn around at the intersection of Hemlock.

When they returned, the woman had vanished. Ewan ordered his friend to slow down and check out the side streets. As they went past South Chestnut, the streetlights gave her away, and they spotted her walking alongside Coeur D' Alene Park. Ewan instructed the driver to take the next right on Cannon and intercept her on South Coeur D' Alene Street. A couple of minutes later they caught up with her at the corner of the park across from the neighborhood residences. Ewan had his buddy pull up to the curb, and he told him to leave the engine running while he went out to talk to her. "What are you going to do?" asked his friend in the backseat.

"Hey, I'm just going to talk to her," Ewan said. "Don't sweat it, man."

The driver glanced around nervously. "I don't like this," he protested.

"Don't be such a chickenshit," Ewan smirked. "Look, I'll sweet talk her, and maybe all three of us will get lucky. Okay?"

"Don't hurt her," warned the one in back.

"C'mon, would I hurt a fox like that?" Ewan leered. "Give me a break." He jumped out of the car, stuck his head through the open window and said with a knowing look, "I'll be back in a couple minutes with this tuna fish on the hook." Turning from them, he trotted across the street to catch up with the woman who was now heading in the opposite direction.

From the safety of their car, Ewan's two companions watched him as he approached the woman on the sidewalk. At first, she appeared to resist him when he came up behind her and stopped her. She quickly broke away from him to resume her fast paced walk, but Ewan was persistent and kept right up with her. Finally the woman stopped at the end of the block. They appeared to be talking, and from the looks of it at that distance all seemed to be going well. Then Ewan abruptly left her and ran back toward the car. He stuck his head through the window again and announced in a breathless voice, "You ain't gonna believe this."

Lurid curiosity suddenly replaced the fears of both men, and the driver asked, "What's goin' down?"

"This bimbo's car's broken down, and I convinced her I can help her," Ewan rattled off with wild excitement.

"Where's it at?" asked the man in the backseat.

"At the end of Third…right across from Overlook," Ewan answered him.

"You get her name?" inquired the driver.

"Kim somebody," Ewan said. "Now you guys take off for twenty minutes and then cruise back down Coeur D' Alene and pick me up. By then I might have her talked into a little action."

"You going down there alone with her?" his friend in back asked.

"Yeah, I'm going down there alone with her, dummy," Ewan sneered. "What's she gonna do…bite me?"

The driver was again in a hurry to leave. "Okay, Dave, we'll pick you up in twenty minutes."

"You got it, buddy," Ewan said, grinning. "You guys get ready for some action. I've got a feeling this is gonna be a hot one." He took off and ran to catch up with the woman again. His companions drove away past them.

She had patiently waited for him at the end of the block. As he approached her now, Ewan slowed down to a cocky swagger and said as he walked up to her, "Okay, show me where this busted down car of yours is."

For the first time since he had accosted her, she showed him a smile and replied in a low, sexy voice, "Right this way."

"Lead on, Kim."

They took a right on Spruce on their way to Third. The side of the street they walked on this time was residential, illuminated by house and street lights; the park and playground on the opposite side inviting, Ewan thought, for a quickie right there. It was eleven o'clock at night, and the summer sounds of human activity outside had ended to go indoors. They turned left on Third. No one was around, no cars on the street except those parked there. Ewan glanced at each one, wondering if it was hers, but she continued to walk on until finally he asked, "Just how far is your car anyway?"

"At the end of the block," Kim said. Suddenly she stopped dead in her tracks, turned to Ewan and eyed him very thoroughly, starting at his crotch and working her way up. Her gaze fell upon his and stayed there, and a hungry smile grew slowly on her face.

Ewan didn't quite know what to make of it at first, but with that smile he realized she wanted him, and she wanted him right now. He returned her look with a lustful one of his own, filled with anticipation. "Hey, Kim," he drawled. "You haven't got car troubles at all, do you."

"Not anymore," Kim whispered.

"You probably don't even have a car down here."

Kim licked her lower lip. "Oh, it's down the street," she said.

"So what do you have in mind?" Ewan asked as he ran his eyes over her, from her cowboy boots to her head of luxuriously thick, dark hair.

"Let's cross the street to Overlook and talk about it," Kim suggested as she nodded over her shoulder.

"Lead the way, babe."

They crossed South Coeur D' Alene together, climbed over a low retaining wall and hopped down to a narrow grassy berm below. The glow from the street lights above them cast overhead shadows across the trees and allowed them enough refracted light to see each other's features in the darkness. They could hear the rippling sounds of the creek below. Kim reached into her purse and pulled out a pair of latex gloves, which she put on right in front of Ewan.

"What's that for?" he asked with a look of surprise.

"I'm paranoid," Kim answered softly.

By this time, Ewan had already figured out he had stumbled across a kinky one, but this was a bit too much. That was alright by him, though. He'd just play right along with it. "You got anything in there for me?" he inquired.

"Yes," she answered with a smile that glistened in the dark. "Of course I do."

"What?"

"This!" Kim shot back as she kicked him square in the balls with the toe of her boot.

Gasping in pain, Ewan crumpled to his knees like a wet sack of wet rags. Without any sense of urgency, Kim produced a nine inch stiletto from her purse. She stepped around Ewan with calm precision, seized him from behind by his hair with her right hand and reefed his head back so he could take a good long look into her face. Kim had the knife at his throat. Pain and terror rendered his dangling arms helpless; tears rolled from his panic stricken eyes. "Don't," Ewan whimpered.

Kim smiled. "Goodbye, motherfucker," she said as she sunk the base of the blade into his flesh and whipped it back toward her. Holding him up by the hair a few seconds longer, she stared into Ewan's dying eyes that still pleaded for mercy, listened to the blood gurgle in his throat and watched it spill forth from both sides of his gaping mouth. Satisfied now, Kim slammed him face down into the grass. She placed the heel of her boot against Ewan's side, gave him a sharp shove and rolled his body over. Then she bent over him and undid his pants, pulling them down around his hips. She went to work on him with her knife. When she was finished, Kim dug into her purse with the same calmness of presence she had shown throughout and took out a small freezer bag into which she delicately placed her bloody trophy. His friends would be back for him shortly. She put the knife, bag and gloves back into her purse and scuffed up the ground where she had been standing to cover up any tracks. Careful where she stepped, walking on the tiptoes of her feet, Kim returned to the retaining wall and looked both ways on the street. There was no traffic. As she hoisted herself over the wall, she again glanced both ways, then backtracked along Third and through the park to Chestnut where she had her car parked all along.

****

Ewan's companions cruised down Coeur D' Alene right on schedule. When they found no sign of him, they kept on driving, past Spruce, turned on Chestnut, checked out the park and remaining side streets, all to no avail. Finally, after making a complete loop, they decided to come back around one more time and park at the end of Third where they would start the search on foot. Their nerves already on edge, they talked of giving up and going home, but their fear of Ewan's notorious temper forced them to keep on going as they chose now to investigate the area alongside the retaining wall. They walked slowly and remained quiet so they could hear any sounds that might come from the darkness below them. They also did not want to bring special attention to themselves in the neighborhood. Their search hadn't lasted a minute or two when one of them spotted a lump lying in the grass, revealed dimly by the light washing overhead. "What the hell's that?" he asked, the worst fears of his imagination causing his voice to quiver.

"What's what?" inquired the one who had driven the car.

"Down there."

Peering into the darkness, the driver responded in a hushed tone, "I don't know. C'mon, let's take a look."

"Bullshit!" said Ewan's backseat companion.

"You chicken fucker!" the driver rasped. "Get your ass down there with me! Dave could've fallen over the side, and he might be hurt." He leapt over the wall and started toward the shadowy form still a good fifteen yards ahead of him, his companion right on his heels. Suddenly he stopped and gasped, "Oh, my God!"

Not wanting to look and find out what it was, his friend turned and ran, shouting, "Let's get the hell out of here!"

"Oh Jesus Christ!" the driver moaned over and over.

His companion was gone, over the wall and gone, but not before he heard his friend puking his guts out.

****

Curtis received information about the killing the minute he arrived at work the next morning. The body was at the coroners', and he would have to go there later in the day to look it over, but the main concern around police headquarters for now was handling the heat coming down from the mayor's office. Ewan's old man was on a rampage, and McCoy was the man under the gun. The lieutenant wished Joe was there to catch some of the flak with him, but he was not expected back until later that afternoon.

The press was completely out of control. McCoy's phone rang off the hook, and finally he just quit taking calls. "Brad," he said the moment Curtis entered his office, "I have to make a statement to the press at one this afternoon, and right now you and I are going out there to the crime scene and find something even if we have to invent it."

"We got any witnesses this time?" Curtis asked.

"Just Ewan's two asshole buddies who found the body," McCoy grumbled.

"They see anything?"

"They got there too late," McCoy said. "They claimed Ewan was hustling some little sweetie off the street and took off with her on foot. When they went back to pick him up, she was gone and he was dead."

"You get a description?"

"Tall, good looking...wore western clothes, long sleeved shirt...dark hair."

"Anything else?" Brad inquired.

McCoy was busy stuffing some papers from his desk into a large envelope and digging in his drawer for a note pad. He looked back up at Brad again, grabbed his jacket to leave and said, "Yeah. Ewan told them her name was Kim."

Curtis's expression dropped; his color drained.

"Something wrong, Brad?" asked McCoy with a concerned look.

"No...nothing," the young detective told him. He mustered up a smile and commented, "I wish Joe was here."

"You're not the only one," McCoy growled. "When he gets back from his latest little safari, he's gonna keep his ass put right here in Spokane until we nail this murdering little bitch." McCoy glanced around, searched his pockets to make sure he had everything he needed, and then he told Brad,

"You can read the statements those two kids gave on the way out there. I want to check every house in the neighborhood and find out if anyone saw anything or can identify any strange cars parked around there last night. Let's go."

****

The two detectives examined the immediate area where Ewan was murdered and began directing the dozen or so other police officers already there in their investigations also. They found where the ground had been scuffed, not that it would hold a print anyway since most of it was grass. When the two detectives were satisfied they had done all they could do, they let the others handle the tedious job of an inch by inch search for possible evidence hidden in the grass while they began the door to door canvas, starting with some curious bystanders still assembled across the street. Then Curtis worked the south end of the streets around the park and McCoy took the north side.

After calling on nearly a dozen houses, Brad was no farther along than when he had started. He came to the next to the last house down the line on Chestnut, rang the doorbell and waited. A sophisticated appearing man, who looked to be retirement age judging by his white head of hair and moustache, answered the door. Flashing his badge, Curtis introduced himself and said, "I'd like to ask you a few questions, sir."

"Surely," the man replied in a quiet spoken manner. "Please come in, Detective."

Curtis followed him into the small but tastefully appointed living room, looked around briefly and then inquired, "By chance did you see any strangers in the neighborhood last night? Say a man and a woman?"

"No," the man said thoughtfully. "I don't recall seeing any couples. I did see a young lady later in the evening."

"Did you recognize her?"

"No, she was a stranger around here I think. I know most of the people in this area, and I don't remember ever seeing her before."

Curtis opened his notepad and prepared to write. "Can you describe her?" he asked.

"Tall," the man stated. "Long dark hair, dressed in blue jeans. I think she had a long sleeved shirt on too."

"You remember the color?"

"Might have been gray, I believe. Maybe blue, but I can't really say. It was getting dark."

Brad was busy writing. "Anything else?"

"She was very pretty," the man noted, smiling, "although I didn't get that close a look at her. But she seemed to be very pretty from a distance. Carried herself very well."

"How do you mean?"

"Oh, you know," the witness explained. "She had very correct posture, and she walked with a certain…confidence, I suppose would be the best word to describe it."

"Do you have any idea where she came from?" asked Curtis.

The man thought for a moment, then answered with a pensive look, "Yes…possibly. I do remember a car I haven't seen before parked down the street about the same time I saw her. I can't be certain it was hers, though."

"Can you describe it?"

"White…a new model, but I don't know what make," the man said. "Very nice looking whatever it was, and I think it was a convertible."

Curtis stopped writing, and his eyes zeroed in on the witness. "You say you *think* it was a convertible?" he inquired. His look was piercing and dead serious.

"I can't be certain," the man replied. "It was parked across the street at the end of the block, and the top was up. But I think it was a convertible."

Brad's mind was reeling with a barrage of thoughts. After a long pause, he asked, "Do you remember anything else?"

"No, Detective," the man responded. "Not that I can think of."

"Thank you very much for your cooperation, sir. How do you spell your last name?"

The man told him, and Curtis slapped the notebook shut, thanked him again and abruptly departed. One more house to cover, but he had already heard enough.

Brad met up with McCoy at eleven-thirty, and he knew the lieutenant would be rushed to make his press conference in time. "You find out anything, Lieutenant?" he asked.

"Not a goddamned thing worth mentioning," McCoy grumbled. "How about you?"

"Nope," Curtis answered. "Doesn't appear to be anyone who saw anything out of the ordinary last night."

"Isn't that just fuckin' great," McCoy snarled. "Just what I needed to give the press…nothing."

"We'll come up with something on this one," Brad assured him as he managed a little smile. "I got a feeling about it."

"I hope you're fuckin' right," McCoy said. "C'mon, we gotta get going. I want to come back here later and hit those houses where nobody was home. I've got a list of addresses for you."

"You bet," Curtis said.

"And when that goddamned Rummel gets back, I'm gonna put him to work digging latrines all over this city until he comes up with the little shit we're looking for."

****

Joe had six hours of driving time to mull over the troubling information he had inadvertently obtained from Terri. He wanted to go straight to VanTighem the minute he arrived in Spokane, but he thought better of it and went directly to division headquarters instead. What he had on his mind he would share with no one other than Jack for the time being, but he needed to give McCoy something, anything to keep him from having heart failure, short of pointing the finger at Brad's girlfriend. He was too close to them both, and he had to be absolutely certain one way or the other before he told anyone in the police department, even McCoy.

"Oh, goddamn you, Rummel," McCoy greeted him when he walked into the squad room. "All hell's fuckin' broke loose around here."

Rummel didn't need to ask, and McCoy didn't give him a chance to. He motioned Joe to follow him into his office, and once inside behind closed doors, he went over all of the events of the past twelve hours, concluding with, "I damn well hope you brought me something back from Seattle."

That was it. Joe swallowed hard, took a deep breath and said, "I need time."

"What!" McCoy hollered. "That's all you've had is time!"

"Seventy-two hours," Rummel insisted. "I need more, but three days might give me a name."

McCoy eyed his detective suspiciously. "You got someone?" he asked.

"I think so," Joe replied. "But I don't know her last name."

McCoy shifted to his window and stared outside. Without turning around, he inquired, "You by any chance didn't dig up a Kim out there, did you?"

"All the way from Houston to Seattle," Rummel answered him. "And probably here also," he added.

McCoy turned around. "We wouldn't be so lucky that this woman might be left-handed, would we?"

Rummel snickered, saying, "Hell, the only Kim I know who's left-handed lives with me. My daughter's left-handed, and she sure as hell has never been in Houston." His look grew somber. "I don't know if this other one is or not. But I damned well intend to find out."

"So, you know who she is," McCoy pressed him.

"No," Rummel lied. "But VanTighem might by now. This goes all the way back to Indiana, and these past few days he's been tracking this person down for me."

"Jesus Christ!" McCoy exploded. "We've got the FBI helping us out, and you leave it in the hands of that fuckin' reporter!"

Rummel couldn't help but smile with a little amusement over the torment he had in mind. "The FBI will come in handy," he said. "They can cut through the red tape and get us some social security numbers. VanTighem will need them."

McCoy scowled. The anger within him was very real and growing by the second. "I mean it, Joe. If you allow that reporter to fuck up this case, I'll have your goddamned badge for it. And I don't give a fuck how short you are!"

"Seventy-two hours," Rummel repeated with a look that was equally resolute. "If I don't have a name by then, you and the FBI can have everything I've got."

Choosing not to reply right away, McCoy just glared at his detective, then grunted with a note of finality. "That's it," he said. "That's all you get...three days. And it better be good, Joe."

Rummel caught himself hoping it wouldn't be. If his worst fears were realized, the entire police department would be turned upside down, including McCoy, but most of all Brad, particularly if he had been protecting her all this time. And even at this point, Joe still refused to believe it was her. But he had to find out just the same. "I appreciate it, Jim," he said, his voice filled with sincerity.

McCoy sensed something was deeply troubling him, and he responded in kind with a quiet, solemn tone, "You'd better get over to the coroners' and take a look at this last one. You might find a little variation in the theme."

"I'll head right over," Rummel assured him, and he started to leave.

As he was about to go out the door, McCoy called to him. Rummel turned around. "Joe," the lieutenant said slowly, "I wish I could give you more time, but I'm really under the gun now."

"I understand, Jim," replied Rummel.

"This last one blew the lid right off. Is there anything I can do to help?"

Joe thought for a moment and suggested, "Get hold of the FBI and have them start the ball rolling on a complete background check on a John McConey, originally from Auburn, Indiana. I'm especially interested in a daughter of his, probably in her late twenties...maybe a son too who can help us find her. Have them ready to crack the social security files on McConey and his daughter, the boy too if he even exists. I hope to have some names for you in a day or two."

"That all?" McCoy asked after he finished writing the information down.

"For now, yeah."

"You think the daughter is the one?"

Rummel managed a smile. "Jim, right now I'm flying on a wing and a prayer, but my gut tells me she's the one."

For the first time in weeks, a glimmer of hope crossed McCoy's face. He stopped biting his lower lip and stated, "I'll contact the FBI with this right away."

"Appreciate that," Joe told him, and he quickly departed.

Brad was out on the job, which was a relief to Rummel for now. He went straight to his desk and called VanTighem.

"You're back," came the response over the line.

"Yeah, Jack," said Rummel, "I've got a lot of things to cover with you, but first I'm off to the coroners'."

"I heard about the latest one," VanTighem said. "You want me to meet you there?"

"No, McCoy's got his tit in a ringer. I don't want you hanging around official police business. Meet me at Riverfront Park in two hours...by the foot bridge."

"Sure thing."

"You have any luck?" Rummel had to ask.

"I've got some things," VanTighem replied. "McConey did have a couple of kids in Indianapolis, a boy and a girl. His ex committed suicide right around the time the kids were in their early to mid-teens. I'm waiting for more information to track down their high school records."

"That's great," Rummel told him. His enthusiasm was clearly evident over the phone line. "Look, we'll talk about it in the park. I have to get going."

"See you in two hours," said VanTighem.

Joe hung up and let out a sigh of relief. Now there was real hope, but he had to move fast. If this was going to blow up in his and Brad's faces, he wanted it to be within the next three days. He had no idea how much longer than that he could continue working with his partner on this investigation if the doubt still lingered. That was a balancing act he wasn't prepared to handle. And to make matters worse, he had to deal also with his daughter at home, knowing full well her newly found friend might be the killer.

****

The pathologist on the case was Earl Calvert, a short, wizened man with close cropped white hair, a wry sense of humor and the unnerving habit of always holding his head down and looking over the top of his glasses when he spoke. Like Rummel, Earl was on the verge of retirement, and like

Rummel, he was counting the days. "So, Joe, you've come to pay your last respects," he said when the detective showed up at his office.

Rummel had to laugh. "Why? You planning on dying, Earl?"

"Nope," Calvert smiled. "I've discovered the secret of immortality while working here all these years."

"What's that?"

"Double scotch on the rocks," Calvert replied.

"That's what I like about you, Earl. You make me look like a choir boy." Rummel's expression quickly darkened. "Take me to him, would you, Doc?"

Calvert slowly stood up behind his desk and started toward the door, walking right past his visitor. "Come, my boy," he said as he entered the hallway. "Let's go take a look at the fruits of man's accursed addiction to sexual exploits."

Rummel followed the coroner down the hallway to the morgue. Entering, Joe found the body still out on the table and awaiting further inspection. "This one isn't quite like the others," Calvert explained as he pulled back the sheet. "This boy was roughed up before he was killed."

The first thing that caught Rummel's attention was the cut across Ewan's throat. It ran high on the right and sharply down to the left, just the opposite of what he had been accustomed to seeing. "What the hell's this?" he questioned with a puzzled look. "We got ourselves a right-handed killer this time?"

"I'll talk to you about that in a minute," Calvert said in his matter-of-fact manner. "I want you to look down here first."

Rummel's eyes followed Calvert's gloved hand as the pathologist folded back the remainder of the sheet and lifted the victim's testicles. "I realize he was severely lacerated in this area…though not as bad as the others…which will account for some of the discoloration, but this boy's got a couple of dandy achers. Look here at the black and blue in his crotch that's even running down the inside of his thighs."

"Someone kicked him?" asked Joe.

"Good and hard is my guess," Calvert replied. "Now take a look at the top of his head." Rummel and the coroner shifted back to the opposite end of the table, and Calvert pointed out a matted tuft of hair that had been twisted into a cowlick. "I would have to say someone grabbed our friend here by the hair and gave it a yank," he went on. "If you look close enough, you can even see a few loose ones still left in there."

Shaking his head with amazement, Rummel observed, "He got it from behind then."

"Which means you still have a left-handed killer," Calvert concluded for him. "Except the murderer's getting rougher now, a whole lot rougher."

Rummel looked his old and trusted associate straight on with a probing gaze and asked, "What's that tell you, Earl?"

Calvert didn't answer right away. He just momentarily stared up at the detective over his glasses before he noted, "I'm no psychiatrist, Joe. But if you want an educated guess, I'd have to say your killer is getting more brazen. I'd say he's got his confidence built up, and he may even be getting a little reckless. He was definitely in more of a hurry this time."

That was good news, Rummel figured; if a reckless homicidal maniac could be considered good news. "Her," he told the pathologist. "It's a her."

"That's right," Calvert said, smiling. "I was told you suspected a woman was the culprit. That's one tough broad."

"You got that right, Doc. Tough and very slippery."

"You want to look at anything else?" Calvert inquired.

"Nope. Wrap him up and put him back in the cooler."

"Your new partner was just by," Calvert commented. "That's why I had him out. I figured you wouldn't be far behind."

"What did Brad have to say about this?" Rummel was very curious.

"About the same as you, Joe. Seems to me, though, he's getting a bit more squeamish as these stiffs start to mount up." Calvert showed a sly smile. "This case is putting a few years on the kid, Joe...just like you and me."

There very well could be more truth to that statement than he realized, thought Rummel. Without further comment, he thanked his friend and made a hasty exit to meet VanTighem.

****

VanTighem was already waiting for him when Rummel arrived at the park. The sounds of the nearby waterfalls and ensuing rapids made their conversation difficult, and the two men started to walk away from the Spokane River to escape the noise. "How was Seattle?" Jack asked.

"Good," Rummel answered. "Managed to sneak in a little fishin'."

"You peckerhead," VanTighem declared. "You leave me here to do all the work, and you sneak off on a fishing trip. I suppose that means you tied up with Terri."

Absorbed as he had been the past several hours, Joe had almost forgotten about her. A rush of sweet memories suddenly filled his head, and he flushed when he answered his friend, "Yeah, we took a day out on her uncle's boat. You ought to see that barge...thirty-two footer."

"You do any good?" VanTighem inquired.

"Huh?"

Jack caught that bit of hesitation, realized his friend had been tripped up by the double meaning of his question. But he was still savoring his own pleasant memories and saw no need to pry. "Fish, fool," he said. "You catch any fish?"

"Oh...yeah," answered Rummel. "Terri caught a couple nice ones, and so did her uncle. I sorta bombed out."

Shaking his head, VanTighem commented dryly, "Glad to see you had fun." He could tell Joe was rattled, caught up in a whirlpool of thoughts, so he decided to come right down to business. "Okay," he started, "let me tell you where I'm at so far. Like I told you over the phone, my old buddy nosed around the clerk of court out there and came up with a marriage and a divorce. Birth records aren't so easy to obtain, so he dug way back through newspaper vital statistics during that period and found two birth announcements for Susan and John McConey... a boy, Mark, born November 5th, 1958, and the girl, Linda, was born October 24th, 1961. Pair of Scorpios like me, so watch your ass with these clowns, Joe," VanTighem added with a smirk.

Rummel offered him a thin smile and noted, "You're the 4th, aren't you?"

"You betcha," Jack grinned, then took a deep breath and continued. "The marriage lasted thirteen years, which seems like kind of a miracle if you ask me. Three years later the mother took a one-way trip on a bottle of pills washed down by a fifth of booze. He did get me the coroners' report on that one, and I have it at home along with a FAX of the obituary. The two kids and their old man are listed as survivors, but that's about it, except for her parents who also lived in Indianapolis. Pretty ritzy address according to my buddy. McConey's whereabouts was not listed...just said formerly of Indianapolis."

"What about the kids?" Joe asked as he came to a stop. "They still in Indianapolis at the time?"

"Yeah, but here's the catch. You'd figure the grandparents would at least fall heir to the girl because she was a juvenile and it looks like her father took off, but my buddy got hold of them, and they told him they haven't seen her since she was just a kid. She completely disappeared shortly after her mother's death. He also told me the grandparents weren't too eager to talk about it."

"Shit," Rummel said. "We're gonna need social security numbers to track them down now, and that takes too much time...way too much."

VanTighem was puzzled. "How much time we got?" he asked.

"Seventy-two hours and counting," Joe grumbled. "McCoy put me on the clock, said if you and I couldn't come up with anything in three days, he's turning the whole thing over to the FBI."

"What's wrong with that?" VanTighem inquired, still perplexed.

Rummel wasn't quite prepared to tell his friend his reasons just yet. Instead, he started to walk again and continued to put their situation into perspective. "We could go to the IRS for their old tax records, but even at that, it's possible at her age the girl hadn't worked yet. We might be able to track down the brother that way and find out if he knows where she's been hanging out all these years, but that'd still take way too much time…especially without social security numbers to go by. If we end up turning everything over to the FBI, they could get all that done a helluva lot faster anyway. That's where I'd expect them to start." The detective hesitated a moment before adding, "Unless…"

"Unless what?" Jack asked him.

Rummel took a few more seconds to think before answering. "Let's just suppose these two kids wanted to walk completely away from all their troubles," he suggested. "From the sounds of it, life was not all that easy for them to start with."

VanTighem was eager to know where this was leading. "I'm listening," he said.

"Okay, let's just do it this way based on the amount of time we have," Rummel went on. "Suppose one or both of them dummied up phony birth certificates and started all over…new names, applied for new social security numbers, new lives. Hell, it's possible we could never find them without the help of family members."

"So what are you saying?"

"I'm saying we go with what we got. We track the two kids from their last known whereabouts backwards, and hopefully come up with some photographs of them."

"Then use artist enhancements to age them," VanTighem concluded for him.

"Exactly," Rummel said. "We can bring the girl right up to current age and see what that leads to here in Spokane."

VanTighem looked worried. "I don't think I can get my pal to do all that in seventy-two hours," he pointed out.

"He's not going to," Joe told his friend. "You are."

"Me?"

"That's right. You wanted to play detective, so I'm asking you to hop the next available flight to Indianapolis and find out everything you can about that girl. Start with her last known address and hit the local high schools up for their old annuals. Then go after the grandparents and see if you can't get something, anything out of them, hopefully a photo for starters."

"What about you?"

"I'm staying here," Rummel said. "I've got a first name now from a witness…and maybe a possible suspect. I'll know more when I subpoena her personnel file."

VanTighem's expression glowed with excitement. "Care to tell me who she is?"

Joe pondered that for a few long moments. He knew he would have to confide in his friend, but he wasn't anxious to do so. "Kim Wintrode," he stated at last.

Stopping dead in his tracks, Jack slowly turned to him with shock written all over his face. He looked like he had just been gut shot. "That…that can't be," he stammered. "She couldn't have done this."

"That's what I keep telling myself," Rummel admitted and then he asked him, "What's the matter, Jack. You look like you've seen a ghost."

"I feel like it too," VanTighem mumbled. He stared at the ground, then out toward the river, and finally he looked back again at his best friend. "We got problems, Joe," VanTighem said softly.

Rummel could almost guess. He had known Jack too long, before the time of Cindy, and all he needed now was hear a confirmation of his suspicions. "Okay, Jack, out with it," he said.

VanTighem glanced around one more time, took a deep breath and finally confessed, "Night before last…I ran into her at a charity benefit. She…well, she came on to me…and I…I mean we…well, we spent the night together."

"You dumb son of a bitch!" Rummel yelled. "Didn't I tell you to stay the fuck away from that?"

"I know, I know," VanTighem acknowledged with his palms held outward in defense. "She said it would be alright. She told me her and Brad had an open relationship."

"What the fuck's that supposed to mean?" Rummel snapped.

"It means she and Brad have this arrangement to get it on with whoever they feel like," explained VanTighem.

"You better fuckin' well hope they do," Rummel growled. "Or that kid's gonna kick your fuckin' head in…and I might just stand back and let him do it."

That pissed VanTighem off. "Ahh, don't you be so damned self-righteous," he fired back. "Just what the fuck you been up to these past few days?"

Rummel felt like decking him, more to wake him up and protect him from future harm than anything else. If his guess was right, the least of his worries right now would be a kung fu boyfriend. But Jack had a point. It would be a little hypocritical to fault him for taking advantage of a situation like that. He fumed a moment longer, glared at the writer like an enraged grizzly towering over him, then a slight smile slowly appeared, and Joe said,

"Well…at least you're still alive with your dick still intact. At least I think it is."

VanTighem smirked at that remark, but he didn't find it one bit funny. He wasn't worried about Curtis, and he knew his best buddy couldn't hold a grudge against him too long. It was the streak of pain that had punched his heart and now settled in the pit of his stomach that troubled him. Suddenly he had to admit something to himself he had kept buried the past forty-eight hours. He cared for Kim. He was drawn to her, and she had preoccupied his mind much more than he would have ever expected at this point in his life. To think that she might be a vicious killer and imagine now what kind of sordid past she might have had hurt him to the core. "I gotta tell you something, Joe," he said at last. "I'm kinda smitten with her."

Rummel rolled his eyes skyward. "Can't say I blame you," he admitted. "The truth is I was a little taken with her myself all this time."

"Are you sure about this? VanTighem asked. His light green eyes blazed in the sunshine and pleaded for the right response.

"No, I'm not sure. But we damned well can't take any chances." Joe paused, then added, "We've got a woman who has lived in Houston, Seattle and now Spokane. We have a witness who says the woman who killed Ewan was named Kim. We've got someone who certainly has access to information about police procedures and ways to counter an investigation. Circumstantial as that might be, you tell me if we should just overlook this."

"No," Jack said sadly, his gaze again lowering. "No, we can't overlook it." Suddenly his eyes snapped back with a look of resolve written in them. "Besides," he concluded, "I have to know now myself."

"I suppose you do," Joe agreed. His smile managed to return again, bigger this time. "Since you're on intimate terms these days, I don't reckon you'd know if Kim is left or right-handed, would you?"

VanTighem had forgotten all about that. That would make a huge difference, and he struggled with himself to remember the moments of their recent evening together. He envisioned the table where they had been sitting in the bar, which hand she had used for her drink, which hand she had placed on his that night. Maybe it was wishful thinking, he told himself, but he honestly thought she had used her right. "If memory serves me," he noted finally, "I think she's right-handed. I can't vouch for that for certain, but I think she held her drink in her right hand."

"What else did she hold with her right hand?"

"Don't rub it in, please."

Rummel just shook his head wearily. "For your sake and that of all the rest of us, I fuckin' well hope you're right, Romeo." He slapped his friend on the back and started to lead him toward the parking lot. "C'mon. Let's get the hell out of here. I want to give you a list of things to look for out there, and I'd like to see you on a plane tonight if at all possible."

Still dazed, VanTighem allowed himself to be led away without further comment, his head spinning with a myriad of possibilities and doubts.

****

After sending VanTighem on his way, Joe headed straight to District Court to obtain an investigative subpoena to access Kim Windtrode's personnel file at Seafirst Bank. He arrived there near closing time on a Friday afternoon. Considering the little incriminating evidence he had, it was a long shot, but he had friends there, a long-standing reputation with them, and this was a case everyone wanted solved. Following some persuasive talk, he had his subpoena and a judge lined up to sign it. An assistant DA with considerable legal standing in the community even promised Joe he would personally contact Wintrode's boss that evening and pave the way for swift access to her records. By seven o'clock, Rummel had the judge's signature.

It had been one long and hectic day. Wound up as he was on nervous energy, Joe dropped by one of his old hangouts on the way home for a couple of beers and some time to think over his strategy. He had the district attorney's pledge for absolute discretion in dealing with Wintrode's employer. Now he had to come up with a good lie to back his actions up. The last thing he wanted to do at this stage of the game was spook her, not before VanTighem arrived back with, hopefully, the information they needed anyway. Something else came to mind just then. When he could manage it, he planned to sneak a look at Brad's personnel file also.

Rummel returned home late that evening. Kim's car was gone when he pulled up to his apartment. He could only think the worst of it, that she was out with Wintrode again. A little more than twenty-four hours ago that wouldn't even have caused a passing thought. Now he was walking a tightrope between tipping his hand and worrying himself sick.

Entering his apartment, he rushed to the kitchen where she left her notes posted for him on the fridge. His heart sank when he found one that read she was indeed out with Wintrode and planning to spend the night at her apartment. It said not to worry, they were just having a girls' night out. She left a phone number for him in case he needed anything and told him there was some leftover homemade lasagna in the refrigerator. With the note clutched tightly in his hand, Joe went for another beer instead and wandered into the living room where he paced and stared at the phone for what seemed like a very long time.

Finally he decided to call, just to let his daughter know he was back if nothing else, but in reality he wanted to hear her voice and know she was alright. Rummel picked up the phone and dialed. It rang three, four times, an eternity. The fifth time an answering machine cut in. Joe swallowed hard. The butterflies raised havoc in his stomach. He heard the beep and said, "Kim, this is Joe Rummel. I wanted Kim to know I'm home. Have her call me later if she gets a chance." Rummel hung up. He was tense, actually trembling. He told himself there was nothing to worry about, but his fears would not go away no matter how much he tried to rationalize them.

Feeling very much alone now and totally helpless, Joe forced himself to think of other matters. He wondered if VanTighem had made it out of town yet, and he thought of calling him just to sidetrack his anxieties, but that was no solution. If he was still in town, they would surely talk about the primary source of his apprehension anyway. He thought of calling Julie, but it was late there. And what would he tell her? Terri came to mind next, and then he remembered she wouldn't be back for another day. Twenty-four hours ago he was still with her. He tried to relive those moments in order to bury this torment he was now experiencing. But it didn't work. Amid visions of tender passion with Terri, Kim Wintrode's face kept creeping into his thoughts along with the faces of those victims, their torn throats, their gaping mouths, those eyes still wide with fear. His eyes too revealed a similar fear now as he wondered and worried about his daughter in the company of a possible serial killer.

This night was one Joe would have to ride out alone and endure through every lingering minute that ticked away like a death row clock. Perhaps later, sleep would mercifully rescue him, but for now, it was just a matter of waiting and hoping the phone would ring. Rummel knew he would need help through all this. He turned on the TV and went for another beer.

CHAPTER FOURTEEN

Saturday morning at nine sharp Rummel was rudely awakened by a call. He scrambled for the phone, thinking it was Kim, fumbled the receiver and answered. It was the senior vice-president of the bank. Feeling like he had just been caught by a surprise general inspection, Joe had all he could do to keep from jumping to attention. He tried desperately to shake the cobwebs from his head and erase the grogginess from his voice.

The man on the other end of the line sounded businesslike but pleasant enough. He agreed to meet Joe at one o'clock that afternoon at the bank. That was perfect. Being the weekend, it was ideal to ensure their privacy without fear of Wintrode spotting him there.

After he hung up, Rummel's thoughts immediately raced back to his daughter. He was still worried about her, but in his heart he knew she was okay. His guess was the two of them had gone out on the town and really tied one on, which was exactly the way he felt after the number of beers he had consumed before finally falling asleep.

****

Spokane's heat wave had let up the past ten days or so but was back now in full force to herald August in true fashion. Rummel was stripped down to the bare minimum for his line of work--his old standby dress Dockers, which today were tan, and a light blue short-sleeved knit shirt, no jacket or police issue hardware and characteristically no tie, which for this occasion he actually considered wearing. Why ruin a perfectly good track record at this stage of the game and wear a tie? There was also no need for the gun or the attention it drew on a day like today, he figured. All of his time now was devoted to slipping and sliding in a trail of shit left in the wake of this one case, not in the apprehension of the person responsible. Why worry about a Glock 9mm and all that extra gear? He might as well go civilian for awhile and feel like a human being again.

Joe waited patiently in the outer lobby of the bank, which was open for access to cash machines and the weekend tellers. With his hangover, the air conditioning in there was a real life saver, as opposed to the other alternative of standing outside on the scorching pavement. The minutes ticked away approaching one o'clock, then passing it. Only the muffled voices of business transactions behind glass and the annoying beeps of money machines kept him company. It was now ten after, and he was beginning to wonder if his man was ever going to show up.

A few minutes later someone dressed much like Rummel, except he was wearing expensive slacks, entered the bank. He was tall, had an athletic build and carried himself very well. His dark hair, clearly styled, was splashed with streaks of silver, and he possessed strong, confident features which made him a very imposing and handsome man. Despite all of that, he looked a little harried. He caught Joe's look of close scrutiny, approached him and asked, "Are you Detective Rummel?"

"Joe Rummel," came the reply with a warm smile and a friendly handshake, followed by the presentation of his badge and the subpoena.

"Joe, nice to meet you," the banker said as he took the subpoena. "I'm T.A. Harper...I go by T.A. Sorry I'm late. I promised the kids I'd take them swimming this afternoon, and with this change of plans I had to wait for my wife to get back from a hair appointment so she could do the honors. Let's head to my office." Harper unlocked the main door leading to the corporate offices, allowed Joe to slip inside, then closed it and locked it behind them. They took the elevator only to the fifth floor of the twenty story building. As Rummel followed T.A. down the hallway, he couldn't help but glance at the names on the doors, finding the one he was looking for right next to Harper's.

When he entered T.A.'s large, corner office, Rummel was greeted by a good view of the city center and Canada Island in the river below, a view he knew was partially shared by the office next door. These people were living right, the detective figured, and for the life of him, he couldn't understand why someone like Kim Wintrode would do something so crazy to screw all this up. "Please sit down, Joe," said T.A. as he gestured toward a richly upholstered leather chair. Rummel sat down, sunk into the plush, soft cushion, and the bank officer told him he would be right back.

In Harper's absence, Joe took the time to look around and see how the other half lived. Windows filled the office, and on the walls hung three pieces of western art that appeared to be originals. It was art Rummel could relate to; the same could be said for the overall look of the room itself, masculine and homey. Obviously the man was a trap shooter and duck hunter, judging by the trophies on top of his bookshelf, the standing wood duck mount on its private pedestal in the corner and the miniature handcrafted decoys that lined another shelf. He also had a photograph of a black lab on his desk, which Rummel had sneaked a peek at and, of course, the obligatory family portrait. When Harper returned carrying a folder, Joe remarked, "I take it you're a duck hunter."

"My passion," the bank executive said. "How about you?"

"I'm a pheasant man," Rummel replied.

Parking himself momentarily on the edge of his desk, T.A. put the folder down and said with a relaxed smile, "I can't hit those damned birds for squat. They rattle the hell out of me when they come busting out right at your feet."

"We're lucky," Joe noted. "My hunting partner's got a pair of Brits that do all the work. If you're used to ducks and a duck gun, it can be tough. Try a double with improved and modified cylinders."

"I've been thinking about switching guns for chinks," Harper said. "I just don't get after them that much." He stood up, handed Rummel the file and sat down behind his desk. "I hope she's not in any kind of trouble," T.A. commented as the detective started to go through her records. "Kim's a topflight bank executive with a big career ahead of her."

"No trouble," Rummel lied as he looked up from the folder in his lap with an innocent smile pasted on his face. He took his notebook out of his front pants pocket and started to write while he continued with his fabricated story. "It's her brother we're looking for, and we just want to take the necessary precautions not to inadvertently alert him. You know...blood's thicker than water no matter what kind of upstanding citizen you are."

"I understand," Harper replied.

Rummel already had her social security number, birth date and other particulars recorded and was now jotting down notes about her work history, which showed employers only in Seattle and Houston, nothing else listed going back to Indiana. "I see she's got both a bachelors and a MBA from Baylor," he commented.

"Straight A student," T.A. pointed out. "A copy of her transcripts is in there also."

Joe was still concentrating on his notes. "I see that," he said. After a minute or so of writing, he closed the folder, looked up and remarked, "Kim's been with you here in Spokane about a year now, hasn't she."

"That's right...a little over ten months to be exact."

Rummel rubbed the side of his face. "Tell me something," he said. "Has she taken any business trips back to Chicago since she's been here...say, particularly within the past four months or so?"

Harper thought about that for a few moments, then responded, "No, not Chicago. I can't think of any reason why she would have gone there anyway on bank business. We haven't had any conferences there recently."

"Anywhere nearby Chicago, maybe Indianapolis?"

"No. She travelled to Seattle a couple of times...and Portland once. Unless she went to Chicago on her own time," Harper added. "Why do you ask?"

"Just curious," Joe answered. That put a sizeable hole in his suspicions, he speculated. If he couldn't place Wintrode in Chicago back in April, he may well be drawing a big blank here. All he needed now was to discover she was right-handed, and he'd be back to square one, with McCoy climbing right up his backside again. But it also filled the detective with a brief rush of relief over his concerns about his daughter being out all night with her and not reporting in as of yet. There was still one other possibility, however, and he inquired, "Would it be possible for you to do me a favor?"

"What's that?" T.A. asked.

"Just between the two of us, could you find out if she took any personal time off in April? It'd be a big help."

Hesitating briefly, T.A. replied, "I suppose I could do that. You mind if I call it in to you early next week?"

"That'd be great," Rummel said. He handed the personnel file back to Harper, saying, "Thank you very much, T.A. It's a pleasure doing business with you. I'm sorry I screwed up your plans with your kids."

Harper looked concerned. He slipped Kim's file into his middle drawer and inquired, "You sure she's not in any kind of trouble?"

"Nothing to worry about," Joe said with a confident grin. "I happen to be acquainted with her myself, and I feel the same way about Kim you do."

The senior bank executive appeared relieved. "Glad to hear that," he said.

"But there is one thing I want to ask of you," Rummel brought up, his expression turning very serious. "I need to keep our little meeting here in the strictest of confidence."

"Of course," agreed T.A.

"I appreciate that."

"Glad to be of help, Joe." Harper paused a moment, then suddenly changed the subject and asked, "What do you shoot?"

"I bought this Spanish made over/under called a Lanber. Ugly thing, terrible looking wood, but I got a helluva deal on it, and it's the best damned shotgun I ever owned. As far as I'm concerned, it's balanced better than a Browning."

"I'll look into one," T.A. said.

"You won't be sorry," Joe assured him. "Well, I have to get going." Rummel stood up, and Harper did also, joining him. The two men shook hands again, and together they left the building.

****

Next stop was division headquarters. Rummel had already arranged access to the personnel files, having acquired a key on the sly for a previous devious mission a few months beforehand. He wandered around the squad room making small talk with the officers on duty, checking just to make sure Brad wasn't around or expected in. Being Saturday afternoon the place was pretty well deserted anyway, and no one would be working in human resources. Satisfied he had free reign, he went into the personnel office and pulled the file. For expediency, he ran everything through the copier, bundled up his papers, put Curtis's folder back in place and returned home to review what he had obtained.

Kim's '86 beige Ford Taurus was parked out front, and Joe's heart jumped with relief. "Hey, Kitten, I'm home," he called out as he entered the apartment. "Tried to call you last night, but all I got was one of those damned machines instead." No answer. Rummel looked around. No one in the living room or kitchen; maybe she was in the bathroom. "You here?" he called out again. Her bedroom door was partially closed, and he could hear the faint signs of life stirring in there. "Kim, you alright?"

A trailing moan came from the bedroom followed by, "Ohhh, my head."

Rummel rapped lightly on the door. "You okay, Kim?"

"Nooo," came the agonized reply.

Joe peeked into the bedroom and asked, "You sick, Kitten?"

A big lump underneath the covers answered, "I hate alcohol. I'm sooo hung over."

Rummel had to chuckle. "Yeah, I'm a little queasy today myself too," he told her. "You need anything?"

"No, not now," Kim replied. She peered up at her father with half shut eyes and forced a feeble smile. "I've already ODed on Tylenol. I just need some sleep."

"I'll leave you alone, Kitten," said her father gently, but he couldn't resist a parting shot. "How about pizza for dinner tonight?"

"Ohhhh…"

Joe laughed and left the room. He returned to the kitchen, made himself a sandwich and started to go over Brad's personnel file. No chance of being interrupted by his daughter.

Curtis was born in St. Louis; there was a copy of his birth certificate attached to an I-9. His application form for the Spokane PD revealed he had attended high school in St. Louis, no copy of a diploma enclosed.

College transcripts from four different schools, most affiliated with the military, were included, but no degree. His DD214 showed he had enlisted in the Army at age nineteen to serve as a MP. He had taken basic at Ft. Polk, AIT at Ft. McClellan, then he had been assigned to Ft. Benning one year, Germany for two, back to the States at Ft. Ritchie to complete his enlistment. His ASVAB scores were good, 120s to 130s. After his discharge, he had worked briefly for the sheriff's department in Alexandria, Louisiana, and from there he had gone to work for the Houston Police Department for six years, nary a blemish on his record. He had been decorated for valor twice. An Internal Affairs report revealed he had killed one individual in self-defense during the commission of an armed robbery and had received a clean bill of health following a routine investigation.

Seattle was pretty much the same, including another citation for valor. The only exception was another Internal Affairs report concerning excessive force, but that was dropped without any action taken. It did mention a past verbal warning in reference to another case, which was also dismissed, no formal written warnings or reprimands, scarcely enough to warrant his transfer to vice unless he had requested it himself. All in all, pretty clean.

Aside from his social security number and past addresses, Rummel had nothing he could sink his teeth into. The best he could do was match Brad's addresses with those he found in Kim's file to determine how long they might have been together, although that might not mean anything either since they currently were not living together. He didn't dare run any kind of further checks on a fellow officer without departmental approval. For now all he could do was turn over Wintrode's social security number to the Feds for an employment and tax history search. He gathered up the papers and put them away in a locked file cabinet, which he kept in the entryway to his attached garage, away from Kim's eyes or anyone else who might come wandering through the apartment. Then he flopped down on the couch and flipped through TV channels in search of a fishing program, settling instead for a rerun boxing match.

Three hours later Kim staggered into the living room looking like death warmed over. Joe was in the kitchen making dinner. "How you feeling, Kitten?" he asked.

"Terrible," Kim growled.

Rummel's sympathies were with her. Many a time in his life he had been in the same boat; too many, in fact. It made him thankful he didn't go on binges anymore. Now his hangovers were confined to the middle-aged variety, no energy to put one foot in front of the other and annoying little eye aches that dragged on all day. "You'll feel better after you have something to eat," he said to her.

"What's for dinner?" Kim forced herself to ask.

"Smoked salmon and macaroni and cheese."

"Yuk!"

"Hey, it'll fix you right up," her father laughed. "Seriously, it works. Take it from an old pro."

"I'll stick with salad," Kim said as she sagged down on the couch next to her father.

"What'd you guys do last night?" Joe inquired. His question came out of more than just mere curiosity.

"What didn't we do," Kim moaned. "Brad drove us around to some night spots and took turns dancing with us. Poor guy must be dead today. Then we went back to Kim's and stayed up all night listening to music and getting very, very drunk on just about every drink imaginable." She let out a big groan and added, "I hate alcohol. Never again. I hate it...hate it...hate it."

"Brad stick around with you guys?"

"No, he left for his place about one."

"I haven't seen him since I got back," Rummel noted.

"He's been working real hard on that murder case of yours," Kim commented weakly.

"When did you get home?"

"I must've passed out 'cause I woke up on Kim's couch about noon. She nursed me back to health with some orange juice and barley soup, and I guess I got back here about two."

"Brad mention anything about the case?" Rummel quizzed her, curious as to what might have been said.

"Oh, Pops, he's not like you," Kim scolded him. "We just danced all night and talked about other things."

"Like what?"

Kim sat up and glared at her father. "What is this...the third degree?"

"No," Joe said, laughing it off. "You know me...always the cop." His look turned serious and he told her, "I was just worried about you, Kitten. To be honest, I was real worried."

Smiling, Kim replied, "I appreciate that, Pops. I'm sorry I caused you to worry. I've been a bad girl." She grabbed her stomach, dropped back onto the couch and moaned, "Ohh, have I ever been a real bad girl."

Rummel was certainly happy to have her back and in one piece, even if she was sick and not much company. He knew they didn't see enough of each other, and that was his fault more than hers. He couldn't hold it against her that she had found new friends and spent most of her free time with them. Under any other circumstances, he would have approved wholeheartedly.

Tomorrow he was going to make sure they shared the entire day together, just the two of them, maybe go out to lunch and take in a movie.

There wasn't much else he could do on a Sunday anyway, other than wait to hear from VanTighem and hang on the hopes he had come up with something conclusive, one way or the other. For his daughter's sake and his own, he hoped Kim Wintrode would be let off the hook. For Jack's sake too.

There was just one other item on his agenda for this weekend. Terri would be back tomorrow night. He would give her a call then. Joe wanted to hear her voice, and he had a favor to ask of her.

****

Sunday turned out just as Joe had hoped it would. He and Kim slept in late, went downtown for brunch and did a little shopping for him, under Kim's strict supervision, rather than catch a matinee. Then they took a walk down by the river and talked about things important to father and daughter. He confessed to her he had met someone in Seattle, and Kim was overcome with delight. She hit him with one prying question after another, some of them downright embarrassing. These 90s women were something else, Joe figured, flat out pushy, now that he had forgotten how much he had been enamored with the 60s versions who possessed the same traits. To avoid the uncomfortable grilling, he quickly shifted the conversation to another topic. They talked about Kim finishing college, but at this stage neither wanted to be parted from the other, so they just left school up in the air. She could always finish at Gonzaga or Eastern Washington. Rummel promised her he would take her to Seattle sometime soon, offering her the tantalizing prospect of a fishing trip on Terri's boat. Kim again told him she wanted to meet Terri very much.

That night Kim went to bed relatively early, around ten. She had to be at work the next morning, and she was still worn out from her Friday night escapades. It provided Rummel the ideal opportunity to call Terri and discuss something with her in private. He waited a little while for Kim to settle in, then picked up the phone and dialed.

Terri had just arrived home.

"Sorry to call you so late," Joe opened. "I figured I wouldn't catch you until now."

Her voice sounded excited when she replied, "Joe...I'm glad you called. I've been thinking about you all weekend."

"How was fishin'?"

"Ah, you incurable romantic," Terri said. "I should've guessed that'd be your first question."

Rummel laughed, at himself more than at her comment. She made him feel good, brought out laughter in him, something long since missing. "Can't teach an old dog new tricks," he apologized.

"We did about the same as when you were out with us," Terri informed him. "Biggest went eighteen pounds."

"Rub it in," Rummel said. "I've been telling my daughter about your fishing boat. She loves to fish, and I told her maybe we could get together sometime."

"Bring her on out," Terri offered, her enthusiasm rolling across the phone line. "Would love to meet her."

"She'd like to meet you too," Joe replied. His tone was soft and sincere.

"You told her about us?"

"Not everything," Rummel chuckled. "She tried to pry it out of me, but I didn't have the guts to give her the details." There was a pause on both ends of the line, and then suddenly Joe found some courage he never knew he had. "I miss you, Terri," he said.

"I miss you too, Joe. Very much."

"When this thing's cleared up around here, I'll take some time off and come out to see you," he promised her.

"How's it going?"

Rummel hesitated a few seconds, then said, "That's the other reason I called you. We had another one, and I'm under the gun big time." Another pause, then, "I need a big favor, and I need this kept strictly between you and me."

"What is it?"

"I want you to nose around and see if Brad took a trip to Chicago sometime in April. If by chance he did, I need the flight information to find out if his girlfriend went along with him. Her name is Kim Wintrode."

Terri's concern came across clearly over the phone. "What's this all about, Joe?"

"I'd rather not say right now, Terri," Rummel told her. "It could really complicate things for Brad if anything got out. You're just gonna have to trust me on this one. All I can say is it's important...it's really important."

"I'll see what I can do," Terri said. "It might take a few days."

"That'll be fine," Joe replied. "I've got Jack back East right now working on something to tie this in. Hopefully he'll have some answers in a couple of days so I can see if I'm barking up the wrong tree or not."

"Is Curtis in any trouble?" Terri had to ask.

"I don't think so," Rummel said. "But his girlfriend might be. That's all I can tell you for now."

"I understand."

"I knew you would." There was a long pause before Joe commented, "You're a good cop, Terri. I don't say that about a lot of cops."

Terri could hear the sincerity in his voice. "I appreciate that," she said. "You want to know something?"

"What?"

"You're a good man."

Rummel couldn't respond to that right away. He was not accustomed to being flattered like that, and a little bashful about it. "Thanks, Terri," he said at last. "I needed that, but sometimes I wonder if it's true."

"Take it from me, I'm right about this one," Terri assured him. "You're just too used to beating yourself up. The rest of us think you're one helluva guy."

"The same goes both ways, Terri. I'm pretty fond of you too."

"Glad to hear that, Joe."

"Well, I suppose I'd better let you go," Rummel said. He was feeling a little uncomfortable about their conversation, not that he wasn't pleased with it because he was, but he found himself wanting very much to be with her right now and not talking to her over the phone.

"Yeah, I still have to unpack. You take care, Joe."

"You too, Terri…and thanks for the help."

"Any time."

"See ya soon," said Rummel.

"Bye, Joe."

Rummel hung up and experienced a sudden rush of relief mixed with a feeling of missing her already. He knew he was acting like a school kid, but it felt sort of good. It had been a very long time since he had felt this way.

CHAPTER FIFTEEN

VanTighem had contacted his reporter friend before he had left Spokane the previous night and now awaited him in the lounge of the Holiday Inn where he was staying. It was two-thirty Saturday afternoon. He was dead beat from a late night flight and an early wake-up call so he could get to work first thing in the morning.

Earlier that day, he had gone to the public library where he had searched old city directories and phone books for Susan McConey's last known address. Finding what he had needed, he had been able to identify nearby high schools her daughter would have most likely attended, but he still wouldn't be able to see any yearbooks until Monday morning. Now it was just a matter of a waiting game until Dan Gustine arrived and gave him some of the particulars he needed before taking his next steps. It had been twenty-five years since VanTighem had seen the man, who would now be in his early fifties, and Jack wondered if he would recognize him when he did arrive. Already he was a half hour late, and already VanTighem was getting sick of 7UP on the rocks.

A stocky man about the right age entered the lounge and glanced around at the booths and at the bar where VanTighem was sitting. He had a good head of long, unkempt, wavy hair, which was what Jack had remembered, though it was thinning just a little and almost totally white. The real tip-off was the pair of dark rimmed glasses which perpetually rested halfway down his upturned button nose. The set jaw, cynical mouth and middle linebacker sense of urgency completed the picture for VanTighem. Jack left his bar chair and started toward the man, asking, "Dan, is that you hiding behind all that white hair?"

Gustine laughed, smiled broadly and replied, "Hell, Jack, twenty-five years hasn't changed you a bit. You still look like a weasel." The two men vigorously shook hands, slapped each other on the shoulder, and Gustine remarked, "So why hasn't your rotten lifestyle turned *your* hair white?"

"I dye it on occasion," VanTighem fibbed. "C'mon, I'll buy you a drink."

"I'll have what you're having," Gustine said. "I trust your judgment."

"No, you won't," VanTighem snickered. "This is 7UP."

Making a face and sticking out his tongue, the reporter commented, "Yuk…what is it with you middle-aged guys these days? You're all on some sort of fuckin' health kick. I'll have a gin and tonic and make it a double."

"Some things never change," VanTighem noted as he wrapped his arm around his old friend and led him to the bar. Jack ordered a drink for Gustine, passed on another for himself, then came right to the point. "I'm on the clock with this thing," he explained. "We've got a serial killer back in Spokane, and I need some answers fast."

Gustine looked surprised. "I didn't know you're still working for the paper. I thought you were fat and happy writing shitty novels." He flashed a smile following that last remark.

VanTighem ignored it. "I'm not working on this as a journalist," he explained. "I've got a good buddy who's a cop, and I'm helping him out."

"Why?"

"So I can write another shitty novel, you dumb son of a bitch," VanTighem remarked, grinning.

Gustine nodded agreeably. "That makes sense. So, you think this little sweetheart I've been researching might've had something to do with it."

"It's a possibility," Jack answered. His expression showed cool resolve, although hidden inside the thought of a connection to Kim Wintrode still hurt.

Gustine downed a third of his drink, lit a cigarette and noted, "Well, she had a good start."

His interest piqued, VanTighem's look narrowed in on the reporter. "How do you mean?"

"She's got a police record…of sorts."

"What do you mean of sorts?"

After taking another drink, Gustine answered, "She got busted as a juvenile for prostitution. After I talked to you, I dug a little deeper…just out of curiosity, mind you…but I couldn't resist. I figured if you were looking, then there might be something of interest there for me also."

"How the hell did you get hold of a juvenile record that old?" asked VanTighem. "They're sealed, and it should've been destroyed by now."

"How right you are," Gustine said, "but there is no juvenile record on her." He smiled and added, "She wasn't busted as a juvenile originally. The cops booked her as an adult, because they thought she *was* an adult. Her IDs proved it."

In an instant, Jack was ecstatic. "Holy shit!" he exclaimed. "You mean to tell me you have a police file on her with mug shots and all?"

Waving him off, Gustine explained, "Hold your horses, ol' buddy. The cops *had* a police file on her. They fucked up and maintained an adult record for a few years, then one day they got a call from some fancy mouthpiece down South who said he represented a very rich client who wanted to make sure all records on this Linda McConey were sealed and properly disposed of, or the department would be facing a big time lawsuit."

"Where down South?" VanTighem pounced.

Gustine scratched the back of his head, studied his friend's intense look for a moment, then said, "Funny you should ask that. My source in the department actually remembered that, which I thought was a little odd. He said it was Houston."

That bit of information set off all sorts of alarms in VanTighem's head, but he didn't want to let it show. He eased back a little, preparing for his next question which could be a bit delicate. "You mind telling me the name of your source?"

The reporter finished his drink and replied, "I'd rather not, Jack. You, as much as anyone, know all about this professional ethics crap we abide by. You see, my source is the poor dumb cop who busted her in the first place and ended up eating shit for it down the road." Gustine cracked a cynical smile, noting, "That's why he remembers it all so distinctly after all these years...that, and one other reason."

VanTighem was back on the edge of his seat. "What's that?" he asked.

Putting out his cigarette, Gustine inquired, "You still buying?"

"Sure."

Gustine ordered another drink and said to Jack, "This Linda McConey was not your typical sixteen-year-old street hooker. She was already a two hundred a trick call girl, and my source tells me the sexiest little fox he'd ever laid eyes on. Cops don't forget things like that...particularly when they've had their peckers run through the blender over it by some hotshot lawyer."

Sitting back in his chair again, VanTighem shook his head in frustration and concluded, "So all the records are kaput."

"Sorry, Jack," Gustine said as he started in on his second drink.

"What about the grandparents?" VanTighem posed.

Dan Gustine thought about them for a moment. "Well, that certainly explains why they don't much care to talk about her," he observed. "I gave you their address and phone number. Feel free to ask them yourself."

"I intend to," Jack stated. "That's where I'm heading tomorrow." After a momentary pause he asked, almost as an afterthought, "You find out anything more on the brother?"

"Vanished," Gustine flatly replied. "The grandparents told me he worked in a hospital as an orderly for a little while after high school, then packed up and disappeared shortly after his mother's suicide. No scrapes with the police. I checked."

A connection suddenly flashed in VanTighem's mind, and it started him thinking. He toyed with his empty glass for a time, seemed to ponder it and nothing else, then he tilted his head back a bit and conjectured to the back bar, "How hard do you suppose it would be to get your hands on birth certificates if you worked in a hospital?"

Gustine was somewhat intrigued by the question, and curious also why it had been asked. "I don't suppose it'd be that hard," he said, rubbing his chin. "Buddy up to the right person, maybe bribe them, dummy up some paperwork, that's all. Why do you ask?"

VanTighem turned to the journalist. "Oh, I was just wondering," he said. "I seem to keep coming up with two ends and no middle. A phony birth certificate could create a whole new person in the right hands...new social security number, new identity, the works."

"Hospital birth certificates don't mean squat," Gustine noted. "The hospital provides the information to the clerk and recorder, and that's when the record becomes official."

"I know that," Jack agreed. "But what if someone submitted a whole new set of information from the hospital and then had it swapped out in the recorder's office? There's where your bribe comes in, or even blackmail. You yourself said she seemed to have some real juice from down South."

Gustine thought about that for a moment. "Who the hell knows what she might have been able to do," he remarked. "She sure as hell fucked over the police department royally."

"You got anything else for me?"

"That's it," the reporter said. "Except you'd better cut me in on the story if you guys bust some serial killer from all this. I could use a good crime piece that has a local twist." Gustine revealed a friendly smile, but behind it, in those hazel eyes of his, there was the probing look of a seasoned newspaperman.

VanTighem broke down and ordered another 7UP, looked at his friend's drink, which was nearly empty, and asked him if he wanted another.

"No, I have to drive," Gustine told him. "That's how I've avoided a DUI all these years...two drinks max. Say...when did you quit?"

"About three years ago," Jack answered.

"Why?"

VanTighem smiled. "It's a long story. You're too old. If I told you, you wouldn't have enough time left to live through it."

Gustine laughed. "Yeah, I suppose that's true. I remember you back in school at Benjamin Harrison. You were hell on wheels." Reaching into his pocket, Gustine pulled out his pack of cigarettes, lit one and said, "These are the things a guy should quit. I've been trying. I'm down to a pack a day. I suppose you quit smoking too."

"Yup."

"Jesus, next thing you'll be telling me you're going to church."

VanTighem just chuckled. "Who me?" he asked innocently.

"Yeah, you're right," Gustine said. "The roof would cave in." He finished his drink and asked, "What you got planned for the rest of the day?"

"Not much," Jack answered. "The weekend's pretty much got me on hold, except for getting in touch with those grandparents."

"Why don't you come over to my place," Gustine suggested. "If you don't mind bachelor digs, we can swap a few old war stories, and maybe you can fill me in some more about this murder case. I might even be able to give you a few fresh ideas. I make a mean burger," he added.

VanTighem thought about that before responding. There wasn't much else he could do right now, and he was open to any new angles that might help out his investigation. His only concern was a nagging feeling that told him the past was gone, and reliving it with people who knew him then was a little depressing. They never seemed to forget his antics. It always left him with one foot trapped back there somewhere and the other trying to push himself free.

But this was an old friend, and he was curious about what twenty-five years had offered him, although he figured he knew most of the answers to that question already. At one time, this was one of the best damned reporters the Army ever had, and VanTighem wanted to compare some notes on Vietnam, find out if he had shared the same experiences over there and afterwards Jack had lived with all these years. Not that he wanted to relive the past or Vietnam anymore, but they did have common beginnings and parallel careers. He thought it might be interesting to observe someone now who had remained on the same path over all this time. It made him recall the old adage, 'There, but for the grace of God, go I.' With an affirmative nod, Jack told the reporter, "I'd like that, Dan. I'd like that very much."

****

The next morning VanTighem drove his rented car out to what he thought would be the suburbs but was instead the rural countryside to visit the grandparents.

The little get-together at Gustine's apartment the previous afternoon and evening had reaffirmed one conviction in him--he didn't like hanging around drunks. Joe was the only one, and that was because he rarely got drunk. He and Gustine had hashed over the war, speculated about the investigation, bitched about politics, jobs, ex-wives, and as the evening wore on none of it had made any sense. He had left early under the pretense he had some business back in Spokane to take care of over the phone. Instead, he had called the grandparents from his motel room and had all but demanded they see him the next day, telling them this was a matter of upmost urgency and lives depended on it. Reluctantly, they had agreed.

Expecting a farmhouse, VanTighem came upon an estate instead. These people had money. He drove the long, curved driveway past impeccably kept grounds and parked right in front of an elegant colonial home, complete with white porch columns two stories tall. He climbed out of the car, walked to the front door and rang the bell. Perhaps a minute or more passed before a woman answered. She was a tall and exceptionally attractive white haired lady in her early to mid-seventies, very sophisticated in both appearance and manner, and she was dressed for formal Sunday activities. VanTighem was actually surprised a butler hadn't come to met him, but possibly that wasn't the style of these Midwestern people after all. "You must be Mr. VanTighem," she said in a reserved though pleasant tone.

Jack stuck out his hand, followed by his best social smile, and he replied, "I am, and you must be Mrs. Erickson. I'm very pleased to meet you, Mrs. Erickson."

The woman shook his hand lightly and asked him to please come inside.

He followed her down a hallway and into an expansive living room which was decorated with what looked like family heirlooms rather than expensive store bought furniture. In one corner, near some tall windows where the light filtered in past richly embroidered maroon and gold drapes, a rugged and very striking gentleman sat in a well worn wing chair. He was a big man who had coarse grey hair and wild eyebrows that were darker in color, and with the sunlight breaking over him, he looked like a Viking king perched on his throne. But that image was quickly dispelled by the walker parked in front of him. He struggled to his feet when VanTighem approached.

VanTighem quickly crossed the living room to save his host the inconvenience of moving, shook the man's hand as he steadied himself on the walker and said to him, "Please, sir, don't trouble yourself. I'm Jack VanTighem."

"Nice to meet you, Mr. VanTighem," the man greeted him with a deep, rumbling voice completely in character with his craggy appearance. So was his grip, which was iron strong, and Jack could feel the rough calluses of a lifetime of hard work on those big hands. "My name is Rodney Erickson. Folks around here just call me Rod."

"My pleasure to meet you, Rod." He may be rich, Jack thought, but he sure as hell hadn't inherited it. He had worked for it all his life.

Erickson abruptly let go of VanTighem's hand and dropped back into his chair. "You'll have to excuse my condition," he noted. "I had a little stroke last year, and it kinda messed up my wheels."

VanTighem instantly liked this man. This was a man Joe would have liked also. This was someone he'd like to take fishing with them. "I can sympathize with that, Rod," he said. "About seven years ago I experienced a little shot to the head myself that completely knocked out my right ear."

"You had a stroke?" Erickson asked, surprised.

"That's what the doctors said."

"You're too damned young to have a stroke," remarked Erickson in that resonant voice of his.

"Don't I wish," Jack replied with a smile.

"Please, Mr. VanTighem," said the woman. "Have a seat." She moved closer to her husband, took a chair next to him and gestured that their guest take the Damask upholstered couch opposite them.

"Thank you, Mrs. Erickson." VanTighem made himself comfortable.

"May I get you some coffee?"

"No thank you," Jack said. "I hope not to trouble you folks too long."

Erickson came right to the point. "Evelyn said you wanted to ask us some questions," he stated. "Something about our grandkids I believe it was." The note of disdain in his voice when he mentioned the grandchildren came across clearly.

"I know this might be difficult," VanTighem began, "but this is a matter of extreme importance. Police business, I'm sorry to say."

"You a policeman, Mr. VanTighem?" asked Erickson. His manner had noticeably cooled.

"No," Jack answered with an amused little smile. "Believe it or not, I'm a writer. But I'm working with the Spokane Police Department on this particular case. Sort of a special assignment, you might say."

"I guess Evelyn must have told you we haven't seen those kids for close to twenty years. There was another fellow asking the same questions just last week, and we told him the same thing."

"I understand that, sir," VanTighem replied. "Fact is he's been helping me out. But there are some questions I need answered on my own. I hope it won't be too difficult for you folks," he added, looking back and forth between the two of them.

"We've long put it behind us," Evelyn Erickson said softly.

Her husband mellowed a little and leaned back in his chair. "It's water under the bridge for us," he sighed. "But you look like a decent fellow, and we're always willing to cooperate on police business."

"Thank you both," VanTighem told them, and then he began his questioning. "Would you care to tell me why it's been so long since you've seen your grandchildren?"

Rod Erickson opened his mouth to respond to that, but his wife cut in. "Our daughter married someone we didn't approve of, and she ended all ties with us…may God rest her soul. We tried, but she was too far gone with that man."

"John McConey," VanTighem said.

"Yes."

VanTighem wanted to tell them McConey was dead, but he thought better of it and went on. "So the last time you saw your grandchildren, they must have been, maybe, around nine and twelve?"

"That's right," Erickson replied.

"Did you ever receive any pictures of them when they were older?"

"We never saw or heard from them again," Erickson stated. "The truth is we had started proceedings to have them removed from their household and placed in our custody, but Susan told us if we tried that, we'd never see them or her again." Lowering his head, he sadly finished, "As it is…that was the case anyway."

"And no one tried to contact you over all these years," VanTighem concluded.

"No one," Mrs. Erickson said.

"I don't suppose you'd have any idea where they went to high school then."

"Fact is I do," said Erickson when he looked back up at the writer. "We have some friends in the city who knew Susan and kept us posted from time to time. Mark graduated from Washington High and went to work in a hospital for a short time afterwards. Linda went to school there also, but we never heard if she graduated or not. Not long after…Susan died." Erickson paused a few seconds to regain his train of thought, then concluded with, "Following Susan's death, they both just disappeared."

VanTighem's research had proved right. He would be at that high school first thing in the morning. What bothered him now was why hadn't the two grandchildren attempted to make contact with their grandparents on the own, particularly in light of the potential wealth available for them here. Perhaps their mother had concocted some story about them dying or moving elsewhere. That was a possibility, but something else was coming to light now also.

Disappearing off the face of the earth like they had, it made VanTighem ponder the possibility they might have purposefully schemed it all up in advance, and one way to ensure their success was to cut all ties, no matter how painful. If he and Joe could just get their hands on that brother, a lot of these questions would be answered. But the way it appeared, he was even more elusive than the woman they were actually tracking

Not wanting to cause these people any more trouble than they had already suffered, Jack carefully worded his next question. "Have the police ever contacted you regarding Linda for any reason?"

The Erickson's glanced at each other, and Rod Erickson responded, "No...we've never been contacted by the police...other than you. Why? Was Linda in any trouble?"

"Not really," VanTighem lied. "I just have reason to believe she dropped out of school at a relatively young age and thought maybe the juvenile authorities had followed up on it."

"Last we heard from our friends," Mrs. Erickson said, "Linda was a straight A student. She even skipped a grade."

That was interesting, Jack thought. He had figured he'd probably find her in the sophomore class, but more than likely she had been a junior when she had left school. Other than that, he was just about at the end of his rope here. He stood up and thanked them both for their help.

"I'm sorry we couldn't offer you more," Erickson said. His tone was still gruff, but there was sincerity in it and a natural kindness of spirit.

"You've both been a big help," VanTighem told them again.

"Mr. VanTighem," said Evelyn Erickson. "I know it's been a very long time, and maybe they don't know or even care we exist." She paused as her voice started to quiver a little. Taking a deep breath, she continued with measured words, "I still have vivid memories of them when they stayed with us here, them playing down by the creek out back and such. If you do find them, Mr. VanTighem...please tell them we're still here...that we still care."

"I will do that," Jack assured them both. He walked over to Erickson and shook his hand again, saying, "I've enjoyed meeting you, sir." To her he added, "I've enjoyed meeting you both very much."

"Folks around here still call me Rod," Erickson reminded him with a growing smile.

"Rod, if you ever get out to Spokane, the fishing trip is on me." VanTighem reached for his wallet, pulled out a business card, which he used on rare occasions, and handed it to the man. "The number's unlisted, so you'll need this." He turned to Evelyn Erickson, who was now standing. "Mrs. Erickson, you are a very lovely lady. I know this has not been easy for you dredging up old memories, and I appreciate your help and kind hospitality very much."

"You're most welcome, Mr. VanTighem," she replied with cultured graciousness.

VanTighem thought her refinement seemed a little out of character with the surrounding farm lands and the down to earth nature of her husband. "Well, I must be going," he said.

"I'll show you out," offered Mrs. Erickson.

Turning to leave, Jack was suddenly captured by a thought that had not occurred to him before, and he faced them again. "There is one other question that just dawned on me," he noted.

"What's that?" Mrs. Erickson asked.

"I've come across a rather unusual name. Does the name Wintrode mean anything to either of you?"

A look of shock suddenly flashed across Evelyn Erickson's face, and she glanced at her husband, then back at the writer. "Why...yes, Mr. VanTighem...yes, it does. My maiden name is Wintrode. How did you find that out?"

VanTighem was practically stricken speechless. If there had ever been any doubts in his mind, which there had, they were gone now. He felt like he had just been stabbed in the heart, and the knife was twisting. The Ericksons looked at him with puzzled expressions, and from their faces he could tell also they expected an answer. They deserved one. Scrambling for his composure, he replied, "Oh, nothing...really. It's just that I know someone in Spokane by that name. Like I said, it's rather unusual." He paused, uncomfortably, adding finally, "For some reason...you sort of remind me of her, Mrs. Erickson."

"All my relatives are back East," she told him. "I don't know of any family living out there."

"It's probably just a coincidence," VanTighem commented with a quick smile. "Thank you both very much again." He left the living room with Mrs. Erickson escorting him to the door. As he stepped outside, he said goodbye to her and headed toward his car.

Evelyn Erickson stood in the doorway. "Mr. VanTighem," she called out to him.

Jack turned around.

"If you see Linda, please convey that message I gave you to her."

Realizing his expression betrayed him, that she could read it and knew much more already than he was willing to reveal, VanTighem hesitated before he answered her, "I will, Mrs. Erickson. If I see her, I will give her your message."

"God bless you, Mr. VanTighem."

Jack paused again as he became besieged by an uneasiness brought about by the woman's look, which was both tender and grieved from all those years of separation and painful memories, an uneasiness triggered also by those words which represented the never ending struggle within him. Why couldn't those words come easy for him? Why was it easier to bed this woman's granddaughter than it was to respond in kind to her simple blessing from the heart? When would this struggle ever end? Coming from his mouth, his response seemed almost hypocritical. "God bless you too, Mrs. Erickson."

VanTighem left the Erickson's in a hurry to return home, not to his motel room, but to Spokane. He would first try to locate a photograph in some high school annual, but in his mind the answer was already imbedded. Now he had business to take care of in Spokane.

****

The next morning VanTighem headed straight for George Washington High School, which was located in Haughville, a working class neighborhood near downtown Indianapolis.

It was a school of the older style and tradition, a big brick fortress, though not terribly run down by any means and certainly well monitored as VanTighem soon found out. He went straight to the administration offices, introduced himself to a squat, older lady behind the reception desk and inquired if the school maintained a collection of yearbooks. Eyeing him suspiciously, years of battles with school kids etched across her severe expression, the woman told him to stay put and she would be right back. She disappeared into another office, and Jack waited patiently while he entertained himself casting a critical eye on some very depressing old photographs on the walls that featured people and places of supposedly some local significance.

Students wandered in and out, and VanTighem found himself feeling sorry for them trapped in this cold environment for four years of their lives. He had hated high school and had always felt he should have gone from his sophomore year straight into college. He still hated the confinement, the drab atmospheres, the meanness of adolescence, the unbearable rules and regulations, the whole sad comedy of plodding through puberty on the road to adulthood.

After some long minutes, the receptionist returned with a woman who looked to be in her late thirties or early forties, a petite and rather attractive blonde who wore her hair short, very efficient, and who obviously downplayed her looks for this environment. She introduced herself as Sarah Miller, assistant principal.

"Jack VanTighem," he responded along with his best friendly smile and handshake. "I'm looking for a couple of people, and I just wanted to go over some of your old yearbooks to see if I can find some pictures of them."

"Are you a policeman, Mr. VanTighem?" the woman asked with cool reserve.

"No, actually, I'm a writer, and..."

"A reporter then."

This third degree was rapidly becoming a little frustrating, but VanTighem didn't let on, and his charm continued to flow. "Actually, fiction," he said, the smile never fading. "But I am on police business out of Spokane, Washington."

"Do you have any documentation to that effect?" Sarah Miller inquired.

Of all the hurdles he had overcome so far, to come up against an overly officious school administrator was a bit too much. His look turned very serious, and VanTighem replied, "No, I don't, Ms. Miller. But we can make a phone call right now to the Spokane Police Department and a Detective Joe Rummel, and he'll clear this thing right up. Use my credit card to make the call." Softening a little, Jack added, "This is very important, Ms. Miller. Some lives have already been lost, and we're trying our damnedest to prevent that from happening again."

His sincerity mellowed the woman a bit, yet she said nothing for a few seconds as she stared straight at him with her remarkably large and richly hued brown eyes. "Have I met you before?" she asked finally.

That jarred VanTighem's solemn expression loose, and the smile returned. "I can't imagine where," he said.

"You look familiar."

"Maybe you saw my picture somewhere," the writer suggested, dropping a subtle hint. "I assure you it wasn't in the post office."

For the first time since their meeting, Sarah Miller smiled. It was a very pretty smile, making her all the more attractive. "You said you're a writer," she noted. "You by chance didn't write *Soul Mates*, did you?"

"I did," beamed VanTighem.

"Mr. VanTighem...you are an incurable romantic."

"Guilty as charged," VanTighem allowed. He blushed a bit. "Call me Jack."

Sarah's smile held strong. "C'mon, Jack," she told him. "I'll take you to the library myself."

They left the office together with the assistant principal asking VanTighem a steady stream of questions, both of them followed out the door by the disapproving scowl of the school clerk.

VanTighem had a fairly good idea of which annuals he needed, '76 and '77, but just to be on the safe side he took the classes of '75 through '80 off the shelf.

"You're lucky," Sarah noted as she watched him spread out the books on a nearby table. "Many of these end up stolen. Who are you looking for?"

"A girl by the name of Linda McConey," VanTighem replied as he thumbed quickly through the alphabetical listings by class.

"That name certainly sounds familiar," Sarah said. "I've been here fifteen years. I must have come across her at one time or the other."

"Here she is," Jack suddenly announced. He looked carefully at a page from the sophomore class of 1976, at one photo in particular, nothing more than a small mug shot of a cute kid. Maybe, but not conclusive. Snatching the 1977 yearbook, VanTighem raced to find the junior class. She was there again, but this time the cute kid had blossomed into a lovely young lady, more than that, in fact. She was a beautiful woman far beyond her years. Though styled differently, the hair was the same, and those piercing eyes sought out VanTighem from the page. Underneath the obvious makeup, a bit more than usual for a high school girl, her features were still young and not yet totally formed, but it was more than enough to tell him this was Kim Wintrode.

"I remember her," Sarah stated. "I had just started here as a teacher."

VanTighem quickly turned to her. "You do?"

"That was a tragic case," the school administrator went on. "She was in trouble over something…it never did come out. It all happened just after her mother committed suicide."

"You ever know what became of her?" Jack eagerly asked.

"Just disappeared," Sarah told him. "Dropped out of school and vanished."

VanTighem scrambled again for the '76 annual and searched through the seniors. No Mark McConey. He found his name listed in the index, but no page number for a photograph. Out of desperation, he went for the earlier books. The best he could come up with was a sophomore picture that could have passed for a sixth grader. It made no difference at this point anyway. He had found what he had come for. Clutching the '76 and '77 books, he asked Sarah in a tone that was almost pleading, "Can I borrow these two books? It's extremely important."

She hedged a few seconds, answering, "Well…I don't know if we can…"

"I'll give you a deposit," VanTighem insisted. "How about a hundred bucks cash? I'm not kidding you, Sarah…this is vital."

She thought about it a few moments more, then said, "I suppose that would be alright. You'll have to provide me an address and phone number and the name of that detective...what was it?"

"Joe Rummel," VanTighem hastened to tell her. "I'll give you his number too."

"That should be enough," Sarah concluded. "You can keep your money."

Jack wanted to kiss her right then and there, but thought better of it. Under different circumstances, he would have asked her out for lunch, but not now, not with what he had weighing on his mind. He had a plane to catch later that afternoon, and he had an urgent phone call to make as soon as he found the privacy to do so.

****

With five hours to kill before his flight, VanTighem drove from the school straight into the heart of the city to find a decent place for lunch and a pay phone. Parking wasn't near the problem he thought it would be, and soon he was walking the streets looking for a restaurant that suited him. After a leisurely stroll, he came across a small bar and grill that featured an interesting menu posted outside and some appealing smells when he entered. It was one of those red and white checkered table cloth places with spindly oval chairs painted black and the obligatory ferns throughout. He was still a little early for lunch, so VanTighem ordered a 7UP at the bar and headed straight for the pay phone inside.

He dialed police headquarters first, only to discover Rummel had been out all morning, no return time expected. His next attempt was Joe's apartment, hoping at least he could catch Kim there and have her pass on the message he had found what they were looking for, nothing more than that, no details. The phone rang six, seven times before Jack hung up. Damn him, he thought. Why the hell couldn't he step out of the Stone Age just once and get himself an answering machine like everyone else? Frustrated, VanTighem picked out a table and waited to order.

Following lunch, a very decent burger and great fries, the writer tried to phone again, this time amid the noise of a now crowded restaurant. Again the same results, and VanTighem had all he could do to keep from slamming the receiver down. He paid his bill and left.

With time to kill still on his hands, Jack decided to take a little tour of the downtown area and allow his nerves to settle a bit. He would try his calls again later at the airport. It was a beautiful day in Indianapolis. The sky was a bright blue without a cloud in sight, and on the streets some very attractive young women whiled away their lunch hours. This certainly beat sitting in an airport, he concluded.

Passing a book store, VanTighem suddenly thought of something and went inside. He browsed around until he found what he was looking for. He took the hardbound copy of *Soul Mates* to the cashier, paid for it and wrote on the inside cover:

> Sarah--thank you again for all your help.
> If you ever get out to Spokane, dinner is
> on me. Cheers--Jack VanTighem

"Would you do me a favor?" VanTighem asked the store employee. She asked what it was, and he told her, "I have a friend here in town who would like this. I have to leave for the airport right away, and I'd appreciate it if you'd give her a call and tell her this book is waiting here for her."

"Sure, I'll do that," the cashier said cheerfully.

"Her name is Sarah Miller, and she works at Washington High School not too far from here. You got a phone book?"

The cashier reached under the counter and produced a directory for VanTighem. He looked up the number and wrote it down for her, then dug into his pocket and handed her a twenty dollar bill. "This is for your trouble."

"I can't take that," the young woman protested.

"I insist," VanTighem said. "This means a lot to me."

Reluctantly, the cashier took the money. Jack thanked her and left. When he was gone, she dialed the number he had given her and asked for Sarah Miller, turning the book over as she waited for Sarah to come on the line. VanTighem's face stared back at her. Smiling, she said to herself, 'There's one lucky woman.'

CHAPTER SIXTEEN

Monday morning found Rummel and Curtis driving out to Newman Lake and a remote site off Thompson Creek Road. A car, with a body in it, had been discovered parked in the woods, no additional information. The sheriff's people had already been dispatched, and the two detectives were to meet them there.

After two or three wrong turns with Brad driving, they came upon two county squad cars and an unmarked parked alongside the road where a trail of tire tracks led across a meadow into the woods. George Sept was standing next to the unmarked car waiting for Rummel.

They pulled up and parked behind Sept's vehicle. Rummel hopped right out and caught the glint of a windshield reflection about a hundred yards away in the trees, exposed by an already blistering eleven a.m. sun.

"Déjà vu all over again, like the great philosopher once said," Sept remarked with a shrug and a look of resignation as Joe approached him. "This time we didn't take any chances. We haven't driven back in there, and we stayed off the trail when we went back to investigate."

"Good man," Rummel replied.

Brad joined them. "Who found the body?" he asked.

"Some kid out fartin' around with his .22 plinking ground squirrels," Sept told them. "He ran home and had his mom call us, then led us back here."

"Where is he?" inquired Rummel.

"He's over there in a squad car with one of the guys," answered Sept, pointing. "I wouldn't bother him right now. He's one sick puppy. This guy's been dead at least forty-eight hours."

"Ah, fuckin' great," Rummel moaned. He turned to Curtis with a pleading look. "Brad?"

"My turn again, I take it," Curtis remarked.

"Seniority trumps beauty," Joe winced. "Besides, I've had my share for a lifetime."

"Short-timer's prerogative," Sept interjected with a self-satisfied smile.

"Let's go," Curtis grumbled.

The three men struck off, following the tire tracks on both sides and scanning the ground ahead of them for any signs of someone who might have been on foot in the area. They hadn't gone very far when a putrid smell warned them about what they could expect. Covering their faces with handkerchiefs, or in Brad's case the palm of his hand, they approached the vehicle. Its passenger door was still open. What they saw in there was the ghastly remnant of a bloated human being surrounded by swarming flies.

Rummel handed Brad his handkerchief, which the young detective gratefully took after he put on a pair of rubber gloves. Brad covered his nose, scowled at Joe and shook his head with disgust. Rummel cupped his nose with his hand and stepped back several yards to join Sept.

As Curtis stuck his head into the beat up, late 60s Plymouth Valiant, Rummel made the muffled comment to Sept, "Looks like our little lady has taken a step or two down the social scale."

"How's that?" asked Sept through his handkerchief.

"That old beater there," Joe said. "She may have tagged more than her share of sleazebags, but all of them could at least afford better than that."

Sept briefly lowered his handkerchief. "Maybe she was in a hurry this time," he noted.

That was a thought Rummel had to consider. Could it be the pressure was on, that the killer knew, or at least sensed, he was on to her, and she wanted one last quick one? Maybe the first dumb son of a bitch to come along? "You get a good look at the victim earlier?" Joe asked the sheriff's detective.

"Some guy who looked to be in his late forties," Sept told him. "Hard to tell, though. Some drunk from the looks of it. The back seat was full of empty beer cans."

"Hey, Joe!" Curtis suddenly called out. "You won't believe who this guy is!" Rummel hadn't the foggiest idea, and he didn't have the time to ask either because Brad answered for him. "It's Alan VanTighem. Your buddy's cousin!"

"Oh shit no!" Rummel shouted as he raced forward to take a look for himself. He slapped on his own pair of gloves and peering over Brad's shoulder he could scarcely recognize the once thin face now bloated and scaly like a rotten cantaloupe, or those eyes, which had always sparkled with intelligence but now bugged blindly out of the man's skull and appeared to settle only on him.

"Here," Curtis said as he handed Rummel a wallet behind his back. "And look at what we got here!" he exclaimed.

Without even a glance at it, Joe put the open wallet down on the roof of the car. "What'd you find?" he urged his partner, trying not to gag on the stench. Then he backed away to allow Curtis out of the car.

With the handkerchief still held over his nose, Brad turned around and proudly displayed a long, wavy hair.

Forgetting the smell, Rummel immediately dived into his jacket pockets with both hands to search for something to hold this long awaited piece of evidence. "George!" he shouted. "You got an envelope or something?"

"What you got?"

"A hair! A woman's hair, I'll lay odds!"

Sept stepped forward with a small plastic bag he always carried. "Here you go."

Carefully, Rummel held the bag open while Curtis slipped the hair into it, and then he handed it to Sept along with VanTighem's wallet, and covering up his nose with the handkerchief Curtis had returned to him, he crawled into the car to take a closer look for himself. "Where'd you find it?" he yelled to Brad who was now standing a safe distance away.

"Between his fingers on the right hand!" Curtis shouted back.

Rummel probed the dead man's fingers, careful to avoid the fingernails which this time might just hold skin traces. He found nothing more there, but just a few inches away, stuck in the dried blood that covered the victim's thigh, there was a second hair that appeared identical to the first. "Well, Alan," Rummel said in a low voice, "you may never have amounted to much, but you might have just given us what we've needed." Then he added softly, "Sorry it had to be you, old buddy." As he was about to crawl back out of the vehicle, the detective suddenly spotted something else. A button was lodged in the edge of the floor mat on the passenger's side of the car. "Hey, Brad!" he called out. "Bring that bag back over here and get this for me!"

Curtis was back at the car in an instant. "You find something else?"

"Yeah, I've got another hair and this button here. Looks like it could have come off a shirt or a blouse."

Curtis handed Rummel the plastic bag, and Joe carefully put the newly found evidence inside and gave the handkerchief back to his partner; then he took the bag back to Sept while Curtis took another look inside and around the car. When he approached him, the sheriff's detective inquired, "What else did you find in there?"

"A second hair," Rummel replied, "and a button too that doesn't look like it belongs to the victim."

"Say, maybe she was in a hurry after all."

"I sure as hell hope so."

"Did I hear Brad say you knew that guy in there?" asked Sept.

"He was my best buddy's cousin."

"Sorry to hear that," George replied.

"He was living on borrowed time anyway," Rummel noted sadly. "I just hate to see him go this way."

"Nobody should have to go like that," Sept sympathized.

"Something just ain't right here though," Rummel added.

"What's that?"

Joe thought for a moment, and his gaze momentarily drifted off before he said to the county detective, "Alan was a crafty bastard. He knew this shit was going down, and he would've been smart enough to stay clear of it. I just don't see him ending up all the way out here with that woman unless he was forced to do it."

Just then Curtis returned to them. He let out a long breath of air and announced, "I don't think I want to go back in there for anything else."

"Don't blame you," Joe said. "Let's call in the forensics people and get this place sealed off."

"Fine by me," Brad gladly agreed.

"You taking this stuff straight back to the lab?" Sept inquired. "If so, I'd like to tag along."

"Be my guest, George," said Rummel. "Why don't you meet us there in an hour or so. I've got to stop by the apartment for a few minutes and check the mail."

"You expecting a love letter?" Sept teased him.

Stonefaced, Rummel replied, "Something like that." Turning to Curtis, he asked, "You don't mind taking a little side trip, do you?"

"Not at all," Brad answered.

The three men started back toward the road, again following the vehicle tracks as they went. After going only a few yards, Rummel stopped and noted, "You know something...there's only been one car in here. That means she walked out of this place," he concluded.

"But if she came out here with him," Sept offered, "it's too damned far to walk all the way back to town."

Rummel didn't respond right away. He looked back at the car, then to the road, and finally at his two companions. His expression was dark and troubled. "Unless someone picked her up," he suggested.

Curtis and Sept just stared at each other and shook their heads. The thought of two of them out there was too mind boggling to comprehend.

****

Rummel drove on the way back to town, and after taking the little detour and arriving at his apartment, he saw Kim's car parked in front. That was expected. She often walked or bicycled to work. He pulled up behind it, asked Brad to stay put and said he'd only be a minute. Getting out, he walked between the two vehicles. Suddenly he stopped and glanced around with a repugnant expression that contorted his face.

Curtis stuck his head out the passenger's window and asked, "What's the matter?"

Joe shrugged it off and replied, "Ah, that stink must be sticking with me. I can still smell it."

"I know what you mean," Brad said.

I'll be back in a minute."

Rummel trotted up to the front door and checked the mailbox for appearance's sake. Taking out a couple of bills, he then unlocked the door and went inside to do what he had come home for in the first place. The detective headed straight for the phone and dialed VanTighem's number. On the fifth ring, the answering machine kicked in. Rummel hated them, but he hadn't expected Jack to be back yet anyway, not this early in the day. "We've got another one," he said to the nemesis machine. "But this time we've also got something to work with. I'm gonna need you to get me one of Wintrode's hairs. That should be right up your alley." Rummel hesitated before saying next, "I've got some bad news about your cousin. I'll explain it all when I talk to you in person. Call me the minute you get back. It's important, Jack. I think we've got her." Joe hung up and left the apartment.

As he retraced his steps, Rummel again stopped by the trunk of Kim's car and sniffed the air. "Goddamnit," he said to Brad. "There's something rotten around here, and it's not stuck in my nose."

"I thought I noticed something too," Curtis commented from his open window, and he climbed out of the car to join his partner.

Rummel was looking all around on the sidewalk and in the back of Kim's car trying to trace down the source of that odor. He even checked the bottoms of his shoes to see if he had accidentally stepped in some dog crap, but that wouldn't be the right smell anyway. This was something rotten, dead. "I wonder if a squirrel crawled into her car and died," he remarked to Brad finally. "Maybe got in the trunk somehow."

"It sure as hell seems to be coming from there," Curtis noted as he pulled at his nose. "You by chance don't know where her car keys are, do you?"

"She's got an extra set in the house. Hang on…I'll be right back."

After he scrounged around a minute or two for Kim's keys, Joe returned to her car and opened the trunk. A putrid blast of stench from that hot, enclosed space slapped them both squarely in their faces, and Curtis turned quickly away, gagging. Joe spotted a black athletic bag he had never seen her use before, and he took it out, holding it in front of him arm's length. "What the hell did she do?" he grimaced. "Leave her lunch in here?" He balanced the bag on the edge of the trunk, unzipped it and peeked inside.

Rummel's eyes shot wide open. With a tormented roar, he bellowed, "Oh, my God!" In a fit of rage and anguish, the detective backhanded the bag into the trunk, and in the next instant he reeled to one side, bent over and heaved his guts up all over the street.

Curtis grabbed the bag, and fighting for his breath also, he forced a look inside. "Holy shit!" he exclaimed.

A blood splattered, nine inch Italian stiletto glistened in the overhead sunlight that sneaked inside, and a pair of blood stained rubber gloves lay crumpled in the bottom. Curtis shook the bag. A severed penis caked with blood flopped into view.

"Oh, Jesus!" Rummel was gasping now. "Oh, Jesus fucking Christ! Not this! Not her!" He gagged on his vomit and tears and coughed up the residue from his gnarled stomach.

Brad dropped the bag back into the trunk. His face drained, he turned to his partner and placed a gentle hand on Joe's doubled up body. "There's got to be an explanation for this, Joe," he said. His words were hesitant and without conviction. "C'mon, we've got to get this taken care of."

Rummel slowly straightened up and lifted his tear soaked eyes to the sky. He had to struggle for every breath. Suddenly he spun around and fell against the side of Kim's car, burying his face in the crook of his arm while he rhythmically pounded the roof with his tightly clenched fist, sobbing over and over, "It's not her. It can't be her."

In a show of compassion, Curtis approached him and laid a hand on his shoulder, saying to him softly, "Kim's going to come out of this okay. C'mon, Joe…get in the car. We've got to go downtown."

Rummel could take no more. All those years of restraint in the face of human fungus finally came to a head and exploded within him, and he swung his arm backwards with violent rage, catching Brad across the face and sending him sprawling onto the pavement. "You fuckin' rights she's gonna be okay!" he roared at his partner who was now wiping blood from his nose. "I'm gonna get that fuckin' bitch who did this! And I'm gonna kill her!" He started for his police sedan.

Brad jumped to his feet. "Hold on, Joe!" he shouted. "We'll get her…okay?" With an outstretched hand, Curtis took a few cautious steps toward him.

Rummel readied himself for a surprise shot from those feet. "You stay out of this, Brad," he warned. "I'm gonna take care of this myself."

"Okay, okay," Curtis said as he took a couple more steps closer. "But let's do this by the book." He paused a moment, ran the back of his hand across his bloody nose again, then continued in a calming tone of voice. "Someone set Kim up...okay? Maybe she is in trouble right now, but she could also be in danger more than anything else. Let me go get her. Let's go downtown first, and then I'll drive out and pick her up at work and bring her back to you."

Knowing damn well who was behind all of this, Rummel wasn't about to trust her boyfriend. "Bullshit!" he snapped. "If anyone's going to get Kim, it'll be me!"

"You're in no shape to do that, Joe," Curtis argued. "And we can't have her wandering around until you get ready." A couple more steps forward, and Brad stopped, stalled for time to let reason sink in. "Look," Brad went on, "any clown can crack a lock and stash something in some poor unsuspecting soul's trunk. We've got the hairs, Joe. They can clear Kim. We've got enough evidence now to find the real killer."

The detective's head was spinning. There was wisdom in what Brad had said, but right now Joe trusted no one, not even himself. What could he do, anyway? Go out and drag Kim Wintrode in by the hair, screaming? Or would he kill her? He wanted more than anything else to have VanTighem back in town with the information he so desperately needed. That was all it would take, and with luck that was only a matter of hours away.

There was another thought also that slashed away at his heart like that knife in the black bag. Just what if it was his daughter? Rummel hated himself for even thinking that, and for considering the many more questions that now rushed into his mind and tugged his emotions in every which direction like a pack of starved hyenas ripping away at his carcass. Chicago. Kim had been there then, and she had abruptly left. The murders had started up in Spokane while she had been off wandering around the country somewhere, but it was possible she could have been right here all along. The Seattle killings last summer--vacation time from school. And Kim was left-handed. These were the things his colleagues would be looking at with a much more objective point of view, and that would not be good.

Rummel would hear no more of this from himself. Brad was right. He was in no shape to handle this rationally, and the truth was he could muddle it up more if he went to her himself. She would be cleared by the evidence they had found, and then he, with VanTighem's help, would settle the score once and for all. The tension and rage slowly subsided in Rummel, and he lowered his eyes to the pavement. A new wave of tears streaked his cheeks. He brushed them away with the back of his hand and said to Curtis, "Go ahead and take me downtown, Brad. You go get her and bring her to me." Looking up, Joe added, "And you go easy on her. No embarrassment, no cuffs...you hear me?"

Brad stepped forward and grasped his partner by both arms. "Joe, trust me," he said. "Kim's my friend too, you know. I'm just bringing her in for questioning." Pausing, he forced a smile. "Tonight you two will be home together watching TV. She's going to come out of this okay…I promise you that."

Rummel sadly shook his head in face of this new onslaught of frustration and fears and said nothing in response. Instead, he just slowly walked around to the other side of the car, steadying himself with one hand against it as he went, and climbed inside.

Curtis considered retrieving the black bag from Kim's car, then thought better of it. It was best to leave everything in place for the crime scene people. It was also best to get the hell out of there as quickly as possible in the event his partner might be harboring second thoughts. Without another word, Brad hopped in and drove straight away to division headquarters.

****

After dropping Joe off at police headquarters and putting him in the hands of McCoy, Curtis went to the crime lab where he met George Sept and explained to him Joe wouldn't be able to make it due to some new developments, no details. He turned over the evidence they had collected earlier and told the medical examiner he would be back in a couple of hours with another hair sample for comparison. Sept opted to stay there and wait for any possible preliminary results. Then Curtis went out to pick up Kim.

Joe was sitting in the squad room trying his best to avoid going outside and chain smoke when Brad arrived with Kim. She looked scared, and she ran immediately to her father, throwing her arms around him. "Daddy, what's this all about?" she pleaded. "Brad said you found something in my car, and they need to ask me some questions."

Rummel hugged her hard. "It's okay, Kitten," he assured her as his tears began to form again. "Some son of a bitch played a dirty trick on you, that's all."

Kim pulled back from him, looked into her father's tormented face and asked in a voice breaking with emotion, "What…what did you find?"

Rummel couldn't answer her, not right now. It was too much for him to handle. He drew her close to him again and whispered in her ear, "It'll all be taken care of, Kitten. This is just a big mistake, and in no time we'll get it straightened out." He held her by her upper arms and looked into her tearful eyes for a moment, then kissed her on the forehead and told his daughter, "Brad's going to need some things from you. He's going to ask you some questions, and I want you to help him out the best you can."

"What things? What questions?"

Rummel could see she was terrified. "Just routine, Kim," he explained to her. "Tell him everything you know, and it'll all work out."

"I don't understand, Daddy," Kim persisted.

"In an hour or so, it'll all be over," Joe promised her. "Then we'll go home." He looked over his shoulder and gave Brad the go-ahead nod to take her for questioning. "I'll be waiting here for you, Kim." Rummel hugged her again, hard and long, then gently turned his daughter around toward Curtis and pointed the direction for her to go. "Brad will get this straightened out for you right now. I'll be right here when you get back."

With hesitation in her steps, Kim went to Curtis, and he put a reassuring arm around her shoulder to lead her away to the interrogation room. "I hope the fuck you have some answers for me," Kim grumbled to him under her breath.

Brad had to laugh at that remark. "I'm glad someone in your family can handle this little ordeal," he chuckled. "Your dad slugged me earlier over this whole mess."

Kim's fears suddenly vanished under a wave of curiosity. "No kiddin', Brad?" she said with surprise. Her look was mixed with confusion and concern. "Just what the hell happened?"

"I'll explain it all to you in private," Curtis answered.

They started to leave the room together, but Kim stopped and turned one last time to her father, showing him a brave smile. Rummel mustered up a little smile for her in return, and then, when she was out of sight, he sagged back into his chair. Down the hallway, Curtis continued his conversation with Kim. "You got a hair brush on you?"

"Sure," she replied, puzzled. "Why do you ask?"

"I'm going to need a hair sample from you to bail you out of this situation," Brad told her. "I'll explain it to you in interrogation."

The minutes crawled by while Joe waited in the squad room. McCoy came in to visit him briefly and assure him they would get to the bottom of this, then he returned to his office and closed the door. A half hour later Brad reappeared with Kim. He asked her to stay with her father while he talked to the lieutenant. Kim rushed into her father's arms, and they sat down together on a small vinyl couch as Rummel wrapped his arm around her and Kim laid her head on his shoulder. They waited.

"I just got the coroners' report over the phone," McCoy was telling Curtis. "Said the victim was killed late Friday night or early Saturday morning."

"I was with Kim and my girlfriend Friday night," Curtis informed him.

"How late?"

"About eleven-thirty," Curtis said. "I left her at my girlfriend's apartment where she supposedly spent the night."

"Can your girlfriend verify that?" McCoy asked.

"Let's give her a call at work and find out," Brad replied. He quickly wrote down her name and both a work and home number and handed it to the lieutenant.

McCoy took the paper from him and said flatly, "I'll do that." Then he commented, "The lab people also informed me they've got prints all over that knife. Have we got anything on Kim?"

"No, but I think I can take care of that," Curtis told him.

"How do you plan to do that? She hasn't been charged with anything yet."

"I think Joe will let me into the apartment for some samples of things she's handled if he feels it will help her. Which I'm sure it will," Brad quickly added. "I also want to check her clothes for any missing buttons."

"Did she give you a hair sample?" inquired McCoy. He was back to biting his lower lip again.

"No problem...right here." Brad handed McCoy an envelope which contained several hairs from Kim's brush. "Gave them to me voluntarily."

"I'll have someone get these over to the lab right away," McCoy said. "It may take some time to come up with an exact match, but at least we'll see if there's a class match or not."

"I'll need at least an hour over at Joe's," Curtis noted.

"Take someone with you from the crime lab to help."

"I will."

"We've got the green light all the way down from the top to push this through as quickly as possible," McCoy remarked. "They're on standby in the lab right now."

"I'll be back as fast as I can," Curtis said. He started to leave. As he opened the door, Brad heard his name called, and he turned around. "You need something else, Jim?"

"Close the door, Brad," McCoy said softly. The lieutenant hesitated, glanced out at the hallway as the door was being shut, then looked down at his desk while he searched for the courage to ask the question that had been plaguing him since this all unfolded. His eyes returned to the detective, his expression both solemn and worried, and McCoy inquired, "Brad...do you think she did it?"

Curtis also lowered his eyes momentarily and replied, "I don't know." When he looked back up at McCoy, he stated, "But there's one good place to start and find out."

"What's that?"

"Call my girlfriend. She should be able to confirm Kim's alibi."

"I'll do that right now," McCoy said, and Curtis left the office.

Once outside, Curtis took Joe aside and explained to him what he needed. Rummel immediately started to protest, but Brad quickly convinced him this had to be done sooner or later anyway, and it might as well be sooner so they could all go home. Knowing if he was in Brad's place he'd do the same thing, Rummel reluctantly dug into his pocket for the house keys and handed them over. "I'll be back as soon as I can," Brad promised him and left.

"Am I under arrest?" Kim asked her father when he returned to her.

Rummel looked into those teary eyes, saw the worry in her face that furrowed her brow, the tension that tugged at her mouth and aged his little girl right before his eyes. He knew he must be mirroring that same expression with his own dread, but he had to be encouraging, even if his gut told him otherwise. "No, Kitten, you're not under arrest," Joe replied in a soothing voice. "Look at it this way," he continued. "We've finally got some decent breaks in this case...I mean real evidence that will give us a conviction when we find the killer. You just got in the way, that's all. Some rotten bastard broke into the trunk of your car and planted that crap on you. When they compare the hair samples and fingerprints, you and I are going to go home, and this will all be over."

Kim laid her head against her father's chest and said softly, "I hope so, Pops. I really hope so."

It was nearly five o'clock when Curtis returned. He had been at the lab longer than expected. Seeing him enter the squad room, Rummel jumped to his feet and rushed to meet him at the door. "What'd you come up with, Brad?" he pounced.

Curtis's look darkened, and he glanced from side to side as he offered his evasive reply. "I've got to go in and talk to McCoy first. I'll be back in a bit."

Rummel's hand shot out and seized Brad by the arm when he started to move away from him. "I want to know now!" he demanded. "You've left us sitting here all goddamned afternoon, and we're entitled to an answer! Is Kim being charged?"

Grabbing his partner's hand, Curtis wrenched it from his arm and answered him in a tone that was cold and forceful. "I'll be back in a minute, Joe. Then you'll have your answer." With that, he walked away and entered McCoy's office.

Kim was by her father's side now. "What happened? What was that all about?"

Joe sheltered his daughter with a big, secure arm around her and growled, "Cops. That's what it's all about."

Inside McCoy's office, Curtis was detailing the preliminary lab results. "We have what looks like a near match with the prints we lifted from some of Kim's items back at the apartment and those on the knife. But that won't mean a damn thing until we actually print her and make the comparison. The hairs are a class match, and the lab people are running more tests right now to see if we might have an exact match. Judging from the color and curl, they expect to have it, short of waiting forever on DNA results." Pausing, he noted next, "And I found a blouse missing a sleeve button that looks identical to the one we found. I left that at the lab too."

"McCoy shook his head sadly and turned to stare out the window, his hands clasped behind his back. "I talked to your girlfriend," he said to his reflection there in the glass. "Kim, is it…helluva coincidence."

"What'd she say?"

The lieutenant continued to look straight ahead at nothing in particular, answering at last, "She told me she went to bed around one a.m. and let Kim sleep on the couch. When she awoke the next morning, Kim was gone." Turning back to Curtis, he took a deep breath and sighed, "Let's go out there and book her."

Rummel knew by their expressions, as the two police detectives approached him, that the verdict was in, and it wasn't good. Before he could get a word out, McCoy told Brad to take Kim downstairs, and he asked Joe to join him in his office.

Curtis grasped Kim gently by the arm and said, "C'mon, Kim, we've got to go."

Kim swung her arm free from his grip and screamed, "What are you doing?"

"Come on, Kim," Brad repeated, reaching for her arm again.

"Let go of her!" Rummel bellowed as he broke in between them, poised to strike.

"Daddy, make them stop!"

McCoy butted in. "Kim, you're being charged with the murder of Alan VanTighem. You have the right…"

"Don't give me that shit!" Rummel roared.

"Joe, you stay out of this!" McCoy yelled.

"Fuck you! Nobody's putting my daughter away!"

"Brad, take her!" McCoy ordered as he bulled into Rummel and pushed him out of the way. Holding up his hands to stop Joe if need be, he added, "And read her her rights!"

Curtis hurried Kim away. She looked back over her shoulder at her father, crying, "Daddy, I didn't do anything! Tell them, Pops…I didn't do anything!"

"That's okay, Kitten!" Rummel shouted past McCoy who was now holding him back. "They can't make this stick, Hon! I'll get you out of this, Kim! We'll get the son of a bitch who did this to you! I love you, Kitten! I'll get you out of this!"

"In my office, Joe!"

"Go to hell, McCoy!"

"You're off the case!" McCoy shot back. "As of right now, you're on sick leave!"

"I'll get the fucker who did this to her! I'll kill that fuckin' bitch!"

McCoy threw his hands up and said, "That's it, Joe. Go home. Do you want somebody to drive you…maybe stay with you awhile?"

Rummel just glowered at the lieutenant, his dark eyes burning with hatred at that moment for everything under the sun except his daughter. "I'm gonna get her, Jim," he rasped. "I'm gonna get her."

McCoy's heart went out to his detective. He knew, if he was in the same situation, he'd be acting the same way. All he could do now was try to calm the storm. "Go home, Joe," he said again. "Get Kim a good lawyer and take a long look at this thing in the morning when you can reason it out."

"Don't patronize me!" Rummel snapped. "I've already reasoned it out! You'll have your killer even if I have to bring her head in here and dump it right on your fuckin' desk!"

"Don't you go takin' the law into your own hands, Joe," McCoy warned him. "Or I swear I'll lock you up too!"

"Go for it, Jim," Rummel sneered. "Give it your best shot." He whirled around and stormed toward the exit.

"I mean it, Joe! I don't want any more trouble!" But McCoy's words fell on deaf ears as Joe disappeared out of sight.

****

Rummel hung around downstairs for ten minutes or so in hopes of seeing his daughter, but Curtis, accompanied by two uniformed officers, kept him away and tried in vain to calm him down. Brad promised him he'd arrange a meeting with her first thing in the morning if he would just go home now and cool down. He told him he'd do everything he could to help. Rummel would have none of it. He left headquarters in a rage.

Once he arrived back at his apartment, Joe started drinking heavily and making phone calls to both VanTighem and Terri, neither of whom was home. All that was left for him to do was smoke, drink and wait.

At eight-thirty the phone rang, jolting Rummel out of his drunken stupor on the couch. His condition was obvious when he answered.

"Joe? What the hell's wrong with you?" VanTighem demanded on the other end of the line.

"They arrested Kim," Rummel slurred.

"They got Wintrode?"

"No, Kim…my daughter."

"What for?"

"They think she killed them people."

"What people? You fuckin' drunk?"

"Fuckin' right." Rummel mumbled. "I'm gonna kill her."

"That's enough!" VanTighem shouted over the phone. "You sober your ragged ass up right now! I'm on my way over, and you'd better be drinking coffee when I get there. You hear?"

Rummel flopped his head back against the couch and scrambled for his senses. "You get her?" he managed to ask.

"I got her," Jack replied. "You have your goddamned act together by the time I get over there. We've got work to do."

That was all Joe needed to hear. He shook his head hard and hung up without saying goodbye. After two futile attempts to get up off the couch, he forced himself to his feet the third time, stumbled over the coffee table, picked himself up and staggered into the bathroom. He turned on the cold water full blast, stripped down and lurched into the shower.

****

VanTighem banged on the door and then walked right in. He caught Joe coming out of the bathroom, naked from the waist up, a towel tossed over the top of his head in such a manner it made him look like a half asleep Arab. He was a mess. "Well, aren't you a pretty sight," Jack remarked.

"Don't lecture me," Rummel grumbled. "I feel like shit."

This was no time to trade barbs, VanTighem figured, and he came right to the point. "So, what's this about your daughter getting busted? Who's she supposed to have killed?"

"Sit down, Jack," Rummel said as he crumpled onto the couch like he'd been pushed. "You'll have to forgive me," he noted with an apologetic smile. "I'm still drunk."

VanTighem took a chair.

Coughing, Rummel reached for a cigarette and lit it. "Your cousin was the latest victim. They're charging Kim with it...along with the others, I expect."

Shock dropped VanTighem's mouth wide open, not so much over the fact his cousin was dead, which he had already assumed from Joe's telephone message, but that Kim was being held responsible for it. "Alan's been murdered? How the hell can they pin that on Kim?"

Joe leaned back and watched a languid trail of smoke from his cigarette reach for the ceiling. "Someone planted an athletic bag in her trunk. It contained a bloody knife with her prints all over it, rubber gloves and..."

"And what?"

Rummel abruptly sat up, bent forward and lowered his throbbing head. "Makes me want to puke every time I think about it."

"So puke and tell me!" VanTighem snapped.

As tears again moistened his eyes, Rummel looked up at his friend. "Alan's pecker," he quietly said.

"Ahh shit!" Jack exclaimed. He jumped to his feet and paced for a few moments behind his chair, then leaned over the back of it and stated, "And so they're hanging Kim for the whole series of killings."

Rummel glared up at him. "She didn't commit the last one either," he snarled.

VanTighem threw his palms up, saying, "Hey, don't get me wrong. I didn't say she did. So someone planted the bag...the who we probably both know...end of story."

"I wish it was," Joe remarked wistfully, adding, "They've got a pretty good match of hair found at the scene of the crime, a button off her blouse found in Alan's car, and to top it all off, she *is* left-handed."

VanTighem flopped back down in his chair. "Whew," he sighed. "Talk about a stacked deck."

"Too stacked," Rummel commented. "I might've been drunk these past couple of hours, but I've still been thinking. You remember what Terri told us in Seattle?"

"What?"

"About the crimes being too perfect, like a cop had pulled them off...or someone who knew all the angles of police work." Rummel paused for a quick drag off his cigarette and said, "Well, so is this setup. It's too perfect."

VanTighem had already caught his drift. "Kim's been hanging around with Wintrode again," he concluded for him.

"Exactly."

There was a long, heavy moment of silence, and then Jack flatly stated, "Kim Wintrode is McConey's daughter. She is Linda McConey."

Rummel felt such a genuine smile coming on it almost hurt. "My good friend, that's just what I wanted to hear from you."

"Yeah, well before you go striking off to nail her, we'd better think about Kim first. You're going to need a good lawyer, the best money can buy. I'll call him first thing in the morning and don't worry about the expense. It's on me."

Despite the hurt he was still feeling inside, the uncertainties he was still experiencing, having a friend like VanTighem was indeed a comfort to Joe's soul. "At this point, I ain't arguing with you, old pal," he said. "And I appreciate the help very much."

"Nah, it's the least I can do," VanTighem brushed it off. "It's worth every cent of it. This thing's got me pissed off too, now that they've dragged Kim into it."

"Then you know how I feel," Joe nodded.

"Yeah, I do...but getting drunk won't help matters any. You've still got to corner Wintrode, and that ain't gonna be easy."

"Particularly since McCoy relieved me of duty today," Rummel added with a smirk.

Throwing his hands up in the air, VanTighem remarked, "Oh, that's just great."

Rummel took a few moments to think. "Maybe that's not so bad after all," he suggested. "It gives me a free hand to trace Wintrode to all the other murders. I've got Terri working on something right now that could possibly put her in Chicago." The detective revealed a devious, bitter smile. "And now her guard's going to be down with Kim in jail. If I can come up with enough circumstantial evidence to squeeze her a little, she might just trip over herself."

"But you said it right there," Jack argued. "Circumstantial. That's not enough to get Kim off the hook."

Rummel took a last drag off his cigarette and stubbed it out in the ashtray. "It might," he concluded, piecing it together as he went along. "Considering the fact Kim and Wintrode were together when your cousin got killed. Kim told me she got plowed and slept over at Wintrode's...and Brad was with her too for awhile. My guess is Wintrode will either deny that, or she'll give McCoy a little different accounting of the time frame."

"If Kim actually passed out," VanTighem speculated, his words carefully chosen, "Wintrode could've had a field day creating evidence, couldn't she."

"You got it," Rummel replied. "Including enough time to commit the murder in the wee hours of the morning and plant her handiwork in Kim's trunk. Like I told Sept, I don't think this was a random killing like the others. I think your cousin was forced out there, and that could've been part of the plan to start with."

"So where do we go from here?"

"First, we start by you telling me everything you found out back East. Then we take it all to your lawyer tomorrow and let him start building his defense." Rummel stopped for a few seconds, plotting. Suddenly he showed VanTighem something the writer had never before seen from him-- a mean, vindictive smile. "When I'm through, every finger that gets pointed at Kim is going to get pointed right back at that fuckin' bitch. I'm going to take her down...no matter what it costs me."

CHAPTER SEVENTEEN

The next morning VanTighem and Rummel met with Jack's attorney. They laid out the entire story for him, pieced together by what concrete information they did have. Jack had brought along the yearbooks which supported their contention that the identity of Kim Wintrode was, in actuality, that of Linda McConey. Rummel was amazed at the difference only one year could make, but he too was positive that the person in the junior year photograph was indeed Kim Wintrode. Based on their research and the credibility of both men, the attorney agreed to take the case and promised to see Joe's daughter that afternoon. Rummel was delighted and could hardly wait to break the good news to her.

VanTighem went home, and Joe headed straight for the police station where he spent nearly an hour in lockup reassuring his daughter, being careful, however, not to tell her too much. Considering the circumstances, Kim was holding up very well; her steadfast trust in her father bolstered her spirit. Finally Rummel told her he had a phone call to make that might shed some more light on her case. They said goodbye, and Joe took off for home.

Rummel was lucky. He caught Terri at work just as she was about to leave for an investigation. "Terri, this is an emergency," he explained. "I don't want to go into any details right now, but my daughter's in big trouble, and I need that information on Kim Wintrode pronto."

Terri was immediately concerned by the desperation in his voice, and a little shocked. Joe had never struck her as being a man who could become so rattled. It made her appreciate his need. "I did some digging around," she informed him, "and I found out Brad spent three days in Chicago around the middle of April. But I haven't been able to obtain a flight manifest from the airline yet to find out if she was with him."

'Eureka!' Rummel thought. "Was it business?" he hastened to ask.

"Yeah," she replied. "We sent him out there on an extradition."

"Then all we're waiting on is the manifest," Rummel said.

"I'll subpoena it if I have to," Terri assured him. "Since it's that important."

"It is," Rummel asserted. "It's damned important. Try to get it as soon as you can."

"I'll see what I can do, Joe."

"Terri, you're a champ." Rummel paused a moment, adding, "I owe you big time for this, Terri. You name it."

"How about you getting your big sexy body out here for a little free-for-all," Terri said softly over the phone.

Joe could feel himself blushing, but he was no longer feeling shy about her, which he figured was a vast improvement. "That's a date, Kid," he responded, almost shouting it. "When I get this mess straightened out, you and I are going to have a private little party and celebrate. What's the chances of you stealing your uncle's boat for a long weekend?"

"Excellent," Terri answered him. "He's been asking about you."

"Then we're on," Rummel promised her.

"I gotta go," Terri said. "I don't want to, but if I'm going to find time today to get your information, I'd better be off."

"Thanks again, Terri."

"Any time, Joe. See ya."

After he hung up, Rummel let out a little hoot and punched the air. He had a feeling about this one. Somehow he sensed this would nail Kim Wintrode right to the wall.

****

VanTighem was restless that evening. Something was troubling him, and he couldn't put his finger on it. He wandered around the cavernous rooms of his home trying to occupy himself, but nothing seemed to hold his attention for very long. He went into the kitchen with the idea of making dinner, but opted for a grilled cheese sandwich instead. He then tried to work on some notes for this next novel he would soon be starting. That lasted only fifteen minutes, and he was restless again. He flipped through the television channels and abruptly shut off the set when nothing caught his interest. Some relaxing music appeared to be a better remedy, yet that didn't last long either, and he was up again, pacing. VanTighem thought of calling Joe just to check in and see how things were going, but he decided not to bother him at a time like this when he had matters weighing so heavily on him. If Rummel wanted to talk to him, he would call.

At nine o'clock the doorbell rang. Jack figured his friend must be paying him a surprise visit, and he hurried to answer it. Opening the door, he found Kim Wintrode standing there instead. Stunned silence greeted her warm smile, and the cool reception she received quickly clouded her look. "May I come in?" she asked, her manner precise.

Hesitation gripped VanTighem. For a few long and unsettling moments, he didn't quite know what to say. The struggle within him that sought an answer to his real feelings about this woman again erupted. Obviously she was dangerous, but was she also so irresistibly appealing he would risk it all? Even his life? His heart took a little jump, and Jack experienced a flutter in his stomach. These were the warnings of deeper feelings he had known before, when common sense had also called and he had failed to listen. This night was no exception. He mustered his composure and said at last, "I'm surprised to see you here, Kim."

Without asking again to be invited in, Kim walked right past him into the foyer and turned to face him. "I needed to see you tonight," she stated. "I have to talk to you."

VanTighem closed the door. "Please," he said to her, gesturing toward the living room. "Make yourself comfortable."

"Thank you." Inspecting her environment as she walked with slow, poised steps toward the fireplace, Kim again looked up at Jack's portrait before she turned to him at the door where he still stood. She looked very professional in her two-piece navy suit with red tee and matching scarf in her breast pocket, and VanTighem suddenly felt a little self-conscious in his Levis and frayed grey sweatshirt. Kim remained businesslike. "Are you going to join me?" she asked.

Jack approached her with a forced self-assurance of his own to try to regain command of the situation. Aloofness was now his best defense. "What's the occasion, Kim?" he asked in an indifferent tone of voice.

"I expected a little better reception than this," Kim responded.

"It's been a tough past three days," VanTighem hedged.

"How was your trip?" she inquired with a smile.

"How'd you know I was on a trip?"

"I tried calling you, Jack. You left a message on your answering machine saying you'd be out of town for awhile...something about seeing your publisher." Kim paused, then added, "I didn't know your publisher was in Indianapolis."

VanTighem felt like he had just been punched in the stomach, and he knew his reaction gave him away completely. Yet this also presented an opportunity that had been farthest from his mind. Perhaps she had come here to confess, though likely not, but the least he could do was face her with honesty and hope for some of the same in return. He managed a sly grin. "How'd you know I went to Indianapolis?" he asked.

"It stands to reason," Kim flatly told him. "You and Joe have covered New Orleans, Houston and Seattle. Indianapolis is your next logical choice." Showing him a warm smile again, Kim approached him and said with a knowing look, "Besides…those are my high school annuals you have over there on the coffee table."

So much for any secrets between them, Jack thought. But what about Chicago? She didn't mention that. He needed to hear more. "I'm glad to see you're being up front with me," he commented. "I'd have been a little disappointed in you if you were not."

"I have nothing to hide," Kim told him. "Not anymore." She glanced toward the bar. "You mind if I have a drink?"

"Sure. What do you want?"

"I'll get it," Kim said as she walked to the antique liquor cabinet. She opened it and took out a bottle of vodka. "You care for anything?" she asked.

"Why not," VanTighem said. "There's a jug of Kool-Aid in the fridge underneath the bar."

"You keep mix there too?"

"Should be plenty to choose from in there," VanTighem replied.

"Thanks." Kim mixed herself a drink and poured him a glass of cherry Kool-Aid. "Where are the dogs?" she asked.

"Outside," Jack said. "I was driving them nuts pacing around, so I thought I'd give them a break and let them rest in the kennel."

Kim returned to him with a drink in each hand, and at that moment Jack remembered to observe which hand she used. She gave him his drink with her left and cupped both hands around her glass. "Shall we sit down?" she asked.

"We can do that."

Kim sat in the center of his modern, ivory colored couch, and VanTighem pulled up a matching chair to be a little closer to her without sitting next to her. She placed her drink down on the chrome and glass coffee table with her right hand, and glancing toward the yearbooks she said, "I won't bore you with the details, but those were very difficult times for me."

"I'll bet they were," Jack remarked. "I did my research."

"Yes," Kim said sadly, "I suppose you did." She looked up at him and added, "You're good at that, aren't you."

VanTighem took a drink. "I try my best," he responded in a manner that was detached, even cold.

"I'm sure you do," she said as her eyes searched his. "Just how much do you know?"

With a deep breath and a little sigh, VanTighem answered her. "I talked to your grandparents, and they gave me enough to fill in the blanks."

"They're still alive then," Kim noted. "How are they?"

"Your grandmother told me to give you their love if I ever ran across you," Jack replied.

Kim briefly lowered her eyes, then reached for her drink, again with her right hand, which was a minor relief for VanTighem. She took a sip and looked back at him. "I've always regretted that," she confessed. "They are very sweet people. We just did what we had to do."

"We?" VanTighem inquired. "You mean your brother and you?"

"That's right," Kim said.

"Whatever happened to him?"

"He left for the Army, and I lost track of him over the years."

VanTighem wanted to hear more. "When's the last time you saw him?"

"In Houston," she replied. "We spent some time together there."

"You ever get in touch with your father?" Jack ventured to ask.

Kim looked a little surprised at first, then her expression darkened. "I wrote him once and tried calling him a couple of times," she volunteered. "I'll be honest with you, Jack. I wanted to kill him, even planned to do so at one time in my life. But someone beat me to it."

Sensing he was on a roll here, VanTighem couldn't have stopped even if he had wanted to, though he could clearly see this conversation was difficult for her. He took another drink and asked, watching her face closely for any telltale signs, "Do you know who did it?"

"No," Kim said. There was a look of honesty in her eyes that was hard to deny.

With that realization, Jack paused to weigh his suspicions and then followed up. "You think it's possible your brother might have done it?" he inquired with a probing look.

Kim glanced away, hesitating. Finally her eyes returned to his, and she replied softly, "The thought has crossed my mind from time to time. He disappeared not long after it happened."

"And you haven't seen him since," VanTighem reiterated.

"Not since Houston," Kim again stated.

"That's not to say he couldn't be following you everywhere you go."

Kim looked shocked. "That'd be crazy. There's no way he wouldn't get in touch with me."

VanTighem leaned back in his chair and stared up at the ceiling for a time. He wanted to believe her, and what she said was starting to make sense. Maybe they were chasing the wrong person all this time, but that was Houston and New Orleans, not Seattle and this most recent rash of murders in Spokane and Chicago. Joe's daughter was on the hook for them, at least the ones here, and Chicago didn't look good either. He knew full well his first priority was to clear her--if she could be cleared. He was beginning to wonder.

Kim interrupted his thoughts. "I came here tonight to tell you these things myself. Everything...if you want to know."

Looking back at her, Jack said in a quiet, comforting voice, "What's past is past. Some of it's none of my business."

"You found out about my police record, then," Kim remarked. Her look clouded.

VanTighem's face revealed his understanding. "Like I said," he told her, "that's water under the bridge. I don't get uptight about skeletons people have in their closets. If you opened mine, it would look like the Roman Catacombs."

Kim knew then what she had feared all along. At some point, if she continued seeing this man, she might one day just fall in love with him. There was no place for that in her plans; not now, not ever. She had to go on with her life as it was. "I appreciate that," she told him. "You're a very kind and understanding man."

VanTighem had to chuckle. "You wouldn't have said that if you'd known me a few years back."

"I think you were always that way," Kim observed. "You just tried hard not to let it show."

"I've heard that before," Jack commented with a nod of his head. He finished his drink.

Kim stood up and walked over to him. She took his glass and said, "Here, I'll get you another. I want a refill anyway."

"Catering to my addictions, I see," VanTighem smirked.

"Yeah, some addiction," she answered him. "You're a bad one alright."

VanTighem laughed, and Kim went to the bar to prepare another round. Returning, she handed him his glass and sat back down on the couch. "I heard what happened to Kim Rummel," she noted to break the ice for a topic she knew must be troubling VanTighem. "She was with me that night it happened, you know."

"I'm aware of that," Jack said.

"Yes, I figured you would be by now," Wintrode commented. "We partied together up to one o'clock or so" she continued. "I guess I had too much to drink, and I went to bed. When I woke up the next morning, Kim was gone." She looked at VanTighem with that same undeniable sincerity in her eyes. "I had to tell them the truth, Jack. I don't see how she could have done it, and I don't believe she did. But I just don't know what time she left the apartment. That's what I had to tell them. Personally, I think she was too drunk to even drive home, but who knows." After a pause, she added, "There's no way I'd believe Kim was capable of such a thing."

"Would you testify to that in court?" VanTighem asked her.

"Of course I would," Kim said. "If it would help, you bet. But Brad tells me the evidence is stacked up pretty heavily against her. He wouldn't give me any details, but he indicated it doesn't look good."

"No, it doesn't" Jack agreed, his tone pensive.

"You don't think she did it, do you?"

VanTighem wasn't eager to answer that question. Right now he was totally confused. Finally he said, "I'm like you...I just can't believe Kim is capable of doing something like that. I've known her since she was a kid," he pointed out with a smile. "She's never given her dad any trouble, other than being headstrong and extremely independent...which in my opinion is a character quality rather than a defect. But then, I'm not her dad."

"I like her too," Kim said. "A lot."

"To be honest with you, Kim," VanTighem told her bluntly. "I thought you did it."

"I know you did," Kim replied sadly as she lowered her eyes to the drink she now clasped in her lap. Looking back at him, she added, "And I don't blame you. If I was in your shoes, and particularly Joe's, I'd have thought the same thing...considering my background and the places I've been."

"I take it you're right-handed then," VanTighem probed as he pretended to conceal his interest with a joking grin.

Kim smiled. "Always have been," she said and held up her drink in her right hand.

Jack was totally relaxed now, perhaps a bit too much so, he wondered, but he was comfortable with this woman, and in his heart he had to believe her. He only wished his gut feelings would confirm that rather than give him no indication whatsoever about her. They spoke instead of Kim Rummel, and he didn't like what he was hearing. His confusion and uneasiness about *her* involvement was clouding his mind a little, he thought. He shook it off and returned to matters regarding his guest. "I'm happy to see that, Kim," he smiled. "I've been fighting these conflicting feelings about you for days."

"You care to talk about it?" Kim inquired, curious.

Jack's look grew serious. "I don't think now's the time," he answered her. "Considering the circumstances."

"I think it is," she asserted. "That's the main reason I came over here...to talk to you about *my* feelings."

VanTighem braced himself. Either way this was going to be difficult. He took a drink and told her to go ahead.

Kim had difficulty starting, and she shifted nervously on the couch. "Brad and I have been together a long time," she began. "I've had a few other relationships, and so has he." She paused, trying to find the right words, and then she continued. "We've never let that interfere before, and

I suppose that's one of the reasons we've been together so long. We give each other the space."

"I can understand that," VanTighem allowed, nodding.

"Good. I'm glad you can because I've been experiencing feelings for you that won't let it be both ways...not anymore." After another moment of hesitation, Kim finally said, "I've spent a lot of time thinking about this, Jack. I've even talked to Kim about it. I hope you don't mind. You've got a big fan in her, you know."

VanTighem showed her a gentle smile and asked her to go on. He was feeling a little lightheaded and suddenly very hot.

"To be honest with you, Jack, I have a lot invested in Brad. I think if we continue to see each other, I'm going to forget about that investment...and I can't afford to do that. I can't risk falling in love with you, Jack." Kim stopped for a moment to gauge his reaction, which had remained stoic all this time. In his eyes she seemed to find understanding, but she sensed she had also triggered an old hurt in him that he fought to conceal. It troubled her that he didn't let the pain out now. Her look drifted downward, and she finished what she had to say. "Maybe someday I'll regret this decision. I think maybe I will." She looked him straight on again, adding, "But right now...I'm afraid to take the chance."

Jack never moved a muscle. He had taken it all in very thoughtfully, and now that it had come down to the moment for him to respond to her, he felt nothing but emptiness inside, a total void of anything except disappointment. He had learned to live with that all of his life, and at this point he was thoroughly fed up with it. He was left again with only one thing on the face of this earth. Himself. He looked down at his glass cradled listlessly in his hand, and he was reminded of something missing from his wrist. His mind wandered back to a time when he wore a bracelet on that wrist, to the many years that bracelet and alcohol had served as ironclad defenses against times like this.

VanTighem slowly stood up, and he felt his head spin a little, his knees wobble. He turned to gaze upon his defiant portrait above the fireplace, and his eyes remained fixed there for painfully long, silent moments. Then he faced Kim, and a smile gradually formed. "I was a photographer in Vietnam," he commented completely out of the blue. "A photographer and reporter. Did I ever tell you that?"

Kim's expression registered surprise over what he had just said, and she replied, "No...you didn't."

"One of the best," VanTighem said proudly. "One year military and two years civilian. I wore this Montagnard bracelet on my wrist to commemorate the first time someone took a shot at me. I wore it for over twenty years after that," Jack added softly. His stare started to drift with the memories that were beginning to return. "It protected me." He glanced around the room, seized the seconds to search for his words. "That whole time," Jack continued as his eyes again found the beautiful woman who was staring back at him, "I wanted to go back. I loved the excitement, the adrenalin rush. I loved Vietnam. I loved the war. This may sound a little strange, but I felt nothing could hurt me over there as long as I had my camera. The war was happening to all the rest of them, and I was just there to document it...to show the entire human race what fools they really were to start a war like that in the first place. I was, in my own twisted sense, above it all...and invincible."

After another pause to collect his thoughts, VanTighem said, "For more than twenty years I loved and longed for all of that again. And then one day, I found someone I loved more. It was a real shock to my system, I'll tell you," he snickered, but his expression quickly grew serious again. "That and sobriety," he noted quietly.

"One night I was lying in bed all alone, and out of the blue something inside my head said very clearly, 'Give Cindy the bracelet'." Jack smiled and remarked to Kim as an aside, "I've got this little problem with these voices inside my head telling me what to do, and I'm getting damned tired of it." His smile subsided. He took a quick drink and went on with his story. "I waited some time before I did anything about it. Parting with that bracelet was a big step for me. Cindy was leaving for a job back East, a temporary thing, but a big opportunity for her. As she was getting on the plane, I suddenly felt compelled to get rid of that bracelet, and I handed it over to her. I told her to do anything she wanted with it...throw it away if she wanted...it was hers now. She protested a bit but took it, and as I left the airport, this incredible wave of relief suddenly rushed right through me. Vietnam was gone...the war was gone. Just like that. It's never come back. And for all practical purposes...Cindy never came back either." Shaking his head, VanTighem looked around the room and commented, "Boy, it sure is getting hot in here."

"Was that the end of the relationship?" Kim asked.

"It ended after she got back," Jack told her. "We stuck it out a few months, but she got scared and had to run." VanTighem halted a bit more to let that last remark sink in. "Just before it was over," he continued, "that same voice told me to let her go. I didn't want to do that, but by then it all seemed completely out of my hands anyway. She fought with herself over it. She always wanted things both ways," Jack smirked. He hesitated, his eyes suddenly moistened, and his expression grew very sad as he said, "I just told her to go...just like I'm telling you to go."

Tears had started to appear in Kim's eyes also. She didn't want to lose him, but she feared even more what would happen if she allowed herself to give in to her emotions. "You want me to leave right now?" she asked.

VanTighem wouldn't answer her directly. He rubbed his wrist where the bracelet had been all those years, and he remarked with a bitter smile, "You know…it's amazing. One little bracelet can make an entire war go away. It's crazy. But nothing, it seems, can make the love for her go away…nothing. Not even God."

Kim stood up, crossed the room and put her arms around the man who she wanted to be with. She rested her head on his shoulder, and she inquired in a very soft and gentle voice, "May I stay…just this one last night?"

Jack's vision was growing a little fuzzy; his head was starting to spin again. He had heard that very same line before, and he had said no. VanTighem was almost tempted to tell her that, but he thought better of it. Instead, he put his arms around her and held her close to him for long, comforting moments. That driving need for her was back again in full force, as were his feelings for her, and he knew the lightheadedness he now felt came from her touch and not some mysterious ailment he had been experiencing, probably from the lack of food.

Kim laid her head back to look up into Jack's eyes, which were now filled with sadness. Her hair flowed over his hands, and he ran his fingers lightly through it. "Well?" she asked. "I don't have your answer yet."

"Why not," VanTighem replied with a brave little smile. 'What the hell could it hurt?' he said to himself.

CHAPTER EIGHTEEN

Rummel tried calling VanTighem first thing in the morning, but no answer. He figured he must be working out at the health club already, and he'd try later. His schedule that day was tight, and he was already running behind for his appointment with the lawyer. Kim was to be arraigned later that morning, an event the media had eagerly awaited, and he would be there to lend her his support, particularly in light of all the publicity, much of which he knew would be aimed at him. As he hurried out of the apartment, he hoped Jack hadn't somehow forgotten Kim's court appearance and that he would be there to provide them both his much needed presence and assurances.

The court hearing was as tough as Rummel had expected, but the media blitz afterwards was far worse than he had ever dreamed. And VanTighem never showed. McCoy was there, however, and despite the fact he hated such spectacles, he pitched right in and shouldered the brunt of the barrage, allowing his detective the opportunity to escape the press wolves. That was a favor Joe wouldn't forget, and while he was at it, he was going to have a few choice words with his best friend for ducking out on them.

After briefly visiting with Kim and her lawyer, Joe went home exhausted. He tried calling VanTighem again, but still no answer. He left a brusque message on Jack's answering machine, bitching him out for not showing up, although it was a bit halfhearted. He was beginning to worry about him. Rummel cracked a beer and flopped down on the couch. He needed a little nap, but he was too keyed up to sleep. A cold beer and his feet up on the couch were about the best he could do to relax for now. A half hour passed and another beer, and the detective was just beginning to drift off when someone rang the doorbell. Must be VanTighem, he thought, and immediately he was alert and on his feet. Rummel opened the door to find McCoy standing there.

"Joe…can I come in?" the lieutenant asked.

Something was wrong. Joe could see it written in his eyes and all over his downcast expression. "What's the matter?" he pressed. "Something happen to Kim?"

"No, Kim's fine," McCoy said slowly. He hesitated and bit his lower lip, more fiercely than usual. Finally he came out with it. "Joe…I've got some bad news. Jack's dead."

Rummel staggered back like he had been gut shot. Shock drove him speechless. He turned away from McCoy and lurched toward a living room chair to grip the back of it with both hands. His head dropped.

McCoy stepped inside the apartment and slowly approached him.

"I knew he couldn't stay away from her," Rummel gasped in a hoarse whisper. "I should have stopped him." Suddenly he shot upright, and his quick move startled McCoy. "Goddamnit!" he shouted as he pounded the back of the chair with his fist. "I should have stopped him!"

"Who you talking about?" asked McCoy.

"Wintrode!" Rummel roared as he turned to face the lieutenant. His dark eyes raged with hatred. "That fuckin' bitch Kim Wintrode!"

"Wait a minute, Joe," McCoy tried to explain. "This isn't what you think. Nobody killed Jack."

Rummel was stunned even more. "What?"

"No," McCoy went on, gesturing for calm. "Jack ran his car off the road out on North Indian Trail early this morning." He paused before finishing what he had to say. "Joe…it looks like he was drunk."

"I don't believe it!" Joe bellowed. "He'd never take another drink! Never!"

Shaking his head solemnly, McCoy told him, "The blood alcohol says otherwise, Joe. Point one four."

"Where is he now?" snapped Rummel.

"Probably still in the morgue," McCoy said.

"You order an autopsy?"

"Saw no need to. This is a clear case of DUI auto fatality."

"Order an autopsy!" Rummel demanded. "Get on the phone to Earl right now and order an autopsy! And have him put a rush on it!"

"Joe, I…"

Rummel's anger collapsed into imploring. "Please, Jim, you've got to do this. If nothing else, please do it for me."

McCoy's feelings went out to his detective's emotional pleas. With nothing to lose from it, he agreed to an autopsy and went to the phone to call Earl Calvert. In a minute, it was done. Turning to Joe, he asked, "Satisfied now?"

"Not quite," Rummel said, and he headed into the kitchen where he had left his jacket and gun. Returning, he asked McCoy, "You been over to Jack's place by any chance?"

"No," McCoy answered. "Why would I do that? I came to you as soon as I heard. He doesn't have any relatives around here."

"C'mon," Rummel said. "I've got a key. Let's go take a look and find out what really happened." Joe was already out the door before McCoy had even made up his mind to accompany him. Considering all his troubles these past forty-eight hours, the least McCoy could do now was humor him.

****

The dogs were barking in the kennel out back when the two detectives arrived at VanTighem's. Rummel let himself in, with McCoy right behind. They looked around the living room and found nothing out of the ordinary; then Rummel marched straight up to the bedroom.

An empty bottle of vodka was on the nightstand along with a glass. The bed looked like an army had bivouacked in it. On the opposite nightstand was another glass, and Joe went to inspect it. There was lipstick on the rim. She was getting bold, he thought. And why not? There was no crime in shacking up. He could just hear her story now. They went to bed, he got drunk and she left. In his despair, Jack must have taken his Mustang out to look for her or race down lonely roads late at night. Maybe he even killed himself. It all made perfect sense, particularly to those who knew the old Jack VanTighem. But Rummel wasn't buying this little scenario, not one bit. He had another picture of what had happened, and he was banking on the fact an autopsy would prove him right.

"I don't know, Joe," McCoy commented as he glanced around the room. "Looks to me like he had a party in here last night."

"I wouldn't take bets on that," Rummel growled.

"You really think he was with Brad's girlfriend?" inquired McCoy.

"I know so."

McCoy tried to be reasonable. "Don't you think they just got it on, and for some reason he decided to take off?"

"Not a chance."

"What makes you so certain?"

"Jack would never drink," Rummel flatly stated. "I know him, and that's a fact. And if he ever did, it would have been beer or whiskey, not vodka."

McCoy just shook his head in disbelief, but he would give Joe the chance to prove him wrong. "Why don't we head out and see Earl?" he suggested. "There's nothing else we can do here."

Rummel turned around and stormed out of the room.

"Where you going now?" McCoy asked, a little perturbed by this whole episode.

"I gonna take care of the dogs!" Rummel shouted. As he rampaged his way downstairs and through the living room, Joe suddenly stopped for a moment and looked around. He was wondering just where the hell Jack had stashed those high school yearbooks.

****

Alone in the coroners' office, Rummel paced like a caged tiger while he awaited the autopsy results. McCoy had business back at the department and couldn't hang around any longer. They had already run some preliminary lab tests that they should be ready by now. Ten more minutes passed before Early Calvert entered his office. "Joe," he said, "I'm really sorry about your buddy. I didn't know the guy, but I've heard he was one of the last great mavericks."

"Thanks, Earl," Rummel replied solemnly. "You two would have hit it off. What'd you find?"

"Well, the initial blood alcohol indicates Jack was drunk as a lord. He'd been out there a couple hours before they found him, and even then he was way over the limit. But that ain't all."

"What else?" Joe quickly asked.

Calvert peered over his glasses. "To start with," the pathologist explained, "he had taken a pretty healthy dose of barbiturates, and of all things…acid."

"LSD?"

"Yup. And some traces of amphetamines too. A real nasty mixture of uppers and downers"

"Were the barbiturates enough to knock him out?" Rummel inquired.

"Hard telling in those combinations. I can tell you this, though. He was so fucked up he didn't know the difference between topside and the bottom of the sea. This was the best one man party I've seen in years."

"He wasn't alone."

"Well, whoever was with him, I sure as hell hope they didn't try drive home."

"Trust me," Rummel said. "I'm sure she was fully capable." He thought for a moment and added, "But if that was the case with Jack, how do you suppose he drove?"

"Beats the hell out of me," Calvert responded. "I know I couldn't have. But I've written in the report cause of death was an auto fatality. He had a broken neck, head trauma and some internal injuries. No seatbelt and thrown from the car according to the accident investigation. There was no need to do a full autopsy, but you ordered it, so that's what we're doing."

"I think you've given me everything I need to know," Rummel told the coroner. In his own mind, that *was* all he needed to know. From here on, he'd take care of the rest himself. No one else, just him. The time had come to break a few laws, even pay Kim Wintrode a personal visit. Joe thanked Calvert and asked him to provide McCoy a complete report when he had it all put together, no rush, not right away. Looking a little skeptical, Calvert nevertheless agreed.

Then Rummel left. He had much to do before this day was finished. Although he didn't exactly know how he was going to go about it yet, he'd come up with something, play it by ear as he went along. But one thing was clear in his mind. One way or the other, he was going after her.

****

It was nearing four o'clock by the time Rummel arrived back at his apartment. He went immediately to his cramped storage space in the back entryway and started to tear through the file cabinet drawers where he thought he had stashed a breaking and entering kit he hadn't used since Chicago days. Finding it hidden in a pantry instead, he packed it all into an attaché case and quickly changed into his best suit, with a tie even, to upgrade his appearance.

On his way out, Joe suddenly remembered he should call VanTighem's attorney and inform him about what had happened. He felt a responsibility to do just that, but he was in a hurry, and for the moment he didn't want to face the complications brought about by Jack's death. It was probably all over the news anyway. Rummel had already made up his mind to cash in part of his pension to help pay for Kim's defense, but that was a practical matter, like helping to make arrangements for Jack's funeral. Right now there wasn't time to deal with such things. With luck, he would soon resolve the issue of Kim's defense on his own.

Wintrode lived in a luxury apartment complex located in Fairwood, not far from Jack's house and also not far from where he had been killed. It had a central garden and private underground parking but nothing in the line of extra security other than the standard spread of surveillance cameras, which made Rummel grateful. Still, it would be risky. By the time he arrived there, it was close to five o'clock, giving him less than an hour to search her apartment, maybe much less, and in fact she could show up at any time. If so, they'd have their meeting sooner rather than later. Pretending to be there on legitimate business, he strolled through the courtyard and straight into the lobby like he owned the place and took the elevator to the fourth and top floor where she lived. Joe knew right where he was going. Kim had left the address posted on their message board in the kitchen. When he found the right apartment, he went to work on the lock. It was a piece of cake, which surprised the detective since he'd figured he had probably lost his touch over these relatively straight-laced years working in Spokane.

Once inside, Rummel knew he had to move fast. The apartment was large, airy and, fortunately, sparsely furnished. He systematically checked the layout of all the rooms first, then started with the kitchen. Joe rummaged through every drawer and cupboard space, not forgetting the refrigerator, and especially the freezer where he hoped, with squeamish reservations, he would find the missing parts of the other victims. Nothing, not even a hint of incriminating evidence.

Next, he examined the living room. He looked under the sofa, pulled away the cushions, and he thoroughly searched her desk and computer work station in the elevated library portion that afforded a picture window view of the downtown area. Rummel also went through the bookshelf there very carefully, hoping to perhaps find those high school annuals that might have been taken from Jack's house. Nothing.

The bedrooms were next. The detective scrounged through her dresser drawers, searched the closets in both bedrooms, looked under the beds, under the mattresses, behind curtains, everywhere, but all he derived from his efforts was the conclusion the woman was very fastidious, a little Spartan in her furnishings and very extravagant in her wardrobe. Except no western wear, save an obligatory pair of blue jeans.

Rummel's last stop was the bathroom. One of the items he was intent on finding was a box of latex gloves, and the bathroom would be the most likely place for that. The bathroom, it turned out, was also the most time consuming. It was more than ample in size, and Wintrode had it stuffed with every cosmetic and feminine hygiene product imaginable. But no gloves and no prescriptions for barbiturates. In fact, she must have been as healthy as a horse because a bottle of Tylenol was about the most powerful drug he could find.

Frustrated, Rummel went through the apartment one more time quickly, this time checking the utility and hallway closets for anything. He even looked behind her numerous paintings, careful to straighten each one out before he went on to the next one. He found nothing.

Joe took one last look around, hoping to spot something he had overlooked. It was already past five-thirty, and time was against him. He could think of nothing he hadn't already covered. The woman was squeaky clean, and that angered him very much.

The detective now had some hard choices to make. He could wait around for Kim to come home and confront her, but he realized that would do him little good and probably a lot more harm. His presence here was not official police business. Besides, what would he confront her with? Her real identity of which he now had no proof? Rummel decided he would come back later, after dark, hopefully for the chance to go through her car in the parking stall. Then, if he found nothing, he would go to her under the pretense he needed her help to clear his daughter. He would also tell her about VanTighem's death. Between the two subjects, she might make a mistake, say something that would give him a clue, or the excuse to beat the truth out of her if he had to.

For the next hour, Joe wandered the streets of downtown Spokane to think before he settled down at Flaherty's for a couple of beers just to calm his shattered nerves. Not wanting to drink too much, he finally ended up on a bench in Riverfront Park where he watched the joggers pass by and the crowds of people who gathered there for that beautiful summer evening. He marked time by the setting sun and the steady parade of visions that marched through his mind. The thought of Kim in that jail cell tore him apart inside, yet the memories of his best friend hurt even more. He saw the faces of the victims, and he remembered that afternoon he had first met Kim Wintrode at Brad's for dinner. Recalling his first impressions of her, how much he had liked her, Rummel wanted now to rip those images from his brain and crush them underfoot, just like he wanted to crush her skull. Somehow she had killed Jack. There was no doubt about that in his mind whatsoever. But how could he prove it? When he discovered the answer to that question, then he would also be able to free Kim and avenge his best friend.

Terri came to mind, his only pleasant thought of the past two days. When this was over Rummel promised himself he would go to her, let his defenses down and allow fate to play its hand. But even the memories of Terri brought him back to the cruel reality of the moment. She had not yet contacted him about that flight manifest which he knew would place Kim Wintrode in Chicago. Right now he desperately needed that; he needed anything he could get his hands on to pin that woman down once and for all.

A red fireball sank out of sight in the West leaving an orange sky swept with the brush strokes of purple clouds. Realizing he couldn't stay there forever to mull over his dilemma, Rummel decided to go home for awhile and maybe make that phone call to VanTighem's attorney after all. As he stood up and stretched his exhausted body, he was suddenly stricken by another thought. The dogs. There was no one at Jack's to look after the dogs. They should at least be fed and watered. With quickness in his step, Joe headed for his car to do just that.

****

Rummel turned on the foyer lights and surveyed the big empty living room filled with ominous shadows. It was deathly still in there, and without his friend around, the house appeared cavernous and cold. He flicked on the living room lights and began to relive memories as he slowly walked toward the kitchen where Jack kept the dog food. With a plastic bucket filled with dry food from the sack in the pantry, Joe went out the back door to the kennel. The last vestiges of sunset sneaked through the serene branches of some weeping willows in the backyard. Overhead, the sky was turning indigo to reveal its treasure of stars.

"Hey, Woody, Bridgette," called Rummel. "How you guys doing?" The two Brittanies stood on their hind legs against the hard chain-link kennel fence, their friendly barks and innocent enthusiasm welcoming their old hunting buddy. "Okay, you two," Rummel announced, "it's chow time." He opened the gate, entered and filled the bowls in front of their individual houses. The spaniels bounced around him with the exuberance of pent-up energy, and Joe decided to allow them to run in the fenced quarter acre backyard for awhile. They chased each other across the lawn for a minute or so, but quickly opted to follow their old friend around as he dragged the garden hose to their kennel and filled their water bowls. When he was finished, Rummel wandered over to the stonework patio and sat down on the steps to watch after them while they ate and exercised. He needed the rest anyway.

As if sensing something was wrong, both hunting dogs chose to ignore their food for the time being, and they joined Joe instead. With their heavy heads resting on his thighs, they stared up at him with sad faces that seemed to plead for an explanation. Rummel wondered as he petted them both how he could reassure them when he too was lost for an answer. "Well, you guys," he sighed, "it looks like it's just the three of us now." Tears started to fill the detective's eyes when the gravity of that truth finally struck him fully. He took a deep breath and continued talking to the dogs and an empty night. "I don't know what I'm going to do with you kids. My place is too small, and they don't allow pooches there." Joe looked into their attentive faces. He could almost believe they understood every word he said. "I know this banker who'd commit armed robbery to have a pair like you two. What do you think about that? Would you like to live with a banker? You'd have a respectable home for a change. You wouldn't be associated with some goofy writer who hears voices. It'd do wonders for your reputations." Rummel paused, chucking to himself over a thought that had just occurred to him. "Just think of the career opportunities. Hell, I know of this opening coming up real soon for a bank vice-president."

Joe had their undivided attention. "Nah," he drawled, "we'll figure out some way to stay together. I'm the only friend you guys got now." Suddenly his tears became unleashed and raced down his cheeks. But he went on, even though the words were beginning to catch in his throat, and he was choking on his emotions. "We gotta stick together and do right by your old buddy. Won't be long now, and we'll be out there again after those birds. He'll be expecting us to bag a few extras for him." Sniffing back his runny nose and trying to catch his breath, Joe momentarily pulled his hand away from Woody to rub his eyes and brush away his tears. "We need each other more than ever now," he added in a soft, broken voice.

He looked up at the night sky and the sweep of stars. "It's a good thing your dad got religion after all those years," Joe told the dogs after a long pause. "Someday you guys can all be together again. Jack would like that. I just hope the Good Lord can forgive him for that fuckup of his at the end. I'm sure He will. I'm not sure I ever will...but what the hell do I count? I'm just a dumb cop who likes dogs better than people."

Rummel struggled to his feet, every bone and muscle in his body aching with fatigue, and he said, "Well, kids...I guess we'd better get you back. I've got some business to attend to." Both Brittanies jumped up on him, one on each side, and Joe petted them one last time, saying as he looked up again at the vast night sky, "You look after him now...okay? We're gonna miss him down here." The tears again fell freely from his eyes, and he just let them run.

Rummel stormed into the house after putting the dogs back in their kennel. His grief had given way to rage, and his rage had left him trembling and in desperate need of a drink. He tore open the door of the refrigerator beneath the bar and yanked out a bottle of Miller, popped the cap and threw it to the floor. Then he barreled his way across the living room to the fireplace and glared up at VanTighem's portrait, vowing to them both he'd have their revenge. Joe was shaking violently all over. His head and insides screamed for a cold beer to calm him down. He raised the bottle to his mouth and glanced up again at his best friend. Something gripped his wrist and held his arm motionless, the bottle still at his lips. Rummel froze, and suddenly he remembered VanTighem's words that night they had been fishing. Jack had said how easy it would be to make the hurt go away. All he had to do was take a drink. But he couldn't. And now, for some inexplicable reason, Joe couldn't either. He had to face the hurt, no matter what it cost him, just like Jack had done. It seemed forever he stood there paralyzed with his eyes locked on that bottle in front of his face. There was no miraculous calm within him, no divinely inspired warmth from this sudden revelation, just burning hatred for the person who had caused all of this to happen and now for that beer he held before him also. A new wave of tears returned in force and clouded his vision. Free from mysterious restraint now, his hand slowly lowered. Then, out of a sudden burst of anger and frustration, Rummel cut loose. With a huge roar and all of his weight behind it, he smashed his beer against the fireplace in an explosion of spray and glass, and he yelled at the top of his lungs, *"I'm going to kill that fucking cunt!"*

****

Blind fury carried Rummel on its wings straight back to Kim Wintrode's apartment building. He drove directly into the underground garage, found her blue BMW, distinguished by its personalized plate INVEST, and parked behind it to block its path. Joe snatched his attaché case off the passenger seat, climbed out of his truck and walked right up to her car without a care who saw him. His hands were trembling and fought his ability to pop the lock with his slim-jim. After only a halfhearted attempt, Rummel gave up, went back to his pickup and tossed his attaché case inside. Reaching behind the seat into the storage compartment, he pulled out a tire iron and returned to Kim's BMW. Without a second's hesitation, Joe smashed out the driver's window with a quick series of fierce blows that were accompanied by the instant, repetitive blast of the car alarm, and he stuck his hand through the broken glass to open the door. He then pulled the hood release and went around front to open it. With another series of hard shots from the tire iron, he struck the negative post on the battery and reefed the cable off with the lug wrench. The detective carried a Maglite in his breast pocket, and he used it now to search Wintrode's car.

The commotion he had caused brought a few curious spectators down to the basement, and one of them called out, "Hey, man, what the hell you doing?"

Ignoring him, Rummel continued his search.

The same bystander who had spoken found the courage to approach the car, and this time he threatened, "You'd better knock it off, or we're gonna call the cops!"

By now Rummel was finished with the interior of the BMW. He had checked the glove box, console, under the dash and seats, visors, and he had even yanked the backseat out enough to run his hand along the seam there. He backed out, went to the trunk and with a vicious thrust, he plunged the pry bar end straight into the metal just below the lock. He began to reef on it with a vengeance.

"That's it!" the bystander shouted. "I'm calling the cops!"

Joe stopped for a moment and glared at the man, then marched right up to him. He reached into his pocket for his identification, stuck his badge squarely in the man's face and snarled, "I *am* the cops!" Intimidated and shocked, the man staggered backwards several steps, and Rummel went back to work. With one beefy heave, he sprung the truck lid open. Satisfied after a minute or so of inspection there was nothing of consequence in the trunk, Rummel tossed the tire iron back into his truck and ran up the stairs to the main entrance of the apartment building. He had his badge out again to ward off anyone else who thought they might play good citizen and try to stop him.

Joe pounded on Kim's door several times, rang the doorbell and banged again. He waited. After he rang the bell again, he put his ear to the door to catch any signs of activity inside. No sounds. He knew she wasn't the type of person to hide from him anyway, and he concluded she must be at Brad's. If her car was here, he must have picked her up.

Rushing back down to the basement garage, Rummel barged through a crowd of a half dozen or so people who had gathered to check out the ruckus, and he climbed into his pickup as if nothing had ever happened. His tires squealed as the detective backed up into the driveway, spun around and raced off.

****

By the time he arrived at Curtis's apartment all the way across town, Joe had calmed down a little and regained some of his wits about him. He pulled up slowly across the street, killed his lights and shut off the engine. For a minute or so, he scanned the units in the building and the surrounding neighborhood. The lights were out in Brad's place; his car wasn't parked on the street. It could be in the attached garage, Rummel speculated, but why no lights on? This time he would take some precautions.

He climbed out of his truck and walked around back to the small guest parking lot to see if the white Chrysler convertible was there. It was gone. Returning to the walkway leading to Brad's apartment, Rummel decided to take a chance on the door first before using his kit. He looked around one more time, cautiously walked up to the entry and tried the door. It was unlocked. Joe pulled out his flashlight and quietly entered, closing the door gently behind him.

Soft moonlight spread into the living room like melted butter and outlined clearly most of the furnishings in the shadows, enough to allow Joe to wander through without the use of his flashlight. It suddenly dawned on Rummel he didn't know what he was looking for here. He had come for Brad's girlfriend, not to search his partner's apartment, but while he was here his natural curiosity tugged at him to take a look around. Passing through the open dining area and then the kitchen, he stuck his head around the corner just to make certain he was alone before he began to grope his way into the hallway, which was unchartered territory for him. As his eyes became accustomed to the darkness, he thought he could make out three rooms, probably a bathroom and two bedrooms from the looks of it. Rummel took soft, calculated steps toward them.

When he peered around the corner into the bathroom, Joe flicked on his flashlight. The beam searched all around from ceiling to floor, coming to rest on a large medicine cabinet trimmed in oak. He could justify the discovery of latex gloves here, but he also wanted to take a look at the pharmaceuticals. He entered the bathroom, then stopped dead in his tracks. His light switched to the shower curtain. A victim of the movie *Psycho* since his youth, Joe approached the shower on his tiptoes, stood back and nudged the curtain aside with the end of his Maglite. He let out a sigh of relief and went straight to the medicine cabinet. His light scanned the labels. Now here was a drug collection if ever there was one, he thought. Some he recognized, some he didn't, but it was more than enough to spurn his interest further.

Rummel stepped back into the hallway, looked toward the entry to the kitchen and dining area where there was a set of patio doors. There was enough outside light coming through those doors and the kitchen windows to creep into the hallway and familiarize him again with the layout in that direction. He turned around to follow his flashlight the rest of the way into the bedrooms.

The first bedroom on the left appeared to be the guest room. It was furnished, though sparsely. Rummel's flashlight sought out the closet, and again he stood aside as he cracked open the doors. It was relatively empty except for the standard issue of police uniforms and an old Army uniform. When his light fell upon the lapels, he noted the crossed pistol insignia of military police. Satisfied there was nothing here, he left to make his last stop down the hallway, the master bedroom.

It was spacious and, like the rest of the apartment, very tidy, not an item out of place. One of the dressers displayed an 8x10 photograph of Brad and Kim together in some idyllic setting with an ocean or large lake in the background. Surrounding it were at least a dozen other photos, all of Kim taken in various locales. His flashlight swept over the brass bed stand and king size bed, neatly made up with a flowered comforter over it, and landed on a large portrait of Kim hanging on the wall, this one being of topflight studio model quality. Joe couldn't help but think she should have been a fashion model. She could have made it in any market, and he definitely understood how she had commanded such fees as a teenage hooker. That, he figured, was probably how she had launched her career in the first place.

Checking out the double closet, Rummel opened the left door first. There appeared to be nothing out of the ordinary. The cowboy boots were there, but that meant nothing in this country. He opened the right door, gradually, cautiously. The narrow flashlight beam started marching right down the row of garments one by one, and Joe's jaw dropped open. "Shit," he whispered. Then he said to himself, 'She must be moving in here.' A woman's wardrobe filled the entire side of the closet.

He turned away and quickly went to the nearest dresser and rummaged through its drawers. They were filled with Brad's clothes, so he shifted to the other dresser on which the photographs were displayed. The drawers were stuffed with women's wear--panties, hose, slips, tees, the works. Suddenly the pharmacy in the bathroom took on a whole new meaning and explained why Kim's medicine cabinet had been as pure as a Christian bookstore. Rummel began to wonder what else she had stashed around here.

As he retraced his steps down the hallway, Joe was driven by the haunting fear he had experienced earlier in Kim's apartment. The freezer. He went to the kitchen, shined his light on the refrigerator and started to open the freezer compartment.

A car pulled up in the parking lot out back. He could hear it, and there was a brief shot of refracted headlights that sliced through the kitchen window. Gently closing the freezer, Rummel cut his flashlight and edged his way back toward the living room, along the dividing counter to the patio doors where he could catch a glimpse of the parking lot below.

Standing off to one side to blend in with the open drapes, he watched for someone to come up the back way. Rummel heard a car door slam. He waited, his heart starting to pound, the palms of his hands growing sweaty. For the first time all day, Joe reached under his jacket for his gun and cautiously drew it, fearful any quick movement might be detected from outside. The seconds ticked by with a throb, throb, throb in his chest and a ringing in his ears from the stillness all around him. His throat was dry, and he had to swallow hard. If it was just her, he was going to go for broke. If it was Brad or both of them, he didn't know what he would do, but he had the gun, and he had the vengeance burning in his soul. One way or the other, someone was going to talk. A sweat broke out across his forehead. His eyes watered as he searched the darkness.

Behind him, a woman's form stepped out of the shadows in the living room and stood silhouetted against the picture window, a single street light and a full moon providing her backdrop.

Rummel listened hard. He thought he heard footsteps through the glass doors of someone coming up the sidewalk below the patio deck. He slipped away from the doors and with his eyes still fixed outside, he took some steps backwards through the dining area and into the living room. A sudden chill raced up his spine, a warning cops learn to heed. Rummel whirled around.

She was right in his face. Her smile flashed in the pale light that perfectly outlined her dark figure. That same light betrayed the glint of a knife blade Rummel suddenly saw coming for him.

Instinct threw the detective's arm across his throat, and the blade ripped his forearm full length. Shock and pain tore the gun from his hand as it sailed over his left shoulder into the dining room. Rummel jumped back just in time to avoid a thrust to his midsection, but he didn't move far and fast enough, and the knife slashed over his ribcage. Staggering backwards, he tripped over his own feet, lost his balance and crashed into the dining room table. Fear forced him to keep scrambling, and he rolled to one side the same instant his attacker came down on him. The knife stabbed the table top with an ominous thud, just inches away. She let out a groan as the edge of the table caught her in the midsection, and Rummel jumped to his feet only to hit the right side of his face on the corner of the dining room hutch. Dazed, he made it a few steps forward, spun around and dropped to his knees. His hands instinctively searched the floor for his gun.

Joe managed to look up. She had straightened up, retrieved the knife and was now standing by the table glaring down at him. A foreboding blue luminescence filled the room from the outside light that filtered through the patio doors and living room window, capturing her in between. Her face was still streaked with shadows and heavy wisps of long, disheveled hair. She was breathing heavily, resting for a few moments before she came after him again. Rummel's good hand frantically swept the floor in search of his gun, his own gasps for breath drowning out any sounds his rustling fingers might make.

This brief timeout gave him the vital seconds he needed to evaluate the situation. She was wearing a tight fitting dress, which was to his advantage. Huddled over, he was at least better protected from a fatal stab wound. To her left was the corner of the kitchen dividing counter. If he timed it just right, had the courage to wait this out and make her come to him, he might be able to spring up and tackle her, hopefully force her into the edge of that counter. It meant waiting to the very last instant and giving it all the strength he had left. Joe felt the warm, sticky dampness that saturated the side of his shirt. His right arm burned, and his hand was growing numb. Luck had not been with him to find his gun. Any moves he might make to look for it further would put him off balance and jeopardize this last chance he might have. All he could do now was wait.

Her heavy breathing subsided and drifted into silence, a controlled, intentional silence Rummel knew was aimed at unnerving him and forcing him into a stupid move. In an attempt to level himself out a little also, he took a deep breath and let it out slowly. She took a couple of steps forward. Joe didn't move. His heart hammered at his chest, screamed at him to get the hell out of there, but he just froze and fought all those fears that raced from his brain to every part of his body urging him to run and protect himself. He braced himself for what would come next.

She took another step, then stopped. Rummel slowly rocked back on his haunches, trying not to telegraph his intentions. His eyes remained locked on hers. They burned with his hatred through the darkness. They waited patiently for her to make a move, any move, even the slightest twitch that might signal her attack. Although he was still unable to see her face clearly through all that hair, Rummel sensed her inner being completely as if she had become a part of him after all this time he had spent hunting her down. Mustering every last fragment of his courage, he flashed that big grin of his to taunt her into making the first move.

She was on him in a second, and Rummel charged off the floor with every shred of strength he had left, grabbing her around the middle with such ferocity her knife hand flew backward rather than forward. Putting his full weight behind it, he bulled her into the dividing counter. The crash of their bodies there was explosive, but the struggle had forced a slight miscalculation, and he had missed slamming her squarely into the corner of the counter. She bounced off to the left into the dining room, and Rummel rolled to his right toward the kitchen.

Despite the fact he was badly hurt, Joe knew he had to move now if he was ever going to move at all. Staggering to his feet, he pushed himself further into the kitchen where he would find a knife of his own. Fear told him to turn around instead, head for the front door and try to escape, but rage ruled him now.

He almost made it to a rack of knives on the kitchen counter.

She came out of the opposite direction, from behind a dividing wall that separated the living room, out of the darkness of the hallway. In an instant she was on him and plunged her knife high into his chest when Joe spun around to confront her. Shock and searing pain blasted the detective's eyes wide open to stare right into her deranged face. She jerked the knife back out, and Rummel stumbled backwards to lean against the kitchen sink. With his arms dangling helplessly by his sides, he just stood there a moment gazing at her shadowy figure and wondering how he could have let this happen to him. He had always believed it would be the other way around, that he would kill her, not her killing him. Joe's head started to spin, his vision blurred, his legs buckled. He dropped to his knees.

Like a cat she paced slowly toward him, then stopped in front of him and glared down at her defeated victim. The subtle light in the room caught her smile again. Rummel couldn't take his eyes off that smile. He knew it would be the last thing he ever saw.

She quickly stepped to one side, grabbed a handful of his hair to twist his head around and laid her knife at his throat. Only a desperate instinct for survival and a still smoldering hatred gave him the strength to move his injured arm and grasp her wrist just as the knife point cut into him. She was strong, stronger than him by now, and the knife slowly began to dig into his flesh and creep its way across his throat.

Strange things go through a dying man's mind. Rummel suddenly realized he was holding her left wrist in his hand. He had been right all along. She was left-handed.

A sharp explosion, an ear shattering crack and a flash filled the darkness. Her wrist went limp. The knife dropped to the floor. She keeled over sideways, pulling Rummel over with her, his head now cradled in her arm.

A light came on that blinded the detective for a moment. Lifting his head a little, he tried to focus his eyes on the person who stood at the entry to the dining room. He couldn't make any sense of it. That couldn't be right. What he was seeing wasn't right. It was impossible. Kim Wintrode was standing there with outstretched hands holding a smoking .357 magnum. "He was my brother," was all she said.

Rummel's head flopped back down. He pushed himself away a little, over the arm underneath him, and turned to take a look at the face. The bullet had blown away the backside of his assailant's head and knocked the wig off center. Rummel still swore it was a woman, but behind the makeup the features began to form in his mind, as impossible as they seemed. The shape of the mouth, the nose, all of it came together, and gradually Brad's face appeared.

CHAPTER NINETEEN

McCoy was the first person in the hospital room when Rummel was finally taken out of ICU. Joe was still weak and groggy. His body felt like it had been used for target practice on a live hand grenade range. He had no idea how many hours or days he had been out.

"Welcome back to the living, Joe," McCoy beamed.

"How…how long's it been?" the detective asked weakly.

"This is your fourth day after surgery," McCoy told him. "For awhile we thought we might lose you."

"Nah," Joe said softly, "I wouldn't miss my retirement over a little thing like this."

McCoy laughed and announced, "Hey, you mean son of a bitch, I've got someone here to see you."

"Huh? Who?"

Without further explanation, the lieutenant went to the door, opened it, and Kim walked in. She rushed to her father's bedside with tears streaming down her cheeks and threw her arms around his neck exclaiming, "Pops! You scared the hell out of me! I was worried sick about you!"

"Ouch…Oooo!" Rummel cried out from the weight of her on his chest, but he wouldn't let go of her with his one good arm no matter how much pain her affection caused him.

Kim jumped back. "Sorry, Pops. Did I hurt you?"

Rummel smiled. "Maybe I'm just not as tough as I used to be, Kitten," he remarked. "It doesn't hurt anymore. Come here." Joe held out his hand and wrapped his arm around the back of her head to pull her cheek next to his. His tears mingled with hers now, and he said to her, "I love you, Kitten. Seeing you here makes it all worth it."

McCoy approached, and when Kim stood up straight again, he placed his hand on her shoulder saying, "I'm returning this wildcat to you, Joe. We can't afford to feed her anymore."

Rummel started to laugh, coughed instead and grabbed for his chest. "What makes you think I can?" he finally managed to ask.

Kim glowered at them both. "You guys think this is so damned funny. I've been rotting in that damned jail cell, and my dad almost got himself killed, and all you two can do is make stupid jokes." She couldn't help but crack a smile though, despite the fact she was a little put off. She concluded her mock tirade when she huffed, "That does it. I'm finished with men."

"That's my cue to leave," McCoy chuckled. "This is mild, Joe…compared to what she's said to me these past few days."

"I can imagine," Rummel grinned. "That's my girl."

"I'm sure you two have plenty of catching up to do," McCoy said. "You take care of yourself, you hear? I still have a few good months to get out of you." He started for the door, reached for the handle but turned around with an afterthought. "Oh, by the way, Joe…I have them at my house now."

A puzzled look swept Rummel's face. "Huh? What are you talking about?"

"The dogs. I'm looking after VanTighem's dogs until you get on your feet."

"How the hell did you know about that?"

"When they first brought you in," McCoy explained, "I came right to the hospital. You were out of your head, mumbling something or other about who was going to take care of the dogs. Then I remembered when you went out to feed VanTighem's dogs." The lieutenant paused a moment, smiled broadly and added, "I take back everything I said about him. Anyone who can raise dogs like those two is alright in my book. You'd better damned well get on your feet soon, or you ain't gonna get those two pooches back."

"Thanks, Jim," Rummel said softly.

"No problem," McCoy replied. "After all the bullshit I've put you through, it's my pleasure. Anything you need, you just holler."

Rummel thanked him again, and McCoy left the room.

Kim gave her father a long, solemn look. "I was just sick when I heard about Jack," she told him.

Joe showed her a gentle smile. "It's okay, Kitten. I'm sure he's off in some other world now coming up with all kinds of schemes. For the oddest reason, I have this weird feeling he'll be back some day."

The tears again filled her eyes, and Kim grabbed her father's hand saying, "I'm sorry for all the trouble I've caused you, Pops. I somehow feel responsible for this."

Squeezing her hand hard, Rummel replied, "Huh? I don't recall any trouble."

Kim found laughter amid her tears. "I love you, Daddy," she cried. "I'm so glad this is all over."

Rummel held her head close to his again, his eyes fixed on the ceiling, his thoughts telling him this wasn't quite over yet.

****

A week later Joe was home and doing well. Although he had lost much of the feeling in his right arm, he exercised it constantly, and bit by bit his strength in it was coming back.

Kim Wintrode had been very cooperative providing information about her deranged brother. She had freely admitted she had harbored her own doubts about his sanity, but categorically denied any knowledge of the murders or Brad's involvement in them. She was, after all, credited with saving Rummel's life which more than overshadowed any suspicions McCoy or the district attorney's office may have had about her. The grizzly evidence the police had found in Curtis's freezer capped off their case. No one could figure out the connection to an ancient, dried up rose in a plastic bag also in there.

Wintrode also testified on behalf of Kim, telling the police that the night the three of them had been together, Brad had returned to her apartment about five in the morning. Kim had, in fact, passed out on the couch, and that could have given him ample opportunity to apply her fingerprints to the knife. She also told them Kim had complained about losing a button off her blouse earlier in the evening. Brad must have popped it loose while they were dancing, she speculated. Due to the closeness of their relationship with Kim, hairs from her head would have been no problem to collect. Wintrode claimed she had gone to bed after Kim had passed out, and when Brad had returned, he had inadvertently awakened her. She remembered it had been shortly after five a.m. because she had glanced at the clock. Her only crime, as far as the police could see, was initially lying about the time frames. Considering her subsequent actions and cooperation, plus the fact Brad was her brother and it was understandable she would try to protect him, the authorities decided not to pursue the matter. Her testimony tied it all neatly together, and McCoy took great pleasure in informing Joe his daughter was officially and completely exonerated. The case was closed. No one in City Hall or the police department ever wanted to hear about it again. One of Spokane's finest had caused them enough grief already. No one, except Rummel.

****

Kim had her car packed and was ready to leave for the long trip back to Chicago.

She and her father had talked it all over shortly after Joe had arrived home from the hospital. It was a decision she had found very difficult to make, but Rummel had encouraged her to return to school and start a life of her own.

That decision still hurt him but it was time, and soon there would be nothing left for her in Spokane anyway. Joe was toying with the idea of moving to Seattle if he could ever swing it. Kim was very pleased her father had found a romantic interest in his life, and she encouraged the move.

For her, the difficulty stemmed from the feeling she didn't belong to either place anymore. Spokane had left her with so many troubled memories she felt she could never be comfortable there again. Chicago was just a means to her end, a degree. The truth was deeper than that, however. The two cities represented the separate lives of her parents, not her life. She still felt unwanted by her mother in Chicago, and now her father was gently nudging her out of the nest also. As frightening as it was for her, Kim had already made up her mind to make the best of it and find that niche she could call her own. In the meantime, she vowed to herself she would attempt reconciliation with her mother and perhaps even establish a common understanding between them. If she could accomplish that, then she figured her life would be a success up to that point. It would also help offset the fading ties to her father she sensed would one day come.

Standing by her car on that late August morning, they said their goodbyes. From the looks of it, the summer heat wave had finally passed. There was even the hint of fall in the crisp, clear air. Rummel was trying his best to be strong and keep from being choked up, but he wasn't being very successful at it. He knew in his heart this was much more than just the end of another summer vacation for them both. His little girl was going out on her own now, and it would never quite be the same again.

Kim stuffed her overnight bag into the already cramped car and turned to her father with tearful eyes, saying, "Well, Pops...I guess I'm ready to go."

"You drive carefully now, Kitten," Rummel instructed her in his best fatherly manner, "and don't stack that stuff up so high you can't see out the windows."

"I won't," Kim promised him. A prolonged and painful silence followed. She didn't want to leave him. It wasn't right. He wasn't completely healed; in fact, his arm had just come out of a sling. He needed her. All those reasons she had already argued over with herself dozens of times before. Also--she was afraid to go. These thoughts stifled the words in her throat which was tight and dry, and she had to swallow hard before she could continue. "I'm going to miss you, Daddy."

"I'm going to miss you too, Kitten," Joe replied in a quiet voice.

Kim tried to delay the inevitable. "Think you'll be out in Seattle by the time I graduate?" she asked.

"Maybe," Rummel told her. "I know one thing…I'll be *in* Chicago *when* you graduate."

"Promise?"

"That's a promise."

"Well, I guess I'd better get my butt in gear and graduate then," Kim said, forcing a smile.

Her father smiled too. "Good idea," he agreed. He didn't want to drag this out any longer than he had to. If he did, he might just try to keep her there with him, and that would do neither of them any good. They both had their plans now, and they both had to stick by them. "You take care, Kitten," Joe said, his voice cracking. "Just remember, your old man loves you a whole helluva lot, and he's just a phone call away."

"I love you too, Daddy," Kim replied. She was crying openly now. She threw her arms around his neck and said again, "I really do love you."

As he hugged his daughter tightly, Joe had a gut feeling it may never quite be like this again so make the best of it. They held each other for a very long time, until finally Rummel forced himself to back off a bit and hold Kim at arm's length. "You've got a long drive ahead of you, Kitten, so it's best you be going." He snorted his runny nose and wiped it with the back of his hand.

Kim's smile glowed out of her tears. "What a guy," she remarked.

As he gently turned her around, Rummel did something he had not done since she was a kid. He slapped her on the butt and said, "Get…before your old man breaks down like a blubbering idiot."

"Okay, I can take a hint," Kim laughed. She trotted around the car to the driver's side and blew him a kiss over the roof.

"You call me as soon as you get to Chicago," Joe reminded her.

"I will."

"Call me collect from a payphone tonight."

"I will."

"And you drive carefully."

"I will."

Their eyes locked, and their smiles grew sad. "I want you to have the best damned life you can ever have," Joe said to her in a quivering voice.

Kim hesitated and then answered, "I will. You too."

"Count on it, Kitten."

"Love you."

"Love you too."

Kim climbed into her car and slowly drove away. As she tried to look back behind all that luggage and wave goodbye at the same time, she almost ran off the road. Rummel cringed, shook his head incredulously and waved back. When she was out of sight, he lowered his aching arm and walked slowly back to his apartment, listening all the while to that disconcerting voice inside him telling him it would never be the same again.

****

"How are you and the dogs getting along?" Joe asked McCoy as he entered his office.

McCoy jumped to his feet. "What the hell are you doing back here so soon? You're supposed to be on sick leave."

"I am," Rummel grinned. "I'm just checking on the dogs."

"I suppose you want them back," McCoy grumbled good-naturedly.

"I can't keep them at the apartment," Joe told him. "I'll have to make some kind of arrangements."

"Well, don't just stand there," McCoy said. "Sit down." Rummel took a chair, and the lieutenant sat back down behind his desk. "You know," he suggested, "you could always move into Jack's place and look after the pooches there. You'll probably inherit the whole damned works anyway."

Rummel chuckled. "Not if his ex-wives have anything to say about it." Joe's look grew solemn, and he remarked, "I never heard anything about the funeral while I was in the hospital. You know how it went?"

"Big celebrity event from what I heard," McCoy commented. "Packed house, plenty of women."

"The way things have gone these past couple of years, I don't know if Jack would've liked that or not."

"No offense, Joe, but I'm surprised the church roof didn't cave in."

Smiling, Rummel replied, "No offense taken, Jim. The fact is Jack was a deeply religious man."

"Nah, you gotta be kidding me."

"No, I'm not," Rummel said quite seriously, and then he quickly changed the subject. "But checking up is not the real reason I came here. I need a little favor, Jim."

"What's that?"

"You still have Brad's ID and badge?"

"Yeah, I do," McCoy said. "They should be right here in my drawer somewhere."

"Mind if I borrow them for a bit?"

McCoy was suddenly very curious. He detected the old, devious Rummel. "What for?"

Joe tried to look embarrassed. "This may sound a little corny," he explained, "but I made a promise to myself when Jack died that I'd find the killer. I just wanted to take that badge out to his grave and show him I did what I'd promised."

McCoy gave his detective a weird look, but it seemed like a reasonable request--of sorts. "I guess that wouldn't hurt anything," he nodded, "if it means that much to you."

"It does."

Digging through his desk drawers, the lieutenant produced a black leather folder and handed it over to Rummel. "Here you go."

"Thanks," Joe said as he stuffed the wallet into his pocket. "Well, I guess I should be going. That's about all I wanted…that and see how the dogs were doing." He stood up to leave.

Standing also, McCoy said, "Now you take care of that old beat up body of yours, Joe. I still need you back here for those few remaining months before you retire."

"Don't worry about me," Rummel assured him. "I'm too short to do myself any harm. Besides, I want to go out without wrecking my track record."

"What track record?"

"Not wearing a tie, for one thing," Joe grinned.

"That's no surprise. What else?"

"For being the only cop over six-three and two-thirty who's never won a fight."

"Ah, bullshit," McCoy scoffed.

Rummel just smiled. "See you later, Jim."

"Take care, Joe." Rummel left, and McCoy sat back down, thinking. He told himself there was nothing he should worry about. Everything had worked out just fine. McCoy started chewing his lower lip. Why then, he asked himself, was he worrying?

CHAPTER TWENTY

Rummel rang the doorbell to Wintrode's apartment and patiently waited.

Shortly, Kim answered. Her look registered instant surprise when she saw him standing there. "Joe. I didn't expect to see you again."

"I have some things I'd like to talk to you about," he told her in a pleasant manner. "May I come in?"

Looking nervously over her shoulder, Kim answered him, "I was just in the process of trying to get some things done. The place is a mess, and..."

"This won't take long," Joe interrupted.

Wintrode hesitated a moment longer, finally agreed and opened the door all the way for him to enter. "Like I said," she reminded him, "I'm a bit rushed."

Rummel stepped inside the apartment and glanced around at all the boxes laid out in her nearly barren living room. "You must be moving," he noted.

"I'm leaving Spokane," she replied crisply.

"Where you heading?"

"I thought I'd try New York," Kim said. Her tone was impatient. "I've never been there, and that's where the action is for my line of work. Now what can I do for you, Joe?"

The detective didn't answer right away. He wandered around the living room, taking his time to look the place over. Finally, he turned to her and remarked, "I thought I should thank you for saving my life."

"No need to thank me, Joe," Wintrode quickly responded. "If I could have handled it any other way, I would have."

"I guess I should also apologize for trashing your car," he added.

Kim folded her arms and flatly told him, "The insurance company took care of that."

"Well, you know, I was under a lot of stress with Jack's death and all," Joe continued as he purposefully dragged out his words. "I guess I just lost my head."

"Yes, Jack's accident was very tragic," she agreed. "Now what is it you really want, Joe?"

Rummel smiled, first to himself and then to her. He had triggered the right reaction in her. "Oh, I've just been doing some thinking," he rambled on. "I know you were with Jack the night he died. He told me all about you two, and it was obvious he had company that night. There's no doubt in my mind that company was you."

Wintrode chose not to respond. She would let him have his say. He was going to have it anyway, whether she listened or not.

Taking another look around the room, Rummel strolled over to an empty bookshelf and drummed his fingertips on it. His back turned to her, he explained, "I went through Jack's place the other day looking for some books. I know it's a big house, and maybe I overlooked them...but I don't think so." He faced Kim. "A couple of high school yearbooks. They were from Washington High School in Indianapolis. You wouldn't know what happened to them, would you?"

"I don't know what you're talking about," Kim replied, her voice and manner icy cold.

"No, I don't suppose you would," Joe commented. He started to wander around the living room some more, talking as he walked. "The reason they're important is that there was a young lady in there by the name of Linda McConey. Now let me tell you about Linda. She and her brother had a pretty tough life. Their father was an unsavory character, and one day those two kids just disappeared right off the face of the earth."

"What's your point, Joe?" Wintrode snapped. "I'm in a hurry."

Rummel stopped pacing. He flashed a knowing grin at her and stated, "My point, Kim, is that you are Linda McConey, and your brother's name was actually Mark. Unfortunately, Mark doesn't have a recognizable picture in any of the yearbooks, but it makes no difference. I know who he was. Your brother ran off to the Army, and a few years later you two ended up together in Houston." Joe paused to let his words sink in, and then he said, "About five years ago your father was killed in New Orleans. The interesting thing about that killing is that it was almost identical to these other murders we've had around the country...including Houston. But not quite identical," he intentionally added.

A smile slowly appeared on Kim's face. "You wearing a wire, Joe?" she asked.

Rummel chuckled. "Nope. Never even thought of it. Besides…I'm not on duty. I'm on sick leave."

"Well then, I suggest you go home and be sick," Kim told him. "I'm busy."

Rummel wasn't about to budge. "You know, Kim… one thing's for certain. Only two people knew the complete truth…just who committed what crime. Now one of them is dead. That leaves just you, Kim."

Wintrode's eyes narrowed in on the detective, and her impatience turned to anger. "If you came here for a confession, Rummel," she shot back, "you're wasting your time. I told the police everything I know."

"No, you didn't," Joe said to her in a calm voice and with a lingering smile. "You didn't tell the police who killed your father, and you didn't tell them who killed Jack. For that matter, I'm also convinced there were two people involved in the murder of his cousin. Someone had to drive all the way out there and pick up the killer. The way I see it, Alan didn't go out there on his own free will. He was too crafty to get picked up by a strange woman, particularly with things going down in this town the way they were. Besides, I never figured Alan was much for women. He was too easily distracted by a six pack of beer. No, I think Alan was tagged at closing time, probably at gunpoint and probably by a cop, and then hauled out there in his own car with an accomplice close behind." Joe stopped a moment to let Kim relive that night in her own mind. He went on. "Same can be said for Jack. You may be superwoman, Kim, but it usually takes more than one person to keep a car straight and push it off the road into a ravine."

Kim was defiant. "You through?"

"Not quite," Rummel said.

"Well, I am," she stated. "The movers are coming in an hour, and I have to finish packing. If you'll excuse me?" Without waiting for his response, Kim spun around and stormed down the hallway toward her bedroom. Rummel gave her a minute and then followed her. Blocking the doorway of her bedroom, he silently observed her, with her back to him, while she stuffed a suitcase on the bed with clothing. As she started for the closet, she suddenly noticed him watching her. "Didn't I make myself clear?" she snapped.

Joe ignored her hostility. "I almost forgot," he said. "I brought something for you. It's Brad's badge." He reached into his jacket pocket and produced the leather folder. "I thought you might want it." Kim stood fully facing him now not much more than ten feet away. Rummel gently tossed the case to her.

Wintrode let it drop to the floor right between her feet. "Cute, Rummel," she sneered. "Too bad it wouldn't have proved a thing. I could have caught it equally as well with either hand. I'm ambidextrous."

Frowning, Joe realized his deep-rooted suspicions were warranted after all, and there were many questions that would go unanswered, not just those about her father and Jack.

Having had just about enough of his intrusion, Kim showed him a nasty smile and said with a certain sadistic delight, "Brad always wanted to be like me. Even when we were kids. The problem was he eventually lost control. He wanted to *be* me. Actually, it all turned out for the best the way it did."

"Just how many did you kill?" Rummel asked. His palms were clammy, and his forehead was starting to break out in a sweat.

Kim flashed him a coy look and said sweetly, "Detective, I don't know what you're talking about. Brad killed all those people. Houston, Seattle, Chicago…I've never been to Chicago…and right here in Spokane. You know that."

His control regained, Joe gave her a smile of his own, just as nasty. "Oh, I know you were the one who did in your old man. But what'd you do in Houston? Teach your cub how to kill?"

"I've had enough of this shit," Kim responded as she turned her back on him again. "Get the fuck out of here, Rummel!"

"What about Jack?"

Wintrode slowly faced him. "What about him?" she asked in a much calmer tone. "He was an interesting guy. I was actually growing very fond of him."

That was all Joe could take. Once more the rage built inside him, and he glared at Kim Wintrode with a murderous look. "You killed him!" he shouted, although he quickly struggled with himself to regain his composure. "Jack would never drink," he continued in a tightly controlled voice, almost a hoarse whisper. "I know that for a fact. You drugged him out of his mind, poured booze down him, and you and Brad drove him out Indian Trail and ran his car off the road."

Kim egged on his hostility with a wicked grin. "That's your theory, Joe," she taunted him. "You think whatever you want." Pausing a few seconds to let her words eat away at him, she added with biting viciousness, "If it's any consolation to you, Joe…I fucked his brains out before he died." She turned away to take a suit from the closet and fold it neatly in her arms, and then she looked at the detective and calmly remarked, "Actually, it was a rather fitting way to go. Booze, drugs, the sex…certainly the sex…and that black Mustang of his. I thought it was a very appropriate tribute to him." Her sarcasm instantly collapsed into fury, and Kim snarled, "Now get lost, Rummel!" She turned her back on him and packed her suit away.

"Hey, Kim."

Wintrode sighed heavily and asked, "You still here?" Her manner expressed frustrated boredom when she slowly faced him. Kim looked straight down the barrel of a 9mm. Without the slightest hint of fear in her piercing blue eyes, she stared defiantly at Joe and stood her ground, challenging him to do something. "You haven't got the guts, Rummel," she mocked him with a contemptuous smile. "You kill me, and you can kiss your retirement and everything else goodbye. It'll all go right down the toilet, Detective. You walk out of here right now, and you can go live your shoddy little life somewhere on a fishing boat. No one will ever be any the wiser."

She was right. Joe knew he would be risking everything he had ever worked for on just this one decision. Even he wasn't certain he had enough to make his case stick. His hand began to tremble as his eyes strained down the sights that partially covered her head. His injured arm ached, and his worst fears, those she had just shoved down his throat, invaded the pit of his stomach and assaulted his brain.

Then he thought of his daughter and what this woman had almost done to her. Suddenly Jack's face came to mind, that devil-may-care smile of his chasing away Joe's anxieties. Rummel's hand stopped shaking. It was all over now. Joe eased the trigger back and fired.

AUTHOR'S NOTES

The story continues in Seattle where Detective Terri Long investigates some bizarre and ruthless murders, but this time the people being murdered are the police. The case takes a twisted journey into the local underworld and uncovers a turf war within an Asian crime syndicate. The hunters become the hunted in this life and death investigation that takes one wrong turn after another in a maze of intrigue that leads to a shocking ending and turns good and evil upside down.

Look for *Police Brutality* coming soon on Amazon Kindle and available in paperback.

www.ingramcontent.com/pod-product-compliance
Lightning Source LLC
Chambersburg PA
CBHW060922180626
46817CB00004B/1349